KING OF MIST

STEEL AND FIRE BOOK TWO

JORDAN RIVET

Copyright © 2016 by Jordan Rivet

All rights reserved. No part of this publication may be reproduced, distributed or transmitted in any form or by any means without the prior written permission of the author.

This is a work of fiction. Names, characters, places, and incidents are a product of the author's imagination. Any resemblance to actual people, living or dead, or to businesses, companies, events, institutions, or locales is completely coincidental.

Contact the author at Jordan@jordanrivet.com

For updates and discounts on new releases, join Jordan Rivet's mailing list.

Cover art by Deranged Doctor Design

Editing suggestions provided by Red Adept Editing

Map by Jordan Rivet

King of Mist, Steel and Fire Book 2/ Jordan Rivet – First Edition: May 2016, Updated Edition: January 2019

❋ Created with Vellum

For Kaylee Peelen.
Thank you for your friendship, encouragement, and all the bookish conversations.

CONTENTS

Map of the Continent	vii
1. The Fourth Good King	1
2. The Council	11
3. The Firesmith	19
4. The Ladies	28
5. Encounters	37
6. The Guardsman	44
7. House Denmore	51
8. The Caverns	58
9. Night	67
10. Plans	74
11. The Army	81
12. House Zurren	94
13. Training	104
14. The Fire Warden	112
15. Harvest Festival	118
16. The Lantern Maker	126
17. Aftermath	133
18. The Queen	141
19. The Parents	148
20. Farewell	159
21. Fireworks	166
22. Scouting	171
23. News	180
24. The Phoenix Leaf	186
25. The Bottle	194
26. Firetears	199
27. Preparations	204
28. The Engagement Feast	212
29. The Mountain	224
30. The Fire Guild	231
31. The Castle	235
32. Lantern Maker's Daughter	245

33. Flight	249
34. Daybreak	255
Epilogue	263
Acknowledgments	267
About the Author	269
Also by Jordan Rivet	271

MAP OF THE CONTINENT

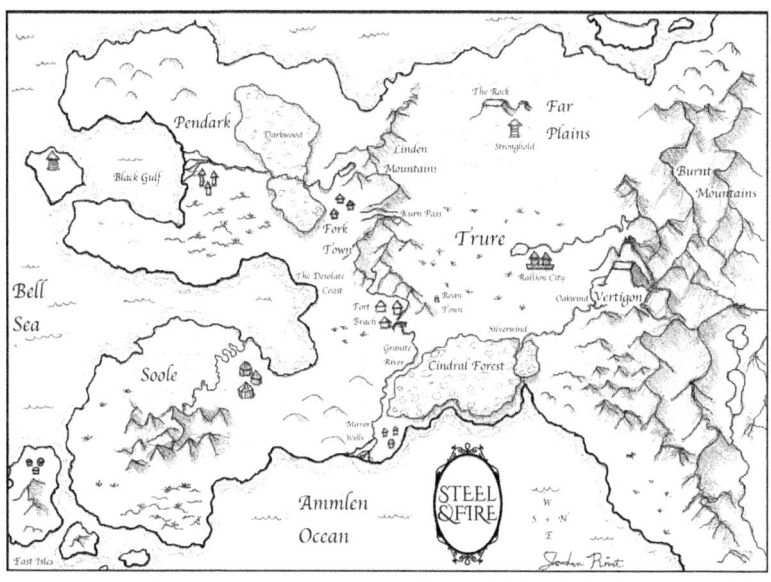

1
THE FOURTH GOOD KING

KING Sivarrion Amintelle tossed his crown onto the floor. The tarnished silver rang against the stones. He grumbled to himself and crossed the library to retrieve it. He'd been aiming for the table.

Siv picked up the crown and ran his fingers around the inner band, feeling the metal worn down by three—now four—generations of Amintelle kings. It was a heavy thing, weighty like the duty of the kingship that now rested on his shoulders. He tossed the crown again.

"Point for Amintelle!" The crown rang like a bell as it caught on a candlestick, then it landed on the table with a satisfying thunk. "Amintelle takes the lead! Will he be able to defeat his opponent?" Siv deepened his voice. "I don't know, Dun. After his recent setbacks we weren't sure we'd ever see another Amintelle victory. He looks in peak form now, though, wouldn't you say? He's winding up for another toss."

Siv retreated to the door of the library and spun the crown across the room. The Firejewels set in the band flashed in the lantern light. The crown landed on the candlestick again. A perfect shot.

"It's a ringer! Amintelle wins! Amintelle—"

The door burst open. "Sire, did you summon me? Are you in peril?" Pool ran into the room, a long knife in his hand, deadly focus on his face.

Siv snatched a book from the nearest shelf and leaned against the bookcase.

"Of course not, Pool. I'm busy preparing for the council meeting." He quickly flipped the book so it was right side up. "Why? Did you hear something?"

Pool looked around the library, eyes narrowed. He took in the crown resting around the candlestick and raised an eyebrow.

Siv cleared his throat. "I'm very busy being king, Pool, so if you don't need anything..."

"Of course, my king. I wish only to prevent any nefarious and untoward things from happening to you as they did to your father."

Siv grimaced. "I know. It's okay." He put the book back on the shelf and strode to the table to retrieve his crown. He sat, turning it in his fingers. It was just a piece of metal and a handful of jewels, but it had changed his whole world.

He looked up at Pool. "Any word from the investigation?"

"Not since we cleared the last of the kitchen staff of any wrongdoing, Sire," Pool said. "We will discover the perpetrator of your father's murder."

Siv hadn't thought it was one of the servants, but they had to cover all the possibilities. He'd been king for a grand total of one month, but they were still no closer to discovering who had slipped Firetears into his father's tea. The poison took a while to kick in, so any of the dignitaries King Sevren had entertained the morning of the Vertigon Cup could have been responsible. Many of them had been visiting from the Lands Below to watch the dueling competition and pay their respects to the King of the Mountain. Some were rulers in their own right. Siv would have to be very careful whom he accused of regicide. This could go bad faster than dumping a jar of zur-wasps onto a sleeping velgon bear.

Even though the traditional mourning period had only just come to an end, Siv had spent the past few weeks meeting with the heads of noble family after noble family, trying to establish a rapport with each of them. No one had expected the king to die so young, and many of the old nobles still considered Siv an irresponsible youth. They thought he could be contained and controlled. He couldn't let that idea fester and take root amongst his people too.

Being king was burning difficult. Not for the first time, he wished he could ask for his father's advice. King Sevren had tried to teach him when he was alive, but Siv had missed too many opportunities. He frowned at the crown in his hands, willing away the grief clutching at his belly. His father was gone. It was up to him to take care of their mountain.

"Where's Dara stationed today, Pool?" he asked. Pool still lingered inside the door to the library as if he expected whatever had made that noise to jump out from behind a bookcase.

"Miss Ruminor is guarding the entrance to the cur-dragon cavern today," Pool said crisply.

"I'm going down there."

"Don't you need to continue your preparations, my king?"

"No, I'm ready now." Siv grabbed some scribbled notes from the table and stuck them in his coat pocket. There were only a few items of business that required notes. Today was more about establishing the dynamics of the new royal council. He didn't need notes on how to be charming.

Siv and Pool made their way down the winding staircase from the library. Siv hadn't planned for Dara to spend her days guarding doorways when he asked her to join his Castle Guard, but too many guardsmen had been involved in the plot against his father, and the remaining few had to take up the slack. A month before the king's murder, Captain Bandobar had recruited a dozen men to reinforce the aging company. They'd been perfectly positioned by whoever had truly hired them to betray the royal family. They had incapacitated the loyal guards and tried to abduct Siv and his sisters. Only Dara, his training partner and friend, had been able to save them.

Siv had to figure out who was responsible for the treacherous guardsmen soon. The plot had failed, but unless they could root out the source, his father's murderer was sure to try again. He would have to keep a close eye on the nobles at the council meeting for any signs they were disappointed to have a new Amintelle king.

Meanwhile, Pool was vetting replacements for the short-staffed Guard. It had been safest to fire all the new recruits, whether they were sure of their involvement or not. He'd sent Captain Bandobar away too. Rot and mold had been allowed to infiltrate the Guard—and the kingdom—for too long. They needed a fresh start with people they could trust. Such people were in disturbingly short supply in Vertigon these days. But Dara Ruminor was one of them.

Dara did footwork back and forth in the entrance to the tunnel. The stone stretched flat and straight as a dueling strip. No one would be able to get past her, and it was just the right length for her exercises. Advance, retreat, advance, lunge.

Her steps echoed through the tunnel, and a Firebulb on the wall vibrated with the rhythm of her movements. She kept her black-hilted sword in its sheath at her waist, pointing her fingers as she lunged and stabbed at the air. She imagined a shadowy opponent, blade sharp and eyes deadly. She bounced on the balls of her feet, anticipating a rapid attack or a vicious feint. She had to remain ready, ever on the defensive. She lunged, driving her invisible blade into her imagined enemy. Then she resumed her guard stance and started again.

The light from the Firebulb cast a muted glow around the tunnel. Every once in a while she glanced down the passageway, but the only people likely to come up that way were the dragon keepers. The entrance to the cur-dragon cave opened above a sheer cliff. No one could threaten the prince from there.

Not the prince. The king. She had to keep reminding herself that Siv was now the ruler of Vertigon. She had been a member of the Castle Guard for a month, but she'd spent most of that time guarding the castle's various orifices rather than the king himself. He hadn't been outside of the castle much, as they still didn't know the identity of his enemies or where they might ambush him.

Or at least, the king didn't know his enemies. Dara had a pretty good idea about one of them.

She stabbed the air, a light sweat breaking out on her forehead. Her footsteps rang loud in the empty tunnel. She was beginning to wonder whether she might have been a more effective protector if she had stayed at home. At least there she could have gathered proof of her parents' involvement and maybe learned about their new plans instead of guarding unassailable hallways. But she couldn't stay under her father's roof, not when she was fairly certain he had been the one to kill King Sevren.

At first she had doubted her suspicions. She thought the whirl of adrenaline and fear when she foiled the kidnapping—and possibly the murder—of the prince and his sisters had made her jump to conclusions. But when she returned to her parents' dwelling long after midnight that fateful evening, her fears had been confirmed.

Dara trudged up to the house, shaken and numb from the events of the day. Her mother and father were sitting at their large stone table, talking in low voices. She paused on the porch to listen through the kitchen window.

"Where is Corren?" Lima said. "He should be finished with the bodies by now."

"Have patience, my darling." Dara's father sounded calm.

"We must find out who stopped Farr."

"Corren will do everything he can. He has to make it look like Farr's death was unrelated to the others."

"Stupid boy." Lima made a strange sound, partway between a snort and a sob. "How hard could it have been to stab the young—?"

"Lima. The job isn't done. We must be careful for a while yet."

"At least your part succeeded. And good riddance." A chair scraped across the floor. "Where is Dara?"

"I expect she is with her dueling friends."

"I'm going to . . ."

Dara hadn't heard the rest. She stomped on the steps by the porch to alert them to her presence, hoping they'd think she just arrived. She had heard enough to confirm that their assistant, Farr, had failed at an important mission—one they had sent him to carry out. They already knew he wouldn't return.

He wouldn't return because Dara had killed him.

Her parents had looked up when she entered the room, taking in her fractured, exhausted appearance. She wasn't even sure whether what she had overheard or the fight she had barely survived had shattered her more. She told them she'd gone for a run to clear her head after hearing the news of King Sevren's assassination. Fortunately she hadn't been injured in the clash, so there was no reason for them to suspect she had been outside the Fire Guild at the crucial moment. Her parents had offered her a bowl of porridge and sent her to bed. They'd been kind and nurturing, as parents should be. If only she'd learned the truth about what they were capable of before she faced Farr on that boardwalk.

Dara gritted her teeth and picked up the pace of her footwork as regret squeezed her like a hand around her throat. There was no point thinking about that. Farr had made his own decision. He'd been trying to abduct young Princess Selivia, and his companions were about to stab Siv to death when she stopped them. She had no choice.

That didn't save her from seeing Farr's face in her dreams, his eyes going wide and then lifeless. He had seemed like a nice person, and she'd thought him harmless. But he had fallen under the thrall of the Ruminors, and they were a force to be reckoned with. Dara was only just coming to understand how dangerous they were.

The morning after the king's murder, she had moved out of her parents' home to live with their enemy. She didn't reveal what she suspected, simply saying she'd been offered a job on the Castle Guard. She had long failed to live up to their expectations anyway, and her departure would just be one more disappointment. Her father had given her a cold stare and turned his back as she left through the Fire Lantern shop. But her mother had flown into a towering rage. She screamed about how Dara would never be as good as her sister, Renna, who had been killed in a surge of Fire a decade ago, and how she was betraying their family name. Dara trudged down the slope of Village Peak with her mother's shouts hammering her like hailstones, desperately fighting the urge to cry. If Lima hadn't been so harsh, Dara might have turned around and decided to stay. Instead, her mother had treated her with the same derision she'd experienced for the past decade—and her father had done nothing to ease the sting.

She was fairly certain the only reason her parents hadn't marched to the Castle Guard barracks and dragged her back home was because they didn't want to draw attention to themselves while the investigation into the king's murder was underway. The relative ease with which she'd walked away from them only helped to confirm her suspicions.

She'd tried to sort out what her parents wanted as she got used to living away from them for the first time. Her father resented the restrictions placed on his power by the Fire distribution system. Her mother believed in the Fireworkers' natural superiority—even though she didn't have the ability herself. But Dara knew it was about more than that. Her parents wanted revenge for Renna's death. Zage Lorrid, the Fire Warden, had been responsible for the accident, and the Ruminors' hatred of him was well known, but they held a deeper grudge—one that was much worse than Dara had realized. The king had pardoned the Warden and denied them justice. Now they wanted the king and his children to pay the price.

Dara intended to atone for what they had done in turn and prevent them from trying again—if she could. And if she ever got to do more than guard an empty passageway.

Her boots shuffled and scraped against the stone floor as she moved, switching directions as rapidly as possible. A cold breeze drifted from the cur-dragon cave, carrying a hint of mist through the corridor. Autumn had been cold and rainy so far, and it was threatening to be a vicious winter.

"Do you never rest?"

Dara spun to face the entrance to the castle. Siv—the king—leaned in the doorway. He wore a deep-blue coat and a sword buckled at his hip. Dara recognized it as a Fire Blade, even from this distance. Pool's tall form loomed a few paces behind him.

"I have to stay in shape," she said.

"You make me tired just watching you."

"You should be training too," Dara said, wiping the stiff, too-long sleeve of her guard uniform across her forehead. She was having new coats tailored to fit her better, but this one would have to do for now. "You'll be too slow next time we duel."

"I am in wonderful shape," Siv said, putting his fists on his hips and posing with his chest puffed out. "You should spend more time admiring me, really."

Dara fought a grin. He wasn't wrong. He had a strong, slim waist and broad shoulders, and the shadow of a beard on his jaw emphasized his high cheekbones and intelligent eyes.

"I'm too busy keeping my eyes on this passageway in case the cur-dragon keepers rise up against you."

"I've always suspected them," Siv said. "They're sneakier than burrlinbats under an Eventide moon."

"Did you need me for something?" Dara asked. "Or are you just here to critique my footwork?"

"There's no way I'd be as critical of your footwork as you are of it yourself." Siv stretched his arms over his head, joints cracking. "I happened to be walking in this general direction and thought I'd say hi."

Pool made a sound very like a snort behind him.

"Don't you have a council meeting soon?" Dara asked.

"Yeah, but I'm making them wait. It's all part of the plan."

"Right. Today's the day you're going to demonstrate your brilliant political maneuverings."

Siv nodded sagely. "It will be a council meeting for the ages. You should come. I'm sure to be very impressive."

"I am on duty, Your Majesty," Dara said.

"Majesty. Ooh, that's a new one."

"Would you prefer 'Your High and Mightiness'?"

"That is very tempting, but seriously, it's just me and Pool. I wish you'd go back to calling me Siv." The king's voice was casual, but there was sadness in his eyes, something that had been there too often of late. Dara's chest tightened at the sight. She knew how much Siv's father had meant to him. And his life wasn't supposed to turn out this way.

"I'll see what I can do," Dara said.

"Good. Now, when I'm done with my meeting I want you to come with me to talk to Zage about that Fire Blade we picked up during the attempt against my life."

The image of a tall, mysterious swordsman flashed before Dara's eyes. They had faced him together. Dara had feinted, opening the man up for Siv's killing blow. They'd made a good team, despite the fear rattling both of them.

"What about it?"

"I thought it was standard Guard issue, but I had a closer look recently and now I'm not so sure."

"Is that it?" Dara gestured to the dueling blade buckled at Siv's waist.

"Nope, this one's Bandobar's. They're different. Check it out." Siv drew the sword from his own sheath and handed it to Dara. "Captain Bandobar had his blade custom Worked by the army's Firesmith, and it has the castle seal."

Dara took the rapier and hefted it, feeling the perfect balance of the weapon. She ran her finger over the stamp in the cold steel hilt. Or at least, it was cold when she first picked it up. Within seconds, warmth spread from the weapon into her fingertips. She nearly dropped the blade as the heat seeped into her blood and crept up her arm. Without thinking, she spun away from the king and dropped into a lightning fast lunge. The blade sang through the air.

"You can show off your perfect form later," Siv said, but he sounded impressed.

The blade came alive in Dara's hands. She could barely help herself as she thrust at an invisible target. The Fire imbued in the steel and the Fire sense in her blood worked together to make her movements uncannily fast and sharp. But when she felt a connection forming to the Fire seeping through the stones of the passageway too, she quickly straightened and handed the blade back to Siv.

"It's good steel." She didn't meet his eyes, hoping he hadn't noticed the difference when she wielded it compared to a normal blade. It was the first time she had held a Fire Blade since she discovered she could Work the magic Fire flowing through Vertigon Mountain. She hadn't realized how different a Fire Blade would feel in her hands. It was little wonder Fire Blades were forbidden in competitions.

"I want to see if Zage can tell anything by comparing it to the one we found," Siv said. "That one doesn't have a maker's mark at all. It might help our investigation if we know where the blade came from."

"No, don't give it to Zage!" Dara said quickly. She hadn't gotten a good look at the blade of the swordsman they had defeated together the day of King Sevren's murder, but there was a chance it could lead right to her parents. They had sent Farr, and it was possible his companion got the Fire Blade from one of their allies. The assassin who had attacked Dara and Siv near Fell Bridge had carried a knife with a Firegold hilt too. It could very well have been a Fire Blade from the same source. Too much of the evidence pointed toward the

Workers—and her parents were chief among them. She didn't want the Fire Warden to be the one to discover the link. As much as she deplored her parents' involvement in King Sevren's murder, she didn't want them to be executed either. She hoped to find some other way to stop them.

"I mean, I can look into it," she said, blushing when the king raised an eyebrow at her. "No need to bother the Warden."

"Is guard duty that boring?" Siv asked.

"I know a lot of the Firesmiths," Dara said. "They would probably be able to give us more useful information."

"That's a good point," Siv said.

"I'll have to wait until my shift is over, though."

"The blade is in my chambers. You sure you don't mind doing some investigating?"

"Of course not," Dara said. "I'll do anything to figure out who's responsible for what happened to your father." She dropped her gaze to the stones. She didn't add that she desperately hoped she was wrong about her parents.

"Thanks," Siv said. "I can always count on you." He reached out as if to nudge her, but instead he circled her arm with his hand, just above the elbow. Warmth spread from his fingers. He met her eyes, and his grip tightened, as if he was contemplating pulling her closer. Dara's heart did a slow, painful flip.

"Yes, Your Majesty," she said.

Siv dropped his hand abruptly. "Come see me when you're done. I'll tell you all about my brilliance at the council meeting."

He turned to stride back into the castle, and Dara found herself missing him before he was even out of sight.

2

THE COUNCIL

SIV was still kicking himself by the time he arrived at the council chambers in the castle's central tower. He shouldn't have gone to see Dara. All that did was remind him of their hours in the dueling hall together, of the night she had danced in his arms, of what he could never have. He was the king, and kings didn't think about kissing their guardswomen. He may care for Dara, he may owe her his life, but he couldn't let his father's legacy down.

Pool opened the door to the royal council chambers with a flourish, as Siv had instructed. The double doors banged against the walls, making the tapestries hanging from them shudder. The bodyguards who had accompanied the noblemen waiting within stepped aside to make way for the king.

A long oval table made of polished oak all the way from Cindral Forest filled most of the room. High-backed chairs inlaid with Firegold surrounded the table. A Fire Lantern hung from the ceiling, casting warm light over the men and women seated around the table. The chamber had no windows, and the tapestries on the walls muted the echo of Siv's boots on the stone floor.

He strode to the far end of the table, keeping his head high as the noblemen and women stood. He had invited the heads of all the most important houses in Vertigon. He had to establish his hold over the nobility before they could begin to maneuver against him, especially because he wasn't sure which ones might want him dead. It was just like dueling, except potentially more deadly.

The heads of Houses Morrven, Samanar, Rollendar, Denmore, Roven, Farrow, and Nanning watched him expectantly. A few had brought their advisors along, and Lord Nanning had brought his rather fearsome wife. They were all at least twenty years older than Siv, except for Lady Tull, the beautiful young widow who was now head of House Denmore. The council members represented houses that had followed his father for many years, and they were powerful in their own right. Siv would have to convince them to respect him if he was to carry on the Amintelle legacy.

He fought down a jolt of nerves as he faced the nobles. *I'll have them all in hand before First Snow.* He cleared his throat, about to launch into his opening speech, when another man entered the chambers.

"Sorry I'm late, Your Highness," Bolden Rollendar said as he strode in with barely a nod at Siv. The doors slammed behind him with a resounding bang. He flipped a hand through his sandy-blond hair and took a seat beside his father, Lord Von Rollendar. The other nobles followed his lead and sat down before Siv could say anything. Siv grimaced as the scrape and screech of shifting chairs filled the room. He'd planned some inspiring words about how they'd all stand together to ensure a prosperous future for Vertigon. Too late for that now.

"Right. Well, shall we begin?" Siv sat in his throne-like chair as the nobles shuffled papers and muttered to each other, not paying much attention to him.

Bolden caught his eye and winked, as if they shared some sort of joke, but Siv didn't smile back.

"We need to discuss the coming winter," Siv said, diving into the first item in his notes, underneath the part about the rousing opening speech. "I understand from my advisors that we will have a particularly harsh winter this year, and we need to make sure the people have enough food. Lord Morrven, how fares the plum harvest?"

"The plums are as good as ever, Your Majesty," Lord Morrven said. He had a gravelly voice that was at odds with his plump-cheeked appearance. He glared across the table at Bolden's father.

King of Mist

"But the Rollendars have been clogging up our access roads and delaying the workers."

"Nonsense," Von Rollendar said immediately. Like his son, he had sandy hair, graying at the temples, and his nose was pointed and cruel. "Our men keep to roads owned by my estate. You must be mistaken."

"I know which roads belong to the crown and which are private," Lord Morrven snapped. "The plums will rot if we can't get them over to the drying grounds in time."

"Your accusations are baseless," Lord Von said. He straightened the sleeve of his red coat, which was embroidered with his family's sigil in black thread. "My house has the right to do what we wish with our holdings."

"The road isn't yours."

"We acquired a portion of the Silltine Estate some time ago." Lord Von waved to his son, and Bolden pulled out a map showing the roads along the southeastern ridge of King's Peak, near where Orchard Gorge opened into the Fissure. Their landholdings were clearly marked with red ink. "You'll find that we own orchards on both sides of the road. Therefore, it is ours."

Lord Morrven barely glanced at the map. "How are we supposed to get our plums up to market if we can't use the road?"

"Surely that's not my problem." Lord Rollendar smiled and turned to Lord Samanar across the table, a distinguished gentleman with coarse gray hair and luminous eyes like a morrinvole. "Wouldn't you agree that I should decide who travels on my own land?"

"Of course, Von." Lord Samanar glowered at Lord Morrven. "Besides, Morrven plums are barely fit for the mountain goats."

Morrven's face darkened. "Why you—"

"I think," Siv said before the argument could get any worse, "that the law makes it quite clear the road itself belongs to the crown. You can't prevent Lord Morrven from transporting his produce along it, Lord Rollendar."

"I pay for the road's maintenance," Von said. He met Siv's eyes steadily, and Siv remembered a particularly vicious lecture the man had given him when he and Bolden had been caught throwing rotten fruit at passersby on that very road as boys. "If the crown

13

wishes to care for it, perhaps the crown can compensate me for the work I've done on the cobblestones over the years."

Siv opened his mouth to respond, but others started chiming in, not allowing him to get a word in edgewise.

"If the crown is going to pay for your cobblestones," Lord Farrow said, "it can burning well fix up Orchard Bridge down by our holdings. It gets too much traffic as is."

"Now just a minute," said Lord Tellen Roven. "We've been in line for bridge maintenance for months now. You can't leap ahead to—"

"Enough," Siv said, raising a hand for quiet. It took longer than he would have liked for the nobles to fall silent. "If you have complaints about the bridges, compile a list I can examine in depth. We'll find the firestones for it if the maintenance is essential before winter. In the meantime, Lord Rollendar, you must allow Lord Morrven's workers access to his orchards. We need to get the harvest in before First Snow."

"Are you going to dictate what we can do with our own lands?" Bolden said suddenly. He met Siv's eyes for five full heartbeats before adding, "Your Majesty."

The council fell silent. The noblemen looked at Siv expectantly. Well, they were all expectant except for Bolden, who met his eyes across the wide table, smirking like a povvercat. Siv resisted the urge to glare back at him. Mostly.

"I will do what is best for the people of Vertigon," Siv said. "As landholders, it's your responsibility to ensure that our mountain's industries run smoothly. For now, that means making sure all of our produce can be preserved before First Snow." He looked around at the noblemen, intending to fix them each with a kingly stare, but they were already losing interest in what he was saying. How had his father gotten them all to pay attention so well? Siv cleared his throat loudly. "As for the rest," he met Bolden's eyes, "I'll put the younger Lord Rollendar here in charge of surveying every bridge in Vertigon and reporting any repair work needed. Bring your requests to him. It's a sizeable, tedious job, but I'm sure Lord Bolden can handle it."

Bolden's smile froze, and you could have chilled a bottle of wine in the space between him and Siv.

After what felt like an hour, he said, "Yes, Your Majesty."

"Good," Siv said. "Now, how about those goat farms?"

When the council meeting ended, Siv felt like he'd been circling his dueling hall at a dead run for the past two hours. Why did politics have to be so complicated? Worse, it was damn boring. Every single nobleman had a request for funds or special treatment from the crown. As often as not, at least one nobleman was mortally opposed to whatever another required. Siv spent the whole time settling disputes and parsing out what each party really wanted. And that was when he wasn't being forced to call the council to attention again as they squabbled and chatted amongst themselves. So much for his plans to captivate the nobles through sheer force of personality.

The council members milled around the chambers after the meeting, speaking to each other in tight groups. None of them approached him. They seemed all too willing to carry on the business of the kingdom without much input from the king. That didn't bode well for Siv's future as ruler. He had hoped they would appreciate a little youthful energy on the council. In truth, they didn't take his suggestions all that seriously, especially with Bolden thwarting him at every turn. He was going to have to do something about that man—and soon.

He wished he had an uncle or other relative on the council, someone to be a guide and an ally. His father had been an only child, and his mother's family all lived down in Trure. He felt exposed and vulnerable without his father, even without the grief that still snuck up on him when he least expected it. House Amintelle held the throne, but its landholdings were relatively small. They had won the crown by virtue of his great-grandfather's strength as a Firewielder, but the days when magic workers held political power in Vertigon were long gone. The other nobles owned the entire kingdom's orchards, goat and pony farms, and many of the Fireshops, and demonstrating his family's power was difficult.

As the nobles shuffled out of the council chambers, Lady Tull Denmore lingered at the door, speaking to her advisor in a quiet voice. She was a beautiful woman, young and delicate and sad. She was also the fabulously wealthy head of a major noble house, one that had blended with her own House Ferrington when she married Lord Denmore. The Ferringtons controlled one of the major access roads to the Fissure, and the Denmores owned most of the goat paddocks on Village Peak. Since the tragic death of her young husband, Tull had become very powerful indeed. Siv had intended to propose to her just before his father's death—or else find a powerful bride in his mother's home country of Trure—but that scheme had fallen by the wayside. Something—or rather someone—kept holding him back.

Siv wasn't in the mood to talk to Lady Tull after his underwhelming performance at the council meeting, but he spotted Bolden waiting for her outside the doors, perhaps to escort her home. Siv couldn't allow a Rollendar-Denmore alliance to take hold right now. He straightened his coat and strode over to her.

"My lady."

"Your Highness." Tull offered him her smooth, white hand, and he bent over it, deep enough to be both kingly and gallant.

"Thank you for attending the council meeting," Siv said. "I hope it wasn't too boring for you."

"Not at all, Your Highness."

Bolden edged sideways in the entryway so that he was fully in Siv's view, looking about as happy as a furlingbird with a cold as he tried to listen in.

"Would you like to dine with me tomorrow night?" Siv asked the young widow, not bothering to keep his voice down. "Your company and your presence in the castle would honor me." *There. That sounded suitably regal.*

"Thank you, Your Highness. I'd love to."

"Good. Until tomorrow, my lady."

Tull curtsied, looking up at him through delicate eyelashes. She really was lovely, and it was high time for him to renew his courtship before Bolden secured any promises himself. Before his father's death, Siv had thought there was a chance he could insist on a certain non-noble marriage, but now that he wore the crown himself, he was starting to see how important marriage alliances could be. The nobles would dismiss him as long as they saw him as weak, and an Amintelle-Denmore-Ferrington alliance could be truly formidable.

But as Lady Tull left the council chamber, accompanied by her retainers, Siv already had a different woman on his mind. He hoped to get back to his chambers in time to catch Dara before she headed off on her investigation. Unfortunately, his sister Soraline intercepted him before he'd gone more than five steps.

"Siv! How did it go?"

"Hey, Sora."

"Tell me everything." She grabbed his arm eagerly. She had dark hair, round features, and light eyes like their Truren mother's. "Did you discuss the Ringston Pact? Did Lord Farrow mention the—"

"It was fine. Nothing too exciting happened."

"But—"

"I have to get back to my chambers," Siv said. Dara might have come and gone by now. He wasn't sure what time her shift ended.

"But you have to tell me what happened," Sora pleaded. At seventeen, she loved politics more than just about anything. Siv tried to squeeze past her and her hulking red-haired bodyguard, Denn Hurling, but he stopped at the look of desperation on his sister's round face.

"Okay, okay. I'll fill you in."

"Yes! You know, you could let me actually attend the council meetings. I might be able to help."

"You're a seventeen-year-old girl," Siv said. "I don't think having you whispering in my ear will help my credibility with the nobles. They already think they can walk all over me." *Even the young ones.* He hoped Bolden contracted a very nasty case of gut rot in the near future.

"I know more about the kingdom than you do anyway," Sora mumbled.

"If you don't want me to tell you what happened, I can—"

"Never mind!" Sora said. "Sorry, Siv. Start at the beginning."

He filled his sister in on the discussion as they walked. To his immense surprise, talking it over actually made it easier to process everything that had happened, and Sora even had some good insights.

"Why do you think Lord Rollendar wants to control that road so badly?" Siv asked. That had been bothering him since the beginning of the meeting. "He doesn't grow plums, and Lord Morrven isn't his direct competitor. He shouldn't care."

"Hmmm . . ." Sora considered for so long that Siv thought she must be lost down a morrinvole hole in her head. Finally, she said, "What did Lord Samanar say? He's Morrven's biggest rival."

"He supported Rollendar," Siv said. "But like you said, Samanar and Morrven are competitors, so that's expected."

"But Lord Samanar has never been particularly friendly with the Rollendars," Sora said. "In fact, they're barely supposed to be on speaking terms."

"You think it's a new alliance?"

"Sure sounds like it."

"Great. That's the last thing I need." The Rollendars were making new friends left and right. Siv had to rein them in quickly. And he couldn't have people ignoring or interrupting him in meetings. He had to do something to establish his hold on the council soon. And he had to figure out what was so important about that road.

3
―――――
THE FIRESMITH

WHEN Dara's shift ended, she jogged up the winding stone stairwell of the castle's central tower to retrieve the Fire Blade Siv wanted her to investigate. It was still strange that he lived in the king's chambers now, far away from the beautiful dueling hall he had constructed outside his original rooms in the western end of the castle. Dara had never actually been inside those rooms, but she had spent hours in the dueling hall over the summer. She still went there sometimes to practice with the training dummies. She hoped Siv's duties would eventually let up enough to allow him to train with her again. She missed how uncomplicated their friendship had been within the dueling hall.

Dara slowed at the landing at the top of the stairwell. The young Castle Guard stationed outside the king's chamber was a new recruit, one of the first men hired in place of the treacherous guards who had tried to kidnap Siv and his two sisters.

"I need to get something from inside," Dara said as she approached. "King's orders."

"Of course." The guardsman stepped aside, heels clicking. "You're Nightfall, aren't you?"

"Huh? Oh, yes. Or at least I was."

"I've seen you duel. You're brilliant."

"Thanks." Dara said. "Do you compete?" The young man had the look of a soldier rather than a sport duelist, all strong arms and sharp edges. His dark-brown hair was cut in a clean military style.

"When I was a kid," he said. "Had to quit when I joined the army. I still follow the sport, though."

"Me too," Dara said.

The young guardsman stuck out his hand. "I'm Telvin, by the way. Telvin Jale."

"Dara."

"Are you going to keep dueling now that you're on the Guard?" he asked.

Dara hesitated, glancing down at the sigil on her uniform. She felt so far removed from who she had been just a month ago, when she had adopted the Nightfall persona to help her obtain a dueling patron.

"I can still go to competitions when I have Turndays off, but my duties don't allow me as much time to train."

"I hear you." Telvin rested a hand on the sword hilt at his belt. "It also changes your game when you learn how to fight to kill. It can mess up your competition strategy."

"I guess it can." Dara was more afraid her competitors would surpass her as they continued to train full time and she slowly lost her edge. She would rather lose to a worthy opponent in peak form than have her skills slowly atrophy.

"You were hitting your stride at the time of the Cup," Telvin said. "I was sure you were going to win it all."

"Things are different now," Dara said quietly.

She already missed the thrill of competition, the tap of her boots on a stone dueling floor, the clang of blades. She missed her dueling friends too, their hours doing drills and cheering each other on, their trips to the Stone Market on Village Peak for pies and salt cakes. She'd barely seen them since she moved into the barracks.

She hadn't had a chance to get to know the other guardsmen yet. The Guard was so short-staffed that there usually weren't many of them hanging out in the barracks behind the castle. Pool had been very busy since his promotion to the head of the Castle Guard after Captain Bandobar vanished. They would need more good men soon. The king and his family remained vulnerable.

Telvin Jale held open the door to the king's chambers for Dara to enter. "You should try to get to some competitions," he said. "It would be a shame to waste your talent."

"Thanks. Maybe I will."

Dara had never been to the king's antechamber before Siv's ascension. Most of the tapestries and decorations were still an old-fashioned style. She would have expected more dueling weapons adorning the walls and maybe even a duelist's banner or two now that Siv had been living here for a while, but he had hardly touched the room since he moved in. There were lots of books, though, spread over the low couches and lying open across the tables. That didn't surprise her at all.

Dara found the Fire Blade on a side table beside the door to the bedchamber. She sensed its location from across the room thanks to the Fire core buried deep within its metal. From the outside, it looked like a normal rapier with a hint of gold running down the blade, but Dara could feel the difference.

She picked up the weapon, accidentally knocking a length of black cloth onto the floor. She bent to pick it up and realized it was a duelist's banner after all: hers. She held up the stretch of black cloth emblazoned with her name, remembering how it had felt to stride into the King's Arena with the crowds calling her name, how it had felt to see Siv cheering for her from the royal box. She didn't know he had kept this. He hadn't brought it with him when he left the arena after the Vertigon Cup, so he must have sent someone to retrieve it specially. Dara felt that slow, painful flip in her chest again, but she ignored it. There was no use thinking about how things had been before or how they could have turned out if Siv hadn't become king so suddenly. She would keep her feelings wrapped up tighter than a bandage over a stab wound.

She put the banner back where she had found it and examined the Fire Blade. It felt like Bandobar's, which she'd held earlier, except it was more powerful. The weapons were about the same size, but this one felt more substantial somehow, as if the extra Fire added weight to the steel.

Dara made sure Telvin Jale couldn't see her through the partially open door. Then she took a deep breath and reached into the blade with her will, trying to touch the Fire core. She wasn't sure exactly how, but after a few minutes she connected with the blade, almost like her veins had fused with it and her heart pumped blood through flesh and metal and back again. The sword would be lightning in her hands, fast, searing, and deadly. This was why no one was allowed to create Fire-infused weapons except the king's own smiths, why no one but soldiers and Castle Guards were permitted to carry them. A Fire Blade in anyone's hands was dangerous; a Fire Blade in a Fireworker's hands was utterly lethal.

Dara focused on the blade, willing the connection to sever. It took concentration, but eventually she managed to hold the blade without letting the power seep into her. She didn't know whether a Fireworker would be able to sense the connection while she held such a blade, but she had to be careful. Her ability was still a secret, and it had to stay that way.

She had grown up believing she couldn't Work the Fire like her father, Rafe Ruminor the Lantern Maker, and her sister before she died. Dara had tried to draw on the Fire countless times, but her fingers had remained cold long past the age when the Firespark normally manifested. She had resigned herself to a life apart from the Fire and found dueling, a passion that had more than replaced the missing power.

But less than two months ago she had discovered that she could access the Fire after all. She hadn't told anyone at first. No matter what she decided to do with her newfound talent, it would change her entire relationship with her parents. They had always been disappointed in her for not being able to Work and for not wanting to be involved in the mundane aspects of the business. She needed time to process what her new Fire ability would mean for her future. She hadn't anticipated that she would end up keeping it a secret after the Vertigon Cup was over. She couldn't let her parents find out now. They would expect her to rejoin their business—the business that was responsible for the assassination of the king—and she would have to explain why she didn't want to be involved. She couldn't let them find out she knew about their plot against the Amintelles if she hoped to thwart their efforts.

The Fire tempted her with every pulse, though. Dara wanted to feel more of the heat, of the molten power that had flooded her veins just a few times now. There were a handful of access points in the castle, and it was becoming harder and harder to stay away from them. The only thing keeping her grounded was the knowledge that Siv would be in even more danger if her parents found out what she could do. And she would never let anything happen to him.

Dara shook off the thought and turned her attention to the Fire Blade. The king was right: there was no mark of any kind indicating who forged the weapon. During the fight, she had been too relieved that none of them had been stabbed to think about where the weapon came from. But it was definitely not army or Guard issue, so one of the traitorous Castle Guards hadn't simply given the mysterious swordsman his blade. Besides, the swordsman had fought like the blade was a part of him.

Fire Blade in hand, she left the king's chambers, nodding to Telvin Jale on the way out. He didn't comment on the weapon she carried. He, along with the other Castle Guards, must know Dara had been friends with the prince before. They treated her with respect, despite the fact that she was young and a woman—one of just two on the Guard. Most of the kingdom didn't know Dara had saved Siv and his sisters on the day of the assassination, but the Guard remembered.

Dara left the castle and jogged most of the way to her destination, far off on Square Peak. It was good to get out into the city again. As much as she liked the wide castle halls, she missed running through the crisp mountain air. She darted down the steep stairs and avenues of King's Peak, past greathouses and parlors and official buildings of marble and stone. The lower avenues of King's Peak bustled with noblemen and attendants, travelers and tradesmen. A handful of tough mountain ponies clopped along the cobblestones, snorting irritably as she jogged past. A few people looked askance at a young woman in a Castle Guard uniform. She ignored them and kept running.

She made her way to Stork Bridge, which stretched across the Fissure to Square Peak. Her boots pounded on the wooden slats of the bridge, and mists shifted beneath her feet. The Fissure was the only access point to the mountaintop kingdom of Vertigon. Visitors from the Lands Below had to traverse its length until they reached the steep road that wound up the canyon side. A series of pulleys made importing goods easier—albeit still precarious—but friend or foe had an arduous journey ahead of them if they wanted to enter Vertigon.

Once you were on the mountain, though, bridges spanned the gaps between the three peaks, King's, Village, and Square. The secluded kingdom was a place of peace and prosperity, a place where fighting was reserved for the dueling hall and dangers to the citizens were nonexistent. Or it had been until the king was murdered.

When Dara reached Square Peak, she ran faster. It was broader than King's and Village Peaks, with more room for wide buildings, such as dueling halls and the army barracks. Mountain goats roamed the peak at will, and there were paddocks with enough space for the stocky mountain ponies to exercise. Countless caves pockmarked the lower part of the peak, many inaccessible due to numerous drop-offs and cliffs around the jagged edges of the mountain.

The Firesmith Dara sought worked in one of the shops on a lower slope of the peak, not far from a steep drop-off into the Fissure. She left Stork Bridge and climbed down a winding stone staircase to reach the smithy. For the final stretch, a rickety set of wooden steps led down to the entrance to the shop jutting out of the stone.

Smoke and heat and the scent of molten metal poured out of the opening. Dara knocked politely, but she knew the man inside wouldn't hear her. She pushed opened the door and entered the realm of Daz Stoneburner, the best sword smith in Vertigon.

He was a slight man, more diminutive than his name and reputation implied. He stood just over five feet tall, and he had wispy white hair and a large mustache covering most of his mouth. Despite his short stature, his arms were thick and strong, and they glistened with sweat as he pounded a short blade on an iron anvil. The thud of hammer on steel filled the workshop. As a Fireworker, Daz could hold the red-hot blade with his bare hands. Fire flowed from an access point beside the anvil, making the windowless smithy glow as bright as day. Daz would be adding a steady supply of heat and Fire to the metal in his hands as he crafted the weapon.

Daz turned toward Dara the moment she entered, as if he could sense her coming through the door. But he was not alone.

"Coach!"

Dara's dueling instructor, Berg Doban, leaned against a stone table near the forge, where blades in various stages of completion awaited the work of the master Firesmith. He was a big man, with square shoulders, a bit of a gut, and rough salt-and-pepper hair.

"Hello, young Dara," Berg said, lowering his thick eyebrows. "What are you doing away from the castle? You must be guarding our king."

"He sent me on an errand," Dara said. "And I'm not on duty every single hour."

"What can I do for you, Miss Ruminor?" Daz said. He continued his rhythmic pounding on the weapon in his hands, fixing Dara with a sharp stare. He had forged her dueling weapons for years, but she still found him intimidating.

"I wanted to ask you about a blade." Dara hesitated, glancing up at Berg. He had been the one to ask her to watch out for Siv in the first place, but she still wasn't entirely sure where his loyalties lay. He wasn't even from Vertigon originally, and she found it strange that he was so eager to look out for the royal family. "Uh . . . I can come back later."

Berg simply folded his arms over his chest. "Go ahead, young Dara."

Dara held up the weapon from the mysterious swordsman.

"Can you tell me where this came from, Master Stoneburner? It doesn't have a maker's mark." She eyed Berg again. "And it's a Fire Blade."

Daz's hands stilled, his last beat echoing through the workshop. He set down the still-glowing sword he'd been working on and exchanged an unmistakable glance with Berg as he took the Fire Blade from Dara's hands. The steel reflected in his dark eyes as he examined the weapon from all sides.

He didn't say anything for a long time. Then instead of answering Dara he looked up at her coach.

"Well, that confirms it," he said.

"Confirms what?" Dara asked.

"I am telling you this," Berg said to the Firesmith. "You see what you must do."

Daz didn't answer. He ran his fingers along the tang of the blade, studying its smooth, Fire-forged surface.

"Do you know who made this?" Dara asked.

"I cannot help you." Daz put the weapon back in Dara's hands and shuffled over to his anvil.

"Why not? What's going on?" Dara said. "Coach?"

Berg frowned at Daz as the pounding of the hammer resumed, then he turned to Dara.

"This blade came from the prince's attacker, yes?"

"Yes."

Berg scratched his wide jaw. He considered her for a long time before speaking again.

"I must ask you, Dara, a very important question. Are you loyal to the Amintelles?"

"What? Coach . . ."

"You must answer. You are Castle Guard now. You have sworn your life to protect the king. You even stopped your training to do this. But are you loyal?"

"Yes," Dara said without hesitation. She wasn't sure what Berg was getting at, but this much was clear. She may miss dueling, and she may wonder whether she'd done the right thing by leaving her parents, but some things were simple. Her hands tightened on the blade in her hands, warming the steel. "I won't let any harm come to Siv."

"Good," Berg said. His frown deepened. "There is a plot, a plot that goes deeper than you know. This blade is a part."

"What kind of plot?" Dara asked. She barely dared to breathe, heat and nerves humming in her stomach. Surely Berg didn't know about her parents. Otherwise, why would he have asked her to train with the prince all those months ago? "And how do you know about it?"

"I will show you," Berg said. "Tomorrow night you must meet me by the school at midnight. As to what kind and who, that question is more difficult."

"You must have some idea."

"Is not a conversation for today," Berg said. He glanced at Daz Stoneburner again. "Some people are not as loyal as they should be."

"I swore an oath, Doban," Daz snapped, his hammer stilling. "I will not break it, even if your cause is noble."

"You must!" Berg said. "You see this blade." He gestured to the weapon in Dara's hands. "You know what they will do when they have more."

"Stop them, then," Daz said. "Stop them, but do not ask me to add yet more illicit Fire Blades to this mess."

Dara expected Berg to keep arguing, but instead he stalked toward the exit, jerking his head for Dara to follow. Daz Stoneburner hadn't resumed his work, and he watched them with narrowed eyes. But it wasn't Berg who had the Firesmith's attention. Instead, he stared at the Fire Blade growing warm in Dara's hands.

She quickly returned it to its sheath and left the forge without looking back.

She shouldn't have come to see Daz, even though he was the most talented Firesmith she knew. She shouldn't trust any of the Fireworkers. Some must support her parents' efforts against the king, though Dara wasn't sure how extensive that support was. Master Corren the Firespinner—and Farr's original employer—was on their side, and Farr had been taking the princess straight to the Fire Guild's headquarters. The Workers had good reason to resent King Sevren. He had enforced a policy of regulation that diminished and diluted their access to the Fire of Vertigon. The tension had been increasing for some time now. She'd thought Daz was staying out of it, though. What if he was on their side now too? If he was, why had Berg come to see him today?

Dara tried to ask her coach what was going on as they climbed the rickety stairs leading away from the smithy, but he brushed off her questions with a roll of his heavy shoulders.

"We talk tomorrow," he barked. "Do not be late."

4

THE LADIES

WITH Sora trailing him and chattering in his ear, Siv didn't make it back to his rooms in time to meet Dara. The new Castle Guard at his door informed Pool in crisp tones that Miss Ruminor had already come and gone. Siv did his best to hide a scowl of disappointment as he strode into his antechamber and flopped down onto the couch.

He pulled off his crown and twisted it between his fingers as Sora began digging through the books and papers on the table, still lecturing him about everything he should have done differently at the council meeting. He felt unbearably restless. He wanted to go for a run, of all things, and he *hated* running.

"Where's Sel?" he asked his sister, cutting off whatever enthusiastic diatribe she'd been on for the past half hour.

"With Mother."

Siv sighed. Their mother had spent the past month secluded in her chambers. Last time he had visited her, she informed him she would be returning to Trure now that her husband was dead. She wanted to take her youngest daughter, Selivia, with her. It wouldn't be the worst thing in the world for his sister to spend some time with her cousins and grandfather in the Land of the Horse Keepers, but Selivia adamantly refused to leave the mountain behind.

"What do *you* think about sending Selivia to Trure?" Siv asked his other sister. Sora may only be seventeen, but she could be wise. Sometimes.

To his surprise, Sora said, "I don't think you should make her go."

"Really? Not even to lay the groundwork for future marriage alliances with Trure?"

"I think she would be more use here," Sora said. "You can hint to the nobles that you're thinking about promising her hand. It'll keep the ones with young sons in line for years until she's actually old enough to marry any of them."

"Can't I do that with your hand?" Siv said with a grin. Sora gave him a flat look in return.

"*I* have plans for my own hand," Sora said. "And I think Sel will end up being more enticing than I am when she gets older. She'll be the greater beauty."

Siv blinked. "That's very . . . noble of you."

"I'm stating facts," Sora said. "There's nothing noble about that. Besides, Selivia's still pretty sad." Her voice softened. "I don't think it's fair to make her leave so soon."

Siv agreed with that at least. He hated seeing the grief on his young sisters' faces. It was too much of a mirror of his own. They had all loved their father, and his loss shadowed their family like a winter storm. But Siv couldn't let his emotions reign. They all had to do things they didn't want to do.

"Speaking of people's hands," he said with a sigh, "I've invited Tull Denmore to dinner tomorrow night."

"That's wise," Sora said, "though it may be too little too late. She has been visiting the parlors with Bolden almost every night."

"What?" Siv leapt from his chair and paced across the room. *Firelord take Bolden Rollendar all the way to his burning realm.* "Every night?"

"Yes. I had tea with Vine Silltine recently, and she filled me in on the parlor gossip. The prevailing belief is that they'll announce an engagement soon."

"So while I've been busy with the aftermath of our father's assassination Bolden has been . . . oh that's low, lower than a cullmoran nest in . . . *every night*?"

"You'll have to act quickly," Sora said.

"I guess I will." Something niggled at the back of Siv's mind, something besides Bolden and his sneaking maneuverings. "Wait a minute. What are your plans for *your* hand, Sora?"

Sora frowned at a map spread across Siv's table. Dimples wrinkled in her round cheeks. She may not be a great beauty, but she was reasonably cute. And she cared about their family and their kingdom as much as he did. Siv should really appreciate her more.

"I am going to marry the Crown Prince of Soole."

"You are? Since when?" Siv stopped at the table, looking down at the map where far-off Soole was outlined. Located beyond Trure and Cindral Forest on a rocky peninsula, it was as far from Vertigon as blasted Pendark.

"I've had it in mind for a while now," Sora said. "The Soolen ambassador was here during the Vertigon Cup. She said the Crown Prince has not yet been promised to anyone."

"Isn't he nine?"

"He's fifteen. Honestly, Siv, you're supposed to know these things. He was nine when we met him six years ago."

Siv rubbed a hand through his hair, thinking back to the grand visit from the Soolen royal family. Siv had been fourteen, and he and Bolden had spent most of the time trying to capture a jar full of zurwasps to release in the Soolen queen's rooms. She had not been very nice at all. The Crown Prince hadn't impressed him either.

"Wasn't he a bratty little thing?" Siv said. "He can't have turned into a particularly appealing fifteen-year-old."

"As I recall," Sora said dryly, "you were a rather bratty little prince at the time too. And you're doing all right."

Siv raised an eyebrow.

"Why, Sora, that's the nicest thing you've ever said to me."

"Soolen queens have more power than Vertigonian ones," Sora said, ignoring his comment. "And assuming you live long enough to produce an heir, it's the only way I'll ever be queen."

"Oh." Siv studied his younger sister. She really did love the workings of the kingdom. He had often thought she might make a better ruler than him. Not that he would ever tell her that. "Well, I feel sorry for the little guy. You'll make a formidable Queen of Soole, Sora."

King of Mist

"Thanks. So, have you worked out how you're going to woo Lady Tull away from the dashing Lord Bolden?"

Siv sniggered, but Sora only folded her arms and fixed her light-blue eyes on him.

"Oh, come on," Siv said. She had to be joking. "You think it'll be hard? What woman could possibly favor Bolden over me?"

"It may surprise you to hear this, Sivarrion," Sora said, "but you are not the only handsome and eligible young man in Vertigon. Bolden is a bit dark and brooding, but many women like that. And he's ambitious. Lord Denmore was too, and Tull picked him first."

"I'll keep that in mind," Siv said, "but Bolden is going to have to rein in his ambitions. Him and his father."

"I agree. I'll keep my ears open in any case," Sora said. "If the Rollendars have a new alliance with the Samanars, it won't be good news for us." She went back to rearranging the papers spread across his table. "And you'd better work on being your most charming self tomorrow night. It wouldn't hurt to take every opportunity to remind Lady Tull that if she chooses you she'll become queen."

"Sure," Siv said. "Apparently some women like that sort of thing."

Sora looked back at the map and traced Soole with her fingertips. "Apparently they do."

THE FOLLOWING NIGHT, Siv strode toward the eastern tower, where he would be hosting his dinner with Lady Tull. He didn't think he had anything to worry about in his pursuit of the comely widow. All he had to do was be kingly and fascinating. And actually ask for her hand. That was the part he was still working up to.

As Siv reached the eastern stairwell, Dara marched up to intercept him. She bowed and snapped off a salute to Pool.

"Your Highness, I may have news about the investigation you asked me to conduct."

"That was quick." Siv had a full complement of Castle Guards in tow and decided he didn't know them well enough to be sure they were trustworthy. If only he could read the minds of all the men who were supposed to protect him. "Walk with me. We can talk in the tower."

"Yes, Your Highness," Dara said, falling in beside him as they started up the stairs. She was always extra formal around him in front of her new comrades. Siv found himself wondering whether she fancied any of them. The Guards were all spry and athletic, and doubtless very good with their swords.

He rolled his shoulders, not wanting to think too much about that. Maybe he shouldn't have invited her to join the Guard and live with all those men in the barracks. He could be a burning fool sometimes.

He studied Dara out of the corner of his eye. He wouldn't object to being able to read her mind either. She looked professional and serious in her Castle Guard uniform. She had acquired a new coat since yesterday, one that was tailored to fit the curves of her tall frame better than the standard issue one. Her trim black trousers fit her well too. If she noticed him noticing, she didn't let on. Her golden hair was pulled back in a tight plait, but a few wisps had escaped it and framed her proud face. She kept her eyes on the stairs ahead. She had been unfailingly proper since taking the job. He supposed he should be grateful that she was making things easier by keeping him at arm's length, even if it wasn't that easy after all.

He forced himself to look straight ahead as they climbed the stairwell. A glass-encased parlor jutted out from the tower on one of the upper levels. It would be the perfect setting for his evening meal with Lady Tull. With luck, the moon would rise over the peaks of Vertigon and bathe the mountain in a muted glow. It would be damned romantic, and Tull wouldn't be able to help saying yes to him. She was the only woman he should be thinking about tonight.

But Dara strode beside him with her usual confidence, and he wished the other Castle Guards would disappear. He wanted to walk a little closer to her, to look into her intense eyes, to take her hand just so he could feel her skin against his. When they reached the door, he asked Pool to wait outside.

"I'll fill you in later," he said, not giving him a chance to protest.

They entered the parlor, where a serving woman was finishing up the final preparations for the meal. She fussed over a small table set with polished stone plates and goblets, not the fanciest set the castle owned, but nice. In the center sat a pure Firegold vase filled with artfully preserved apple blossoms. The glass windows revealed the deep shadows spreading over Vertigon as the sun began to set. Mists boiled deep in the Fissure and spread tendrils around the bridges. They might not have the clear, romantic night Siv had hoped for, but it was still one of the best views on the mountain.

If Dara was impressed, she didn't let on. She waited until the serving woman placed the final piece of silver on the tablecloth and shuffled out.

"I have a lead," Dara said as soon as they were alone. "I went to see a sword smith about the Fire Blade, and Berg was there."

"Doban?" Siv hadn't thought about his dueling coach in weeks. He'd had many more important things on his mind. "That's normal, right? To find a sword master in a sword shop."

"They weren't talking about swords, exactly." Dara filled him in on the conversation she had witnessed. There wasn't much to go on. Berg had been talking about plots against the Amintelles for months now. Little good that had done Siv's father.

"They weren't surprised to see a Fire Blade without a maker's mark," Dara said. "Someone is forging them for your enemies. I think Berg wants Daz to do the same for him."

"This is Daz Stoneburner?" Siv asked.

"Yes. He said he wouldn't break his oath." Dara studied him with those intense eyes of hers. "I'm not sure what he meant."

"Wouldn't that be the oath not to forge Fire Blades for anyone except the king and army?"

"That's the only Firesmith oath I know of," Dara said, "but I'm not sure that's all he meant. And why would Berg ask him to make weapons rather than working directly with the army and the Guard if there's a real threat? Something doesn't add up."

"Hmm." Siv paced across the small parlor. There wasn't much room for pacing with the table and chairs in the way. His arm brushed Dara's as he passed her. "Do you think your parents would have any insight into any other oaths a Fireworker might make?" Dara's father was a prominent Fire Lantern Maker. Siv didn't think Lantern Makers would have much to do with a potential illicit weapons ring, but they must know most of the Workers in Vertigon.

"I'm sure they don't," Dara said. Her response was quite sharp.

Siv knew Dara didn't get along well with her parents, but he was still surprised at her vehemence. "Berg told me to meet him at midnight tonight, and he would show me what's going on."

"Are you sure that's a good idea?" Siv remembered a particularly harsh dueling lesson in which Berg had fought them with a sharpened blade. He hadn't hurt Siv, but he had cut Dara's arm right through her sleeve. Siv didn't like the idea of her going off to meet the man in the middle of the night.

"Why not?" Dara said. "Maybe Berg knows where those weapons are being forged."

"Then why didn't he tell you straight off?"

"I'm not sure. This thing could be a lot bigger than we thought that first time we were attacked."

Dara looked up and met Siv's eyes. A bit of color suffused her cheeks, and Siv wondered if she was remembering the same things he was about that night. He had held her for the first time that night, right before he was almost murdered. He had very nearly kissed her.

Firelord take him, but he wanted to kiss her now. The sun dipped lower, setting the mist creeping up the slopes alight. The mountainside blazed gold and red, and the dying sunlight caught in Dara's golden hair.

With a rather kingly effort, Siv pulled his eyes away from her and resumed his frenetic pacing. It wouldn't be fair to kiss her now. Not when he couldn't offer her anything more than that. He had already asked her to devote herself to the Castle Guard knowing it would take her away from dueling, the thing she loved most. He had no right to ask anything more of Dara Ruminor, not even a kiss.

So something was going on, and Berg knew about it. Siv shook his head. He should think about Berg, with his grumbling voice and his gruff, square face. Think about Berg, not the gorgeous woman standing almost within arms reach.

He imagined that strange practice bout again and the white-hot rage he had felt when Berg cut Dara's arm.

"I don't think you should go out there tonight," he said.

"What?"

"With Berg," Siv said. "I don't think you should meet up with him in the middle of the night. We don't actually know whose side he's on."

Dara frowned. Damn, she was even pretty when she was frowning.

"If Berg was going to do something to me, he's had a thousand chances," she said. "He could have tossed me into the Fissure as we left the Firesmith, and no one would have known. I should see what he wants to show me."

She was right. They needed something new, some sort of breakthrough if they were going to find whoever had orchestrated his father's death. Even if that meant putting Dara at risk. He glared at the table set for his romantic meal, wishing he could call it off. If only he could go along to make sure Dara was safe. She could take care of herself, but he would feel better if he could watch her back.

"Report to me as soon as you return to the castle," Siv said. "I don't care how late it is. I want to know you're safe."

"I'll be fine," Dara said. "Besides, are you sure you won't be busy late tonight?"

Her gaze dropped to the romantic table setting, and Siv winced. He had made no secret of his plans for the evening. Of course she knew he was entertaining a noble lady shortly. Worse, she would understand completely what his end goal had to be with Lady Tull.

"Even if Pool has to pull me by the toes from my bed, I insist on being informed when you return," Siv said. "Besides, you'll have way more fun sneaking around than I will here."

He gave a rueful smile, and to his relief Dara answered it.

"I'll do my best to have more fun than you," she said. Her normally serious face softened as she met his eyes. Her hair fell in wisps from her braid, and the sun caught them like tendrils of Firegold. The curve of her lips and the intensity of her eyes nearly drove him mad. She couldn't possibly know the effect she had on him. She looked so beautiful he wanted to—

"Berg!" Siv gasped. *Think about ugly old Berg. Don't think about Dara.*

She raised an eyebrow. "What about him?"

"Uh . . . ask Berg if he's heard of any dueling schools where the owner of our Fire Blade may have trained. They could be turning out athletes who are a bit too comfortable using deadly force."

"I'll ask," Dara said.

"Good. Be careful. And don't forget to tell me when you're back."

Dara snapped off a salute and headed for the door, ever the professional. Siv watched the door long after she closed it behind her.

5

ENCOUNTERS

DARA crossed paths with Lady Tull Denmore on her way out of the tower. Though they had met before, the noblewoman didn't even glance at her as she swept up the stairs toward her dinner with the king. She was a small woman, but she looked positively regal in an elegant blue dress with a modest cut, her hair piled on top of her head in an intricate style that must have taken hours.

Dara hurried past, ignoring the dull pain that sprang up in her gut at the sight of Lady Tull. She had no reason to be wary—and certainly no reason to be jealous. Lady Tull would make a charming Queen of Vertigon. And Siv had been so sad since his father died. He deserved to have someone who brought him joy. Not that Dara was convinced he had chosen Tull because she made him happy. Siv was doing what he had to for the good of the kingdom. His own feelings couldn't be his main priority. Dara understood that better than anybody.

Still, she couldn't help replaying her few moments alone with Siv as she descended through the tower. Their closeness. The brush of his arm sending a slow blaze across her skin. Just the two of them facing that fiery sunset view. What would happen if she ever told him she felt like burning to a cinder when he looked at her the way he sometimes did? He didn't think she noticed it, but it was all she could do to keep from stepping into his arms when he looked at her like that.

But there was no point in thinking about what could never be. Dara adjusted her new Castle Guard uniform, which had just arrived from the tailor that morning, and straightened her shoulders. She had taken on this duty to atone for her father's actions, not to steal moments alone with Siv. She was a guardswoman, and the king had a duty to select an appropriate queen.

When Dara rounded the corner at the bottom of the stairwell, she almost bumped into Fenn Hurling. In her mid-thirties, the muscular red-haired bodyguard was almost as large as her twin brother, Denn. Fenn folded her arms, the polished buttons of her coat winking, and stared down at her. Dara muttered an apology, but it didn't ease the disapproving scowl on Fenn's face.

Fortunately, Princess Selivia popped out from behind her a second later.

"Dara! I haven't seen you in ages."

"Hello, Princess. How are you?" Dara couldn't help smiling whenever she ran into the young princess. Not yet fourteen, Selivia was a bubbling cauldron of enthusiasm ready to overflow at any moment. Some of that joyous energy had been missing since her father died, but she seemed in good spirits today.

"I saw Lady Tull!" Selivia said. "Her dress is so lovely. Did you see it?"

"Yes."

"Siv wouldn't let me set up the parlor for him. He said I would make it too girly."

"I'm sure it would have been beautiful," Dara said. "It looks nice, though. I just came from there."

"Where are you going now?" Selivia walked with Dara down the wide corridor, her slippers whispering on the marble floor. Selivia had abandoned her black gowns the second the family's mourning period had ended. Today she wore a deep-green dress that looked like it was getting too short for her already. She would be as tall as Dara soon.

"I'm heading back to the barracks for a bit. I have to run some errands tonight," Dara said.

"Ooh, how are the barracks? Mother never lets me explore them."

"They're fine," Dara said. "A bit empty right now. I have my own room for the moment."

"Oh, you mean you might have to share?" Selivia looked back at Fenn, who had fallen in behind them. "You could be roommates when the barracks fill up again!"

"Maybe," Dara said. Fenn grunted noncommittally. She was the only other woman on the guard, but Dara hadn't forgotten that Fenn had been nowhere in sight when the princess was kidnapped a month ago. Supposedly one of the turncoat guards had hit her over the head, but that could have been orchestrated to keep Fenn in the castle if things went poorly. Dara had to be cautious with her trust.

"Can I come see your room, Dara?" Selivia asked. "Please!"

"I don't think—"

"I'll end up sneaking over there anyway. Better for you to take me now than when there are a bunch of new guardsmen making them all smelly."

Dara chuckled. "You might have a point."

"Excellent. Fenn, don't tell your brother."

"Yes, my lady," Fenn said, her tone surprisingly indulgent.

Dara led the way down the corridor leading to the back courtyard, which separated the castle from the guard barracks. It was strange to have the run of the place. Dara had been able to see this castle from the window of her room in her parents' home for her entire childhood. She had never imagined she would one day live within its walls.

When they were almost to the back courtyard, a dark-robed figure loomed into their path. Selivia gave a little squeak, and Dara put a hand to her blade.

"Evening," said a dry, papery voice. It was Zage Lorrid, the Fire Warden. He stared down at them, his face egg white and grim. A bit of silver glinted at his throat.

"Oh, Warden, you scared me," Selivia said.

"Where are you going, Princess?"

"Dara is showing me the Guard barracks," Selivia said.

Zage frowned, his dark eyes glittering. "I don't think that's wise in light of the tragedies your family has faced of late."

"I'm tired of sitting in my room," Selivia said. "Dara will protect me, like she did before."

Zage looked Dara up and down. "I suppose she did." He kept staring, and Dara wasn't sure whether to look away or not. She got the sense that Zage knew every thought in her head and every worry she'd ever had. She shivered. Did he know what had happened with Farr? No, that was impossible. No one had been around to see it.

Dara remembered what Berg always said about making eye contact before a duel: the first person to look away lost. She held Zage's gaze. The Fire Warden didn't blink, didn't waver, but neither did Dara. This was the man who had killed her sister. Over ten years ago, he had unleashed a surge of Fire through the mountain that had burned right through Renna as she was learning to Work. Zage's name had long been a curse in Dara's household. She couldn't forget it, even though they were supposedly loyal to the same family now.

"We'll be quick, Warden," Selivia said, apparently not bothered by the staring match. She tried to edge past Zage to reach the outer door. "I'm finished with my lessons for the day."

Zage finally turned from Dara and looked down at the young princess.

"Perhaps I should accompany you," he said, his expression softening unexpectedly. There was affection there. And concern. He didn't want the princess to be in danger. The realization threw Dara off balance.

"I'll show you the barracks another time, Princess," she said.

"But—"

"I promise."

"Fine." Selivia sighed dramatically. "Let's go to the kitchens, Fenn, and see if they've made any special desserts for Lady Tull's visit."

Zage waited until the princess and her bodyguard marched off toward the lower level of the castle before he swept away in another direction. He didn't give Dara so much as a backward glance.

Relieved to be rid of him, Dara headed out to the barracks, a sturdy building at the edge of the back courtyard. A few practice weapons leaned against the wall, but the quiet of evening had already settled over the grounds. She mulled over Zage's intervention as she climbed the steps to the simple portico outside her room. He clearly suspected Dara was a danger to the young princess. Siv respected Zage as a teacher and maybe even a mentor, but the man had never warmed to Dara. She had every reason to mistrust him—or at least she had until she'd thrown her lot in with the Amintelles.

Zage was her parents' longtime political adversary too. As Fire Warden, he controlled the flow of Fire through the mountain, and they believed he wanted to keep power out of their hands by spreading it thin, leaving it diluted and unthreatening. But now that the Ruminors' desire for power and revenge had taken a dangerous turn, had Dara found herself on Zage's side after all?

She had questioned why her parents went after King Sevren before directly challenging the Fire Warden. She suspected it wouldn't have been enough for them to simply kill him. They would want to obliterate him. They'd demand a public denunciation of his crime, the justice they hadn't received ten years ago. And they wanted a new ruler, one who wouldn't try to keep their powers in check. In that, they had failed. For now.

Dara was sure they would try again. The Ruminors wanted revenge. They wanted change. They wanted a revolution. Dara had vowed to stand in their way. She missed her sister as much as they did, but taking down the Fire Warden and every Amintelle on the mountain would not bring her back. She would do whatever it took to avert her parents' murderous ambitions, even if that meant working alongside Zage Lorrid.

Dara's door creaked as she returned to her room to prepare for her evening jaunt with Berg. The room was austere, with two raised cots, a small wooden table, a stone washbasin, and a few shelves for her possessions. A handful of dueling tokens, a necklace of mismatched Fire-forged beads, and the medal she had won in the Square Tourney last year were the only keepsakes she had brought to the castle. She forced down the memory of her mother screaming vitriol at her as she left her childhood home behind.

She pulled off her boots, which were still shiny and new, and sat on her cot to rub her feet. She'd switch to her old clothes for the midnight excursion. She wouldn't want anyone to recognize a Castle Guard snooping around whatever Berg planned to show her.

Dara's dueling gear sat unused in the corner. She avoided looking at it as much as possible. She could keep competing on Turndays when Pool hired more Castle Guards, but it would be terrible to go to tournaments and see her rivals outstripping her because they trained more. Dueling was an all-or-nothing game, and Dara had decided to give her all to another cause.

She wished she felt more confident that it had been the right decision. Did she really have a place in the castle, especially now that the king was entertaining his possible future wife?

The reminder was like a blow to the stomach. She shrugged it off and unwound her braid, running an ebony comb through her golden tresses. She had to keep her focus, just like in a competition. If Berg revealed some useful insight tonight, she might be able to stop her parents *and* whoever else was plotting against Siv. His troubles likely ran deeper than the Fireworkers. Maybe her parents were only the beginning.

A knock sounded at her door, making Dara jump. She tossed her comb on the bed and opened the door. The young guard she'd met the other day was raising his fist to knock again.

"Hello," Dara said. "Telvin, right?"

"Dara." He gave a slight bow, almost a salute. "Would you like to have a drink in town this evening?"

"With the other guardsmen?" she asked.

"No, just with me."

"Oh, um, thank you," Dara said, surprised at the directness of the offer. "I have business over on Square tonight." She started to shut the door then caught sight of the eastern tower rising behind Telvin. She couldn't quite see the glass parlor at this angle, but she could picture it—and the romantic table setting—well enough. She surprised herself by pulling back the door and calling out to Telvin before he walked away. "Actually, I have time beforehand if you don't mind getting some food too. I'm starving."

"Great," Telvin said. "Are you ready now?"

"Give me five minutes," Dara said. "I'll meet you by the gates."

"Agreed." Telvin smiled and turned crisply on his heels to march down the portico to his own quarters. He had broad shoulders and a strong back, and there was something pleasing about his sharp, serious movements.

Dara looked up at the tower, a gloomy spire in the fading light. Siv was doing what was necessary. Why shouldn't she grab a bite to eat with one of her new colleagues? She needed all the allies she could get.

6

THE GUARDSMAN

DARA changed into a black blouse, tucked soft gray trousers into her old boots, and braided her hair again. She slung her black cloak over her arm. It had been a gift from Selivia, and it was by far the finest item of clothing she owned. She also buckled her Savven blade at her waist. She needed to be prepared for her midnight stroll with Berg.

Telvin Jale waited for her at the small sally port by the main castle gates. He still wore his guard uniform, but his coat buttons were undone, and his shirt hung open at the neck. He greeted Dara with a nod and only the slightest glance at the ornate black hilt of the Savven on her hip.

They ambled down through Lower King's, passing the fine greathouses with elegant balconies and marble-trimmed porticos. A hush permeated the streets at this twilight hour. Dara and Telvin had to step aside to allow the occasional palanquin to pass by, but most people on King's Peak would be at their dinners already, bent over bowls of goat stew, flatbread, and orchard fruits.

"I don't know many good places to eat in Lower King's," Telvin said as they made their way from the residential areas near the castle to a busier street lined with stylish shops and parlors. "My favorite haunts are over on Square."

"Did you live there before you joined the army?"

"No, I grew up on Village," Telvin said. "Not far from the mines. My father and brothers still work there."

Dara reassessed his broad shoulders and strong build. Yes, she could see his mining family roots.

"But you joined the army?"

"It's a better life than my father's," Telvin said. "And Castle Guard is better still."

They peered in the windows of the shops and taverns as they walked, looking for somewhere to eat. Dara stopped at a familiar sign: Bridge Troll Tavern.

"I've actually been here before," Dara said. *With Siv.* She still remembered the cozy warmth of the establishment, the way one patron had smoked a pipe by the window, the tendrils escaping into the night. And she remembered Siv leaning in to advise her about how to act around potential patrons, nearly taking her hand. It felt strange to bring Telvin here, but then Siv would be entertaining—and possibly proposing—to Lady Tull at that very moment. "I don't know if the food is any good, but we could try it."

"Looks fine to me." Telvin pulled open the door for her with a creak.

Dara led the way to a table on the opposite side of the tavern from where she had sat with Siv. The Bridge Troll Tavern was quiet this evening. A pair of travelers sat in a corner booth, and a well-dressed craftsman leaned against the bar and chatted with the tavern keeper. A few men came in behind Dara and Telvin, looking like butlers or noblemen's attendants on their night off. Their voices were soft and sober. Gloom had settled over the city during the past month of mourning. King Sevren had been well loved. Something would need to change soon in Vertigon, or this winter would be very grim indeed.

Dara tried to shake off the somberness of the evening as she settled in across from Telvin with goat pies and ale. She hated the taste of ale, but she took a long sip from her tankard anyway. She was one of the Guard now, and she should embrace her new role. Siv was doing the same.

A small Firebulb hanging above their table created a warm pool of light around them. Dara and Telvin talked about dueling as they ate, but that only made her miss the rush of competition and the roar of the crowds. And Siv waving a black silk banner with her name on it. She forced herself to take another sip of ale.

"What do you think of the king?" she asked.

"Think of him?" Telvin said, forehead furrowing. "He's the king."

"Yes, but what's your opinion of the man himself now that you work for him?"

"I was recruited from the army." Telvin snapped to attention in his chair. "I am loyal to the crown."

"This isn't a test," Dara said. "I'm just curious."

Telvin's shoulders relaxed a little. He studied his tankard, scratching a thick finger along the carving at its base.

"The king is young," he said. "I don't reckon he's proved himself yet, but then he hasn't had a chance either."

"That's true," Dara said. "How old are you, if you don't mind me asking?"

"Twenty-two. Not much older than the king himself, to be fair. Another drink?"

Dara blinked, surprised she had already finished her ale. Somehow it didn't taste any better at the bottom. But she thought of that romantic table setting in the sunset-drenched parlor and accepted a second one.

"These were on the house," Telvin said when he returned with the foaming tankards. "The tavern keeper wanted to know if you're really Nightfall. I was damn proud to say I'm having dinner with one of the most popular lady duelists in Vertigon."

"That's not me anymore," Dara said.

"I was proud anyway." Telvin took a long sip of the complimentary ale, looking at her thoughtfully. "So what do *you* think of the king?" he asked.

"He's a good man," Dara said. "He'll prove himself."

"I hope so. Vertigon deserves a good king."

By the time they finished their meals and their third round of drinks—Dara switched to water for herself when she went to fetch the round—it was past the eleventh hour. She'd have to run to meet Berg on time.

"What do you say we cross to the pubs on Square?" Telvin said. His face was a little red, and he had relaxed considerably. "Tomorrow's my day off, and I reckon a few other barkeeps would love to treat you."

"I have to take care of a few things," Dara said. "Thanks, though." She stood, wavering a bit from the drinks, and dug her fingernails into the wooden tabletop to steady herself. The Firebulb hanging above the table swayed, right at eye level. The tavern door was closed, and there was no draft. It was as if Dara was pulling the Fire in the bulb toward her. It seemed to grow larger before her eyes. Her skin hummed with warmth.

"Did you forget something?" Telvin asked, coming around the table to stand beside her.

The Firebulb swung forward. Dara focused on calming her body, keeping the rush of the drink in her blood from loosening her control. She almost never drank, and it seemed to affect her connection to the Fire. She'd have to remember that.

"No, I'm fine." She pulled her gaze away from the glowing bulb and turned to Telvin. "Shall we?" She strode deliberately to the door as the Firebulb swayed, finally slowing to a stop behind her.

Outside, Dara breathed deeply, allowing the damp breeze to clear her head.

"Are you sure you don't want to come for another drink?" Telvin asked, stepping closer to her in the darkened street. "Didn't you say you're going to Square anyway?"

"Maybe next time," Dara said. "I'll see you back at the barracks."

Telvin looked like he wanted to protest, but instead he bowed over her hand and said, "Good night, Dara."

She gave a quick nod, hoping to discourage a longer farewell, and strode away. He would likely take Stork Bridge over to Square. She'd have to make a detour over Garden Bridge so he wouldn't see where she was heading. She wasn't ready to trust Telvin Jale, however nice he seemed.

Dara jogged all the way to Berg's dueling school on Square Peak. Mist oozed around the bridges. The night was eerie, with the sharpness of autumn in the air. The run warmed her, and the buzz from the ale dissipated. It was a relief to know the warmth came from pure exertion when she thundered across little-used Garden Bridge. It was built of wood and rope, its pathways sparsely lit. She was too far away from the stones of the mountain to worry about pulling any Fire into her body.

That Firebulb had definitely gravitated to her in the tavern. She had to get control of her newfound ability—and soon. It was easier to draw on the Fire when she had steel in her hand to help her focus. The trouble was she carried a sword all the time now, and sometimes the Fire came when she didn't want it to. She needed to figure out how the magic worked so she could train herself to avoid such incidents. Despite being around the Fire her whole life, she wasn't sure where to start. Most Fireworkers trained with a master who guided them through the first dangerous moments while they were still children. Those with the Spark could handle the Fire without being burned, but if they lost control it would still hurt them. The Fire could even kill, as Dara knew all too well. And if she lost control, people might find out what she could do. That would raise more questions than she was prepared to answer right now.

The streets of Square Peak were even emptier than Lower King's. The chill and the mist had driven people indoors, where they'd sit around Fire Gates, warm their hands with Heatstones, and wrap themselves in wool blankets. It was not a night to be out alone.

The dueling school rose before her, a hulking shape in the darkness. The last of the students would have gone home by now, or into the warm arms of a neighboring pub. Dara felt a twinge of sadness as she thought of her friends Kel and Oat, who were no doubt holding forth in one of those pubs. She hadn't seen them in weeks, and she missed them.

Berg opened the door of the dueling school and stepped out as Dara neared. He wore a cloak of mountain bear fur, making him look a bit like a bear himself, apart from the sword buckled at his hip.

"Coach," she said.

He grunted a greeting. "You are armed?"

Dara flung back her cloak to reveal the Savven.

"Good. We must be silent. Tell no one what I will show you. Enemies of the Amintelles have ears. Trust no one."

"Yes, Coach." Dara hesitated and then asked, "Why do you trust me?"

Berg lowered his eyebrows and gave her an appraising look.

"There is a reason you ask this, young Dara."

"It's . . . it's possible my parents are involved," she said. "Do you know anything about that?"

Berg blew out a long breath and cracked his large knuckles one by one.

"You know," he said. It wasn't a question.

"I figured it out too late," Dara said. "I . . . I think my father . . ." She didn't finish the thought, hoping Berg would fill in the details that she hadn't been able to say out loud.

"Yes," Berg said. "But he did not act alone. You are against your father and mother in this, Dara?"

"They're wrong," Dara said. A sharp wind blew over the peak, whistling through the alleyways and rattling the shutters on the dueling school. She shivered. "I wish it could be different, but King Sevren didn't deserve to die."

Berg inclined his head solemnly. "No. The king was good. Come."

He led the way toward the far northern side of Square Peak, heading in the direction of the Burnt Mountains beyond Vertigon. They walked in silence at first, keeping to the shadows between buildings. A feral cur-dragon snuffed and sneezed in an ally, but nothing else moved.

"Coach," Dara said after a while. "Have you told anyone about my parents?"

"I will tell no one unless I trust them," Berg said. "I trust no one."

"What about King Siv?"

Berg looked at her from beneath lowered brows. "You must tell him. When you are ready. There is much to do before then."

"I know," Dara said. Of course she should tell Siv about her parents. She'd known it from the very first day. Something always held her back, though. She couldn't bear to see his reaction when he learned who had killed his father. She pulled her cloak closer, armoring herself against the damp and the mist. She had thought it would feel better to talk about her parents with someone, but hearing her suspicions confirmed out loud wasn't much comfort after all. And Berg hadn't been surprised.

"Did you know about my parents when you asked me to train with the prince months ago?" she asked him. "That was a big risk."

"A risk, yes," Berg said. "But I know my students."

Dara didn't respond. She wondered what would have happened if she had told her parents about the prince from the beginning. Perhaps Berg had been hoping their partnership would lead to an eventual reconciliation between the Amintelles and the Ruminors. If so, he had put too much faith in her relationship with her parents. On the other hand, they could have asked her to spy on their behalf, or even carry the poison to the castle herself. Although, even if she hadn't come to care for Siv, she didn't think she could have done that anyway. Maybe Berg did know her well.

They walked all the way to the northern slope of Square Peak, not far from the largest of the paddocks where mountain ponies were raised. King's Peak and the Fissure were hidden from view here. Instead, the desolate range of the Burnt Mountains spread out in the distance. Smoky clouds hung above them, simmering with red light even at midnight.

The mists continued to drift and curl around Square Peak, and the full moon set them aglow. Suddenly, Berg ducked behind a run-down shack near the edge of the paddock. He blended with the shadows for a moment. Then a rustling, crackling sound came from the darkness, and he pulled back a bundle of dried branches, revealing the entrance to a tunnel leading deep into the mountain.

"We go in here," Berg said. "Draw your weapon."

7
HOUSE DENMORE

DINNER was going well, all things considered. Siv was quite certain he had been suitably charming. He had complimented Lady Tull on her dress and her impeccable table manners. They had talked about the coming winter and even shared the gossip about Lady Samanar's latest antics. The view was magnificent, as expected. It really should have been a romantic evening, but Siv felt as if Lady Tull's crusty advisors had shown up for dinner rather than the woman herself. She kept her cards close to the chest, that one.

"Do you still continue to duel, Your Highness?" she asked as they started in on the baked plum with sweet brandy sauce the cooks had prepared specially for her visit.

"I've been too busy," Siv said.

"Weren't you supporting a duelist for a time?"

"Cheering her on, yes," Siv said. He didn't add that Dara now lived on the castle grounds. It wasn't near midnight yet. She was probably still here somewhere. He hoped she would be all right out in the dark with Berg later. He was most likely on Siv's side, but that didn't mean he wasn't dangerous.

Lady Tull was still looking at him. Right, he was supposed to be wooing her, not thinking about Dara.

"Do you like to watch dueling?" he asked.

"It is too violent for me, I'm afraid," Lady Tull said. "Bolden loves dueling, though. I understand he's also training with the sword."

Siv swallowed a chunk of plum, and it went down the wrong pipe. He choked and sputtered, trying to wash it down with several large gulps of wine. That was news to him. Why would Bolden be training to fight? He much preferred to let other people entertain him than to exert himself directly.

"The Rollendars have always sponsored duelists," Siv said when he recovered from nearly choking to death. "I understand the Ferringtons do not."

"That's true, but my late husband's father did," Lady Tull said. "House Denmore used to support a man called Drimmez."

"*The* Drimmez?"

"I understand he was popular." Lady Tull took a delicate sip of her wine.

"You could say that." Siv barely resisted the urge to blurt out Drimmez's statistics. He had been undefeated for seven straight years before Wora Wenden came on the scene and met him point for point! Drimmez was one of the most famous duelists Vertigon had ever known. Lady Tull didn't sound nearly impressed enough that the house she led had such a legacy.

Dara would have been impressed. Siv took another gulp of wine. He hoped she was all right.

"Your Highness," Lady Tull said, daintily slicing the last baked plum into quarters. "You must know that Bolden has asked for my hand in marriage."

Siv nearly dropped his goblet. He took another sip to buy time. So they were going to take the direct approach, were they?

"I assumed he had," he said as nonchalantly as he could manage. "And have you answered?"

"Not yet, Your Highness."

Lady Tull dabbed at her mouth with a lace handkerchief and met his eyes, waiting patiently. She had a soft gaze, almost as if she were looking past him or trying to remember a dream from the night before. It was too easy for Siv's attention to slip away from her and linger on the mist-cloaked mountaintops outside the glass wall of the parlor.

Dara's eyes were riveting. With her, he could never look away, even when he should.

Siv stood and approached the glass wall of the parlor. Vertigon spread beneath him. The mist-filled Fissure, like a river of milk. Village Peak, with its humble buildings and scattered lights. Broad Square Peak, with the smudged outline of the Burnt Mountains beyond it. His kingdom. Siv thought of the many times he had studied that view with his father. That was why he was doing this. Vertigon had to remain strong.

"My lady," Siv said, his resolve strengthening as he turned his back on the view. This dinner with Lady Tull may not be particularly romantic, but she was a smart woman. She knew why they were really here too. "You must know I had hoped to ask you the same question. Denmore and Ferrington have long been powerful houses."

"Rollendar is powerful too," Lady Tull said.

"Yes, it is." Siv frowned at the implication that House Rollendar already rivaled the crown itself for power. But he carried on before he lost his nerve. "I believe Vertigon would be well served by an alliance between your family and mine. Would you do me the honor of being my queen?"

"I am humbled, Your Majesty," Lady Tull said. "Will you grant me some time to consider your offer?" She didn't hesitate. She had already chosen her words before she arrived, perhaps in consultation with those advisors of hers. "I'm worried about damaging my house if I refuse Lord Rollendar now. We have been keeping company for some time."

"I understand," Siv said. "Take as much time as you need. But I vow to look out for the interests of your house even if you refuse my offer. I want Vertigon to be strong, and Ferrington and Denmore have always been part of its strength."

"Thank you, Your Majesty."

Lady Tull sipped gracefully from her goblet. She smiled at Siv, and there seemed to be real warmth in her expression. He wouldn't go so far as to call it a spark, but it was something. Lady Tull hadn't pretended she was considering the two young men. Like him, she was looking for the best alliance possible—but she wasn't necessarily convinced that it lay with the king. That was a problem.

"If I may say so, Your Majesty," she said, "you have come a long way. I hardly recognize you as the man who used to drink and play mijen with us in the parlors."

"You are too kind," Siv said. "Consider my offer. And I hope you will return to the castle for another visit soon."

"It would be a pleasure."

When the hour grew late, Siv walked Lady Tull to the door of the glass-encased parlor, but he didn't escort her all the way to the castle exit. Despite their surroundings, the evening hadn't been especially amorous. Siv didn't think it would help his case to offer a midnight stroll or a good night kiss. He had officially put in his bid for Lady Tull's hand, and it was up to her to choose.

Siv paced around the parlor, considering what Lady Tull had said about the Rollendars. It shouldn't surprise him that Bolden had already proposed, that sneaking povvercat. He was more worried that House Rollendar had reached such heights that it both rivaled House Amintelle and threatened Denmore and Ferrington. The nobles must truly see him as a child, barely more equipped to rule the kingdom than the teenage princesses. Did the common people feel the same way? He had to do something about the perception of his house—and himself—soon.

The moon rose outside the glass wall, filling the parlor with muted light. Siv poured more wine into his goblet. His head spun, but he gulped it down anyway. He missed the days when he could carouse until dawn with nothing more than a hangover to worry about the next day. Dara was out there investigating nefarious weapons makers, and he was trapped in the tower making business-like marriage proposals. As he had long suspected, being king wasn't much fun at all.

Dara would probably be heading down to meet Berg right about now. There were hours yet before Siv would know what was going on. The restlessness plaguing him rose suddenly, like a true dragon rearing its head to spurt flame.

He didn't want to be stuck in the castle. He had done his kingly duty for the night. He had officially asked for the hand of a suitable noble lady. Couldn't he get away with even the tiniest bit of excitement?

He poured the last of the wine into his goblet and tossed it back.

There was still time. As long as he evaded Pool, there was a chance he could make it to Square Peak before Dara disappeared into the night with Berg.

Sneaking out was surprisingly easy. A steep access tunnel beneath the castle allowed the cooks to bring in food supplies for the kitchens without using the sheer steps leading to the main gates. A pulley system had been installed years ago to reduce the amount of manual labor this required, and the older tunnel had been sealed off. Or at least, it had been sealed until Siv figured out a way to open it. He had used it often for pranks in his childhood—and more recently when he snuck out to watch Dara's duel on Fell Bridge with Vine Silltine.

Getting to the kitchens without arousing suspicion proved easier now that he was the king than it had been for him as the heir-prince. A secret stairwell connected the king's chamber directly to the kitchens, so he didn't have to worry about getting caught in the main corridors.

He retired to his rooms and told Pool he was going to bed. While Pool very diligently guarded the outer doors to his chamber, Siv slipped down to the kitchen through the musty darkness of the secret stairs. If Pool tried to check on him he could always say he wanted a midnight snack. He was pretty sure that was the main reason his father had used the stairs. As long as Pool didn't realize he was out of the castle, he'd be all right.

He still wore his sword, which he'd buckled on before dinner. He cut a dashing figure with it, and he was sure Tull had been impressed. He also grabbed a knife from the kitchens for good measure. He wasn't planning to get in a fight, exactly, but he wanted to be prepared. Dara had looked out for him often enough, and he couldn't shake the sneaking feeling that she wasn't entirely safe with Berg.

A simple brown cloak hung on a hook in the kitchen, left behind by one of the cooks. Siv pulled this on over his ornate blue coat. He was taller than average and rather recognizable, but no one would expect the king to traipse through Square Peak in the middle of the night. With any luck, he would go completely unnoticed.

With a final glance around the kitchens to make sure no one was there, Siv pulled back the cupboard blocking the secret tunnel and descended into darkness. He brought no light, relying on the feel of the dry stone beneath his fingers to guide his path. He loved the musty, earthy smell as he made his way through the heart of his mountain. This was where he belonged, not trapped up in the glass parlor at the top of the tower.

At the end of the tunnel, he listened for noise and then pushed open the creaky door. The street was dark and deserted. The black figure of a zur-sparrow swept overhead. Siv wrapped the brown cloak around himself, hiding his face, and strode into the night.

He made it to Square without incident, arriving just in time to see Dara and Berg leaving the dueling school. He would have felt rather foolish if he missed them after all this effort. Berg's shape was big and square, like a monster from a story. Dara was unmistakable, with her long golden braid and her confident, athletic stride. She always walked like she knew where she was going, even when she didn't. Siv could follow her anywhere.

He stayed at a distance as Dara and Berg made their way through the street. He didn't want them to notice him until it was too late to turn back. They talked in low voices, and he couldn't make out their words. Dara would fill him in eventually, he was sure.

They walked for a long time, leaving the more populated side of Square behind. Siv hoped Pool hadn't discovered he was missing and raised an alarm. He'd have to tell him about the tunnel, and then he'd never get away with something like this again. Siv may be the king and Pool may be the guard, but that didn't mean Pool wouldn't put his foot down and insist on blocking the tunnel to protect him. He didn't want his stairs to the kitchens sealed off either. That thing was useful when he wanted dessert in the evening. No wonder his father had had trouble losing weight!

They approached the outskirts of Square. The houses scattered the slope at sparse intervals here, but the rocks were numerous, making it impossible to decipher anything resembling a true road. Footpaths and winding steps connected the structures seemingly at random. This left plenty of places for Siv to hide as he followed the pair through the darkness. He had to duck beneath the boulders with lightning speed whenever Berg looked around, which was often. This was turning out to be a decent workout. Dara would be proud.

Berg finally stopped beside a humble shack. Siv crouched behind another rock, waiting for something to happen. The rustle of ponies sleeping in a nearby paddock was the only sound. When he peeked out from his hiding place, Berg and Dara were gone.

Siv swore under his breath and approached the shack. It was empty, apparently abandoned. The moon provided just enough light to reveal a pile of branches leaning against the decaying wood like an overgrown crundlebird. Sure enough, when he pulled the branches back there was an entrance to a hidden tunnel. He glanced around one more time then ducked into it and followed Berg and Dara underground.

8

THE CAVERNS

THE pitch dark of the tunnel hovered around them, unnerving in its stillness. Dara stuck close to Berg, his shuffling footsteps her only guide. He hadn't brought an Everlight to illuminate the way, but he seemed to know this passageway well.

They crept through the darkness. Sometimes Berg had to stoop to squeeze through narrower spaces. Dara ran her hands along the rough earthen walls, which eventually gave way to stone. Every once in a while a draft or sudden emptiness indicated more tunnels heading off from their path. Some must lead all the way out to the mountainside, because little pockets of mist flowed through them, moistening their faces.

As they crawled deeper into the mountain, Dara noticed a strange sensation in the rock. She had become increasingly sensitive to the Fire that seeped through the stones of Vertigon, runoff from the channels leading to each access point. It was especially noticeable near Fireworker shops. But here, the fiery residue almost didn't exist. It was as if every drop of Fire had been pulled from these stones. If there had ever been Fire veins running through these tunnels, they were now as cold as a mountain lake.

How was that possible? The Fire Warden's system controlled the flow of the Fire, but you could always find some hint of it. Dara shivered as she trailed her fingers over cold stone, feeling nothing but the rough texture of rock and sifting dirt knocked loose at her touch.

"We are almost there," Berg whispered. "Silence."

Dara nodded, even though he couldn't see her. A few steps later they heard it: the ringing of steel against steel and the tapping of boots, sounds both of them knew well.

A few of the tunnels they passed as they crept forward had lights installed in them. Dara followed Berg's hulking shadow as it formed and dissolved each time they encountered one of the lighted outlets. They still hadn't seen anyone, but they could be discovered at any moment. Passageways deep underground would not be illuminated unless they were used regularly. Dara swallowed, keeping a tight hold on her nerves.

They got closer and closer to the familiar sounds. Berg stalked onward, imperturbable as ever.

At last the tunnel opened up, and they entered a vast cavern. Cheap Firebulbs blazed, casting shadows like daggers from the stalactites and stalagmites. The clash of blade against blade was louder now, along with shouts that were all too familiar.

They exited the tunnel at ground level, but a large rock formation blocked their view of the cavern floor. Hopefully no one could see them sneaking out either. They crept to the edge of the formation and peeked around it, staying as concealed as possible behind its bulk.

It was an enormous underground dueling hall. Dozens of duelists squared off against each other on the smoothed-out floor. Some engaged in partner drills while others sparred, their shouts echoing off the walls. They used blunted sport dueling rapiers, but Dara spotted a long row of wickedly pointed swords in a rack across from their hiding place. She had a sneaking suspicion they were Fire Blades like the one their mystery swordsman had used.

The duelists training on the floor wore protective masks, of course, and the ones waiting their turn to spar wore strips of cloth wrapped around their heads to disguise their appearances. When a pair of duelists removed their masks to shake hands after a bout, they too wore sweat-soaked cloths to hide their identity.

Dara knew many of the duelists on the mountain by their styles alone, but she didn't think she'd ever seen these swordsmen compete in tournaments—and she had spent a lot of time watching those. Some of the mysterious duelists were very good. She would remember them if she'd ever seen them before. They all used a similar style, the mark of athletes who trained with the same coach. Their movements were efficient, brutal. This coach didn't care about racking up points. Most of the hits would have been killing blows.

The pair of duelists nearest to their hiding place was faster than the rest. Their uncanny swiftness suggested these two were using Fire Blades, probably with blunted tips. Dara would need to get closer to find out for sure.

Berg caught her eye and nodded toward another large outcropping of stone. A gap between it and their current location had only small rocks, offering less cover. Berg flattened himself on his belly and crawled toward the next outcropping, surprisingly spry despite his bulk. Dara waited until he was safely concealed before preparing to follow him.

She crouched, adjusting her Savven blade so it wouldn't scrape along the ground. Plenty of noise filled the cavern, so a few additional footsteps shouldn't matter. She held her breath and started to slink out of her hiding place.

Suddenly, a hand covered Dara's mouth and she was yanked backwards into the shadows. She struggled fiercely, clawing at the hands holding her tight. Fear flashed through her. She couldn't reach her blade, and when she pulled frantically for the Fire, there was none to be found in the stones around her.

"Shhh," a voice murmured in her ear. She struggled harder, trying to twist out of the iron grasp.

The grip on her mouth and arm tightened, crushing her back against the broad chest of her captor. Dara was about to bite the hand that held her when two men strode directly into the space where she had been about to crawl.

The swordsmen sat on the smaller stones Berg had hidden behind a moment ago.

Dara stopped fighting. As soon as she was still, her captor released his hold on her mouth.

"It's me," the voice breathed in her ear.

Siv.

Dara bit back a powerful urge to swear at her king for scaring

King of Mist

her, even though he had saved her from being discovered. He didn't release her arm, and his other hand now rested beneath her chin, his fingertips brushing her throat as he clasped her against his chest. The duelists on the rock were directly in their line of sight. They could look over any second and wonder what was in the shadows. Even though she was practically sitting on Siv's lap, Dara didn't dare move.

They must have stayed like that for a full five minutes while the duelists rested on the rocks, sharing a drink from a canteen. There was no sign of Berg. He was astonishingly stealthy for such a large man.

As they waited for the duelists to move on, Dara became more and more aware of Siv's breath in her ear and his heartbeat against her back. He still hadn't released her. She felt dizzy at their closeness. She couldn't help remembering the dance they had shared at the Cup Feast, the night when Siv had pulled her close in the darkness near Fell Bridge. Dara forced her breathing to remain steady. She had to stay alert. They were both in danger here.

Finally, an unseen figure came over and barked at the duelists to get back to training. When they returned to the center of the cavern, Siv finally loosed his hold on Dara.

"What are you doing here?" she hissed, scrambling off his lap and turning to face him.

"Thought you could use some help," Siv said. "Where's Berg?"

"I was following him until you pulled me back."

"There's another way around over there," Siv jerked his head in the direction they'd come from. "Want to check it out?"

"I'll check it out," Dara whispered. "You need to go back to the castle. It's not safe here."

"It's not safe for you either," Siv said. "You almost got caught. Besides, isn't this more efficient than you having to repeat everything you see to me?" He grinned and crawled back in the other direction before she could answer.

Dara gritted her teeth and followed. They couldn't risk attracting attention by arguing, but she needed to get the king out of here as quickly as possible. How could he be so reckless? If they got caught . . . Well, she just wouldn't let that happen.

Siv led the way along the edge of the cavern in the opposite direction of where Berg had disappeared. They passed the tunnel they had come from, creeping forward on careful feet. Taller rocks provided better cover on this side. Other passageways led out of the cavern, some large, some barely big enough for a cat. Dara hoped they'd find Berg eventually. She wasn't sure she'd be able to get out of here on her own.

They discovered an alcove where they could wedge themselves in and have a decent view of the dueling floor over the top of a massive rock. The mysterious swordsmen worked hard, occasionally calling out to each other, but they didn't talk about anything except the moves as far as Dara could hear. A row of stuffed dummies was visible from their new position. Five duelists were busy riddling them with holes with the help of sharpened blades. Again, Dara noticed the efficiency of their movements. Sport duelists fought bouts to ten points. Hits landed on the hand and the knee as often as the chest or gut. Simultaneous hits counted as a point for each competitor. It didn't necessarily matter if your opponent's hit landed as long as you got one too. These duelists didn't settle for simultaneous hits, though, and they both sought and defended against killing blows with every touch.

"Something tells me this secret dueling club isn't focused on winning tournaments," Siv whispered after a while.

"I agree."

"Assassins?"

"Could be," Dara said. "There are a lot of them, though. How many assassins does one kingdom need?"

"There aren't enough of them to threaten the army, though."

"True. But they'd be more than a match for the Castle Guard."

Siv nodded. Dara didn't say the word "coup" aloud, though they were probably both thinking it. He studied the scene intently, and Dara realized this was the most animated she'd seen him since the day of his father's death. The set of his jaw and the light in his eyes suggested he was rather enjoying this despite the danger—and the magnitude of the threat they had discovered.

"We'd better move," Dara said. "Someone's coming this way."

They climbed out of the alcove and continued along the edge of the dueling hall. Dara wanted a good look at whoever was coaching these duelists. A smaller cavern opened off the side of the hall ahead

King of Mist

of them, and something about it drew Dara forward. She picked up her pace. Why did she feel compelled to enter that cave?

Siv stopped her suddenly with a hand on the arm, his face pale.

"That's Pavorran," he breathed.

"What?"

"Pavorran, the general of my father's—of my army." He pulled her down behind another rock and pointed out a stout figure striding into the hall from a tunnel on the opposite side of the smaller cave. General Pavorran was around forty-five years old and powerfully built. He carried himself like a soldier, reminding Dara of Telvin Jale.

Pavorran was deep in conversation with a rail-thin man with dark skin and foreign clothing. If Dara wasn't mistaken, the man was from Soole.

"Think that might be why Berg didn't go directly to the army?" Dara asked. So Pavorran was training a secret army or attack force down here in this cavern. How could the treachery against the Amintelles run this deep?

"Could be," Siv said. "You sure Berg's on our side?"

Dara didn't hesitate. "I'm sure."

She peeked over the rock for another look at Pavorran. He wore his uniform openly here, every crease ironed and button polished. If the army itself was compromised, the purge of the Castle Guard might not have gone far enough. What was he going to do with all these swordsmen?

Something tugged at Dara's senses, and she looked toward the smaller cave that had drawn her attention earlier. Something was going on there, and she was starting to think she knew what it was.

Fire. Someone was using an incredibly strong current of Fire in that cave. She could feel it now, and it explained the strange coldness she had noticed in the tunnel earlier. It hardly seemed possible, but someone had found a way to pull every drop of Fire in this section of Square Peak to a single location. The pull was so strong that nothing was left over in the cracks of stone further away from it.

She edged closer to the cavern.

"Wait," Siv whispered. "Recognize the fellow Pavorran is talking to?"

"Huh?"

"You've met him before."

Dara studied the figure with the foreign clothes, a long silk vest and boots that went over his knees. He wore his dark hair long, an unusual style for men in these parts. Yes, she'd seen him before, but not at any dueling competition. She had played a game of mijen against him once in Lady Atria's parlor. Chala Choven of the Below Lands Trade Alliance. He had mentioned at the time that he supported her father's views on loosening the Fire regulations.

"I remember now," she whispered. "Isn't he your friend?"

"Bolden's friend," Siv said through clenched teeth. "It wouldn't surprise me if we can trace this right back to the Rollendars."

Dara frowned. She didn't understand how all the threads fit together. Was this part of her parents' work with the Fire Guild or not? As far as she knew, her parents didn't have ties to House Rollendar. Could this be a completely separate plot? She felt as if she knew less and less with every discovery. With this small army training here—connected in some way to the real army—their problems were bigger than they first realized.

That strong current of Fire still called to her. Dara wanted to see what kind of Work took so much strength. Her first guess was a forge for the Fire Blades, but she was less certain the closer they got. What if her father was in there? There would be no hiding the truth from Siv then.

He must have seen enough, though, because he tugged on her arm before she could get much closer.

"We'd better go," he whispered.

"I want to see what's in that smaller cave."

"There's not much shelter the rest of the way," Siv said. He was still watching Pavorran, a grim set to his jaw.

Dara looked back at the cave one more time, feeling the incredible pull of all that Fire. He was right, though. They couldn't sneak over to it without some of the duelists seeing them. Their luck might not hold much longer. With a final glance, Dara turned, leaving the pulsing river of Fire behind.

As they started back toward the tunnel, a voice called across the cavern. With a flurry of footsteps and muted conversation, the duelists finished up their bouts and began packing their gear. As Dara and Siv hurried back through the shadows, some were already starting to leave. They all headed off in different directions through the dozens of outlets leading away from the cavern. Some crossed right in front of Dara and Siv, forcing them to lunge for cover every few steps. This was taking too long. Soon the tunnels would be full of these strange swordsmen. They were going to be seen.

"Quick," Siv whispered as a trio of masked duelists started toward their latest hiding place. He pulled her into one of the smaller tunnels leading off from the cavern.

"This isn't the way we came in," Dara said.

"Doesn't matter. We can't get caught."

Dara fought down a stab of claustrophobia and followed Siv into the tunnel. It was smaller—and hopefully less trafficked—than the one they had used on their trip in. With any luck, none of the duelists would come through it on their way home.

They hadn't gone far before they reached a crossing. Voices drifted up the nearest tunnel, coming closer.

"Here." Siv ducked down another passageway to escape the approaching voices.

Dara followed him into the darkness, feeling more and more disoriented the farther into the mountain they got. At every turn clamoring voices and thudding footsteps advanced toward them, the swordsmen oblivious to Dara and the king lurking in the shadows.

The atmosphere grew oppressive. Dara couldn't tell where they were anymore. The drafts and bits of mist and moonlight she had glimpsed earlier were nowhere to be found. Old, dusty air pressed in on them.

When they had walked for almost ten minutes without hearing anyone, she reached out to stop Siv. She kept her hand on his arm even after she had his attention.

"We're lost," she whispered.

Siv didn't answer for a minute. His pulse raced beneath Dara's fingertips.

"I know," he said. "We had to move before they caught us, though. They will kill us without hesitation."

"Are you sure Pavorran isn't doing this to help you?"

"Dara, the kingdom is out of my control." Siv's voice sounded as heavy as the mountain pressing down on them. "This enterprise looks advanced, and I don't know what we can do to stop it, even if only part of the army turns on me. I only have a few guards I can truly count on, and they have as much chance against that little army back there as a morrinvole has against a velgon bear."

It was too dark to see Siv's face, but Dara tightened her grip on his arm. She wished there were some way to help her friend, but she didn't know enough about scheming noble families and treacherous generals. She had always been a duelist, nothing more. Why had she thought she'd be able to save him?

Despite what they had discovered, Siv's breathing remained steady. He was tense, yes, but he wasn't letting fear take hold. She shouldn't either. Siv had supported her and helped her when they barely knew each other, long before she had ever saved his life. She had to think of some way to aid him.

"What about the people?" she said. "They loved your father. I think they'll love you too." She couldn't imagine anyone could get to know this king and not love him.

"The people aren't a match for a secret army of duelists."

"Maybe not, but they might stand up to a conniving nobleman. If you have their support, they could make trouble for any house that tries to rise against you."

"Perhaps," Siv said. "We'll need to get their attention, though."

"You're good at getting people's attention." She squeezed his arm again, and in the darkness he rested his hand on hers.

As they stood there in the lightless tunnel, Dara began to grow warm. It was a familiar sensation now. Something about being around Siv made the Fire sense come alive in her. As he held her hand her awareness sharpened. She realized she could tell exactly which direction they needed to go to find that strange vein of Fire back in the cavern.

"I think I can find the way out," Dara said. "Follow me."

9

NIGHT

SIV followed Dara through the darkness. She kept a tight hold on his hand, and their palms grew warm as they crept back through the tunnels. Every few minutes she stopped to adjust their course or choose a new direction. Siv wondered if she had particularly good hearing. He couldn't make out how she was finding her way.

But she didn't let go of his hand, and that was all Siv cared about. It was foolish of him to come here tonight, but he couldn't bring himself to regret these stolen moments when he got to hold hands with Dara. Besides, if he hadn't come along she might not have recognized General Pavorran, and they'd have missed a vital piece of information.

Siv grimaced. Pavorran. The man had led the army for close to a decade. Vertigon's military was small by the standards of most kingdoms. The long-established Peace of Vertigon ensured that the army didn't see much action. But it was always there if they needed it. The people of Vertigon rested secure knowing that if foreign soldiers ever tried to assault the mountain their men would be ready to defend them. But what of these secret fighters training within the mountain itself? What was Pavorran planning to do with them? And just how deep into the army did his tendrils spread?

Siv considered what Dara had said about the people. If they supported him, if they were loyal, they might be able to stand against a small force. Vertigonians wouldn't take kindly to a coup. They could definitely make things difficult for whichever noble house was behind the plot. He assumed they'd support the Amintelles over the Rollendars, for example. On the other hand, he had also thought Lady Tull would choose him over Bolden as soon as he got around to extending his offer of marriage.

Tull! He had completely forgotten he proposed to her tonight. He dropped Dara's hand as if he'd been burned.

She was concentrating on finding their way, though, and didn't notice. She walked faster. A hint of cooler air drifted through the tunnels now. It was lighter too. They must be almost to the outer edge of the cavern system. Dara walked faster, getting slightly ahead of him. He could see her now, a tall figure silhouetted against the gray of the tunnel.

After what they had discovered tonight, it was more important than ever for him to solidify his hold on the throne. He needed to secure Tull's hand and charm the people. He would win his mountain back from whomever thought they could undermine the Amintelles. He was the Fourth Good King, and he would be burning good at the job!

Siv strode after Dara. Yes, there was definitely mist and light in the tunnels now. They were almost out.

Then Dara walked past a gap in the stone, and a dark figure leapt out behind her. Siv shouted a warning, but the assailant shoved Dara hard against the tunnel wall before she could react. Her head smacked the rock with a sickening thud.

The attacker pulled a sword from his belt. Dara scrambled for the Savven blade at her hip, but she looked disoriented. She wouldn't get to her feet in time. The attacker raised his sword.

"Dara!"

Siv threw himself into the swordsman before he could bring down his blade. They tumbled to the ground, rolling across the sharp rocks, grappling for control. Siv couldn't get his sword out of its sheath. Fortunately, his opponent couldn't do much with his weapon in the close quarters, either.

Siv threw wild punches and tried to get a grip on the man with his legs. They reeled over the sharp stones, fists swinging, struggling for the advantage.

The scramble was nothing like the noble duels for which he'd trained. The mysterious assailant remained utterly silent, but Siv grunted and swore enough for both of them. The other man caught him with a punch to the ribs and dove on top of him, slamming him into the tunnel wall. Siv's head rang, but he managed to flip the man off him and deliver a kick to the knee.

In the seconds before his opponent recovered, Siv grabbed the kitchen knife from his coat pocket. He lunged onto his attacker's back and laid the blade against his throat, grasping him roughly by one arm.

"Don't move," he said.

The man moved, tossing his head backwards and smacking Siv painfully in the forehead. His grip on the kitchen knife slipped. The attacker ducked out of his grasp, diving for his sword, which had fallen to the ground in the scuffle.

When he picked it up, he was facing Dara. She wavered on her knees, as if she had tried to get up but couldn't quite manage it. Blood matted her golden hair.

The attacker lunged toward her.

Siv was faster. He leapt onto the man's back and drove the kitchen knife into his neck. Hot blood spilled over his hands as they fell to the ground.

Silence reigned. Siv listened for more assailants. They—he—had made a lot of noise. They must have attracted attention. But nothing moved in the tunnels except for the drip of blood. They were alone.

Then Dara spoke into the darkness. "I owe you my life, Sivarrion Amintelle." And she slid down to sit on the floor of the tunnel.

Siv wiped off his hands as best as he could on the strange man's shirt and scrambled over to kneel before her. He put his fingers in her hair and gingerly searched for the cut on her head.

Dara winced, reminding Siv that it was now light enough to see. They had to be almost at the surface. He pulled off the brown cloak he stole from the castle kitchen and used it to dab at the wound on Dara's head. It wasn't too deep, but she'd have a headache.

"Are you hurt?" Dara asked.

"No. Maybe a few bruises, but he didn't get a good stab in."

"Good." Dara groaned as Siv shifted his hands to put more pressure on her head wound.

"Do you feel dizzy?" he asked. "Look at me for a minute." He tilted her face up to see if she was able to focus. Some of the usual intensity was missing from her eyes, but when he shifted his position she followed his movements. She should be all right.

"You have nice eyes," Dara said. "I've never told you that."

Siv froze. She didn't sound quite like herself, but her gaze was fixed on him now.

"And you have a nice face," she said.

"You hit your head, Dara." Siv barely dared to breathe. He had always found Dara attractive, but how much did she . . .? Almost against his will, Siv's eyes darted to her mouth. She blinked slowly, and her eyelashes fluttered against the inside of his wrist.

"Who is he?" Dara said, and it took Siv a minute to figure out what she was talking about. Right. The man he had just killed.

Siv moved Dara's hand so she could hold the cloak against the wound on her head, and then turned over the body. The man was Soolen. He was shorter than Chala Choven, though, and he wore cloth wound around part of his face as the other duelists had. Siv breathed a short sigh, relieved he hadn't killed one of his own subjects.

"I don't know him," Siv said. He wished he could have taken the man alive. They might actually get some answers. He looked over at Dara, who still had blood in her hair. The man had almost killed her. Maybe Siv didn't feel that bad about not taking him alive after all. Besides, there had been something odd about this man as they fought. He hadn't made a sound.

Siv picked up the kitchen knife and used it to pry open the Soolen man's mouth. His tongue had been cut out. Siv grimaced. That wasn't a good sign. Soole was the only country on the continent known to cut out criminals' tongues, and they only did it to murderers. He hoped none of the *other* mysterious and deadly swordsmen training in that cavern were murderers from foreign lands. This was not good.

"We'd better get out of here." He wiped off the kitchen knife and tucked it back into his coat, not wanting to leave any evidence of who was responsible for this.

"Check his blade."

"What?"

Dara was on her feet now. She clutched the wall of the tunnel as if still a little dizzy.

"Is it like the other one?"

"Good point." Siv retrieved the weapon that had fallen on the stones. Like the one belonging to the man who had tried to kill them after the Vertigon Cup, it had no maker's mark. It was hard to tell in the darkness, but Siv was pretty sure it was exactly the same as the other one.

Dara reached out to touch the hilt.

"It's a Fire Blade," she said.

"Are you sure?"

"Yes. Let's get out of here."

"Agreed."

Before long, they were hurrying down a final tunnel—not the one they had come from—and emerging into the mist-drenched night. The peak was deserted, but they didn't feel safe until they made it down to Pen Bridge.

Siv supported Dara's arm as they walked, glad she didn't reject his offer of help. She was quieter than usual. He started to worry she was really injured. That, or extra thoughtful. They kept their heads down, hoping that if anyone spotted them they'd assume they were just another couple out enjoying the moonlight.

He liked the chance to hold her, though. As they strolled through the stillness it was almost romantic. Mist seethed in the Fissure and rose around them, pearly and ethereal. Their strides matched, and Dara's arm felt warm in his.

They didn't need to worry about being recognized after all. The bridge was empty, and it was as if they were the only people on the mountain tonight.

Finally, Dara spoke.

"How was dinner?"

"Huh?"

"Dinner. With Lady Tull?"

"Oh." Siv glared at the mist around the bridge as some of the magic fractured. "It went as well as can be expected. I asked for her hand."

Dara jolted, and Siv instantly regretted the words. She strode faster, as if trying to cover her reaction.

"And her answer?"

"She'll consider it," Siv said. "Bolden has already asked her."

"I see."

They resumed their walk in silence. Why couldn't she have waited to bring up Lady Tull? He had to stop doing this, holding Dara close and imagining them as a couple. It only made everything harder. He burning knew that, but he kept letting it happen.

They were almost back to King's Peak, almost back to where he was the king and she was his guard. The castle loomed out of the mist as if it were floating on a cloud. A hint of the Firegold adorning its walls glinted in the moonlight.

"Wait, what about Berg?" Siv said suddenly.

"I'll send word to him in the morning letting him know I got out safely," Dara said. "I think it would be better for both of us if he doesn't know you were out and about tonight."

"Agreed."

"We'll need his help sorting out this mess." Dara's tone was business-like and practical. She was approaching this problem as she would a training session, with no indication that she was particularly bothered by the news of Siv's pending engagement. It was just as well. He had asked her to join the Guard because he knew he could trust her, not for any other reason. He wasn't sure he could trust anyone else at this point. He should really be worrying about that, not about how she apparently liked his eyes. And his face. He could be practical too.

Siv cleared his throat. "Let's sleep on it and figure something out in the morning."

"I agree," Dara said.

They climbed the streets of King's Peak in silence. When they reached the entrance to the secret tunnel, Dara withdrew her arm from his.

"I'd better go back in the way I came out," she said.

"Why don't you stay with me tonight?" Siv knew it was a bad idea, but he said it anyway. "You shouldn't be alone with a head injury."

"That would be difficult to explain to Pool in the morning."

"Let him wonder," Siv said. "I want to make sure you're all right."

"I'll have Telvin check on me," Dara said—rather brusquely, he thought. "I'll tell him I stumbled down some steps on my way home. Too much ale."

Siv blinked. "Who's Telvin?"

"One of the guardsmen. I had a drink with him earlier tonight."

"You don't even like drinking."

"It was okay." Dara shrugged. "He's a decent man."

"Is he," Siv said flatly. Which one was Telvin? Not many of the guardsmen were young. He'd better not be one of the good-looking ones. Why was she having drinks with guardsmen anyway?

"Yes, I think so," Dara said. "I'll keep an eye on him in case he could be a potential ally. He used to be in the army. Maybe he could give us information on Pavorran."

"Information," Siv said. "Sure. Good idea. Just be careful."

"Good night, Siv," Dara said. "And thank you. I needed your help tonight." Then as suddenly as if she were lunging toward a target, she stepped closer to him and kissed his cheek. Before he could move, she strode off through the darkness toward the castle gates.

Siv grinned all the way through the tunnel, the kitchens, and the secret stairwell to his chambers. He was still smiling by the time he fell asleep.

10

PLANS

DARA'S head pounded as she descended through the bottom level of the castle to the cur-dragon cave. She hadn't slept well. Telvin had dutifully woken her up throughout the night to make sure she wasn't slipping into a coma. She had spent her waking hours mulling over what to do about the threat they had discovered yesterday.

In the bright light of day, the solution seemed clear. If General Pavorran and his cronies—whoever they were—had decided to make their own private dueling army, the king needed to do the same.

The Castle Guard had to recruit and train replacements anyway after being compromised during the assassination. It was more important than ever to make sure the new recruits could handle the threat brewing over on Square Peak. They might not have much time. What they really needed was a ready-made group of fit, trained swordsmen who weren't in danger of being influenced by the general.

Fortunately, Dara happened to know some of those.

She nodded to Yeltin, the gray-bearded Castle Guard posted at the entrance to the cur-dragon cave. One of the original guardsmen, he was definitely loyal to the king, but he also wasn't young. They needed fresh blood to meet the new threat.

As Dara strode down the cur-dragon tunnel, claustrophobia

flashed through her at the memory of their adventure the night before. She had been afraid in those tunnels—very afraid—until she felt that river of Fire pulling her like a beacon. She had followed that sensation to get out of the depths of the mountain and back toward the surface. But what was all that Fire for? It presented an even bigger problem than the mysterious duelists.

Pool stood at the end of the passageway, where an iron gate blocked the cavern entrance to prevent unruly cur-dragons from wandering into the castle.

"Greetings, Miss Ruminor."

"I'd like to talk to you and the king about something, Pool," Dara said.

"Certainly. I shall inquire whether he has a moment to hear your entreaty."

Pool opened the gate to the cur-dragon enclosure and shooed away a pair of dragon keepers lingering nearby. The sky outside the cave opening was clear today. The Burnt Mountains stood sharp against the skyline. A cur-dragon launched itself from the ledge and soared out into the crisp blue sky as Dara entered.

Siv sprawled on the floor with his back to her, playing with his favorite cur-dragon hatchling. Rumy was three months old and getting big quickly, already the largest of his litter. He stretched his wings, which had begun to take on a greenish cast, and preened as Siv tossed him bits of morrinvole meat. Siv looked like his old self, not like a king with enemies on all sides. Dara didn't speak, watching him coo at the little dragon and tease it with the treats. Not for the first time she wished everything could go back to the way it used to be.

Then Zage Lorrid stepped out of the shadows, clad in his customary black. A silver leaf pin glinted at his throat.

"What is it, Miss Ruminor?" he said.

"I need to speak with the king."

"About?"

But Siv had heard her name. He leapt to his feet.

"Dara! How are you? How's your h—?" He stopped when she shot him a warning look. "How are you?" he finished lamely. Zage raised an eyebrow.

"I'm fine, Your Majesty." Dara resisted the urge to probe the lump on the back of her head. "I learned something last night, and I wanted to talk to you and Pool about an idea I had."

"Excellent."

Siv waited expectantly. Dara glanced at Zage. "Can we speak in private?"

"No, Zage should hear this."

"Are you sure?"

"Of course."

Siv grinned, apparently not getting the hint that Dara didn't want to talk about this in front of the Fire Warden. Siv trusted Zage unreservedly, but Dara didn't think he'd proved himself worthy of it. When Siv didn't respond to her pointed look in the Fire Warden's direction, she sighed and launched into her tale.

She left out the name of the person who had taken her into the cavern and the part about Siv being there with her. She needed Pool to have all the information if he was going to help them with her scheme, but she didn't want to let on that Berg was their source yet.

Siv acted appropriately surprised as she described the mysterious cavern, playing his part well. He scowled when she got to the part about Pavorran. That betrayal must still burn.

"So we have a squad of swordsmen training in this cavern, possibly with army involvement," Dara finished. "I can't tell how many are from Vertigon and how many are from elsewhere, but there were at least two Soolen men among them."

"This is nearly inconceivable," Pool said when she finished her story, rubbing a hand through the gray hair at his temples.

"It seems a fanciful tale," Zage said.

"I saw it," Dara said.

"I do not doubt you, Miss Ruminor," Pool said. "But are you quite certain they mean the king ill?"

"They definitely weren't training for sport," Dara said. "If it was a normal army exercise, why would they practice in secret?"

"Didn't you go out drinking with another guardsman prior to this?" Zage said. Dara's mouth dropped open. How did he know that? "Is it possible you imag—?"

"Dara isn't lying," Siv said. Zage began to protest, but Siv didn't let him voice further objections. He unlatched Rumy—who had been trying to chew through his boot—from his ankle and turned to Dara eagerly. "You said you had an idea for what to do about it?"

"Yes, Your Highness." Dara resisted the urge to shoot Zage a triumphant look. "You need to build your own army of loyal swordsmen. I don't think we should trust any of the soldiers under Pavorran's sway."

"That is problematic," Pool said. "The candidates I have been vetting for the Castle Guard are invariably enlisted men. I thought the army would be reliable, Your Majesty."

"I thought so too," Siv said darkly.

"Alas, I suppose I can start over," Pool said.

"It takes too much time to train green recruits," Dara said. "These men we—I saw last night were skilled. But I have a better idea. Recruit a new Castle Guard from among the duelists."

"The sport duelists?" Siv scratched at the stubble on his chin. "Interesting."

Pool frowned, thumbing the hilt of the long knife in his belt. "I suppose it would be more efficient to train a company of seasoned athletes in the art of kingly defense. But we must subject them to the same scrutiny as any other candidates for the Guard."

"Of course," Dara said. "But I already know a lot of them. I can vouch for them. And none of them are likely to be Pavorran's men."

"You are forgetting," Zage said, "that many of these duelists are well known in the citadel. It would likely cause a stir if you enlisted a large number of athletes to join the Guard."

"That's true," Dara said slowly. "We could try to focus on ones who are less popular. They're more likely to need the job anyway." Plenty of talented duelists, like Dara just a month ago, were still trying to achieve good enough results to attract a well-paying sponsor. They might be interested in the opportunity.

"Even so," Zage said. "I fear this would only confirm some of the elder nobility's suspicions that our king is young and foolish. Your pardon, my king, but I believe that inviting your favorite athletes onto your royal Guard will not be perceived as a mature step."

Siv didn't respond at first. His eyes glazed over, as if he was concentrating very hard. Rumy tackled his boots again, and he tossed the last chunk of morrinvole to the little creature without looking at him.

"Sire?" Pool said. "Are you well?"

Siv began to pace across the stone cavern. Rumy snapped at his heels for more treats, but he barely noticed.

"Not mature," he said at last. "That's it! Of course." He paced faster. "The nobles see me as a foolish young man. They think I'm not equipped to rule the kingdom. They think they can scheme and corrupt my general and build armies right under my nose. Well, let's give the people what they want."

"Sire?"

"People know I'm a dueling fan, right?" Siv said.

"I believe it has been discussed, yes," Zage said, "especially after your recent enthusiasm for attending tournaments." He shot Dara a look that wasn't entirely friendly.

If Siv noticed the tension between them, he didn't remark on it. "So if I invite all the best duelists to live in the barracks and join the Castle Guard, they'll think I'm being a foolish young man. And people never think sport duelists can actually fight—sorry, Dara—so they won't see all those athletes as a threat. They'll think I'm doing it for the attention, for the pageantry of having pro athletes around me. And we'll give them pageantry!"

Siv whirled toward them, a wild enthusiasm in his eyes that Dara hadn't seen since he first gave her the name Nightfall. She couldn't help grinning back at him.

"They won't realize I'm on to their little scheme," he continued. "The duelists can even keep going to competitions on Turndays. It'll only be natural for them to train right here in the castle."

"We'd have to make sure they get plenty of time to practice anyway, or they might not agree to join the Guard," Dara said. "We'll have them train with sharpened steel at the same time."

Siv clapped his hands together, making the cur-dragons start up in a rustle of claws and wings. "Before long I'll have a powerhouse of trained fighters around me. And everyone will think I'm doing it as a vanity project. Oh, they'll be surprised if they try to come after me expecting a bunch of athletes and instead meet master swordsmen —and women—armed with serious weapons."

"I'm sorry to dampen your enthusiasm, Your Majesty," Zage said, "but you still have the problem of perception. You will not be taken seriously."

"The nobles might not like it," Siv said, looking over at Dara, "but the people will love it. They'll see a king who shares their biggest obsession. They'll see this elite squad of duelists, whom they love to cheer for anyway, and their dashing young king will be right in their midst. We can hold exhibition matches. Festivals. We'll entertain them, court them, show them that King Sivarrion Amintelle is as big a fan as they are. The stuffy old nobles might not like it, but they also won't see it as a threat. And if they try anything, my Guard will be ready for them. At the same time, we'll make sure the people are treated well and their businesses prosper, even during the coldest months of winter. We'll get them on our side in every way possible."

Siv had been pacing so fast he was almost running, but he finally stopped and faced them.

"What say you?"

"I like it," Dara said. She was already making a list of the duelists she knew she could trust. If they made being on this elite force akin to getting a sponsorship and allowed them to continue competing on the side, the duelists wouldn't say no. And none of them would object to the extra attention that guarding King Siv would bring. "I know a dueling coach who would be happy to assist with the training, too."

"I thought you might," Siv said. "Pool?"

"Sire, I don't mean to suggest this isn't a meritorious idea, but aren't some of the professional duelists in this citadel rather flamboyant and, well, difficult?"

"I'm sure you can handle them, Pool." Siv grinned. "And Dara will help keep them in line. She's good at making people be serious. How about you, Zage?"

The Fire Warden didn't answer for a long time. He twisted his pale hands in the folds of his black cloak as he considered the idea. As usual, he scrutinized Dara, blatant mistrust on his face. What else could she do to prove her trustworthiness? She almost wanted to tell him that she'd been alone in the dark with the king last night and done him no harm—although this time he had been the one to save her.

Finally Zage folded his arms, seemingly resigned to the idea, and said, "Very well, Your Majesty. I suppose it cannot hurt. But be wary of your image."

"Oh, I will," Siv said. "In fact, I think my image needed some work anyway. We are going to give Vertigon exactly the young king it wants. And while they're distracted by the pageantry, we'll get the nobles in line." He turned to Dara. "You are officially promoted to recruitment duty. Now, go find me an army."

11

THE ARMY

Siv wished he could be more involved with recruiting his new army of duelists. It would be a lot more fun than holding council meetings, reading reports from his advisors, and having tea with the nobility. He trusted Dara with the task, but it also meant she spent a lot of time out of the castle visiting her athlete friends. In the meantime, Siv's work piled up like sand on the Far Plains of Trure.

His advisors had confirmed that this winter was likely to be particularly harsh. Across Vertigon people worked double-time to harvest all the orchard fruits and prepare the bridges for the extra weight of snow that would soon cover them. A steady stream of imports arrived in the city through the Fissure: grain from Trure, fish packed in ice from distant Pendark, textiles and glass from Soole, rare vegetables and meats from Cindral Forest. In exchange, the Fireworkers sent their Everlights, Fire Lanterns, Fire-forged metal-work, and more down to the Lands Below. Smoke billowed over the mountain as they completed their Works.

Von Rollendar continued to cause trouble over the access road he now controlled. Siv had to deal with him by First Snow or risk having a group of tradesmen stuck in the Fissure with their goods. The council meetings weren't going much better, though. Von grew increasingly bold, and his new alliance with Lord Samanar strengthened by the day. Whenever Siv brought up the road, Von insisted that it was wide open and changed the subject. Siv sent a pair of advisors to check on it, and it was indeed open—at least when his men were there. Lord Morrven claimed that the Rollendar henchmen disappeared whenever the king's men approached, but he hadn't yet been able to prove it.

The other access roads grew clogged the closer it got to winter. Tensions heightened on the slopes and among the council members, but most of the nobles didn't bother looking to Siv to resolve it. They squabbled worse than furlingbirds defending their territory, and he often struggled to get a word in edgewise. He hesitated to trust any of them in case they were behind his father's murder and the secret army of duelists. The mysterious fighters could swarm like zurwasps from the caverns at any moment if he crossed the wrong nobleman.

Siv's continuing courtship of Lady Tull gave him more to worry about. He wished she would just make a decision already. Bolden had started shooting him even dirtier looks than usual, and he was often the first to talk over Siv at the council meetings, which he now attended regularly. Tull must have let slip that she had received another proposal. Siv pretended not to notice Bolden's barbs and focused on getting the kingdom ready for the snow.

Siv was so busy with his duties that he almost missed the first training session with the new Castle Guard. Dara sent him a note to let him know when the duelists would arrive, and he cleared a few hours from his schedule. He was secretly hoping he'd have time to get in a few bouts with the athletes. Council meetings made him want to stab things more than ever, preferably things he could pretend were Rollendars.

Berg and Dara were already there when he arrived in the western wing of the castle. His old rooms hadn't changed since he moved up to the king's chambers. A few of his books were still scattered over the low couch and the simple table. The Fire Gate was cold, though, hinting that the room was no longer in use. He had told Dara to use his antechamber as a headquarters. All the training would take place in his dueling hall because it was more private than the Castle Guard's courtyard.

Siv shook Berg's hand and thanked him for coming. Dara looked better than the last time he had seen her, apparently recovered from her head injury. He had offered to let her move into his old room too, but she informed him it would be better for her to stay in the barracks with the others. It made sense, but he didn't think of her as just another Guard. Dara was different, and she always would be.

He smiled at her and was about to ask her how she was when a young, broad-shouldered man strode into the antechamber.

"Your Majesty." He snapped off a salute.

"At ease."

"This is Telvin Jale, Your Highness," Dara said. "He's going to help with the swordsmanship training. He was a duelist before joining the army."

"Is that so?" Telvin? Was this the same Telvin Dara had drinks with the other night?

"Yes, Your Majesty," he said crisply. "I was the top duelist in my school, and I would likely have gone pro if not for the army."

"I see." Siv glanced at Dara, planning to make fun of Telvin's rigid demeanor, and was surprised to find she was looking at Telvin instead of him. Dara always met his eyes. He could count on her to understand what he was trying to communicate with a look or two. Why wasn't she looking at him now? He turned back to Telvin. Okay, the man wasn't bad looking, but he was so stiff. Top duelist in his school, was he?

"You're dismissed, Jale. I need to speak with Berg and Dara alone."

"Yes, Your Majesty." The man strode out to the dueling hall without hesitation. At least he was obedient.

"I thought he could help with training," Dara said as the door slammed behind the guard. "Are you sure you want him to—?"

"I don't trust him," Siv said.

Dara frowned. "He might be able to tell us about Pavorran. We need to find out who's in on his scheme."

"There's something sneaky about that fellow," Siv said. "Let's keep what we know about Pavorran between us for the time being."

"My king, I am thinking this is wise," Berg growled. "Trust no one."

"Yeah, trust no one, Dara," Siv said. Especially muscular young guardsmen who had been *top* duelists at their schools. "I'm going to watch from the balcony. I'll give you a few minutes to talk to your recruits before I arrive."

"Good," Dara said. "We want to show them you're following their progress. Sponsors often pamper their duelists. We want them to feel like they're on your team. We'll need their undivided loyalty."

"Have you warned them about the stakes?" Siv asked.

"Yes, but I'm not sure they believe me. Those who show up will be prepared to train to kill in your defense, but we'll need them to understand how serious we are."

"They could be hurt if we end up needing them like we think we do," Siv said.

"I know." Dara looked unafraid. Siv didn't know what he ever did to deserve having her on his side.

"We will make them ready," Berg added.

"Okay," Siv said. "Maybe if we have a little time I can even come down to the dueling floor and join—"

There was a knock at the door.

"Yes?"

"Sire? Apologies for the interruption, but Lady Tull Denmore has arrived to visit with Your Majesty. She wishes to join you in viewing the training."

"Firelord take . . . Okay, Pool. Tell her I'll be there in a minute."

Dara's eyebrows rose almost to her hairline. "She wants to view the training?"

"I mentioned what I'd be doing today," Siv grumbled. "She must have decided it would be interesting."

"Sure," Dara said. Her expression didn't give anything away. She saluted and headed for the training floor with Berg. Siv kicked the cold Fire Gate and went to greet Lady Tull. So much for getting to join the duelists. He had been hoping for a respite from the nobility today. Well, if she really wanted to watch the dueling with him, she was welcome to it. It could be a sign she was getting closer to accepting his proposal.

Despite what she'd told the king, Dara feared none of the duelists would turn up. She paced anxiously across the dueling floor while Berg sat in a chair by the washbasin with his large arms folded across his chest. Morning light cut across the smooth stone floor from the four tall windows. The hall felt emptier than usual as they waited for the duelists to arrive.

She had trekked all over the mountain inviting promising athletes to join the elite new dueling squad. She focused on those without patrons and promised that this opportunity would be as rewarding as signing with a sponsor—and it would include free coaching from the legendary Berg Doban. She chose athletes she had known for years, ones with no links to the army or to noblemen who weren't firmly on the king's side. Some duelists might stay away because they didn't want to upset their own coaches, but the prestige of having the King of Vertigon as their patron should attract enough of them.

She paced and paced as the minutes ticked by. No one came. Telvin Jale was doing one-handed push-ups in the corner, but she barely glanced at him. She had decided it would be wise to keep him close due to his connections to the army. And he could help train the duelists if he was as good as he said.

She dropped into her guard stance and did footwork, advancing and retreating across the stone floor. She lunged again and again, counting each one, trying not to stare at the door. What if no one came at all? She couldn't protect the king alone.

Finally, a full fifteen minutes after practice was supposed to start, the doors opened, and the duelists of Vertigon swaggered into the hall in all their glory.

Oatin Wont was the first to arrive, one of Dara's closest friends and training partners and the tallest man on the mountain. He strode in, all swinging arms and legs, and stared at the dueling hall with his mouth open. Luci Belling, a young duelist Dara had been friends and competitors with for many years, followed close on his heels, nervously running her fingers through her short bronze hair. They greeted Dara and Berg and then wandered around the elegant dueling hall, eyes wide.

Next to appear was Yuri, a stocky man with a dark-red beard who trained at a rival school. He'd been friends since childhood with Kelad Korran, another of Dara's close friends. His training partner, Kel's rival, Rawl, was notably absent. Kel wasn't here either, but Dara had expected that. She had other plans for him.

"Hiya, Dara," Yuri said, sauntering up to her. "This is a splendid training space." He nodded toward Telvin Jale, who was now doing sit-ups. "He in charge?"

"No, that would be me," Dara said. "Coach Berg will train us, but I'll command the squad."

Yuri chuckled. "But you're a girl."

"Well spotted," Dara said dryly. "We're still waiting for a few others. Feel free to run laps."

"Sure." Yuri shrugged and went over to speak to Berg. Oat and Luci were inspecting the practice dummies lined up along one side of the hall.

Then Bilzar Ten, Dell Dunn, Shon the Younger (not to be confused with Shon the Shrieker), and siblings Errol and Tora Feln arrived together, jostling each other as they pushed through the door. They had all dressed up for the occasion, wearing cloaks with their signature colors and carrying their best dueling blades on their hips. Dell Dunn even had a sharpened sword, though the hilt was rusty.

Bilzar Ten was the oldest of the group, well into his thirties. He'd recently had a huge falling out with his sponsors, the Morn brothers, who owned a dueling supply shop. He had both talent and sleek good looks, and Dara was a little surprised he'd chosen to come here when he was surely being courted by other patrons. His breakup with the Morns had apparently been rather explosive. Oat had mentioned something about him hurling Morn Brothers dueling supplies across Stone Market. Another version of the story claimed he had hurled one of the Morn brothers. Perhaps the other sponsors had decided they didn't want to deal with Bilzar's drama.

The others were younger than Bilzar, wide eyed and eager. Dara had the most luck recruiting athletes who hadn't yet established themselves with a patron. This was a big opportunity for them, and she hoped they would be loyal to Siv for years to come.

More and more duelists strode in, eventually forming an unruly line that stretched most of the length of the dueling hall. Dara counted eighteen athletes in total. She stood before them, hand on the fine black hilt of her Savven blade.

"Thank you all for coming," she said. "We're here to establish an elite new division of the Castle Guard. If you decide to join us, you will still be able to compete in the duels. You'll have room and board in the castle barracks and a place to train. King Sivarrion will be your official sponsor. In return, you must swear to protect the Amintelle family with your lives. If you can't make that commitment without reservations, you should leave now."

Dara waited. Tora and Errol exchanged meaningful glances but stayed where they were, shoulder to shoulder. The brother and sister had been trying to find a patron who would sign the two of them together for a while now. They needed this. Shon the Younger adjusted the fancifully embroidered cuffs of his coat, hands shaking, but then he was always a little jittery. No one else moved. She had chosen her team well.

"Coach Berg Doban will be our trainer," Dara continued. Berg heaved himself out of the chair and went to stand beside her, glowering at the athletes. Shon's face lit up, and he fiddled with his sleeves some more. He'd flitted around from coach to coach for most of his career, but he'd never had a chance to work with Berg before. "Coach Berg will instruct us in the use of true blades," Dara said. "You must be prepared to draw blood in defense of the king if you join this force."

A few of the duelists nodded. Luci Belling looked pale, but she stood firm. Young Dell Dunn rested a hand on the hilt of his rusty blade and puffed out his chest. Bilzar Ten rubbed his hands together eagerly. Dara wasn't surprised that this part didn't scare them away. Every duelist wondered at one time or another how he or she would do in a bout with real weapons. Now was their chance to prove themselves.

"And the last thing," Dara said. "You are going to work hard here. This job is not for people who want to laze around the castle. You will attend every practice and stay in peak physical condition. Slackers will be cut from the squad without notice. I need your final answer about whether you wish to join us by the end of this practice session. Is that understood?"

"Yes, ma'am," Dell Dunn shouted.

"Can we get started already?" Yuri called.

"Drop your gear and warm up." Dara gestured toward the balcony. "By the way, the king may come in to watch our training. I've told him you're all good duelists, so don't embarrass me."

"You got it, Nightfall," Oat said.

A few of the others chuckled. Dara grinned. They were a motley bunch, but they were her army. Siv's army. She would make sure they didn't let him down.

SIV GRITTED his teeth as Lady Tull leaned over to speak to him for the tenth time. He was trying to watch the exercises, but the dueling didn't hold Lady Tull's interest.

Siv had planned to make a grand entrance. He had prepared a speech about how he wanted the duelists to be comrades in arms and how he would lead their city with justice, wisdom, and mercy in exchange for their loyalty. He'd planned to tell the duelists to come to him if they ever needed help for their families or if they had ideas for the betterment of the kingdom. He wanted to inspire their love and respect by showing them respect in turn. It was sure to be a magnificent speech. Unfortunately, Lady Tull had been hanging on his arm from the moment she arrived, and he couldn't burst onto the balcony lest he accidentally knock her over. The duelists didn't even notice when he appeared. Why were people always ruining his dramatic entrances?

Dara and Berg put the duelists through their paces: rapid footwork drills, a hundred lunges, parry work with partners. Then they divided into pairs for a round robin of bouts, and the pure music of blade against blade filled the hall. The athletes looked great, and Siv would have had fun analyzing their diverse dueling styles if Tull didn't keep interrupting his thoughts.

"These are all professional athletes?" she asked.

"Yes."

"But you're recruiting them for your Guard?"

"Yes."

"Don't they need to spend a lot of time preparing for their competitions?"

"Yes."

"How often will they—"

"They'll be on short shifts, except when I need the full Guard for outings and festivals," Siv said quickly. "In exchange they'll have room to train, a place to live, and all the equipment they need. They'll continue their usual competition circuit as long as a certain percentage of the Guard is on duty at all times. We're signing a larger number to account for the other constraints on their time."

"I see," Tull said, though she didn't sound particularly interested. Siv leaned forward and put his elbows on the balcony, hoping she wouldn't have any more questions.

Dara wore her white competition jacket, and she rotated in to the bouts with the rest of the duelists. He hadn't seen her lose yet. When she swept off her mask after yet another victory, her face was flushed and her eyes bright. Damn, she looked good. And she had just beaten that Telvin Jale fellow. Even better.

"Your Highness," Tull said in his ear. "Do you wish to go for a walk about the castle grounds? It looks like they'll be doing the same thing for a while."

Siv ran through several choice retorts in his head before saying, "Of course, my lady. Please let me escort you." He tried to catch Dara's eye to wave as he left the balcony with Lady Tull, but she was too busy talking to burning Telvin Jale.

Siv had to work very hard indeed not to scowl as he and Lady Tull left the balcony for a stroll around the courtyard.

DARA SMILED as she shook Telvin's hand. He wasn't bad. A little rusty, perhaps, but she wasn't surprised that he had been quite good in his youth. He could be a real asset to the new team. Assuming he proved trustworthy, of course. She was taking a gamble: he was the only person she had asked to join the special dueling division of the Guard whom she hadn't known for years. She was glad to have so many of her friends here, though. And she finally got to duel again!

She surrendered her spot on the strip to young Dell Dunn and strode across the dueling hall to speak to Oat, who chatted with Luci Belling while they waited for their turn on strip.

"Hey Oat, Luci."

"Dara, this dueling hall is brilliant," Luci said. "I've never seen anything so beautiful."

"I know," Dara said. "Do you think you'll join the Guard? You'd get to practice here every day."

"This and the chance to live in the castle and be paid for my time? Dara, how could I say no?" Luci smiled happily. She had just turned eighteen, and her father was a bridge carpenter. If she hadn't earned a patron, she likely would have had to quit dueling to marry or perhaps get a job in a shop. Coaching fees didn't come cheap, and it would be years before she had a shot at a major prize purse.

"How about you, Oat?"

"If Luci wants to do it, I'm in too," Oat said.

"Oh?"

"Sorry, Dar, you haven't been around as much, so you probably haven't heard." Oat put his long arm around Luci's shoulders. Her cheeks turned bright pink. She barely came up to his chest, but they looked sweet together.

"Oh! Congratulations." Dara smiled at her friends, happy to see that some people were finding joy at least. "It'll be good to have both of you around the castle."

"What about Kel?" Oat asked. "I thought he was going to be here."

"He didn't think his sponsor would be too keen," Dara said. Kel's sponsor was none other than Bolden Rollendar. She had gone to see Kel separately after talking to Oat and the others at her old school. But that was a conversation she would not repeat to anyone, even the king, for now.

Dara glanced up at the balcony. She had avoided looking at it for most of the training session. It annoyed her too much to see pretty little Lady Tull whispering in Siv's ear while she was down here sweating away on the dueling floor. The balcony was empty. Siv hadn't even bothered to stay until the end of practice. She told herself it didn't matter. She was just happy to be dueling again.

Dara was stepping up to the strip for a bout with Oat when the doors to the dueling hall flew open.

"Sorry I'm late!" sang a familiar voice, and Vine Silltine sailed into the dueling hall. She wore whimsically embroidered trousers and carried a green velvet gear bag. Her dark hair fell in voluminous waves around her shoulders. She sighed happily and looked around the dueling hall as though she'd designed it herself.

Dara waved for Yuri to take her place against Oat and strode over to Vine. The other duelists around the hall took off their masks to watch them. Dara and Vine had become well-known rivals a few months ago.

"Vine," Dara said, nodding formally.

"Oh, Nightfall, it's so lovely—I mean dreadful to see you. I hear this is where an elite new team of duelists is meeting."

"Who told you?" Dara asked.

"That's for me to know." Vine touched her nose with a finger lacquered in Firegold. She had hinted at hidden sources before, and it annoyed Dara to no end that Vine always seemed to know what was going on before she did.

"You missed the speech," Dara said, "but this is a serious undertaking. We're not training for the tourneys."

"Yes, that's what I hear. We are to protect our dashing young king with our wits and our steel against any threats that may arise. I think it's glorious." Vine smiled around at the duelists. Some of them had gotten back to work, but most stared blatantly at her. Yuri combed his fingers through his red beard, not quite hiding a grin.

Dara took Vine's arm and tugged her into the corner by the weapons rack, farther away from the nearest pair of duelists.

"Vine, you're a noble lady. You can't join the Castle Guard."

"I rather dislike being told what I can and can't do, Dara," Vine said breezily. "I won't have you all participating in this very serious training camp without me. The nobility will have to understand."

"This isn't a training camp," Dara said. "We're preparing to protect the king."

"Excellent. Cross-training is the way to become a well-rounded competitor. I believe it will improve my creativity in the duels if I train with real danger in mind."

"But we—"

"You want this to be serious. I know. My dear Dara, you must remember that I know a lot about what goes on in this city. I hear whispers on the wind that could prove useful. You want me around." Vine smiled and began dancing lightly on her toes to warm up.

"If you're so useful, maybe you can tell me who might be plotting against the king."

"Now, now, Dara. My information is valuable." Vine dropped into a lunge, a miraculous feat considering how tight her embroidered trousers were, and looked up at Dara through long eyelashes.

"Fine," Dara said through clenched teeth. "You can train with us, but I can't have you on the official Guard."

"You're no fun at all." Vine pouted prettily. "Very well, I shall only join for the training."

"And the information?"

"There are many ifs and maybes among the nobility," Vine said. Dara started to speak, but Vine waved at her to be quiet. "I will tell you when I hear more, but suffice it to say that the houses are divided and undecided. Our *dear* king may yet win them over." She slid down into the splits and smiled. "I *can* tell you that a certain Warden of the Fire will be loyal to the Amintelles until his dying day."

Dara wiped a trail of sweat from her forehead, trying to cover her surprise. She expected Vine to know what the nobles were gossiping about, but she'd never imagined Vine would vouch for Zage Lorrid.

"Are you sure?"

"I'm always sure," Vine said. "Now, do invite me directly next time you concoct a scheme like this. I thought we were friends."

Vine didn't wait for an answer before sweeping around the room to greet the duelists as if they were an army of her fans. Dara half expected her to give out tokens. Luci and Tora Feln, the only two women apart from Dara, rushed to greet her like eager hatchlings. At least two pairs of the men forgot to resume their bouts as they watched Vine strut around the hall. Berg had to bark at them to pay attention.

Dara tried to ignore the distraction. She made the rounds of the hall, speaking individually to each of the duelists to confirm their commitment to the cause. Well, except for Errol and Tora. The siblings, both robust with nut-brown hair, clearly came as a pair, so she spoke to them together. By the end of the training session, Dara secured a pledge from each of the duelists to defend the royal family. She hoped they truly understood the potential danger. As they left the dueling hall, already talking about packing their belongings to move into the barracks, she wasn't sure they fully understood how serious this was. But it was a start. She had her team.

12

HOUSE ZURREN

NOT long after the new division of the Castle Guard started training, Siv received an invitation to a different kind of dueling event. House Zurren was hosting an exhibition match between Murv "The Monster" Mibben and Kelad Korran. To his mild surprise, King Sivarrion Amintelle was listed as the guest of honor on the invitation. He had completely forgotten he promised to attend the match. It had been postponed after his father's death, but the mountain was slowly getting back to normal. It would be Siv's first appearance at a large social gathering since he became king.

The Zurren family's white marble greathouse sat at the edge of Thunderbird Square in Lower King's Peak. It had a grand terrace overlooking the square and a broad portico lit with Fire Lanterns. When Siv arrived with Pool and an older Castle Guard called Yeltin, palanquins already gathered outside the house. Lords and ladies disembarked and milled around the portico, and laughter drifted from the second-floor balcony, where more guests braved the crisp evening air.

"My king! Your presence does me great honor!" Lord Zurren flung open the doors and descended the steps to offer Siv a deep bow. An obsequious young man of around thirty, Lord Zurren wore a fine coat embroidered with Firegold and a tall pair of boots, also edged in Firegold.

"Thank you, Lord Zurren. I'm looking forward to finally seeing

Murv the Monster in action."

"He will not disappoint, Your Majesty. Please come in. We are serving our very best wine from beyond the Bell Sea."

"Say no more," Siv said. "You've already made me a happy man."

Lord Zurren bowed and waved for an attendant wearing Zurren house colors to hold the door for Siv and his guards. Pool and Yeltin watched their surroundings with stony faces as Siv adjusted his crown and strode inside.

A massive front parlor stretched the full length of the greathouse. Judging by this and the terrace above, the Zurrens had built the house for entertaining. The actual living quarters must be set into the mountain at the back, with no room for windows. Siv wondered if the Zurrens lived here at all when they weren't having parties. If memory served, their primary holdings were a pair of mines over on Village Peak. He should have invited Sora along. She would know for sure.

Lord Zurren snapped his fingers, and a servant appeared with a goblet of wine for the king. Others circled amongst the guests, offering platters full of soldarberry tarts, salt cakes, and tiny slivers of baked apple drenched in thick caramel. The guests talked and drank, filling the parlor with a pleasant buzz.

Chairs arranged across the parlor floor faced a dueling strip marked out on the tile. The featured duelists were nowhere in sight, but most of the guests had arrived before Siv. When they noticed the king's entrance, they rushed toward him, compliments and commiserations on their lips.

"Good of you to come out this evening," Lord Tellen Roven said. He was a large man, and his voice carried over the others'. "You wouldn't miss a good party, would you?"

"Of course not." Siv raised his goblet. "How are your wife and daughter?"

"Oh, same as ever. My Jully misses your sisters. We hope you and the princesses will come for a meal now that you're out and about again."

"We'd love to," Siv said.

"Your Highness, how is the wine?" Lord Zurren inquired, trying to recapture his attention as the other lords jockeyed for position around him.

"It's superb, Lord Zurren."

"Your Majesty." An elderly noblewoman with more wrinkles than a cullmoran elbowed in front of Lord Zurren. "Do visit House Farrow when you have time. The apple harvest is almost in, and it's high time we had a royal visit."

"Of course, Lady Farrow."

"Don't forget, House Nanning, Your Highness," called another lord. "The goats are particularly plump this year. Make the best pies you've ever tasted."

"I will surely take you up on your invitation, Lord Nanning," Siv said. He drank deeply from his goblet, and a servant materialized to refill it, expertly forcing his way through the throng of well-wishers. "I hear you have plans for a few exhibition duels of your own this winter."

"We do," Lord Nanning said. "We've had a very good year, apart from the recent tragedy. Begging your pardon."

"Of course," Siv said. "We should be looking to the future. And celebrating the good harvest! Perhaps I can host a little festival to mark the occasion. The mountain has been a bit gloomy of late."

"My daughter will love you for that, Your Highness," Lord Roven said. "She's still talking about the last feast she attended up at the castle."

"It's about time we opened our gates again," Siv said. A harvest festival might be just what they needed to brighten the halls again. And it would certainly cheer Selivia up if he got her to help him plan it.

In truth, Siv felt overwhelmed at the onslaught of attention. He used to lounge in corners and drink with his friends at evenings such as this. They all looked at him differently now. Every word he said carried new meaning, and every action was subject to closer scrutiny. He also couldn't help remembering that the last time he'd been at a big event, he had learned his father was dead and then he'd nearly been killed himself. Siv shook off the thought and plastered a kingly smile on his face as he accepted condolences and returned greetings.

"My lords and ladies," Lord Zurren announced. "Now that our guest of honor, His Majesty King Sivarrion, has arrived, let us take our seats. The duelists are warmed up and ready to fight."

Siv took the center chair in the front row, set apart from the others, and the lords and ladies hurried to their seats around him. Siv knotted his fingers in the hem of his fine coat and breathed steadily for a moment. He should have been more prepared for this. Accustomed to the role of the easygoing, rascally prince, it was difficult to present himself as a benevolent ruler, deeply invested in everything his subjects said. He was still getting used to being king.

The last guests climbed down a grand staircase from the terrace and took seats facing the dueling strip. The scrape and shuffle of chairs and the murmur of voices filled the parlor until Lord Zurren stepped to the middle of the dueling strip. He twisted his hands nervously as the audience fell silent.

"Your Majesty." He bowed to Siv. "Lords and fair ladies." He nodded to his peers. "Welcome to House Zurren. We are honored to host you in our humble home. My wife and I hope you will return for many more occasions such as this." Lord Zurren gestured toward a hawkish woman wearing a dress apparently decorated with thunderbird feathers. Lady Zurren acknowledged him with a nod. "Without further ado, allow me to introduce the great and terrible Murv 'The Monster' Mibben."

Drumbeats sounded from behind the spectators. The crowd applauded as a door at the end of the dueling strip banged open and Murv the Monster stomped in. He was a big man and as bald as a baby. Tattoos covered his entire head like a cap. His padded dueling jacket was worn, and the smell of sweat came off him in waves. Siv spotted several ladies—including Lady Zurren herself—covering their noses with handkerchiefs. Murv halted in the middle of the strip and bent his blade over his knee to straighten it, muscles flexing impressively.

Lord Zurren patted his duelist's shoulder, eliciting a scowl from Murv. Then he called, "And now for the challenger, a man who is as precocious on the dueling strip as he is popular with the ladies. Welcome, Kelad Korran!"

The applause for Kelad was quite a bit louder than for Murv, accompanied by a round of giggles from the women in the audience. Kelad entered through the door at the opposite end of the strip and strutted along it, waving to his admirers. He wore a red dueling jacket stitched with the Rollendar sigil in black. He was a full head shorter than Murv, but he looked wiry, sharp, and quick next to Murv's bulk. He bowed to Siv, appropriately formal even though he had spent an evening drinking in the young king's company not long ago.

Lord Zurren waited for the applause to die down then said, "I also welcome Lord Bolden Rollendar, who has graciously sponsored Kelad for the past few years."

Bolden slouched to the front to acknowledge the thanks of the crowd. He met Siv's eyes, his mouth quirking in a smirk beneath his blond mustache. Siv stared at him impassively while Bolden shook hands with Murv, Kelad, and Lord Zurren and returned to his seat.

Kelad and Murv retreated to the ends of the strip to collect their masks and prepare their weapons. Lord Zurren took a seat beside Siv as a dueling official who'd been hired for the occasion stepped forward.

"On guard," he called, his voice a deep baritone.

The duelists saluted and assumed their positions, knees bent, blades at the ready.

The official raised his hands. "Ready?"

Murv grunted. Kelad tensed, a coiled spring preparing to jump.

"Duel!"

And the bout began.

Kelad had a dynamic style that played well against Murv's brutal strength. He bounced on his toes and made quick, teasing feints. When Murv reacted, Kelad struck like a panviper with hits to the hand and the toe. Watching him made Siv itch to get back on the strip.

Murv was good too, though. Every hit he landed made a resounding smack that caused the ladies in the audience to jump. Okay, maybe Siv jumped once or twice himself. They fought two fifteen-point matches (unlike ten-point tourney matches, exhibition bouts were usually longer) and won one each. Murv secured his victory in the second bout with a brutal compound attack, hitting Kelad so hard in the chest that he stumbled back a few paces.

"Point to Murv the Monster," the official called, flinging his hand up. "That's the bout!"

The duelists saluted, and Lord Zurren scrambled to his feet.

"Excellent work," he said, twisting his hands as though he were trying to wring water from them. "Good show! Sire, my lords and ladies, let us take a break for refreshments and reconvene for the deciding match."

A chatter of voices broke out immediately, followed by the scraping of chairs and delighted gasps as the servants reemerged, carrying platters of fanciful foods and beverages. The lords and ladies mingled and drank, their laughter replacing the clang of blades. Kelad quickly acquired a ring of admirers (mostly female), so Siv couldn't get close enough to speak to him. No one particularly wanted to talk to Murv. A space cleared around him as he downed a mug of ale in a single gulp. A Zurren servant mopped the sweat from Murv's shiny, tattooed pate, watching him warily.

Siv meandered around the room, making small talk and generally trying to portray himself as a suitably respectable king. It was damn boring. He felt as if he were slowly suffocating as old ladies gathered around him in clouds of perfume and demanded that he come for tea and talk to their unmarried daughters. He extracted himself from one such ambush and escaped to the far side of the parlor, where a massive portrait depicted Lord and Lady Zurren and their fat-cheeked baby. The child in question was now a toddler, and he ambled through the crowd throwing grapes at people's ankles while a harried-looking nursemaid trailed him.

Siv turned away from the portrait to find General Pavorran standing behind him. Siv jumped as though he'd been stung by a zur-wasp then tried to cover it by snatching another soldarberry tart from a passing servant.

"Pavorran, how do you fare this fine evening?" he asked.

"My king." The general saluted curtly.

"Have you tried the tarts? The soldarberries are excellent this year."

"I don't eat tarts, Sire."

"Your loss. Um, how is your—my—army doing these days?"

"I want more men," Pavorran said. "Vertigon needs a bigger army. I told your father the same."

"I see. Shall we arrange a time to discuss it in more detail? This is a social occasion." Siv grinned. The last thing he wanted to do was promise the general *more* men to turn against him.

"Acceptable, Sire." The general repeated his stiff salute and stalked toward Lord and Lady Farrow. So manners weren't his strong suit. Siv wondered if Pavorran's request for more men had anything to do with that secret training facility. He'd have to delay addressing Pavorran's request for as long as possible—and find out who else in the army might not be on his side.

Siv looked around for the Rollendars. Lord Von and two of his brothers stood on the far side of the parlor with their own ring of sycophants. That wasn't a good sign. The brothers, twins who were wider and darker than their sandy-haired brother, stood on either side of Von like gargoyles, forcing his devotees to squeeze together and face him as if he sat on a throne. Von looked powerful, almost kingly, as he spoke to the noblemen. Siv couldn't have that. But before he could take more than two steps toward the Rollendars and their supporters, Ladies Roven and Nanning accosted him, trapping him between their wide skirts and nattering on about the refreshments until it was time for the duel to resume.

The nobles returned to their seats at an announcement from the dueling official, but Von took his time finishing a discussion with Lord Samanar. The official waited for him, folding his hands patiently and not beginning the final bout until Von took his seat. Bolden and Lord Zurren were deep in conversation and barely glanced up when the duelists stepped up to the starting lines. Interesting. Both Rollendars seemed very comfortable here in House Zurren. Not to mention their lack of concern about making the others—including the king—wait.

The official finally called the duelists to their guard, and Siv turned his attention back to the strip.

"Are you sure you can handle another bout, you big boor?" Kelad called as he adjusted the bend of his blade.

"Shut up, Korran," Murv growled.

"Your last hit was a little weak. I hear your strength comes from your tattoos. What would happen if someone inked a picture of a pullturtle onto your skull?"

"Pullturtle?" Murv mopped the sweat off his shining forehead and pulled on his mask.

"They're very cute," Kelad said. "Would it slow you down or just make you slightly more adorable?"

Murv's face scrunched up in confusion. "Adorable?"

"Ready?" the official said, raising his hands. "Duel."

Kelad launched into a flying lunge and landed a hit on Murv's arm while the man was still trying to figure out what adorable meant. The audience applauded, and giggles and whispers spread through the crowd.

"One, zero for Kelad. Ready? Duel!"

"Hey, Murv." Kelad danced back and forth in front of his opponent, barely staying within the lines of the strip. "What happened to your dueling strategy? Did you forget it at home?"

Murv grunted and attacked. Kelad leapt out of his reach before immediately lunging in with a counterattack. The hit landed on Murv's mask with a thunk. The lady sitting behind Siv gasped.

"Halt! Two, zero for Kelad."

"Learned that move from Nightfall," Kelad said as he returned to his starting line. He met the king's eyes and winked. Siv grinned. So Kelad remembered their prior meeting after all.

"Ready? Duel!"

And so it went. The clang of blades filled the hall, mixed with Kelad's taunts and Murv the Monster's growls. Siv felt envy rolling over him like a hailstorm. He wished he were dueling rather than watching. He'd love to try his skills against Kelad and Murv both. It would be a lot simpler than sorting out which nobles were making power plays and less tedious than establishing himself as a king worthy of respect.

Eventually Kelad wrapped up a decisive victory—though still close enough to be suitably entertaining—and Lord Zurren presented him with a bag of firestones as a reward. Bolden clapped him on the back and promised him a bottle of Pendarkan liquor next time they went out. Siv wondered how close Kelad and Bolden really were. Kelad was Dara's friend. Would she trust him enough to ask him to report on his sponsor's movements? They needed to find out whether the Rollendars had anything to do with the mysterious swordsmen in the caverns. It was tempting to assume they were responsible because he didn't like them, but Siv needed real evidence.

After the duel some of the party moved onto the terrace. It was a chilly evening, but large, freestanding Fire Lanterns warmed the space up like spring. Siv escaped the crowd after exchanging a few suitably regal pleasantries and retreated to the edge of the balcony. He leaned on the stone railing, enjoying the respite from the smothering attentions of the nobility. Thunderbird Square spread beneath him, a steady stream of workers crossing it to climb the steps to Fell Bridge and return to Village Peak for the night. A sharp wind blew across Siv's face, making his hair tangle with the Firejewels in his crown.

"Beg pardon, Your Highness?" A middle-aged man in a neat servant's uniform appeared at his elbow. "Would you like another goblet of wine?"

"Thank you."

Siv took the goblet, but the servant didn't walk away.

"Your Highness, if I may say it, I am sorry for your loss. Your father was a good man," he said. He cleared his throat and stood straighter. "And he was a good king. I was proud to be Vertigonian under his rule."

"Thank you for saying that," Siv said, his throat constricting unexpectedly. He turned toward the man, who had thick, graying hair and a strong nose. Servants in the Lands Below could be obsequious and submissive, and they'd never presume to speak directly to (or about) a king. But Vertigon was different, and Siv wanted it to stay that way. His people were proud, no matter their profession.

"What's your name?"

"Hirram, Your Highness."

"Have a drink with me, Hirram."

"Lord Zurren won't be pleased if I drink his wine."

"I'll tell him I drank both goblets," Siv said. "He'll believe it."

"Very well." Hirram balanced his platter on the rail and took one of the drinks for himself. "This is good, sir."

"Think it really comes from across the Bell Sea?" Siv asked, tapping his goblet against Hirram's before taking another sip.

Hirram glanced around to make sure no one was nearby before answering. "No, sir. Lord Zurren got it from a Pendarkan merchant who's rumored to be unreliable. That's Fork Town wine, if ever I tasted it."

Siv grinned. "I thought it might be. Doesn't mean it's not delicious."

"Aye, sir." Hirram turned the goblet around in his hands, which were spotted with age but strong. A low mutter of voices drifted from the square beneath them. Some of the nobles were beginning to pile into their palanquins to return home. Others left on foot, steps weaving unconcernedly. The mountain was still considered safe at night, despite recent events.

Siv glanced at his companion. "Did you ever meet my father, Hirram?"

"Yes, sir. I served him here a few times. He treated his people with respect. He always spoke to me like a man, something that hasn't been the case with all my employers. I used to work for Lord Rollendar, and he . . . Forgive me, Your Highness, I shouldn't have said anything."

"It's all right, Hirram. So you worked for Lord Von?"

"Aye. I can only say that a man knows when he's being spoken to as a man and when he's being spoken to as little better than a packhorse."

Siv frowned. "Well, I may not be as good as my father, but I swear to always respect my people," Siv said. "All of my people."

"Hirram!" Lady Zurren's sharp voice cut across the terrace. "Attend me."

"Coming, my lady." Hirram drained the last of his wine and picked up his tray.

Siv stopped him with a hand on the arm. "Come to the castle if you ever want a different job, Hirram. I'll find a place for you."

"Yes, sir. Thank you." Hirram met his eyes levelly. "Be as good as your father one day, Your Highness. We are counting on you."

"Aye," Siv whispered as the servant hurried off. One day, he hoped he would be.

In the meantime, he needed to do more to get to know his people —and to get them to know him. He'd spent enough time trying to court the nobles. He wanted to show the people he cared about them too. The mountain had been too depressing of late.

Siv swirled his wine, the Firelight glinting on it like sunshine on rich mountain plums. He really should host a festival to celebrate the harvest. But it wouldn't just be for the nobility. He would throw a party for the people—all the people—and show them the kind of king he planned to be.

13

TRAINING

BERG worked the new Castle Guard as hard as if they were training for the biggest tournament of the season. They had to quickly learn to account for sharpened blades and no boundary lines. He focused relentlessly on defense. Some of the duelists grumbled that the training was too simplistic, but all the fancy attacks in the world wouldn't matter if your opponent ran you through in the first exchange. Dara was glad to get back into the rhythm of dueling. She had faced down death at the end of a sword herself, and it helped her adjust her perspective faster than some of the others.

The sport duelists were an ornery bunch, and training didn't go quite as smoothly as she'd hoped it would. They didn't like taking orders. They had become athletes instead of soldiers for a reason. Dara led the training sessions whenever Berg couldn't make it, and they complained that she was even stricter than Berg, especially when she made them start their lunges over if they weren't perfect and run laps around the entire castle—including up and down every staircase. She could still trounce most of them, but she didn't feel as if she had them in hand yet.

Dara had been relieved of regular guard duty while she trained the recruits, so she rarely saw the king. Siv was busy with his own responsibilities. Occasionally he appeared on the balcony above the dueling hall to check on their progress, but he never stayed long.

He still wasn't officially engaged, and he had to spend time wooing his delicate lady in addition to carrying out the rest of his kingly duties.

Princess Selivia watched the training sessions sometimes, though, and she filled Dara in on the castle gossip. The topic on everyone's lips was the big harvest festival Siv had decided to host. There would be a carnival in the castle courtyard, and the new duelists' division of the Guard would make their official debut at the occasion.

"I think you all should have a special name," Selivia said one afternoon, leaning over the balcony to call down to the duelists, who were resting up after their latest practice session. "And new uniforms! Something to show that you're a special group."

Dara eased off her jacket, rubbing her arm where she'd taken a bad hit in her last bout. "I don't know if that's nec—"

"That's a great idea!" called Yuri.

"Yeah, a team name!" Oat said. "I like it."

"What kind of uniforms?" Bilzar Ten asked skeptically, adjusting the collar of his expensive Morn Brothers dueling jacket over the tattoos twining around his neck.

"Oh, please let me choose them!" Selivia said. "Zala can help me. She has a great eye for color." She indicated her Truren handmaiden, who was supposed to be teaching her the Far Plains language but seemed to spend more time helping the princess dream up new outfits.

"Shouldn't it be Amintelle colors?" Dell Dunn said eagerly. "We're the king's men."

"And women," Luci snapped.

"Wait, what are the Amintelle colors?" Errol Feln asked, scratching at his broad nose.

"Blue, of course," Bilzar said. "Haven't you noticed how often our king wears blue coats?"

"Why in all the Firelord's realm would I notice that?"

"Our king is very dashing," Bilzar said, looking down his handsome nose at Errol, who blinked and leaned over to whisper to his sister—probably asking her what dashing meant.

"How about we call ourselves the Blue Squad, then?" Oat suggested.

"That's boring," Yuri said, throwing a glove at him. "Come on, Oat, you can do better than that!"

"How about the Duel School?" Dell said. The others groaned.

"I wish Vine had come to practice today," Yuri said. "She's good at this sort of thing."

"Oh sure, *that's* why you wish she was here . . ." Oat said, throwing Yuri's glove back at him.

"Hey, I have a great appreciation for all of Lady Silltine's talents," Yuri said.

"How about we call ourselves the King's Men?" Shon said, unlacing his boots with jittery hands.

Luci huffed out a sigh. "We're not all men," she said. "How many times do I need to remind you people?"

"The King's Guard, then?" Shon said, shrinking away from Luci's glare.

"What about us?" Selivia called down from the balcony. "You'll guard the princesses sometimes too."

Yuri leapt to his feet and flung his arms wide, making Selivia giggle. "The Guards and Protectors of the Royal Amintelles, long may they live!"

"How about just calling us the New Guard?" Dara suggested. She still wasn't sure the name was necessary, but she didn't want it to get too flowery and complicated. They had a serious job to do.

"It has a certain simplicity to it," Bilzar said. "We'll be the new blue, the protectors of our king—and his gorgeous and effervescent sisters—and we will be the dawn of a new era for Vertigon."

"Hear! Hear!" Dell called.

"The New Guard," Oat said. "I approve."

"It's easy enough to remember," Errol said with a shrug.

"I love it!" Selivia called from the balcony. "Zala and I will work on your uniforms. They'll have to be a special blue. You're all going to look so gallant!"

She and her handmaiden disappeared from the balcony, already chattering about how they'd help the New Guard make an impression by the time of the grand harvest festival.

With all the training and preparations, Dara had very little time to worry about anything else. She hadn't made any progress at all on figuring out what to do about her parents. She hadn't seen them in over two months, and the longer she waited the harder it would be to approach them. She had asked Vine to keep her ears open for news of the Fireworkers, but she couldn't bring herself to explain why. She still hoped it was a problem she could solve on her own.

And then there was the Fire. Dara had taken to skirting around the Fire Lanterns lining the castle corridors whenever possible. The Fire called to her more intensely than ever. When she was tired, which was often these days, she could barely keep the lanterns from swinging toward her as she passed them. The manifestation of her power may have been delayed, but that didn't seem to have dampened it. Dara still didn't know what to do with her ability. She couldn't ignore it forever.

One afternoon after a particularly harsh practice, Dara trudged down to the castle kitchens in the basement for a snack. Most of the duelists had flopped down on the floor to rest as soon as training ended, and she was alone. She snuck some goat jerky from the kitchens and headed back toward the stairs, planning to take a nice long nap before her evening run.

As she walked through the underground corridor, munching on the jerky, she brushed against a low-hanging Firebulb. Suddenly, Fire shot into her like a shock, and the Firebulb went out. Dara gasped and dropped her jerky. The Fire remained inside her, humming and singing along her bones. It was as if the Fire had sensed her blood could contain it. She shuddered at the feeling.

Dara raised her fingers to the still-swinging Firebulb and concentrated. She gathered the molten heat oozing through her veins, pulling it down her arm and into her hand, and pushed it toward the Firebulb. Slowly, the Fire squeezed out of her and back into the metal vessel. Dara slumped as the last of the heat left her. She had to be more alert so this wouldn't happen again.

She bent to retrieve her jerky. When she straightened, Zage Lorrid stood directly in front of her.

Dara froze. A hundred thoughts went through her mind. She should run. She should draw her blade and warn Zage to stay away. She should pull the Fire back out of that Firebulb and hurl it at him.

Before she could do anything, he said, "So." Then with lightning speed he yanked a burning cord of Fire from the stones and cast it at her.

Dara barely had time to yell before the Fire wrapped around her in a hundred threads. She pulled against them, and though the Fire didn't burn her skin, she couldn't push through it either. It held her firmly as rope.

"Let me go," she said.

Zage watched her struggling against the bonds.

"Curious," he said. "I'd have expected Rafe to teach you how to absorb those threads by now. You must be behind on your training."

"He hasn't trained me in anything," Dara growled. But she stopped struggling. *Absorb.* She could try that. She concentrated on the thread of Fire around her right wrist. She imagined it connecting with her pale blue veins and being absorbed into them. Slowly, the Fire entered her body, and the first bond disappeared.

Zage immediately lashed another bond in its place. But he was staring at her in surprise.

"What do you mean he hasn't trained you?" he said softly.

Dara glared at the Fire Warden, thinking fast. He knew she had the Spark, the innate ability to Work the Fire. It was too late to hide that now. But what else had he figured out? And what was he planning to do to her now?

"I only recently found out I have the Spark," Dara said. "My father doesn't know."

"He doesn't know," Zage repeated. There was something like wonder in his voice.

"Release me," Dara said.

"We must speak first," Zage said. "Tell me. What do *you* know?"

"About what?"

"Your father."

Dara frantically tried to absorb more of the Fire holding her in place, but Zage only added to it, pulling more molten power from the castle walls. He did it automatically, continuing to study her with those glittering black eyes. Zage would tell the king what she could do. Siv would wonder why she'd kept it a secret, wonder whether she knew anything about a bottle of Fireteats that had shown up in the castle a few months ago. Her heart stuttered painfully. Was there any way out of this?

"I don't know anything for sure," Dara said. "But I think my father is a danger to the king."

"Indeed," Zage said. "And you?"

"The king is my friend," she said. "I want to protect him."

"So you say."

"If you don't believe me, then what do you think I'm doing here?" Dara tugged at the bonds again. She was now holding quite a lot of Fire inside her as she absorbed the threads Zage sent at her. The trouble was she didn't know what to do with the Fire next. She had mostly seen Fireworkers making objects. She didn't know how to truly *wield* the power.

"I have long thought you were biding your time," Zage whispered. "Rafe is a patient man, and I thought it clever of him to position his daughter in such a manner. But I've wondered of late what was taking you so long."

"My father didn't position me anywhere," Dara said. "I want to stop anyone who would hurt the king."

"But this ability." Zage watched her as if she were a strange creature from the Lands Below. "I was led to believe you lacked the Spark."

"I did." Dara finally stopped struggling and let some of the Fire drain out of her. It was easiest to direct it through the metal of her sword. It passed through the blade and dripped back to the stones. "It started this summer. I didn't have a chance to tell my father about it before . . . before the Vertigon Cup."

"And you've decided to keep it a secret now?"

Dara met Zage's eyes. It was time to gamble. "I don't think my father has the kingdom's best interests at heart."

"I must agree on that point," Zage said. "But whose interests do you have at heart?"

Dara swallowed. She couldn't believe she was spilling her secrets to Zage Lorrid, of all people. But she was trapped. Her fate depended entirely on what he decided to do with what he already knew.

"Siv's," she said. Her breath constricted as she voiced the truth. Zage must hear her heart pounding. "Not the king, not the kingdom, not the Guard. It's Siv that I . . . that I care about."

Zage sighed, long and low. "I see," he said. The bonds of Fire disappeared from around her wrists.

Dara sagged, rubbing at the warm spots on her skin as the last of the Fire faded back into the stones.

"Are you going to tell him?" she asked.

"Which piece of information?"

"Any of it?"

Zage frowned. "I had hoped to learn the identities of all your father's allies before sharing my findings with the king and preparing for a confrontation. I must admit I expected Rafe to move against me first. I shored up my own defenses instead of protecting Sevren as diligently as I should have. That is a mistake I shall carry on my conscience forevermore." Zage glanced around the corridor, which was darker now that he had stopped wielding Fire to hold Dara in place. She remembered that he'd been close friends with the old king. It must be why he was concerned about the safety of Sevren's children. His devotion went beyond that of a subject. Still, she couldn't forget that it was that same friendship that led the king to pardon him for what happened to Renna in the first place.

"I think my father wanted you to be publicly denounced," Dara said. "He knew King Sevren wouldn't do that."

"Yes," Zage said, his expression calculating. "But Rafe wants more than vengeance against me. Removing King Sevren was the first step of a far more ambitious scheme, I fear." Zage considered Dara, and she resisted the urge to look away from his gaze. "Perhaps you can help me, if you are as loyal to the king as you say you are."

"I don't want my father to be hurt," Dara said.

"Doubtless Siv felt the same way."

Dara felt as if she'd been slapped. She knew. She burning *knew* how Siv would feel about it. But if he sent her away for what her father had done, it would leave him vulnerable.

Perhaps Zage recognized that too, for he said, "Our king needs loyalty. If you can give him that, I will keep your secret for now. But you must help me. Perhaps a reconciliation with your parents is in order, at least temporarily. We must learn how much support they have."

"I know," Dara said. She had been putting off this course of action, but she needed to go home eventually. Her mother's shouts as she left the last time stabbed at her like a Fire Blade. She took a steadying breath. "I need to talk to my father. It's the only way. But if I'm going to help you gather information on his allies, I want something in return." She met Zage's eyes, daring him to say no. "I need you to teach me how to control the Fire. I have to be able to hide it around my father, and I can't do it alone."

"I don't have time for an apprentice."

"I don't have any other options, unless you know another Fireworker you can trust absolutely. It sounds like you're having a problem with trusting them at the moment."

"I suppose I am," Zage said. He sighed, the sound as dry as a desert wind. "Very well. I will teach you to mask your power."

"Good. And I'll tell Siv the truth. But I'll do it in my own time."

"We have an agreement, then. Come to my greathouse tomorrow when you have finished your duties." Zage wrapped his cloak closer and strode away without another word.

14

THE FIRE WARDEN

WHEN Dara arrived at the Fire Warden's grand marble greathouse the following day, she was already tired from practice. Berg had them doing agility training that morning. This involved shuffling side to side as a partner tossed a glass bottle full of wine in random directions for them to catch. They had to change directions at a moment's notice or risk missing the catch and shattering the bottle on the floor. At the dueling school, they used to do this exercise with soft bags full of sand, but Berg wanted to impress upon them the seriousness of making mistakes.

As a result, they spent half the practice cleaning broken glass off the floor of the dueling hall, and they all left smelling like wine. The other duelists decided this was a sign they should go carousing together to christen the New Guard with wine and song. Dara skipped the team-building activity to show up for her first Fireworking lesson.

She stopped before the grand Fireworked doors of the Fire Warden's greathouse. She had never been inside. Even before Renna's accident, Dara's parents had disliked the Fire Warden for how he doled out the power of the mountain. It was one of the things that had kept Vertigon peaceful for so long, but her parents believed the strongest Workers should have unlimited access to the power.

Dara had already declared her opposition to them when she joined the Castle Guard, but she still hesitated before knocking on their oldest rival's door. She was driving a wedge further and further between her and her family. Unless she could get them to abandon their ambitions, she would never be able to return home.

But knock she did. Dara had started down this path, and she meant to finish it. Besides, she wanted to know more about how to use this strange and wonderful ability she had discovered. It had been devastating to attempt to draw on the Fire as a child and feel nothing. She still hardly believed she could Work after all, and she couldn't help feeling excited about the possibilities.

An elderly butler answered the door and led her into the Fire Warden's greathouse. It was an austere place, as cold and severe as the Warden himself. Everything was made of marble and ebony and edges. There wasn't a soft line in sight as they crossed the high-ceilinged entryway. The butler led Dara to an iron door on the far side and unlocked it for her.

"He's at the bottom," the man said. Then he ushered Dara through the iron door and locked it behind her.

Dara swallowed her nerves and descended deep into the realm of the Fire Warden.

The stairs were slick marble, eventually giving way to simple stone. It took quite some time to get to the bottom, and Dara grew warmer with every step. She was getting closer and closer to the Well, the burning core of Vertigon Mountain. This was the source of the mountain's power and industry, the very reason their founders had built their city atop the sheer peaks. And Dara was about to touch it.

She reached another iron door at last. She rapped on it, but there was no answer. Dara pushed open the door, and a wall of heat swept out around her. She had been less affected by heat since the appearance of her ability, but sweat still broke out on her forehead as the door clanged shut behind her. She entered a vast cavern, not unlike the one where she and Siv had seen the mysterious duelists. Instead of stalactites, a smooth arch adorned the high ceiling. Elegantly formed columns were visible around the far walls. This cave was clearly Fireworked, perhaps in the days of the First Good King.

Working stone was far more difficult than forging metal, and it used immense amounts of Fire. No individual Fireworker could mold a space on this scale, but the days were long over when enough of them were willing to collaborate on Works like this.

She stopped on a stone platform just inside the doorway. A raised path led to a narrow stone bridge arching through the center of the cavern. Beneath it, the Fire welled and flowed.

Dara stared down at the Well, the source of the molten power, for the first time. The Fire came from deep within the core of the mountain, like water welling up from a spring. It formed a lake in the center of the cavern, seeping up from the source in a steady flow. Hundreds of channels led off from the lake of Fire, disappearing into tubes and tunnels all the way around the cave. As the Fire bubbled upward from whatever magical source produced it deep within the earth, it was immediately distributed, parsed out through the intricate system originally designed by the First Good King a hundred years ago.

A solitary figure stood in the center of the bridge. Zage. Hands outstretched, he molded and redirected the flows of Fire and sent them into the arteries that would deliver them to dozens of Fireworking shops around Vertigon. Some Fire still seeped and oozed through the stones of the mountain, and strong Workers could draw on this residual power, but for the most part the Fireworkers relied on the flow of Fire they received directly from the Well.

The bigger tunnels had been divided in places, so the Fire now flowed in smaller and smaller quantities to each shop. It spidered out from the source, never enough to make any individual Fireworker a true danger to the ruler of the city.

Dara wondered what would happen if a Fireworker figured out how to meld multiple flows together without the Fire Warden realizing what they were doing. It would require cooperation between Workers willing to give up their shares for a time, but it was possible. It may seem as if the Fire Warden had all the power by controlling the Well, but he was vulnerable too.

Dara remembered the intensity of the channel of Fire she had sensed in the secret dueling cavern. If her father or some other Fireworker was gathering power, there might be no limit to what he could do. That was exactly the sort of thing the First Good King had been worried about when he first created this system.

Zage turned to face her, a narrow silhouette against the intense light of the Well. He wasn't wearing his usual cloak, and Dara was surprised at how skinny he was without it. He wore simple black clothing, with a silver buckle on his belt. He was actually a little younger than Dara's father, but he looked shriveled and ancient before the vastness of the Fire.

"Come," he said.

Dara dropped her own cloak, leaving her Savven blade buckled around her waist, and started onto the bridge. The weapon would be no match for Zage, but she had so far struggled to manipulate the Fire without touching steel at the same time.

Zage glanced at the blade but didn't tell her to remove it.

"You must be alert at all times," he said. "Loss of concentration means death, especially this close to the Well."

"I'm ready," Dara said.

"You are both ahead and behind," Zage said. "Most people learn to Work the Fire from childhood. It becomes as instinctual to them as walking or speaking their native tongue. You will have to work harder." Zage nodded at her blade. "On the other hand, you have proved yourself capable of discipline. And you have urgency on your side. You must seize control of your power and master it. There is no time for coddling."

"Understood," Dara said. "May I ask a question?'"

Zage waited.

"Will it be possible for me to learn everything a Fireworker can do at my age? My father says—"

"I know your father's views," Zage said. "It will be more difficult for you, but not impossible. If you have the potential, you can learn to Work at the same level of proficiency as any other Vertigonian Fireworker. Not everyone recognizes their Spark for what it is from childhood. I myself did not train in the Work in earnest until the age of twenty-two."

"Really? You didn't learn as a child? Is that why my father—?"

"That is irrelevant to our lesson."

Dara swallowed her additional questions. She had assumed she could never become a truly great Fireworker. She had long been taught that Fireworkers who didn't start young would never achieve mastery. She thought she would only be learning to control and hide her ability, nothing more. But hope bloomed in her at the Fire Warden's words. What if she could learn to be a true Wielder, like the sorcerers of old? How far could she go with her gift?

She looked down at the molten Well, imagining what it would be like to draw on that much Fire and mold it into great and terrible Works the likes of which the mountain hadn't seen in a generation.

"Miss Ruminor," Zage snapped.

Dara jumped. She peeled her eyes away from the Fire and focused on him. She was not here for the power. She was here to learn, so that she could do her duty. She would not be like her father.

"I'm ready."

"Close your eyes. Working the Fire is about sensation. You must feel the Fire with your mind before you can touch and shape it." Zage's voice whispered across Dara's skin, and she shivered. "When you begin to combine the Fire with metal and other materials, you must be able to tell exactly what is the Fire and what is the substance it is shaping. This will allow you to control the strength of the item you are Working."

Dara nodded, filing the information in her head just as she filed away Berg's dueling instructions.

"I don't want you to pull on anything yet. Just feel the flow of the power beneath your feet. Sense how it moves. It's like water, but thicker. It is like blood, but smoother. It will shape itself to your needs and will feel different depending on how you focus. Many Workers experience the flow like blood pumped by a heartbeat, but it does not pulse unless you let it."

"How do you experience it?" Dara asked.

The Fire Warden didn't answer, and Dara opened one eye. He was looking away from her, into the Well beneath their feet. The thick light of the Fire swirled in his eyes, which were not black as she had thought but rich brown, like an ancient oak.

"I am a vessel," Zage said softly. "I am a servant of the mountain. I don't seek to impose my own will on it. This power is far too much for one man to hold, and so I make sure it flows to many."

Dara closed her eyes again, feeling the power churning and oozing beneath her feet. The Savven blade grew warm at her hip, and she resisted the urge to touch it and pull a bit of Fire toward her. It was warm, inviting. But this wasn't about her.

"Okay," Zage said. "Let us begin."

15

HARVEST FESTIVAL

SIV leapt out of bed earlier than usual the day of the big harvest festival. He'd been looking forward to it for weeks. His people had worked hard to prepare for winter. The fruits and berries had been harvested and preserved; the bridges had been repaired; the meats had been dried. The workers had done their jobs well, and Siv wanted to reward them. He'd invited guests from all across the three peaks to a grand carnival in the castle courtyard. Too much gloom had filled the kingdom since his father's death, and he wouldn't allow it to carry on through the depths of winter.

Selivia had helped him with the planning, finally back to her usual bubbly self. She enlisted their mother's help with the arrangements. The queen might even stop by the carnival, which would mark the first time she'd been outdoors since her husband's death. Sora tried to take charge of the guest list, and Siv had to remind her not to only focus on her favorite nobles and dignitaries, but to invite tradesmen and miners and orchard workers and artists as well.

They were all excited to introduce the new division of the Castle Guard. Rumors were already spreading about them, and Siv wanted to make sure the whole mountain knew about his new team. He had spent a lot of time thinking about how to establish his image as the Fourth Good King, as opposed to good old Prince Siv. With any luck, the New Guard would help him set the tone for his rule.

Siv had also invited everyone who met with his father the day of his murder to attend the festival. Pool would observe them closely for clues as to who might be responsible. The nobles tended to be on their guard whenever they came to the castle for council meetings, but today they'd be at ease as they enjoyed the entertainment. Maybe one of them would let something slip.

Siv worked in the library while the carnival took shape outside. He kept abandoning his papers to peer out the window as the booths materialized around the courtyard. He had ordered the castle gates thrown open, and unofficial vendors had already begun setting up outside the walls too. The celebration would spread all over King's Peak by the end of the day.

A knock sounded at the library door while Siv had his face pressed against the smoky glass of the window, watching a pair of workers argue over the construction of a colorful awning. He hurried to the table and picked up what was surely an important piece of parchment.

"Enter."

"Are you almost ready?" Selivia bounced into the room. She had taken another Fire Potion to her hair. Red streaks feathered the ends like flames. She wore a deep-orange dress and a belt of maple leaves wrought in Firegold.

"We can't be the first ones there, Sel."

"I don't want to miss a minute of it."

"Well, I need to make a grand entrance," Siv said. "Where's Sora?"

"Who knows? She wouldn't let me pick her dress, so I'm not speaking to her."

"And Mother?"

Selivia shrugged. "She was wearing black again today, but I think she'll walk around a bit at least."

"Good." Siv tossed the parchment back onto the table and stood. "How do I look?"

Selivia bit her lip and studied her brother with a critical eye. He straightened his scarlet coat embroidered with Firegold and struck a pose.

"Flashy," she said. "Don't forget your crown."

"Right." Siv retrieved the circlet from where he'd set it on the table. He didn't know why it was so hard to remember to wear it sometimes. The crown was heavier than it looked.

Selivia danced to the window to look down at the courtyard. "Is the New Guard ready?"

"As they'll ever be," Siv said. "Shall we go check on them? It'll kill time while the guests arrive."

"Sure!"

Siv offered his arm to his younger sister, and they left the library. Telvin Jale guarded the door today, wearing the crisp uniform Selivia and her handmaid had selected for the new squad. The deep blue with subtle embroidery in silver looked sharp on him, Siv had to admit. Damn it. He should have picked some less good-looking guardsmen. The man had been helping Dara train the new recruits, and Siv couldn't help noticing that they were getting along well. Dara had been absent from the castle on several evenings when Siv had casually dropped by the barracks to check in. He'd begun to suspect that she and Jale were spending time together outside of work.

Fenn Hurling marched beside Jale as they descended through the castle, keeping an eye on Princess Selivia. Fenn wore the new blue uniform too. She didn't look quite as dashing as the duelists with her square frame and morose expression, but Selivia had insisted she wear the new coat too. Siv knew Fenn had a soft spot for her young charge. She and her brother Denn had seemed rather unimpressed with the New Guard, but they were loyal. Siv trusted them to look after his sisters.

In the barracks courtyard behind the castle, the New Guard had nearly finished assembling. Dara stood in their midst, making sure every buckle was in place and every shoe and hilt shined. Siv thought she looked a little tired, probably from working too hard. She'd proved every bit as dedicated to training the Guard as she had been to her own dueling. She should really get more rest. He glanced back at Telvin Jale. And she definitely shouldn't be going out in the evenings.

"Your Highness." Dara snapped to attention when she saw him, but she smiled warmly.

"Is everyone ready?"

"Pool is sweeping the grounds one final time," Dara said. "We've assigned several guardsmen to patrol the castle in case anyone decides to sneak in and cause trouble. Otherwise, we will be with you the entire time."

Dara rested her hand on her Savven blade as she spoke, calm and confident. The royal blue looked particularly good against her golden hair. No one would even bother looking at the other guards while she was at his side.

"Good," Siv said. "Let's go show the people their new king."

The Guard fell into a loose formation around him. Though they were all cleaned up and wearing matching uniforms, they didn't look like soldiers. Some had kept their longer hair, like redheaded Yuri with his bushy beard. Bilzar Ten had slicked oil into his locks and made no effort to hide the fanciful tattoos spidering across his neck. A jittery younger fellow—Siv wasn't sure if this one was Shon or Dell—had shaky hands and twitchy mannerisms that would have been stamped out of him in the army. The Feln siblings, Errol and Tora, wore swords with custom hilts swirled with bronze instead of the standard-issue Castle Guard blades. A few others carried their own weapons too, no doubt following Dara's lead. Siv was pleased that she continued to use the black-hilted Savven blade he had given her.

Instead of walking in a rigid box like soldiers, the duelists moved with a swagger that screamed of their confidence in their abilities. Siv adopted a little bit of swagger himself, and as they sauntered through the castle to the front entryway, they cut an impressive figure. They were like a team of old-time, swashbuckling warriors. And more importantly, they had the abilities to back up their bluster.

Pool met them before the front doors in the entrance hall. He looked over the motley assembly with a longsuffering expression.

"My king, the carnival has commenced," he announced. "The guests whose presence you specifically requested have all arrived at this juncture."

"Good." Siv glanced at Dara, who stood to his immediate right. He hadn't mentioned to her that he invited her parents. Her father had been among the tradesmen to visit his father on the day of his death, so Siv had included the Ruminors in his invitation. Even though they didn't get along well, he hoped Dara would be happy for a chance to talk to her parents in a neutral setting. He was more worried about the other people he'd invited.

"Have the Rollendars arrived?" he asked Pool. "And the good general?"

"Yes, my king."

"Excellent." Siv looked around at the New Guard. "Remember you are here to impress," he said. "Keep your weapons ready and your eyes open. And try to have a little fun."

"Yes, King Siv," the Guard shouted in unison.

Dara nodded at him, then she and Pool pushed open the double doors together.

Heads turned as Siv and the Guard strutted into the sunlight. Trumpets blared to announce his entrance (the trumpeters had come highly recommended by Vine Silltine). The company stopped at the top of the castle steps, drawing eyes from all across the carnival. The duelists struck dramatic poses while Siv waved and smiled at the crowd gathering within his walls.

The courtyard had been transformed. The few trees growing between the castle and the outer wall were bursting with color. Leaves drifted from them in a riot of red and orange and gold. Beneath their spreading branches clustered booths for games, bells and whistles and shouts of triumph already ringing from them. In each corner, a different entertainer attracted a crowd of onlookers. There was a juggler, a Worker specializing in Fireblossoms, and even Selivia's favorite storyteller. Siv had spent many hours hanging on the old man's words himself. He had asked the storyteller to proclaim his best tales of heroism and nobility throughout the day. Siv wanted to create a mood of gallantry and prosperity at this festival. Music trilled from another corner, adding to the upbeat, cacophonous environment.

And of course, there was food. Delicious smells mingled with the mountain breeze. Pies packed with every type of orchard fruit, savory stews to take the bite out of the cold air, mulled wine and spiced ale, sweet salt cakes expertly frosted in Amintelle colors. A group of children darted past the castle steps with some of these cakes in their hands, their mouths stained blue from the dye.

The courtyard was already crowded, with more people streaming in through the wide-open gates. Nobles were let down from their palanquins outside, and they came in on foot along with the tradesmen and servants and Fireworkers and miners and students and even a few foreign travelers. The atmosphere was already festive, and they were just getting started.

Siv and his Guard descended the steps and made a full circuit of the courtyard, stopping often to admire the performers and try out the carnival games. Whispers followed them, repeating the names of the duelists the onlookers recognized among the Guard. Lips twisted contemptuously on a few faces, but many people grinned as their young king strode among them. It was a spectacle, yes, but if there was one thing Siv's people loved, it was being entertained.

For his part, Siv was having the time of his life.

He spotted Bolden and his father, both clad in the red and black of House Rollendar. Siv had purposely chosen his scarlet coat to outshine Bolden. There was little doubt whom the people were looking at today. Now, if only the Rollendars would let something slip while they were busy being annoyed at their new king's flair for drama. He could even do something to provoke them. Perhaps it was a bad idea, but when Siv saw the sneer twisting Bolden's face he couldn't help looking around for something that would irritate him.

He spotted Lady Tull by a carnival booth with one of her crusty old advisors. She was playing a ring toss game where she had to throw three circles of iron over a bottle to win a prize—in this case an Everlight small enough to fit in a pocket.

Siv had had plenty of practice tossing rings of metal of late. He strode over to the booth, his Guard strutting along beside him. They gathered a crowd in their wake. Lady Tull looked up, a calculating expression on her face, as Siv offered her a stately bow.

"May I join you, my lady?"

"Your Majesty." Tull dropped a curtsy and looked up at him through thick eyelashes. She too wore scarlet today. Siv wondered if she had been intending to wear the Rollendar colors. To the people gathering to watch them, it must appear that the tragic and beautiful widow had dressed to match their young king. He could almost feel the romantic sighs of the young ladies in the crowd. They were going to love this.

Lady Tull tossed the last of her rings into the booth. It didn't land anywhere near the bottles. She gave a delicate shrug.

"Would you like a turn, Sire?"

"I'd love one."

Siv stepped up to the line beside her. The sullen young man running the game handed him the three rings and ducked his head in a semblance of a bow before slouching back to make sure the bottles were lined up evenly. The crowd of onlookers grew around them.

Siv eyed the target and wound up for the toss. His first ring landed directly over the bottle, clanging loudly against the table. The second one made the bottle totter a bit, but it stayed upright as the ring dropped over it. The spectators cheered. Siv acknowledged them with an easy grin then offered the final ring to his companion.

"Would you like another go, my lady? I'd be happy to teach you."

"Thank you, Your Majesty." Lady Tull stepped closer to him, and Siv put his hand on hers to guide the toss. He looked over at Bolden as he put his arm around Lady Tull and was rewarded with a scowl.

The ring landed directly on the bottle with a clang like a bell. The crowd erupted in cheers.

Bolden said something—no doubt snide—to his father and stalked away through the courtyard. Siv grinned. *That's right, Bolden. Go carry out your schemes. I'm on to you. And she's going to realize that Amintelle is still the strongest house on this mountain.*

He caught Dara's eye, intending to signal for her to follow Bolden and see what he was up to. He was surprised to see a scowl on her face. Siv realized he was still holding Lady Tull's hand. Dara looked away, very determinedly scanning the crowd, her face now blank of any expression whatsoever.

He could not win.

"How about a drink for my New Castle Guard!" Siv called. And he swept up his retinue and dove back into the festival.

Siv made a show of greeting nobles and commoners alike as he paraded through the throng. He ordered a mug of mulled wine for every member of his Guard and handed them out himself. He'd create an image of easy camaraderie. He was a king who got along well with the people who protected him. He'd show everyone that his people were his friends, and that they were loyal. If the schemes against him were even a little bit fractured, he would pour water into the cracks and freeze them by wintertime.

As he handed out the steaming cups of mulled wine, he said a few words to each of the guardsmen, showing them he knew their names and remembered something about each of them. Except for Telvin Jale. He might have accidentally on purpose called him Kelvin Kale. The man nodded and accepted the wine, utterly unperturbed. Burning soldiers.

When he reached Dara, Siv caught her hand as he handed over her mug. Steam infused with spices rose between them.

"Can you see what Bolden is up to?" he whispered. "And now for Nightfall, the leader of my elite new dueling squad," he called in a louder voice. "I'm a lucky king to have Nightfall by my side."

The crowds cheered, and chants of "Nightfall, Nightfall" rose among them.

Then Oat shouted, "Long live King Siv!" and others took up the refrain. The words spread around the courtyard, vibrating through the air like a new kind of song. "Long live King Siv!"

Dara executed a perfect bow and stepped back to let him continue his rounds. As soon as the attention was off her, she disappeared into the multitude. Good. Dara was more than a match for Bolden.

The throng in the courtyard thickened, and the atmosphere grew increasingly festive. Siv swelled with pride to see people enjoying themselves. Bolden and his father could scheme and sneer, but Siv was going to show his people that he cared for them. The people made Vertigon prosperous, and he would show them he knew and appreciated that fact. He set himself a challenge to greet every attendee personally. It was the sort of thing his father would do, and Siv intended to do his memory proud.

16

THE LANTERN MAKER

ONE of the drawbacks of the sharp New Guard uniforms was that it was difficult for Dara to pass unseen through the crowd. She drew eyes and quite a few compliments as she strode by. She wasn't the only Guard not standing in the king's orbit, though. She had instructed the men to rotate between guarding the king and listening to what the crowd had to say about him.

The afternoon sun stretched shadows across the courtyard. Here and there flashes of light disrupted the shadows as artisans demonstrated simple Fireworks. A few bolder Workers even sold their wares in the courtyard itself. More had set up outside, along with opportunistic food vendors and entertainers who hadn't fit inside the castle gates.

Dara steered clear of the Workers as she searched the crowd for the sandy-haired Lord Bolden. His father, at least, should have been easy to find. Lord Von usually commanded a ring of space around him as people tried to fawn over him without getting too close. Von Rollendar's reputation for cruelty was well known in the citadel. But she didn't spot any such bubbles in the crowd, except for the very visible one around the king himself.

Dara had reached the corner where the Fireblossom Worker was creating glowing plumes in the air for an awestruck crowd when she saw them. Her parents.

They stood side by side not far from the castle gates, looking as if they weren't sure whether or not they actually wanted to join the carnival. This was not the sort of event they typically attended. Dara froze, unsure how to unravel her feelings.

Her parents were here. At the king's festival.

Rafe wore his finest coat, the very same one he'd been wearing the morning of King Sevren's murder. He stood tall and straight, looking a bit like a king himself. He had a strong jaw and golden hair, just like Dara's. Other Workers began to notice him, and they approached him one by one to offer greetings.

Lima wore an austere black gown that Dara had never seen before. It was threaded with Firegold at the collar framing her proud face. Lips pursed, she surveyed the crowds as if they were children getting underfoot while she was trying to work.

Dara clutched the hilt of her Savven blade tight, her heartbeat quickening. She hadn't seen her parents since she told them she was joining the Guard. She would never forget the scorn on her mother's face, the resignation in her father's eyes. She had been certain they would never want to see her again.

What were they doing at the castle? Had the king invited them for some reason, or did they decide to come on their own?

Out of the corner of her eye, Dara noticed the Fireblossom distorting in the air, bending slightly toward her.

Breathe. She needed to stay calm. If anything, her lessons with Zage had made her even more sensitive to the Fire, more able to pull it to her at will. But she needed to keep it away, to resist the urge to draw the molten Fire into her body and show her father that she could Work after all. Slowly, the Fireblossom returned to its intended shape. Dara avoided looking at the Worker controlling it, hoping the woman hadn't noticed the shift.

Dara was still fighting a tide of overwhelming emotions when her father saw her. He simply looked at her, no expression altering his proud features. Her mother soon noticed as well and turned to face her daughter.

Dara stood utterly still. Breathed. They were her parents. She thought they loved her in their own way. They must have good reasons for what they had done, but they were playing a dangerous game. Their decisions had been distorted by their grief over what happened to Renna, something that had forever altered Dara's life too. She had to stay calm and try to understand them if there was any way to salvage this.

She released her grip on her blade and strode up to them.

"Hello Father. Mother. What brings you to the castle?"

"Your employer invited us," Lima said. "You didn't know we'd be here?"

"I am not in the king's confidence," Dara said.

Her parents exchanged glances.

"Are you certain?" Lima asked. "The rumors on Village say the king trusts you."

"Rumors can be exaggerated," Dara said.

Her parents looked at each other again, silent communication passing between them. Dara wondered if they had hoped Dara would give them information on the king's movements. Zage had suspected she'd been placed to do just that until he learned the truth.

"How is the shop?" Dara asked. "I'm sorry I haven't been to visit you." And she truly was. She had always felt most at home in a dueling hall, but she still missed the warmth of their kitchen, the coziness of her room, the view of the peaks from their front porch.

"The last of the winter orders have shipped," her father said. "I'm working on improvements to my designs for next season."

"Each lantern is more beautiful than the last," Lima said.

It didn't surprise Dara to hear her father was constantly making improvements. He worked as hard on his Fireworks as she always had at her dueling. He always wanted to be better. He always wanted more.

"And the Fire Guild?" Dara asked. She fought down the image of Farr's lifeless body falling to the ground outside the Guild head-quarters.

"Things were a bit difficult after Farr's tragic accident," Lima said. "But we're back to business as usual."

"That's good," Dara said. *Breathe. They don't know it was you.* "I was sorry to hear about that. I know you were close."

"Thank you," Lima said. She met her daughter's eyes, and they both shifted awkwardly, unsure what to say next. Dara couldn't help hearing the hurtful things her mother had shouted at her when she moved out, the words replaying in her mind like a beating drum.

"When will you be finished with this business, my young spark?" Rafe said.

He took a step closer to her, and suddenly Dara could sense Fire in him. He was holding power. A lot of it. He wasn't Working it as far as she could tell, but he did not walk around with Fire flooding his veins for no reason. Her heart nearly stopped beating altogether.

"This is my work now," Dara gasped. "I'm serving Vertigon. I know it's not what you want me to do, but this is the path I've chosen."

Rafe sighed, exhaling the heat of the power in his body with his breath. What was he going to do with all that Fire?

"Very well," he said.

"You should come home for dinner sometime," Lima said suddenly. "We miss you." Then she leaned forward and hugged her.

Dara was so surprised that she didn't hug back at first. Her mother had never been particularly affectionate, even before Renna died. But there was warmth in her touch. Not Fire, but real motherly warmth. Dara was utterly paralyzed for a moment. Then Lima stepped back, clearing her throat.

"Okay, I'll do that," Dara said. "It was good to see you. I'd better get back to work."

She backed away from them and ducked into the crowd before her father could hug her too. There was no way he wouldn't sense her ability with that much Fire running through him.

As soon as she was out of sight of her parents, Dara ran.

She didn't know what her father was planning to do with the Fire coursing through him, but she wouldn't be able to stop him, and neither would the Guard. She needed Zage.

The courtyard was so crowded now that it was difficult to maneuver. Dara spotted Princess Sora talking earnestly to a group of older noblewomen near the castle steps. Siv and his posse of Guards were all the way on the other side of the carnival from her parents. Dara started toward Sora to ask if she'd seen Zage when a familiar figure stepped into her path.

"Dara! Fancy meeting you here."

"Kel!" Dara threw her arms around her friend for a quick hug.

"Hey now." Kel pulled back and put his hands on Dara's shoulders. He must have seen the worry in her eyes. "Are you all right?"

"No. Have you seen the Fire Warden?"

"Not lately. I'm busy looking for my patron." Kel lowered his voice. "Bolden slipped away a little while ago. One of our mutual drinking companions said he thought he saw the young lord entering the castle."

"No one is supposed to be inside. Can you go after him?"

"He can't suspect I'm—"

"You'll think of something." Dara would worry about Kel later. She needed to find Zage.

Without waiting for an answer, Dara hurried up to the castle steps. She stood in front of the ornate doors and scanned the crowd for any sign of Zage's black cloak.

Princess Selivia stood beside her mother, Queen Tirra, who looked like a ghost in her black dress. Well-wishers came up one by one to offer their condolences for the loss of the king. Siv and his Guards continued to strut through the throng, nearing the center of the courtyard again. Sora was still busy with her noblewomen. Vine Silltine chatted with her own ring of admirers. No Zage.

Dara tapped her foot on the stone step. Who else could she trust who was a Fireworker? Most of the ones she knew well, like Corren the Firespinner, were firmly in her parents' camp. There were a few minor Fireworkers on the castle staff, but none would be a match for Rafe Ruminor.

She scanned the courtyard again and felt a painful jolt in her chest. Her parents were striding directly toward Siv. Her father wore the same determination on his face that she had seen when he was in the midst of the most delicate and important parts of his Work. He was about to act. She had to do something.

"Attention everyone!" Dara shouted. She swept her blade out of its sheath and waved it frantically over the crowd. Heads started to turn toward her. Siv looked up. "It is time!" she called. "Gather around, for our king's new Castle Guards are going to demonstrate their dueling prowess for your entertainment. Come nearer and watch the show!"

The guardsmen looked confused, but to their credit they recovered quickly and headed toward Dara, the king safe in their midst.

Dara ordered a nearby pair of serving men to run to the dueling hall and fetch blunted blades and masks so the New Guard could safely exhibit their talents.

Siv and the Guards got closer to the castle steps and farther away from Rafe Ruminor. Dara didn't dare look at her father as his target moved out of his reach. Finally, as more and more faces turned toward her, she spotted Zage Lorrid. He lurked beneath one of the fiery-leafed trees like a great bat. Dara locked eyes with him, willing him to understand that something was wrong.

Telvin was the first to reach the steps. "You're up first against Bilzar," she said. "Put on a good show."

"Yes, ma'am." Telvin looked a bit bewildered. Dara had begun to think he wasn't the sharpest blade in the rack.

As the Guards cleared the steps for the impromptu exhibition duel, Dara made a beeline for Zage. Most people were too busy watching the duelists to notice when Dara brushed past.

"He's here," she said to Zage when she reached him. "With Fire." She grabbed his arm, jolting as she realized Zage held quite a bit of Fire himself. She let go before any of it could flow into her.

"I will stop him," Zage said.

"Please don't kill—"

"I will protect my king," Zage said.

"Please," Dara said desperately. "If you cause a scene, it'll alert the other conspirators, and we'll never catch them. Neutralize him, but don't hurt him."

Zage's mouth tightened. "Very well." Then he melted into the crowd.

Dara hurried back toward the castle steps, hoping her parents hadn't seen her talking to their enemy. On her way, she nearly knocked over Princess Selivia.

"Great idea, Dara," the princess squealed, clutching Dara's hand. "I can't wait to see the Guard duel for real."

"Me too." Dara couldn't see her parents or the Fire Warden anymore. "I need you to stay close to the steps, Princess."

"Of course. I want the best view possible."

"Good."

Dara continued forward with the princess at her side. Siv stood in middle of the steps, positioned between Bilzar and Telvin. He was exposed, there before the great castle doors. She hadn't meant for him to get up in front of the crowd too.

He raised his hands like a referee and called, "On your guard! Ready?"

An explosive boom split the air.

17

AFTERMATH

DARA dove to the ground, pulling Selivia with her. Screams filled the courtyard. She sensed a massive rush of Fire unlike anything she had ever experienced. It was as if every drop of power in the courtyard had suddenly been sucked away, from the Fireblossoms floating above the artist, to the single beads of Fire in the Everlight carnival prizes, plunging them into shadow.

Then the Fire burst from the tops of the walls surrounding the courtyard in a solid fountain of power. Every shadow vanished in an instant. The screams turned from fear to surprise to wonder. Molten Fire shot into the sky all around the carnival, setting the castle alight. Droplets of Fire fell like rain, landing near the walls and melting harmlessly back into the stones.

Stunned silence descended as the last spouts of Fire bloomed in the sky. Dara scrambled to her feet. Most people had ducked, as she had, so she could see easily over the crowd. Her father stood still in the middle of the courtyard, facing Zage Lorrid head on. Even from this distance, Dara knew he no longer held that reserve of molten Fire. Zage had reached out and sucked every bit of Fire from every Work and Worker in the entire place and sent it outward to the walls.

Rafe and Zage stared at each other for a long time. Loathing crackled like lightning between them.

Then Dara's father turned and strode directly out of the castle gates. Lima followed, and neither one looked back to find their daughter.

"How's that for a show!" came a jovial voice. Siv had recovered faster than everyone else, and he was clapping vigorously. "Magnificent display. It's a new era in Vertigon!"

The crowd turned as one toward the king, awe and delight on their faces, and joined their applause to his. Now *that* had been a spectacle.

"On to the duel!" Siv said. "First up we have Bilzar Ten, the celebrated champion of the Square Tourney for two years running, facing former soldier Telvin Jale, one of Vertigon's own noble defenders. Who will be victorious?"

Bilzar launched into an eloquent recitation of his many talents as the carnival-goers surged forward to watch the duel. As far as they knew, it was all part of the show.

Dara breathed raggedly, relief surging through her. She didn't dare approach Zage. His face was bone white, and he looked as if he'd fall over if anyone so much as said hello. She had never seen anything like that. The level of power it must have taken for Zage to pull all the Fire from the courtyard without hurting anyone was almost unfathomable.

And if she knew anything about her father, the gauntlet had been thrown down.

Dara returned to the castle steps, where the king was busy refereeing the duel and adding his commentary, much to the spectators' amusement. He raised an eyebrow at her as if to ask if she knew anything about the unexpected fiery display. She shrugged and took her place amongst the Guards. There would be time to fill him in later—and time to decide how much he actually needed to know.

But one thing was certain: she wanted to learn how to do what Zage had done. To have the ability to neutralize her father like that and wrench that dangerous power away from him would be a priceless talent. She would work day and night until she had something approaching that level of control.

King of Mist

THE CARNIVAL LASTED LATE into the evening. Siv was in good form, laughing and toasting nobles and tradesmen, guards and ladies, children and servants alike. He played every game and tried every dish, and by the end Dara was sure he had spoken to every individual in the courtyard. Then as darkness fell he gathered the New Guard around him and left the castle walls to join the revelers outside the gates. He strode among his people, a beacon of energy and humor and light. By the time midnight neared, he had established himself as the People's King, the Fourth Good King, who wasn't too good to drink with his subjects, referee duels for his guards, and give children piggyback rides while they laughed and screamed and clutched at his crown.

It was a night that the people of Vertigon would surely remember for years to come. It was the night that King Siv was born.

Dara stayed close by his side, watching for threats and monitoring her men, but also just watching him. He was doing so well. He had worked hard over the past few weeks. She knew his father's death still weighed on him, but she also knew he was a man the people could love. He would do anything for them. And Dara would do anything for him.

The last of the revelers didn't leave until dawn spread fingers of light through the mists. Siv ordered the castle serving men and women to go get a few hours of sleep and forget about cleaning up until later. Then as the last of a rowdy troop of bridge carpenters toasted the king and lurched toward their beds, he finally turned back to his castle.

Dara had already sent most of the Guard back to the barracks. She warned them they would still have to train, but told them they could sleep in for a few hours at least. The princesses had been ordered to bed when they couldn't keep their eyes open any longer. Their mother had long since disappeared as well. Dara and Pool were the last ones left to make sure the king got safely to his rooms.

Siv hummed as they entered the castle and began the long climb up the stairs to his chambers. He'd had a lot to drink with all the toasts throughout the night, but his steps were straight and sure. When they reached the doorway leading to the solitary, fully protected stairwell to the top of the king's tower, Siv stopped.

"You're dismissed, Pool," he said. "Dara can see me the rest of the way home."

"If you are certain..."

"I'll make sure the door guards check his chambers for intruders before I leave," Dara said.

"Thank you, Miss Ruminor." Pool didn't quite hide a huge yawn. "I hope you will allow yourself a lengthy repose as well."

"I will."

Pool nodded to them both and left to seek his own bed. Dara and Siv continued up the winding stairwell alone.

"Any word on Bolden?" Siv asked after Pool was gone.

"He was missing for a while, possibly snooping around the castle," Dara said. She hadn't had an opportunity to check in with Kel yet to find out what Bolden had been up to. "Yeltin saw him and his father leave the grounds before dark, though."

"So he won't be hiding under my bed, then? That's a relief."

"No."

"Any idea what was with that big Fire show? I didn't get a chance to ask Zage."

"The Fire Warden has a flair for the dramatic," Dara said.

Siv chuckled. "You've noticed too? I wish I'd thought of it myself. It was spectacular."

"The whole evening was spectacular," Dara said. "You did well today."

"Why thank you." Siv sounded genuinely pleased. "Careful, Dara, you're going to spoil me with all these compliments."

Dara smiled back at him, and they climbed the stairs in companionable silence. Dara was so tired she couldn't contemplate making any big revelations tonight. Zage had averted disaster with her father for now. She would redouble her efforts to learn the Work, and she would find a way to deter his ambitions. But tonight she was just happy to walk in silence.

Or at least, it was mostly silent. As they neared the top of the tower and the entrance to Siv's chambers, a strange noise made its way down toward them. It was a wet sound, like smacking, mixed with the occasional soft moan.

"Is that—?"

"Shh," Siv said. He stopped Dara with a hand on her arm and

listened for a moment. Then he winked, an unmistakable glint of mischief in his eyes, and crept up a few more steps.

He flattened himself against the wall and edged further around the stairwell, one step at a time. Then he pulled back.

"Let's not interrupt them," he said, grinning widely. He tiptoed back down a few steps.

Dara edged forward so she could peek around the bend as well.

Oat and Luci were on guard duty on the landing outside the king's door. They had their arms wrapped around each other, and they were engaged in a rather vigorous kissing session. As far as Dara could tell they weren't doing more than kissing, but they definitely were *not* watching the door. Someone could walk right up and run the two of them through with a single blade, and they probably wouldn't notice. At least they were leaning against the door, so no one could get into the king's chambers without disturbing them.

Dara was preparing her best imitation of Berg's scolding voice when she felt a tug on her ankle. Siv had slid down to sit on the steps out of sight of the two guards.

"Give them a minute," he whispered.

"They should be—"

"I know," Siv said. "No harm done. We've all had a big night. Let them have their moment."

Dara frowned, but she obeyed and walked down to sit on the step beside Siv.

"You are the king."

"Indeed I am." Siv folded his arms on top of his knees and settled in as if he expected a long wait.

Dara studied him. The gray of dawn feathered the sky outside the tower window, but it wasn't enough light to leave more than vague shadows across Siv's face. His profile looked strong tonight. Kingly. He seemed years older than when they had first met.

But when the kissing sounds coming from a few steps above them grew more enthusiastic he still snickered like teenager.

"I am never assigning them guard duty together again," Dara whispered.

"Probably a good choice."

"Do you think the New Guard made the right impression, though?" she asked.

"They're perfect, Dara." Siv pulled off his crown, which had fallen sideways on his head, and turned it between his long fingers. "A few of the nobles made snide remarks about them, but they're working out exactly as I hoped. And that exhibition match was a stroke of brilliance."

"Good," Dara said.

"I feel very safe indeed," Siv said. "As long as those two up there aren't guarding me together. They're probably about as useful as a pair of pelicans when it comes to guard duty."

"I'll deal with them," Dara said darkly, making Siv chuckle again.

"So the people will love you after tonight," she said. "How about your Lady Tull? Do you think she's leaning toward saying yes to you?"

"I have no idea," Siv said. Then he turned toward her suddenly, startling her with the intensity in his eyes. "You're the only woman I look at, Dara."

She froze. "Siv . . ."

"I know I shouldn't say it. I know what I have to do, what my duty is." Siv took a ragged breath, pinning her with his gaze. "But, Dara, I can't even *see* anyone else when you're there."

Dara struggled against a sudden, desperate desire to throw herself into his arms. The sounds of the amorous activities above didn't help. Not one bit. Her hands found the cold stone of the castle steps, growing warm in an instant.

"We can't," she whispered.

"I know," Siv said. "But I had to say it at least once. And do this."

He leaned in and kissed her. It was a gentle kiss, sweet with the spices of mulled wine. Dara didn't move. It felt like sweet droplets of Fire were falling on her lips.

He pulled back just enough to meet her eyes. Their faces were so close together. Dara could feel his breath on her lips. She could barely move for the heat rushing through her. She wanted more. She wanted him. The kingdom and the mountain and the Fire and the world ceased to exist for an instant.

Dara grabbed Siv's coat and pulled him closer for another kiss. Fire burst in her mouth and roared through her body, and she didn't know if it was actually Fire or if it was just heat, the heat that had been slowly burning and building within her for she didn't know how long.

Siv's crown clattered out of his hands, ringing against the steps and rolling away from him as he put his hands in Dara's hair and drew her closer. All she could feel was his arms around her, his lips against hers, and the heat that filled her and threatened to burn her away into nothing.

There was no sound, no sight, no sensation but the warmth and the softness and the heat of his kiss.

Then something clicked in her like a sudden crack of ice. No sound. She pulled away from Siv and put her fingertips against his mouth. He began to kiss them one by one, and she wanted to melt into the feeling, but she forced herself to listen. The noises from farther up the stairwell had stopped.

"The crown," Dara mouthed, and she nodded toward the stairwell where the two guards had grown very quiet indeed.

Siv seemed to come to his senses with a great deal of effort. "Right. They probably heard that." He leapt to his feet and darted down the steps to where the crown had come to rest. He stuffed it back on his head and started to hum loudly, stomping up the stairs for the benefit of the guards above. "I'm so tired," he said, and executed the loudest, most theatrical yawn Dara had ever heard.

"Yes, Your Majesty," Dara said, not quite hiding her own breathlessness.

Siv grinned and pulled her in for one more too-brief kiss before he continued up the stairs.

"Oh, hello there, Guards," he said as they reached the landing.

"Your Majesty."

Oat and Luci stood at attention, their uniforms mostly straightened. Luci's cheeks blazed red. The pair looked deeply relieved that they hadn't been caught. As far as Dara could tell, they hadn't seen what had just happened a few steps below them and around the corner. Dara could hardly believe it herself.

"Anything to report?" she asked.

"No, Dar—ma'am," Oat said. "All quiet up here."

"Good. Do another sweep of His Majesty's chambers before he enters. Be quick about it."

Oat and Luci saluted and hurried into the king's rooms while

Dara and Siv waited on the landing. He smiled and stepped toward her as soon as the guards were through the door.

She stopped him with a hand on his chest.

"We can't," she said.

"I know," Siv said. "I burning know what we can and can't do, Dara."

There was torment in his eyes for an instant, and Dara knew they had made a mistake. This would only make things harder. They couldn't do this again.

But a glint of mischief replaced the torment in Siv's eyes. Before she could react, he slid a hand around her waist and spun her so her back was to the closed chamber door. He put a hand on the doorknob so the guards couldn't open it without alerting him and leaned in for one more—very thorough—kiss.

By the time Oat and Luci reemerged and reported that all was well, Dara could barely stand up. She ordered them to keep a close watch and then bid the king good night. He gave her a devilish wink as he closed the door.

18

THE QUEEN

SIV slept like a velgon bear in winter that night. Noon was long past by the time he awoke. He had a hangover, and his mouth was dry as Far Plains dust, but he still hummed to himself as he washed and dressed for the day.

He had kissed Dara! More than once. In the harsh light of the next day, he didn't regret it one bit. He should be assessing all the important things he had accomplished by making an impression on his people the night before, but all he could think about was when he would get to kiss her again. It should be easy enough. He could ask to speak to her about very important royal business without the other guards around. As long as they were in a safe room the others would think nothing of leaving them alone together. Or maybe they could sneak out through the secret tunnel and go for a walk on the bridges.

Assuming she wanted to kiss him again. She had seemed enthusiastic last night. Truth be told, he had worried she would push him away. But he had to try it at least once. And she kissed him back! Siv broke into a little jig, nearly knocking over the washbasin. He hadn't just imagined there was something between them after all.

Just before he closed the gap between them in that darkened stairwell last night, a sneaking voice had whispered that it was the wrong thing to do, that it would only make things more difficult. But that hadn't stopped him. And as soon as his lips touched hers he hadn't been able to think about much of anything except her eyes and her skin and her mouth and her...

"Sire? Your lady mother is here to see you."

"Just a minute, Pool."

Siv quickly finished dressing and cleared away some of the books strewn across the couches in his antechamber. He stacked them in a teetering pile on the table and called for his mother to enter.

"Hello, Mother, how are you feeling this fine afternoon?" He offered a gallant bow.

Queen Tirra was a wisp of a woman. If it was possible, she had grown even more ethereal since the death of her husband. She drifted into the room, clad in a somber dress. The black scarf wrapped around her head made her light Truren eyes look almost white.

"I am leaving in the morning," she said. "And I am taking Selivia with me."

Siv blinked, trying to rearrange his thoughts that were still trapped in the eyes of a certain guardswoman.

"She'll be upset."

"Delaying will only make it more difficult for her."

"I'd thought you were going to wait a bit longer," Siv said. "But tomorrow?"

"Your carnival last night reminded me how alone I am now," the queen said. "All those people coming to pay their respects . . . I barely know anyone here. I think it would be best to return to my homeland."

Siv resisted the urge to point out that she would have more friends in Vertigon if she had actually spent more time here while he and his sisters were growing up. But he'd resigned himself to the fact that his mother's heart resided elsewhere long ago.

"Very well," he said. "May I ask why you want Selivia to go to Trure so badly?"

"You seem determined not to take a Truren wife, and Sora has her own plans. I wish to introduce Selivia to potential suitors. She will be fourteen this winter. It's early, but she would do well to begin considering her options. I want to keep the alliance between Trure and Vertigon strong."

Siv grimaced. He hadn't done anything about Sora's suggestion that he use Selivia's hand as a bargaining chip with the nobility. It probably wasn't fair of him to go around kissing guardswomen while simultaneously using his sister to seek a powerful marriage alliance.

"How about a compromise?" Siv said at last. "Take Selivia with you, but promise her she only has to stay the winter unless she wants to extend her visit. And do *not* promise her hand to anyone in that time. That's an order from your king."

Tirra considered him for a moment then inclined her head. "Very well. I will send her back to Vertigon in the spring."

"Good." Siv went over to the side table and poured himself a goblet of water from a silver pitcher. The conversation had sucked away a little of his excitement over finally getting to kiss Dara. He and his sisters all had a royal duty, and now that he was the king he understood even better how important making a good match was.

But his mother wasn't finished.

"How goes the investigation into your father's death?" she asked.

Siv sighed, waving at a pile of papers on the table containing his notes on the suspects. "I'm at a stalemate. Without further evidence I can't make any accusations. The only real clue was the Firetears. It seems that many Fireworkers can make the potion, but no one actually sells it on the mountain itself. Any of the nobles Father met with that day could have privately employed a Fireworker to provide them with the means."

"Have you considered the Fireworkers themselves?" the queen said.

"He only met with one Fireworker that day, and it was Dara's father." Siv shrugged and tipped back his goblet, finishing his water in one gulp.

"Indeed. I know you trust her," the queen began.

"I do," Siv said. "Besides, Dara has saved my life on numerous occasions."

"Darling." Siv's mother reached out a pale hand to touch his arm. "Someone slipped me a note last night warning me to be wary of Rafe Ruminor."

"What?" Siv felt a mist wrapping around his head, making it difficult to think.

"It happened so quickly I didn't see who it was." The queen plucked a crumpled scrap of parchment from her belt and held it out. "It reminded me that I do not feel safe on this mountain. It is time for me to go."

Siv took the note automatically and smoothed it out on his knee. In elegant, looping handwriting it said, "Beware the Maker of lanterns and tears."

"Rafe Ruminor," Tirra said. "I don't know of anyone else the note could refer to. Or anything else. I know Selivia is friends with that girl, and as for you—"

"Dara *is* my friend," Siv said. "And she doesn't speak to her parents anymore. Even if they were involved somehow, Dara has thrown her lot in with me."

"That implies she must know something, doesn't it? Even though she apparently wants to protect you, if she knows who murdered your father—"

"No," Siv said. The note crumpled in his hand. "I don't believe that."

"I'm sorry, my son," the queen said softly. "But it's possible your feelings are blinding you. You have barely considered her father a suspect, even though he was here in the castle that day, and he surely had the means to produce Firetears. Is that logical?"

Siv stood and paced across the antechamber that had belonged to his father so recently. Back and forth. Back and forth. It couldn't be. There had to be some mistake, some unlikely coincidence. Even if the Lantern Maker himself was dangerous, Dara couldn't have known.

But what if she did?

Zage Lorrid had suggested Dara was a danger to him. Zage, who knew more about the activities of the Fireworkers than anyone else in the kingdom. Did he too suspect the Ruminors might be involved in the death of Siv's father?

But what could be their motive? Siv knew about the tragic death of their other daughter, but that didn't have anything to do with his father, did it? The Ruminors didn't like the regulation of the Fire, but would that drive them to regicide? And what did Dara know about it all?

The queen rested a featherlight hand on Siv's shoulder. "I am sorry to put this burden on you," she said. "But I don't wish to stay here any longer, and I want to make sure my little girl is safe. At least ask the Ruminor girl what she knows."

Siv didn't answer as his mother took her leave. The triumphs of the night before didn't seem nearly as sweet anymore. He had invited the Ruminors to the castle. He had thought he was doing Dara a favor by giving her a chance to reconcile with her parents. But what if she'd cut ties with them because she knew they were up to something . . . and she hadn't told him?

He had to talk to her. It was only fair that he give her a chance to explain. Maybe she knew of some other lantern maker who could produce Firetears. Maybe they could tie the whole thing back to that mysterious cavern of duelists, or the Rollendars, or General Pavorran. There had to be an explanation.

Siv shrugged on a coat and left his rooms, sweeping up Pool from the landing without a word.

He hadn't made any appointments for the day after the carnival. The castle needed time to recover from the festivities. A sleepy contentment permeated the corridors. Servants yawned, and guards blinked at bright lights. Siv would have enjoyed the peacefulness of it if a sick feeling weren't taking root in his stomach.

He marched straight to the dueling hall, hoping to catch the end of Dara's practice. His favorite thing was still to watch her duel. Well, that and kiss her. That had already jumped right to the top of his list of favorite things. What if she had orchestrated that kiss somehow? Gotten him to let down his guard in service of whatever her father—*no*. He couldn't start thinking like that. She was Dara. He trusted her. He had to let her explain. And besides, he had been the one to kiss her first.

But when he reached the dueling hall, the guardsmen were already packing up their gear. Telvin Jale saluted, looking as if he had gotten plenty of sleep last night.

"Is training over?" Siv asked.

"Yes, Your Majesty."

"Where's Dara?"

"She left as soon as practice ended," Telvin said. "She said she was going to visit her parents."

Siv stiffened.

"I see. What about Berg?"

"Coach Doban sent word that he couldn't make it today, Your Majesty," Telvin said. "Is there anything I can help you with?"

"No. At ease." Siv looked around the dueling hall at the other guardsmen. They looked worn out, sprawling on the floor or doing half-hearted stretches. It seemed Dara had kept her promise to make sure they trained as usual today. "You all did well last night," he said, forcing himself to sound calm and regal despite the betrayal stinging him like a zur-wasp. "I am proud to have you all on my Guard."

Smiles broke out amongst the duelists.

"Thank you, Your Majesty," said young, earnest Dell Dunn. Siv was pretty sure he could tell him and twitchy Shon apart now. "It's an honor to protect you."

"Long live King Siv!" shouted Yuri.

"Hear! Hear!" called the others.

"If you don't mind, I'm going to use the hall for a while," Siv said. "I hear there are plenty of pies left over from the carnival. Why don't you help yourselves? Tell the cooks I sent you."

"Thank you, Your Highness."

The duelists gathered the last of their belongings and headed for the door. Oat and Luci held hands as they left the hall, and the sight cut at Siv like a knife. The guards greeted Pool cheerfully on their way out, apparently energized by a word of approval from their king. Pool peeked into the dueling hall, giving Siv a pensive look, then retreated to the corridor again.

Siv allowed the stillness to settle around the empty hall. Muted afternoon light cascaded through the tall windows. He shrugged off his coat and tossed it on the chair by the door to his old room. Then he dropped into a guard stance and began to do footwork across the hall, slowly at first, gathering speed as he warmed up. He needed to stay alert. Agile. Like a professional duelist, he had to be ready for anything. He always had to be on his guard.

The rhythmic motion of the exercise helped to calm his mind. It felt good to get back into it, even though his moves were rusty. After he finished his footwork, he retrieved a blade from the weapons rack and did lunges, striking a practice dummy again and again. Dara would explain everything when she returned to the castle. Her father couldn't have been responsible. And she couldn't have known.

Siv worked until every muscle in his body ached and sweat

dripped down his face. He was out of practice and out of shape, but at least his accuracy was still there. He would clear things up with Dara, and he would find whoever had truly murdered his father. He would do what was right for his kingdom.

Darkness had fallen outside by the time Siv finished his workout, and he was exhausted. He cleaned up and retired to his chambers to change clothes. Dara still hadn't returned to the castle. As soon as she did, he was confident she would alleviate his worries.

But his mother had reminded him that he couldn't allow his personal feelings to blind him to what was happening in his kingdom. No matter what he wanted, no matter whom he wanted, he still had to act like a king.

And that evening, Tull Denmore came to see him.

19

THE PARENTS

DARA climbed the steep slope of Village Peak. A sleepy peace covered the mountain in the aftermath of the harvest festival. A lone goatherd ushered his flock along a pathway below her, bells tinkling around the creatures' necks. Muted laughter rose from a tavern set into the mountainside. Smoke from the Fireshops drifted on the wind, and golden autumn leaves swirled across her path.

Dara's muscles still ached from practice. She had worked her team hard that morning, hoping it would take her mind off of Siv and the way it had felt to be wrapped in his arms. But she would never forget that moment, even if it could never happen again.

She didn't know if she wanted it to or not. Well, she definitely wanted to kiss Siv again. It had been wonderful, her senses spinning like a blizzard and crackling like a fire from the instant his lips touched hers. She had hated that the moment had to end. But how could she justify pulling him close again? He was the burning King of Vertigon! There could never be more between them than stolen kisses. And she had bigger problems to worry about right now.

The Fire Lanterns lining the walkway outside her parents' home drew nearer. Dara shook with nerves. She hadn't been here in two months. The last time her boots had trod this path, her mother had yelled about what a disappointment she had been. She as good as said she wished Dara had died instead of Renna. In many ways, her father's cold dismissal had been worse. Dara fought off the urge to turn around and walk away.

She now knew for certain that her father's schemes hadn't ended with the assassination of King Sevren. Her father had brimmed over with molten power when he arrived at the castle last night. He'd been advancing on the king when Zage yanked the Fire away from him. He would try to hurt Siv again. And she might be the only person who could get close enough to stop him.

She climbed the porch of her parents' dwelling, the thud of her boots loud in her ears, and rapped on the door to the lantern shop at the front of the house. Without waiting for an answer lest she lose her nerve, she pushed it open and entered.

"Well, if it isn't the prodigal daughter herself."

Dara stopped at the threshold. It wasn't her mother who greeted her, but Master Corren. The stocky Firegold spinner was known for making elaborate embroidered garments with his golden threads. He was also the original employer of Farr, the man who had tried to kidnap and possibly kill the young royals. He must be in on the plot.

"It's nice to see you, Master Corren," Dara said warily.

The lantern shop was exactly the same as when she left: eight elaborate Fire Lanterns, each a different design, hung from elegant wooden arches around the room. A huge desk covered in drawings and neatly organized papers sat in one corner, with the same hard wooden chairs Dara had spent too many hours in throughout her youth. Corren lounged in one of these chairs with his Firegold-trimmed boot resting on his knee, but her parents were nowhere in sight.

"Where is my mother?" Dara asked.

"She's just gone to fetch your father from his workshop. She doesn't have you to do that for her anymore, eh?"

"I guess not."

"I don't mean to give you a hard time," Corren said. "You have to find your own path, but your parents miss you."

"I'm sure they do." Dara avoided standing too close to the lanterns and focused on staying very calm so she wouldn't accidentally draw on the Fire. She had left her sword behind at the castle. She still hadn't managed to do much with the Fire without metal in her hand, and she didn't want to take any chances.

"How are things up at the castle?" Corren asked. "I hear you're making a name for yourself, along with some of our favorite duelists. Everyone's talking about the New Guard."

"We're doing well."

"I wish I could have seen them at the carnival last night. I hear it was quite the show."

"It was."

Corren smiled warmly, and Dara couldn't figure out if there was more behind his words than polite chatter.

"You know," he said, "I was talking to Daz Stoneburner at the Guild the other day, and he mentioned that he had seen you."

"He did?"

"Indeed." Corren traced a swirl of gold on his boot. "He said you were asking questions about a suspicious-looking weapon. I'm curious: did you ever find out where it came from?"

"Uh . . . no." Dara breathed steadily. *Focus. It's just like being in a duel.* "Why do you ask?"

"Oh, just wondering if you had managed to get your hands on any more of those blades."

"I wasn't . . . No, I haven't."

"So the New Guard isn't armed with Fire Blades, then?"

Corren's question was so casual that Dara almost answered him. Instead she shrugged, as if the distinction between a Fire Blade and cold steel were inconsequential. She was already rushing through everything she and Berg had said in front of Daz Stoneburner that day. If he had been reporting back to the Guild all along, they would know Berg had offered to give her information.

That would mean the Guild knew all about Berg. That wasn't necessarily a surprise. Her father had once stated outright that Berg didn't have their family's best interests at heart.

But Daz Stoneburner had also been watching her very closely indeed when she held that Fire Blade. Was it possible he had noticed she could Work? And if he had, did her parents know too? She fought desperately to control her breathing and the pounding of her heart.

Corren smiled.

Footsteps sounded in the passageway, and Dara's parents entered the lantern shop a second later.

"Corren, we need to discuss last night's—" Lima stopped abruptly when she realized Dara was standing there. Her husband halted beside her, allowing a brief glance at Corren before fixing his gaze on Dara.

"Hello," Dara said. "I . . . I mentioned last night that I would come by for a visit. So . . . here I am."

"Yes, here you are." Rafe studied her from head to toe, and Dara resisted the urge to squirm. How much had Stoneburner told them? Did he already suspect she could Work the Fire? Did he know she had been the one to alert the Fire Warden last night?

"I can come back later," she said. "If you and Master Corren need to talk."

"We do," Lima said, "but it won't take long. Why don't you wait in the kitchen?"

"Yes, ma'am. It was nice to see you, Master Corren." Dara ducked her head and edged around her parents to get to the door. They waited until she had closed it behind her before they started to speak.

Dara snatched a mug from the cupboard and filled it with tea. She set it on the stone table and hurried back to the door. With luck, her parents would assume she was sitting and having a quiet drink while they talked. She pressed her ear against the thick wooden door.

The voices were muffled, but she caught words here and there.

" . . . was nowhere near us, but he knew . . ."

" . . . took me by surprise, and then it was too late to . . ."

" . . . don't think the king even realized how close we were . . ."

" . . . too busy playing the fool . . ."

There was an indistinct murmuring, and then Corren's voice rose above the others.

"What about Dara?"

"She won't help us," Lima said.

"Are you sure? She's your daughter. Maybe if she . . ."

Dara's father responded, his voice a low rumble, but she couldn't make out his words. He would agree with her mother, though. Dara's parents had long since decided she wasn't truly a part of their family, not when she wouldn't dedicate herself to their Work as they wished.

Dara frowned, running her fingers over the grain of the wooden door. She knew it shouldn't hurt her feelings to hear her parents dismissing her. She didn't want to be part of their nefarious activities anyway. They were murderers! But the rejection stung deep down, in a part of her beyond the reach of reason. She glanced around at the kitchen. It looked exactly the same as the last time she had been here. Renna's chair still sat beside her own. The castle was still visible through the window. But this place was no longer her home.

Dara pressed her ear to the door again. The conversation had moved on from Dara and the unlikelihood that she would assist in their next assassination attempt. They were debating what to do next.

"... has the resources in place. It would be easier than getting all the Workers in line," Corren was saying.

"That didn't work as well as it was supposed to last time," Rafe replied. "I still don't trust him."

"And you shouldn't," Lima said. "But you can use him."

"Perhaps," Rafe said.

"It's overdue," Corren said. "We shouldn't have let them walk over us for so long. You are the one to secure our futures. But like I said, he has the resources."

"Very well," Rafe said. "I will visit his greathouse."

"You'll tell him you support his bid for the throne?"

"Indeed." There was a shuffling of feet in the lantern shop, a scraping of chairs against the wooden floor. "It will take some time to prepare. In the meantime, Corren, you..."

Dara pulled away from the door and darted back to the table. It sounded as though Corren was taking his leave. She quickly gulped down half of her tea, which had gone cold. She had just managed to adopt a relaxed posture, her face in her mug, when her mother entered the kitchen.

"Dara," she said.

"Mother."

Lima took a seat across the stone table from Dara. She looked at her for a moment then stood and rummaged in the cupboard for some bread and cheese. Dara stayed silent, still processing what she had overheard. She leaned back a little so she could see into the lantern shop. Her father was shaking Corren's hand.

So they had a noble ally of some kind, someone who wanted the throne for himself. And this ally had resources. Dara thought of the cavern she and Siv had visited, where Pavorran the General had been overseeing the training of the mysterious group of duelists.

But Pavorran didn't live in a greathouse. His quarters were located beside the army barracks on the far eastern side of Square Peak. Whoever her father planned to collaborate with was definitely a member of the nobility. And it sounded as if he was preparing to overthrow the king!

Lima returned to the table and put down the bread and cheese. She met Dara's eyes for a moment then turned away to prepare some tea for herself. She was a tall, imposing woman, not at all prone to nervous activity, but she couldn't seem to think of anything to say to her daughter. *She had plenty to say last time,* Dara thought bitterly. She glanced at her sister's chair, wishing Renna were around to help her understand their proud, cold mother.

By the time her mother finished making tea, Rafe had entered the kitchen.

They sat down across from Dara together.

No one spoke. Dara fiddled with her mug and took another sip of cold tea.

Rafe sliced the loaf of bread and ate a piece of it slowly and methodically, his strong jaw churning. He offered some to Dara, and she took it without a word.

What were you supposed to say to your parents after you overheard them planning a coup? After you last left their home in a hailstorm of bitter words?

After a while, Dara cleared her throat. "Thank you for the bread."

"It came from Tollia's bakery," Lima said.

More silence.

Finally, Lima sighed, a long, heavy sound. "How is your new job?"

"It's going well," Dara said. "I enjoy training with the Guard." She looked up at them. "And the king is good . . . good for Vertigon, I mean. I'm honored to be in his service."

The Ruminors looked at each other.

"Are you so certain?" her father said.

"Yes." Dara leaned forward across the table, catching a trace of her father's familiar scent: fire and metal. "He's a good man," she said. "I'm very sorry for what happened to his father, but I think Siv—King Sivarrion will be a good ruler."

"His reputation—"

"I know," Dara said. "But he needs a chance. He's intelligent and reasonable. I think you'd like him if you really knew him." If only she could convince them to see what she saw in Siv. Perhaps they could work with him instead of against him. There was still a chance.

"Does he still favor Zage Lorrid?" her father asked. The name rumbled in his mouth like an earthquake. Dara resisted the urge to look at her sister's chair.

"I . . . Yes, he does."

"Then I am afraid he will be too much like his father," Rafe said. "Ever since the Warden returned from Pendark he has been influencing the Amintelles to diminish the power of the Fire."

"Pendark? What did Lorrid do in Pendark?"

"It matters little," Lima said. "The damage has been done. And if this young king is like his father, I sincerely doubt he will ever give your father the position he deserves."

"But—"

"Dara, you will understand one day," Rafe said. "Let us leave this topic. You have made your choice, but we needn't discuss it at home."

"Yes, sir." Dara held in a sigh. She shouldn't push them too much on her first visit. "I'm sorry. I . . . I am happy to see you both."

Her mother smiled at her, but it was more like a grimace. Her father studied her pensively. He opened his mouth as if he wanted to say something, but then he decided against it and took another sip of tea.

They finished the bread, cheese, and tea in silence. When Dara rose to go, she promised her parents that she would come see them again. She had thought about inviting them to the castle to meet with Siv in hopes of some reconciliation, but that would be too much of a risk. Her parents wouldn't be dissuaded from their views with one conversation.

She gave them each a stiff hug as she took her leave. She kept her

King of Mist

heart rate absolutely steady when she hugged her father and made sure no Fireworks were nearby. She was relieved to find he wasn't holding onto any Fire himself. He didn't even blink, so she thought her secret was still safe. Unless Daz Stoneburner had said something, of course.

As Dara crossed Fell Bridge and returned to King's Peak, she felt utterly exhausted. She had learned information that could prove useful, but the encounter with her parents left her feeling drained and sad.

The sun sank in the distance, and a light rain began to fall. A sharpness in the air hinted at the snow to come. Soon, the mountain would be wrapped in a deep, soft blanket, and the people would rely on the heat of the Fire to get them through until spring.

Not for the first time, Dara wondered how things would have been different if she had learned to Work the Fire from an early age. She'd be well on her way to being an accomplished Fireworker instead of studying the basics in secret with Zage. Her parents would value and respect her choices. In the fantasy as she imagined it, her sister would still be alive to train alongside her. They would be a real family. But she never would have learned to duel, and she never would have met Siv. If things had turned out that way, she wondered if she'd agree with her parents' actions against the Amintelles.

Dara's father and his associates wanted unmitigated access to the power of the mountain. There was no telling what they planned to do with that power, though. Did her father want to be Fire Warden? Did he want to dominate the other Workers and show them he was the mightiest of all? Or did he set his sights on higher goals? Did he want to be the king himself, to rule the mountain with the magic flowing through its veins as the first Amintelle king had done a hundred years ago?

Dara wasn't sure where her father's ambitions led. The one thing she knew was that her parents wanted to change the balance of power in favor of the Fireworkers. And she might not have opposed them if things had been different.

Dara looked up at the tallest tower of the castle as she approached the end of Fell Bridge, remembering that stolen moment with Siv the night before. As she had known it would, the memory caused physical pain deep within her chest. She could never be with Siv. Not the way she wanted. It might have been easier to throw herself in with her parents' efforts than to split her heart in two.

But there was no looking back now. Dara had made her decision, and she wouldn't let Siv down.

Darkness finished falling over the mountain. She trailed her hand along the railing of the bridge, her fingers going numb from the cold, and descended the steps. Her boots thudded on the stones of Thunderbird Square in a pool of light from a solitary Fire Lantern.

Suddenly, a cloaked figure stepped out of the shadows and grabbed her arm. Dara reached for her sword, realizing too late that she had left it at the castle. She was about to take a swing at her assailant when he yanked off his hood.

"Easy there, Dara." It was Kel.

"You scared me."

"You were pretty deep in thought," Kel said. "Didn't you hear me whisper your name from the shadows like a proper spy?"

"No. Sorry, Kel. I was distracted. You have news?"

"I didn't get a chance to tell you at the festival." Kel glanced around the rain-smudged square and drew her further into the shadow of the bridge guard's house. "I followed my liege into the castle last night."

"Oh, good." Dara had almost forgotten about Bolden Rollendar with everything else that had happened yesterday.

"He was hanging around the kitchens," Kel said. "They were pretty busy with all the stuff for the carnival. He didn't do much, just lurked around for a bit. When one of the cooks questioned him he said he was fetching more salt cakes."

"There were plenty of salt cakes at the carnival."

"My thoughts exactly. Any idea why he might have been snooping around the kitchens?"

"Possibly." Dara was pretty sure Siv's secret tunnel went through the kitchen. He had been friends with the young Rollendar lord in his youth. There was a decent chance Bolden knew about the tunnel. Maybe he had been checking to see if it was still there. "Thank you, Kel. That's really helpful."

"No worries," Kel said. He brushed at the rain droplets on his cloak. "This better be worth missing out on all the fun with the Guard."

"I'm sorry." Dara squeezed her friend's shoulder. "I wish you could join us. If it's any consolation, I make the Guard run laps a lot."

"Maybe I'm better off playing the spy, then. You're probably worse than Berg."

Dara grinned. "You might be right."

"I hope the king is prepared to give me a whole lot of public recognition if I end up helping to foil a coup." Kel pulled his hood back over his head. "I never want to have to buy my own drinks again."

"I'll be sure to mention it," Dara said. "But remember, he doesn't know you're doing this yet. This is just between you and me."

"I know."

"And be careful," Dara said.

"Always am."

Dara nodded and started to leave, then she stopped as another thought occurred to her. "Kel?"

"Yeah?"

"Do you know who makes Bolden and Lord Von's coats, specifically the ones with Firegold embroidery?"

"Corren, I think. I bumped into him at the greathouse a few weeks ago."

"Thanks, Kel. I owe you."

"Sure thing." Kel winked and disappeared into the drizzle.

Dara began the long walk back up to the castle through King's Peak. She had a lot to tell Siv. They might finally be getting somewhere. If her father had decided to work with the Rollendars, stopping him could be straightforward. They could cut off the "resources" Corren was gathering rather than attacking him directly. Dara would feel much better about moving against Von and Bolden Rollendar than against her father. Maybe she could counter his efforts without ever having to confront him.

Dara felt more optimistic the closer she got to the castle. Some of the sadness that had clutched at her during her visit with her parents began to ease as she approached the warm lights of the castle. She always felt wanted here. She felt as if she was part of something. And Siv was here. She wanted to be in the same room with him, work with him on strengthening his position and foiling the plots against him. They were a good team. Unlike her parents, Siv believed in her, valued her, wouldn't let her down.

Maybe she shouldn't kiss him, but she could go tell him what she had learned about the Rollendars. It was excuse enough for them to be in the same room. And if she happened to hold his hand for a minute or two, feel his skin against hers, what was so wrong with that?

Dara strode into the castle entrance hall and shook the rain from her coat. A basket of Everlights and a bundle of colorful awning cloth sat by the door, remnants of yesterday's carnival. The usual hustle and bustle had returned to the castle now that everyone had spent the day recovering from the festivities. Princess Selivia was passing through the entrance hall, chattering with her handmaid. She spotted Dara and darted up to her, eyes bright with excitement.

"Oh, Dara, did you hear?"

"Hear what?"

"Lady Tull is here. She has accepted my brother's proposal. They're going to be married!"

20

FAREWELL

THE kingdom couldn't be more delighted by the news of the royal engagement. The markets and taverns were already buzzing with talk of the carnival. Adding the prospect of a royal wedding on top of it was sure to keep the gossips of the mountain busy all winter long.

The people loved that Lady Tull's tragic story would have a happy ending. They loved that she was beautiful. And her allies loved that she was going to be the queen. Where they had been hesitant to throw their weight behind Siv before, they now supported him enthusiastically.

He received a steady stream of noble visitors and invitations to dine and drink, view orchards, and admire livestock. He might as well fire the castle cooks because it looked as if he'd never have to eat at home again. He took advantage of the opportunity to assure the nobility of a prosperous and peaceful future under his kingship. Tull accompanied him on many of these excursions. She was a smart woman, and she did her part to charm the nobles. Siv almost felt as if they'd rather have her in charge than him.

He was surprised his performance at the carnival had been enough to prompt her to accept him. He'd expected her to keep him and Bolden waiting for weeks or months longer. He'd been stunned when she turned up at the castle to say she wished to marry him, so stunned that he'd nodded dumbly and said, "Sounds good. Let's do that, then."

She had shaken his hand and kissed his cheek, and suddenly the whole castle knew about it. It left Siv feeling winded, defeated, and kind of miserable.

The wedding wouldn't take place until spring. They needed to invite dignitaries from lands near and far, and Vertigon wasn't the easiest place to visit in winter. Besides, Princess Selivia had warned her brother that she would personally murder him if he dared have the royal wedding while she was away in Trure.

The queen delayed their departure for a few days amidst the excitement, but a sudden cold snap reminded her that First Snow would arrive all too soon. So she packed up the youngest princess and prepared to leave the mountain.

Siv, Sora, and Tull accompanied them to the road into the Fissure to give them a proper send-off. He decided it was a good time to take his growing cur-dragon out for a stroll. Rumy was now bigger than his mother, though his muscles hadn't thickened fully and his scales were still a bit soft. He nearly reached Siv's waist when standing on all fours, and he might end up being larger yet.

Siv guided him in a harness as he escorted his mother and sister down through King's Peak. Rumy tugged at the lead, sometimes leaping into the air and flapping his wings for a few paces before falling back to the ground. He also enjoyed snapping at the heels of the tough little ponies that would carry Tirra and Selivia's luggage down the mountain, making the animals snort and shuffle nervously. Siv had to pay close attention to keep the little guy from flying away or accidentally setting someone on fire.

The queen, the princess, and their guards and handmaids would spend a few days traveling the steep road down the Fissure on foot. It wound back and forth along the sheer canyon wall, far too precarious for most people to feel comfortable riding down it. When they reached the bottom, horses sent by Siv's grandfather would be waiting to take them the rest of the way to Trure. For a brief moment, he almost wished he could go with them. That was a first. Siv hated visiting Trure.

The top of the road into the Fissure led through Ferrington-Denmore land, so there had been no way for Siv to avoid inviting his betrothed along. Tull was the perfect lady, as always. She dressed demurely and assured the queen that she would look out for her son. They all knew this was a purely political marriage, but the two played their parts well. Workers from the Ferrington-Denmore Estate gathered to watch them, thrilled to see the lady in her capacity as the future royal consort.

Between them and the onlookers stood the Guard. The duelists had embraced their role enthusiastically, and they now operated like a well-maintained Fire Gate. They formed a loose circle around the king and his party, allowing an appropriate amount of space for their farewell. Siv gave Rumy's lead to Oat while he hugged his mother and sister. Dara was among the guards escorting them today, but she stood facing the steep path into the Fissure, one hand on her Savven blade, and didn't look at him at all.

"Send word when you reach the palace," Siv said. "And watch out for burrlinbats in the Fissure."

"Those don't exist," Selivia said.

"Do too. I've seen them myself."

Selivia stuck her tongue out at him then seemed to realize it wasn't quite appropriate for a princess who was nearly fourteen years old. She blushed and said, "Don't do anything too fun without me."

"I intend to hold a feast in the Great Hall every night you are away," Siv said. "We will all be far too tired of parties to have any more when you get back."

Selivia made a face then hugged him around the waist. When she pulled away there were tears in her eyes.

"You'll be fine, Sel," Siv said. "You won't be gone long."

"I know." She sniffed and turned to say good-bye to Sora, who was busily adding to the list of all the Truren nobility she had asked Selivia to visit while she was in the Lands Below.

Selivia may be crying, but their mother looked as happy as she always did when she left for Trure. She adjusted her long velvet traveling cloak and reached out to squeeze Siv's hand.

"Stay warm this winter," she said. Then with a glance over at Dara, who still had her back to them, she pulled him close for a quick hug. "And be wary of the Lantern Maker."

"Have a safe journey."

The queen smiled, looking positively cheerful as she headed toward the steps leading down the mountainside. Zala, Selivia's handmaid, followed close on her heels, no doubt happy to be returning to her homeland. Fenn Hurling took leave of her twin brother, Denn, looking as stoic as ever. Selivia commenced another round of hugs, beginning to look a bit more excited about the journey.

For his part, Siv was burning miserable. He hadn't spoken to Dara in private since the engagement. He had wanted to tell her about it in person, but word traveled too quickly. By the time he saw her, she had adopted a professional demeanor that hadn't slipped once since. He still hadn't asked her about what had occurred between their fathers on the day of the Vertigon Cup. They needed to have that conversation, but it would surely be like pouring salt in a wound. *Here, Dara, let me kiss you. By the way, I'm getting married. Oh, and do you think your father is a murderer? Thanks so much for the chat.*

He hadn't yet gotten up the nerve to have that particular talk. Dara had been busy anyway. He learned from some subtle questioning of the other guards that she often left the castle when she wasn't on duty or in training. No one knew where she went. She might be spending even more time with her parents. The possibility left him feeling hollow.

Siv took Rumy's lead back from Oat as his mother and sister and their guards and servants began the trek down the mountain. Selivia kept turning back to wave, her still-dyed hair floating over her shoulders like autumn leaves, until she disappeared from view.

"I will return to my estate now, Your Highness," Tull said.

"Very well, my lady," Siv offered her as much of a bow as he could manage as Rumy picked that moment to lunge against his lead. He was a strong little guy, and Siv had to use both hands to keep him from soaring out over the Fissure.

Lady Tull took three mincing steps backwards. "Shall I come to the castle tomorrow to discuss preparations for our engagement feast?"

"Sure," Siv said. "Please do."

When Lady Tull took her leave, the onlookers who had gathered to watch the queen's departure dispersed. Within a few minutes, Siv,

Sora, and the Guard were the only ones left on the road overlooking the Fissure. A wind picked up, howling through the canyon. The queen and the princess would have a cold journey ahead of them.

"Do you wish to return to the castle, Your Majesty?" Dara asked, finally turning to face him. She sounded so formal that she might as well be Pool.

"Yes, sure," Siv said. "You have anything you need to do while we're out, Sora?"

Sora shook her head. She was staring after Lady Tull and her retinue as they made their way toward her greathouse, visible through a line of apple trees.

"What's on your mind?" Siv asked his sister as they started back toward the castle.

"Lady Tull," she said. "Isn't it odd?"

"What?"

"How quickly she accepted your proposal?"

"Um, she took weeks to answer."

"Yes, but there was an obvious strategy behind that," Sora said. "She was waiting to see whether you could stand up to the Rollendars."

"And?"

"You didn't," Sora said, her round face pensive. "Not really. You made a good start of getting people to like you, but none of the key players had actually thrown their support behind you when she said yes."

"She's a smart woman. I'm sure she had her reasons for thinking I'm a good catch," Siv said wryly. He noticed that Dara had fallen into formation on her other side. Her hair was pulled back in a tight braid, and her blue uniform was crisp and pressed. He couldn't quite catch her eye.

"I know she's smart. That's what I mean," Sora said. "It doesn't make sense. What do you think, Dara?"

"The engagement did come out of the blue," Dara said curtly.

Siv was so surprised at her tone that he stopped short and stared at her. The Guards slowed as well, but they didn't crowd too close, giving them space to talk.

Dara seemed to realize what she had said, for she cleared her throat, her cheeks going pink.

"I mean, of course it was in the works, but she didn't look like she was on the verge of accepting your proposal at the carnival. If she was that impressed, why wait until the next day? You could have been engaged before you returned to your rooms that evening." Then Dara skewered Siv with such a sharp look that he was surprised he wasn't bleeding. "Your Highness."

Oh, she was mad. If there had been any doubt before, it was dead and buried. She was mad at him for kissing her. He *knew* it had been a mistake.

"I didn't know she was anywhere near saying yes that night," Siv said. "I didn't think she would say yes at all. I certainly didn't expect to be engaged within twenty-four hours."

"It was really more like twelve hours, Your Majesty," Dara said.

"That's hardly fair," Siv said.

"Okay, we've established that it was a surprise," Sora said impatiently. "But what does it mean?"

"I'm not sure." Siv knelt to adjust Rumy's harness. The back of his neck prickled at the thought that his position might not be as secure as he had hoped. He had believed he was making progress. But what if Lady Tull had some ulterior motive that didn't include the security of Vertigon and House Amintelle, which she supposedly wanted to join?

To his surprise, Dara knelt on Rumy's other side and scratched his scaly head. She shifted closer to Siv and said under her breath, "Bolden was snooping around the kitchens that night. I haven't had a chance to tell you."

"The kitchens?"

Dara glanced up at Sora, but she seemed lost in thought.

Dara leaned a little closer. "Does he know about . . . ?"

"Oh!" The secret tunnel! Siv smacked himself in the forehead, causing Rumy to start. The creature sneezed out a jet of flame, making everyone but Dara take another step away. "Of course. He could have been checking to see if it's still open."

"You need to have it sealed," Dara said.

"I agree," Siv said. "By the way, is there anything else you haven't had a chance to tell me?"

Now Dara was the one who started, but she recovered quickly.

She let Rumy rub his scaly snout in her palm. "Only theories. I don't have anything concrete."

Siv could read her expression plain as day. She was keeping something from him. His mother's suspicions couldn't be right after all, could they?

"Well, let me know when you do have something to talk about," he said. The words came out sounding harsher than he meant them to, but it was too late to take them back.

"Yes, Your Majesty." Dara stood and saluted. Then she resumed her position amongst the Guard.

21

FIREWORKS

AS soon as the king was safely back in the castle, Dara dismissed the extra Guards and headed to her lesson with the Fire Warden. He met her in the underground cavern with his usual dry greeting. As they did every time, they walked to the center of the bridge over the molten Well to continue her training in the Work.

Dara practiced with Zage every day now. He was guiding her through the basic set of Fireworking skills at a breakneck pace. Apprentices normally spent years becoming comfortable with the simpler tasks before learning a specialty. The Fire was used entirely for the production of useful and beautiful objects in Vertigon, so the specialties were along the lines of spinning thread and making decorative inlays from Firegold, shaping steel, and imbuing Firebulbs, Everlights, and Firesticks with lasting heat and light. The craftsmanship of the objects mattered as much as the wielding technique.

But Dara had already decided on the only specialty she wanted to learn. She wanted to be able to suck all the Fire from a place—and a person—as she had seen Zage do. She didn't want to make weapons that would throw the mountain into turmoil. She didn't want to wield the Fire against her father. She wanted to be able to neutralize him. Nothing else would more effectively protect the king, and she feared nothing else would successfully counter her father.

Training at this brutal pace was hard, and it left her exhausted each day. She was all too aware of the danger of wearing herself too thin. What if she missed some important detail, such as what Sora had said about Lady Tull's strange timing for accepting Siv's proposal? Dara had been far too distracted by the confusing tangle of her feelings to think there was anything suspicious about it. Of course Tull would want to marry Siv. Anyone would want to marry Siv.

"Concentrate," Zage hissed.

The bead of molten Fire Dara had been rolling around on her right palm suddenly grew three times in size, picking up power like a snowball rolling downhill. Dara gripped the hilt of her Savven blade in her left hand, trying to regain control of the bead, but it grew hot on her palm. Panicking slightly, she sucked the Fire into her hand, shuddering as it passed into her veins.

"No, no, don't drop it," Zage said.

"It's too late. It—"

"Pull it back out," Zage said. "Focus."

Dara gritted her teeth and stretched out her hand. The Fire pooled in her palm again, slowly welling out of the cracks and lines in her skin.

"Good," Zage said. "Now, make it square."

Dara concentrated on the ball. Slowly, she started to mold it between her fingers.

"Not with your hands," Zage said. "That is for children. You must skip that part of the lesson. Concentrate!"

"Yes, Coach!—I mean—Fire Warden."

Zage made a disapproving sound in his throat. Dara avoided his gaze, her cheeks reddening.

Her fingers twitched, but she resisted the urge to shape the Fire with her hands. She was supposed to control the Fire with her mind, but all she had managed to do so far was make the bead wobble into an egg shape. Zage could control Fire at a great distance. She herself had once managed to throw a bead of Fire like this one and then pull it back toward her, but she had been gripped by panic and driven by necessity. She hadn't managed it since. It was too easy to think of the Fire as clay or ore to be kneaded and shaped, but it was more complicated than that.

"See the boundaries in your mind," Zage said. "Don't picture a cube. Picture a force pushing the ball into cube form. That is the true magic within you. The Fire is only the raw material."

Sweat broke out on Dara's forehead, but she tried what Zage suggested. Very slowly, the surfaces of the bead flattened. She pushed those surfaces from all sides, slow, steadily. She breathed evenly as she Worked, the glowing bead burning into her eyes like a tiny sun. Finally, for a brief instant, a near perfect cube of Fire rested on Dara's hand.

"Okay," Zage said. Dara was pretty sure that was the closest thing to a compliment she was ever going to get from him. It was a good thing she was used to working with Berg. She released her grip, and the cube melted into a puddle on her palm. Instead of pulling it into her, Dara let the Fire drip off her hand like water and sizzle into the stone bridge.

"Next time you must hold it for longer," Zage said. "Then we will practice solidifying so it keeps its shape."

"Yes, Fire Warden."

Dara released her grip on the hilt of her sword and kneaded her hands, which had grown sore over the past hour. Zage apparently thought it was time for a break, because he left the bridge and went over to the stone water basin beside the doorway without another word. Dara followed and accepted a drink when he held it out for her.

They rarely took breaks during these lessons, and they never chatted. Zage had been serious when he said he was going to accelerate her training. Fireworkers didn't normally learn like this, but she needed training, and this was all she could get. Besides, she gathered Zage himself hadn't learned in the usual way, and she had seen what he could do.

"May I ask you a question, Fire Warden?" Dara said.

Zage stared at her for a moment, his dark eyes glittering over the rim of his cup.

"Very well."

"You spent time in Pendark, didn't you? In your youth?"

"I did."

"What were you doing there?"

"Studying," Zage said.

"Studying Fireworking?"

"You know very well there are no Fireworkers in Pendark. They do not have a source as we do." He waved toward the Well.

"Then what were you studying?"

"Politics. Literature. Culture. I wished to remain there forever."

"But you came back to Vertigon?"

"Clearly."

Dara waited patiently, and finally Zage sighed. "Very well. I began training as a Fireworker as a child, though only for a brief period. I was apprenticed to a Firesmith, but I hated the repetitiveness of my lessons. And I didn't have any interest in swords."

His eyes cut toward Dara's Savven blade, and she laid a defiant hand on it.

"I wished to see more of the world, and I did not like Working the Fire, so I ran away. I traveled all the way to Pendark, where I lived for many years. During that time I attended school and went to the university by the sea."

"I didn't know Vertigonians were even allowed to go to the university in Pendark," Dara said.

"That is what I did," Zage said. "I never planned to return to the mountain. You recall what Pendark is known for?"

"Watermight," Dara said. "They say it isn't as powerful as the Fire, but it isn't regulated the way the Fire is here."

"That is correct," Zage said. "At least about the lack of restrictions. In Pendark the strongest wielders of the Watermight have the power. Political power. Economic power. And they have the magic itself."

"That's what my father wants," Dara said before she could stop herself.

Zage raised a thin eyebrow. "Yes. I believe it is. He has a great talent, and he knows that if it were a pure contest of strength he would prevail over most if not all of the Fireworkers on the mountain." Zage peered into his water goblet for a moment before continuing. "When I was in Pendark, I witnessed for myself what can happen when a few powerful sorcerers wield their magic unchecked. Many people *can* use the Watermight in Pendark, but they war amongst themselves every few years until the strongest emerge."

"They have a war every few years?" Dara knew about past wars from her schooling, but they had felt as distant as the Bell Sea in peaceful Vertigon.

Zage inclined his head. "Indeed. The strongest rule over their dominions within the city, constantly fighting to strengthen their positions. The king is all but powerless. The districts not directly under the protection of a Waterworker are rife with crime and poverty. The Workers rule over their petty fiefdoms while the city suffers. Those who can't access the Watermight use more and more drastic and violent means to seize power for themselves in their own ways. A territorial war broke out while I was there, and the city streets ran with blood and water and salt."

"So that's why you believe so strongly in this system." Dara nodded toward the carefully regulated channels of Fire spreading out from the Well. "You don't want any Fireworker to become too powerful?"

"I know what can happen," Zage said. "I do not wish that on Vertigon."

Dara sipped her water, which had grown warm, and thought about her father. Was that really what he wanted? Every schoolchild learned that Vertigon had been peaceful since the reign of the First Good King, but the Fireworkers had warred in ancient days. Dara hadn't realized the extent of the struggles other lands had seen—and were still seeing—with other kinds of power.

"Why did you return to Vertigon?" Dara asked.

"The war proved enough adventure for me," Zage said. "And the Fire called me back. You must have noticed that once you begin to touch it you can't simply put it aside. You could have pretended you never discovered your ability. Instead, you asked me to teach you."

"I want to make sure my father—"

"You know that isn't the only reason," Zage said softly. "That is the problem with power. Once you touch it, you must have more. And power is at its rawest form in the Fire."

Dara didn't answer. She knew what he meant about the Fire calling to her. But she didn't want to become enslaved to it. She didn't want to become her father.

"We'd better get back to work," Dara said.

"Indeed." Zage set down his stone cup and didn't look at her as he strode back to the center of the bridge.

22

SCOUTING

ZAGE became more willing to talk to Dara the more time they spent together. He occasionally went off on tangents about the history of the Lands Below and the substances of power wielded by their people. He was a teacher at heart, and Dara didn't think he actually enjoyed Working the Fire. In a way, that made him less dangerous than her father.

As Dara's abilities progressed, Zage set her ever more challenging tasks. They began working with metal, and she learned to melt and shape steel, guiding the Fire into it with both her hands and her will. She now felt confident that she could keep from drawing on the Fire accidentally.

With this new level of control, she visited her parents more often, but she didn't manage to overhear anything of much use. Guilt still crawled through her at the thought that she was spending time with the man who had caused her sister's death. Even though Zage had opened up lately, she hadn't brought herself to ask him about the Surge that had killed Renna a decade ago.

As soon as she was certain she wouldn't accidentally draw on the Fire and expose herself, Dara decided to pay another visit to the mysterious cavern on Square Peak. She needed to count the duelists training there, but more importantly, she wanted to figure out what huge Firework had been taking place in the smaller cave on her last visit.

She chose her most reliable men to accompany her on the scouting mission: Oat, Yuri, and Telvin. They changed out of their Guard uniforms and left the castle under the pretext of going for a drink in a tavern. They crossed the Fissure on the little-used Pen Bridge. Dara thought they wouldn't be seen, but she forgot to account for one detail: Pen Bridge was in full view of House Silltine.

Dara and the three men didn't even make it across the bridge before Vine caught up to them.

"Dara, Dara, I can't believe you're going off without me. Shame on you!" Vine sang as she reached them. She wore flowing trousers and a short brown coat embroidered with swirling green vines. Her dark hair was pulled up in a hasty bun.

"We're not training," Dara said. True to her word, Vine often joined the duelists at practice. So far Dara had managed to keep her from coming along when they had official Guard duties, though.

"Can't she join us, Dara?" Yuri said.

"She's not on the Guard," Dara said.

"What can it hurt?" Yuri had quickly become Vine's biggest fan, though it surely had nothing to do with Vine's impressive figure and lustrous locks. And her tendency to change in and out of her dueling gear in full view of the others.

"We may go into danger," Telvin said with a frown. "We can't put a lady in danger."

"Dara gets to come," Yuri said. "Why can't Vine?"

"Dara isn't a lady," Oat said.

"Excuse me?" Dara said.

Oat shrugged sheepishly. "No offense."

"Dara is a soldier," Telvin said.

"I'm as good a swordswoman as Dara," Vine said with a wink. "Some would say better."

"We are not going to be fighting," Dara said through gritted teeth. "This is a scouting operation. Nothing more."

"Oh, even better," Vine said. "My day has been dreadful. I dined at House Rollendar. I need a cheerful spy mission after that."

"You were at House Rollendar today?" Dara said.

Vine smiled and tapped her nose. "Are you sure you don't want me along?"

"Fine." Dara sighed. "But if you get hurt, it's your fault."

"I'll protect you!" Yuri said. "I am a Castle Guard, you know."

Dara rolled her eyes and led the way into the warren of pathways and stairs crisscrossing Square Peak. As they headed north, she sent Yuri to double back and make sure they hadn't been followed. She mostly wanted to talk to Vine without Yuri strutting around and stroking his red beard to make sure she noticed how long and luxurious it was.

"So," Dara said as Yuri jogged back the way they had come. She waved Oat and Telvin forward, glaring at them when they tried to eavesdrop. "Did you learn anything interesting at the Rollendar greathouse?"

"Perhaps," Vine said. "Tell me about this scouting mission we're on. It's so exciting!"

"You first," Dara said. "The Rollendars?"

"Lord Von is a dreadful man," Vine said, "but then everyone knows that. The more interesting thing was that all three of Von's brothers recently left the mountain."

"They did?" Dara had seen Lord Von's brothers before, the dark-eyed twins and a younger one, Vex, who could have been Bolden's older brother as easily as his uncle. They were tall and proud, like Von, and together they presented an imposing front. The evidence so far suggested that the Rollendars were planning something. Why would some of them leave Vertigon now? "Do you know where they went?"

"Lord Von didn't say, naturally," Vine said. "He wasn't the one who told me. I have an informant in their employ, but I only talk to her when I visit. It's the single reason I can stomach calling on the Rollendar lords, actually. I don't want her to get caught visiting my greathouse."

"You have an inform—?"

"Of course. But that's not important. The brothers left the day after Queen Tirra and Princess Selivia departed the mountain."

Dara stopped short. "You don't think they'd hurt them, do you?"

"I don't know," Vine said. "I hope not. But the brothers could have other goals in mind. I've heard there is growing tension between Soole and Pendark. I do wonder whether Lord Von might be positioning his brothers in those kingdoms in case he needs them there in the near future."

"What kind of tension?"

"I don't know yet. But my girl also told me a surprisingly large number of Soolen visitors have been hosted at House Rollendar lately."

"Hmm. Have you mentioned any of this to the king yet?"

"I thought you could tell him," Vine said. "You *are* still his right-hand woman, aren't you?"

"I don't know." Dara kicked at the stones on the pathway. "I guess. It just . . . hasn't been the same lately."

"You mean since he got engaged to Tull Denmore?" Vine asked.

Dara glanced at her. Vine had implied she knew there was something between Dara and Siv months ago—back when Dara barely knew it herself. But she wasn't sure how much she could confide in Vine. It wasn't just the engagement, of course. Dara still couldn't shake the memory of the kiss she and Siv had shared in the stairwell after the harvest festival. Siv had been colder to her of late. He must have realized it had been a mistake. Knowing what it was like to kiss him, and knowing that she could never do it again, was little short of excruciating.

But that was a secret she would take to her grave.

"Yes," she said instead. "We've been less . . . close since Siv got engaged."

"Oh, Dara, I'm sorry," Vine said. And there was none of the usual breezy whimsy in her voice. She sounded genuinely sympathetic. "Is there anything I can do?"

"No," Dara said. "But we should tell him about the Rollendar brothers." She met Vine's eyes fiercely. "Even if things are different, I'll still work just as hard to protect Siv and his family."

Vine patted her shoulder. "I know you will, honey."

The scuff of footsteps on gravel announced Yuri's return. He reported that they weren't being followed and fell in beside Vine. He boasted about his results from that year's dueling season as the group continued to the sparsely populated side of Square Peak.

Dara found the entrance to the tunnel Berg had showed her easily enough. She knew of at least one additional exit, the one she and Siv had escaped through last time. But Berg's tunnel had seemed relatively unused, and they couldn't risk being caught again.

The last vestiges of daylight faded away, but the moon hadn't yet emerged. Nothing moved around the quiet paddock and the abandoned shack. The stillness was eerie. Hopefully no one was around to see them sneak underground.

With one final glance at their surroundings, Dara pulled back the branches covering the tunnel. Oat and Yuri took out the Everlights she had instructed them to bring and headed underground. Oat had to duck low to fit his tall frame into the tunnel. Vine went next, and Dara and Telvin took up the rear.

Telvin offered Dara a hand as she climbed in the opening and cleared his throat. "You are a lady as well as a soldier," he announced.

Dara blinked. "Thank you."

Telvin nodded and entered the tunnel after her, pulling the branches over the entrance to hide it once again.

The others waited a few feet ahead, silhouettes against the Everlights. Dara and Telvin joined them, and the five of them descended into the mountain.

"So what are we looking for?" Vine asked as they strode through the cold earth.

Dara told them what Berg had showed her in the cavern. The others grew sober as she explained that the mysterious swordsmen had prompted the creation of the New Guard in the first place, not the king's desire to show off.

"I need you to see what we're up against," she finished. "And I want your honest opinion about whether you think the Guard can defeat the men we are about to see."

"That's pretty serious, Dar," Oat said.

"It'll be more serious if they catch us unawares," Dara said. She sometimes wished she hadn't gotten her friends involved in this, but they were the only people she could trust. And she had started to plan how to end this scheme decisively. She turned to the former soldier. "Telvin, I need your knowledge of military strategy here. I want to go on the offensive and strike the swordsmen in the cave instead of waiting around for them to launch a coup."

"I will do my best," Telvin said.

"Good." Dara didn't mention General Pavorran. The more she got to know Telvin Jale, the more she thought he was on their side, but she wanted to see his reaction if and when he saw his former commander. So far he hadn't let on that he knew anything about the secret cavern. She hoped that was genuine ignorance.

"I like the sound of the plan, though," Yuri said. "Hit them before they hit us."

"We'll have to see if we can take them," Dara said.

"The New Guard can handle it," Oat said.

Dara smiled at her friend's confidence. "I hope so."

As they walked, Dara felt for any sign of the Fire. As before, she didn't sense anything running through the stone nearer the tunnel entrance. In fact, it was uncommonly cold here. But as they approached the cavern she again felt that huge well of Fire up ahead. If she wasn't mistaken, she sensed it much sooner than she had before. The mysterious Work was still underway. And it had grown larger.

"Stay alert," Dara whispered. "Oat, wait here and guard our backs. The rest of you come with me."

Oat saluted and pressed himself against the wall so his tall shadow would be less obvious. Dara figured he'd have the hardest time sneaking around behind the rocks when they got to the cave.

They crept farther down the tunnel. Though the mass of Fire indicated they were close, something was missing. Sound. The familiar clang of blades and scrape of boots was nowhere to be heard.

They reached the cavern and snuck inside, crouching behind the rocks. There was still no sound but the whisper of their own breath. The air was stale, almost musty. Dara held her breath and peeked out at the training floor.

It was empty. The duelists were gone.

"Um, is this what we're looking for?" Yuri asked. He leaned a little further around the edge of a stalagmite.

"Hmm." Vine wrinkled her nose. "How anticlimactic."

"The Guard would have little trouble occupying this space," Telvin said. "If my military training serves."

Dara ignored their chatter, scanning the vast space with a growing sense of dread. She shouldn't have been surprised not to find anyone here. The swordsmen may not practice every night. But the cavern wasn't just empty of people. It was utterly abandoned. All the weapons racks, training gear, and even the water skins were gone. A stray dueling glove on the floor was the only evidence that the cavern had ever been used as a secret training facility. Firebulbs were still affixed to the rough stone walls, but even some of these had started to fade.

"Think they found somewhere new to train?" Yuri asked.

"They must have," Dara said. "But where could that many swordsmen hide without attracting attention?"

The emptiness of the cavern made Dara nervous. She had hoped to strike this cavern and eliminate the bulk of the threat in a single attack. But without knowing where the swordsmen were, it would be even harder to find out when they were about to launch their own attack. It could come at any moment.

Suddenly Dara wished very much that she hadn't left the castle tonight. Siv had plenty of Guards around him, but she couldn't help feeling she'd left him vulnerable. She had to investigate one more thing before they could return, though. The duelists may be gone, but the strange well of Fire was still there, pulsing like a sun at the edge of her senses.

"I'm going to look in that smaller cave," Dara said. "Yuri and Telvin, poke around the other side, and see if you can find anything. Keep quiet, and stay out of the open just in case."

"What's my task?" Vine asked.

"You can come with me."

Dara and Vine crept around to the right of the tunnel. The Fire felt stronger the closer they got. Dara focused on her breathing. She was grateful she'd been training above the Well itself. It made it much easier to resist the pull of a lesser amount of Fire, no matter how large it was.

"Dara, there's something strange in the air here," Vine said.

Dara slowed. They were still about twenty feet from the cave. "What do you mean?"

"You know I meditate to help with my dueling. My senses have grown quite attuned to vibrations in the air. There's something wrong with that cave."

"Would it have anything to do with a whole lot of Fire?"

Vine tipped her head thoughtfully, reminding Dara of a bird. "I imagine that would do it. There's Fire in that cave?"

"Yes."

"How interesting." Vine didn't say anything else, but she studied Dara with a calculating expression. She knew enough of Dara's secrets already. What did it matter if she figured out one more?

"We can't be seen," Dara said.

"Of course."

They approached the mouth of the cave. Just before they reached it, voices drifted out toward them, low and insistent. Dara and Vine dove into the shelter of another rock as two Fireworkers emerged from the smaller cave. One of them was Daz Stoneburner. The other was Dara's father.

Dara pressed herself against the wall. Vine did the same, but she watched Dara rather than the two Fireworkers. She had seen them. She would know Dara's father was involved.

She prayed Telvin and Yuri had followed her orders to stay hidden as the two Fireworkers crossed the empty cavern and headed for an exit tunnel. It wasn't the one Oat was posted in, fortunately. Oat would certainly recognize her father if he walked right past him in a darkened tunnel.

The two Fireworkers spoke softly, but their voices carried through the cave.

"I'm pleased to work with you directly," Daz said. "I was tiring of him."

"Indeed." Rafe Ruminor's voice was rich and strong. "I wouldn't expect an artist of your talents to be content to follow a man with cold fingers for long."

The short, muscular sword smith puffed out his chest. "It's time to return to our rightful place."

"We must be patient, though," Rafe said, "and wait until the appropriate time."

"Agreed. The other Square Peak Workers and I are counting on you to do it right."

"Of course. Thank you for your support. And for the use of this impressive..."

As Rafe and Daz got farther away, the echoes of the cave prevented Dara from hearing the rest of what they said. If the Firesmith had been on the fence about helping Berg a few months ago, he wasn't anymore. He had chosen his side.

"You don't look surprised to see your patriarch," Vine said.
"Dara, you *are* full of surprises. I so love being your friend."

"Please don't mention it to anyone," Dara said.

"Goodness, no." Vine smiled beatifically. "Keeping secrets is among my many talents."

"They're gone," Dara said, checking the cavern again. "Let's take a look."

She darted toward the small cave, leaving Vine to follow. She listened at the opening for a moment before easing around the corner to peek inside. The cave was empty of people. Inside, a massive pool of Fire burned like a melted sun. Heat rolled over Dara as she stared in wonder at the glowing lake. Vine halted beside her, a gasp of awe escaping her lips.

The lake of Fire filled most of the cave, wider than the castle dueling hall. Channels bled into it, hewn recently from the stone, as far as Dara could tell. Unlike the original Well, which sent Fire outward, this lake pulled Fire in, and it was growing steadily. Dara had spent enough time watching Zage maintain the Well to recognize how much Work must have gone into drawing the Fire in like this without alerting him. It was a massive undertaking, doubtless involving multiple Workers, and it had been going on for some time.

So the Fireworkers were gathering power in this cave. The question remained: what did they plan to do with it?

Dara continued to stare, paralyzed by the rush of the power before her, until Vine tapped her on the shoulder.

"Isn't this fascinating?" Vine said. "Positively riveting. If it weren't for the rather inhospitable heat level I should like to install one of these in my garden." Sweat drenched her forehead, and she danced uncomfortably on her toes. Right. Vine wouldn't be able to handle standing this close to so much Fire, unlike Dara.

"That's one way to put it," Dara said, turning to leave the cave. "Let's gather the others and get out of here before someone comes to tend it."

"Wiser words were never spoken," Vine said, hurrying ahead to put plenty of distance between her and the lake of Fire. Dara wished she could do the same, but as they collected their companions and left the caverns, the image of that mass of Fire burned in her mind like the core of a Fire Lantern. What were they going to do?

23

NEWS

Lords Morrven and Samanar shouted across the table at each other. The tapestries lining the council chamber vibrated with the force of their vitriol. Siv wished he could put his fingers in his ears and hum.

They weren't even arguing about anything interesting. The harvest was in, the bridges had been shored up, and the city was in rather good shape for the coming winter. No, the latest Morrven/Samanar argument started over who got to sit next to Lady Tull.

Siv's future wife was turning out to be a real asset on the royal council. Her soft-spoken presence gave the meetings an air of civility. She was always well informed about the affairs of the mountain, and she asked intelligent questions that helped keep everyone on track. Siv was shocked at how effective she was considering how young and relatively inexperienced she was. She was only a few years older than Siv himself, but she managed to appear wise, while he still struggled to make his presence felt.

Unfortunately, she was so popular with the elderly lords that they climbed over each other to fawn over her. Morrven and Samanar had nearly come to blows over who got to shower her with attention during that day's meeting. The argument quickly morphed into an airing of every issue the two lords had clashed over for the past three decades. Siv tried to rein them in at first, but they warmed up like malfunctioning Firekettles. He abandoned his efforts to get through to them when it became clear they couldn't hear him over the blood rushing through their ears. Then it got personal, which proved to be even more entertaining. Morrven's plump cheeks went as purple as his plums, and he recounted the antics of Lord Samanar's wife (who'd left him for the butler at a now-infamous royal feast). Samanar's luminous morrinvole eyes nearly popped out of his head, and he challenged Morrven to an old-fashioned Fire Blade duel.

Siv had decided he was rather enjoying the chaos of the scene when Lord Rollendar stood up and told his contemporaries to be quiet.

Lord Samanar rounded on him. "But Von—"

"I said that's enough, Lord Samanar," Lord Von said. "We have important business to discuss today."

"Very well. You're right, Von."

Lord Morrven scoffed. "Sure, do what he says, you toad-faced—"

Lady Tull laid a hand on the rotund nobleman's arm, silencing him immediately.

"I agree with Lord Rollendar. I'm sure the king would like our full attention."

"Of course, my lady." Morrven took a seat, still glaring at Lord Samanar, who had gone to sit beside Lord Von.

"Right," Siv said. He cleared his throat and rearranged the sheaf of papers in front of him. "Thank you, Lady Tull. Today I'd like to discuss Lord Roven's proposal for a mining..."

Siv trailed off as a messenger burst into the council chamber. Instead of approaching the king, he hurried directly to Lord Rollendar and handed over a weathered parchment. Von read it and glanced at Siv. Then he stood. The council members fell silent immediately.

"Soole has invaded Cindral Forest."

"What?"

"When?"

The noblemen barely glanced at Siv, directing their questions to Von.

"Their army is moving?"

"How many men are there?"

"What do they want with that backward place?"

Siv wished he had time to consider an appropriate response. Why hadn't the messenger given the news to the king first? He tried to get the nobles to quiet down so he could speak. He felt nervous. Not about Soole. They wouldn't dare attack the mountain. But he was afraid he would take the wrong steps, and his people would suffer. He pushed at the crown on his head, which felt as heavy as a sack of stones.

"I propose that we increase the size of the army in light of this news," Lord Von said. "We must be prepared for an attack on our allies."

"You want to fight Soole?" Lord Nanning said, folding and unfolding his hands nervously. "They buy our Works for export across the two seas. We can't move against them."

"If they're in a conquering mood, they won't stop with a few woodsmen in that blasted forest," Lord Farrow grunted.

"Cindral Forest has always been peaceful," Lady Nanning said, laying a hand on her husband's arm to still his fidgeting. "What provoked this attack?"

"Vertigon is supposed to be peaceful too," Lord Roven said. "Let's not get involved."

Lord Samanar stood and pounded a fist on the table. "Von is right. We need a bigger army."

"The mountain is unassailable," Lord Morrven shot back at him. "More soldiers won't make it any safer than it already is."

"We could never match Soole anyway."

"How long before they move again?"

"What does Trure say?"

"And Pendark?"

"We need more information."

"We need more men, I say!"

"Get Pavorran in here."

"It has nothing to do with us. Let us stay out of it!"

Siv was well aware he needed to say something before the conversation got out of hand. The lords and ladies talked over each other, declaring what should be done about the crisis. Soole and Cindral Forest were located far away from Vertigon Mountain. The invasion shouldn't affect them directly. But if Soole was sending armies beyond its boundaries, what would stop it from going after Trure next? Vertigon would have to respond if their closest ally was attacked. Siv curled his fingers around his papers, missing his father with a sudden, surprising ferocity. He stood, but the nobles didn't even notice.

"My lords," Lady Tull said. Her delicate voice somehow carried over the bluster of the others, and they fell silent to listen. "I wish to hear what our king has to say about all this."

"Thank you, my lady," Siv said. "We have to gather more information before we act."

"We need a bigger army," Lord Samanar repeated.

"General Pavorran has already proposed an expansion of the army," Siv said. "But we don't want to become a military state just yet."

"Hear! Hear!" said Lord Morrven.

"Why not?" asked Lord Samanar.

"Firelord take Soole all the way to his burning realm," Lord Farrow grumbled.

Siv raised a hand, but the nobles paid little heed. They broke into half a dozen smaller arguments around the table.

Lady Tull leaned toward Siv. "I believe it would be wise," she said, "to at least consider recruiting a few more soldiers, if only because it will reassure the people."

A few of the others heard her and murmured words of assent. Lady Tull smiled reassuringly. Siv took a deep breath. Maybe a few more soldiers wouldn't hurt anything. He'd keep a close eye on them, though.

"Very well, my lady," Siv said. "I will defer to your good judgment." He raised his voice, trying to imbue it with a regal quality. "I'll give Pavorran permission to expand the army, but we will not consider any troop movements until after the winter. No one will dare threaten Vertigon before then." He looked around the table at each of the nobles in turn, finally drawing their full attention. "Let's remember what makes Vertigon strong: the position of our city high above the concerns of the world. This mountain is unassailable. We must reassure the people that their protection is our highest priority, but remind them they are safe on the mountain."

"Right you are, Your Majesty."

"Agreed! Vertigon will remain strong."

The nobles voiced their approval one by one. It was very like a consensus. Siv had had a damn hard time achieving such uniform approval often enough. He grinned at Lady Tull.

"I'm glad you agree, my lords," Siv said. "In the meantime, we'll gather news from Soole and Cindral Forest and our allies in Trure. Let's avoid making any rash decisions."

"My brothers are on their way to Soole," Lord Von said suddenly. "The Rollendars can provide the information we need."

"Very good, Lord Von," Siv said, not missing a beat. "Thank you for your forethought."

Dara had already warned him about the Rollendar brothers' departure, but it irked him that House Rollendar was once again better positioned than he was. He still couldn't figure out Von's end game. He had sent a message to Hirram, the serving man at House Zurren, asking him to keep an ear open for any news, hoping for hints about the disappearance of the mysterious duelists. It was time he started cultivating some informants of his own.

The nobles talked animatedly as they left the council chambers. Several of them surrounded Lord Von, seeking more information from his mysterious sources. Siv was about to call him back for a private chat, when Lady Tull approached him.

"Your Highness, I hope you don't mind me speaking up in council meetings," she said.

"Of course not, my lady," Siv said. "I value your opinion. And you are to be queen. We ought to work together on matters of state."

"I will do what I can to help." Lady Tull smiled demurely.

"The noblemen listen to you, my lady. You shouldn't underestimate how valuable that is."

"I won't." She dropped into an elegant curtsy. "Until next time, Your Highness."

"My lady."

Siv watched her go, the last of the council members departing close on her heels. The more Lady Tull turned her support his way, the stronger his positioning amongst the nobles became. Perhaps their marriage really would be the right thing for Vertigon.

As the doors to the council chamber closed behind the nobles, Siv ran a hand over the polished wood of the large table. It had come all the way from Cindral Forest. Known for woodworkers and paper-makers, it was supposed to be a serene land with a few small villages scattered within the forest's boundaries. It didn't amount to a proper kingdom. Cindral Forest was no threat to Soole. However, it would provide a secure staging ground for actions against Trure, the country where his mother and sister were now staying. If Soole threw the Lands Below into further turmoil, Siv hoped he could prevail upon them to return to the safety of the mountain. Vertigon was far out of harm's way, especially with the expansion of the army. Siv frowned. He hoped he wouldn't regret that decision. He'd have to make sure the army stayed close to the barracks on the far side of Square Peak. Their presence would reassure the people, but he couldn't have them teaming up with the mysterious missing duelists.

Siv pulled off his crown and dropped it on the table with a thunk. Then he poked his head outside the door and told Pool to summon General Pavorran.

24

THE PHOENIX LEAF

AT her next Fireworking lesson, Dara told Zage about what she had seen in the cavern, including the growing well of Fire and the two men they had seen leaving the cave.

Zage considered the news in silence for a few minutes, his pale forehead furrowing, and then he said, "Your father and Daz Stoneburner were there. Did they mention any other Fireworkers?"

"Stoneburner said something about the Square Workers," Dara said. "That makes it sound like there are a fair number of them involved, doesn't it?"

"There would have to be to accumulate that much Fire." Zage gazed out over the Well, the light flickering in his eyes like twin flames. "They must be redirecting the flow of Fire from their shops, giving up some of their own share to build up the lake of Fire you describe."

"They couldn't tap into the system before it reaches the shops?"

"I'd sense such an attempt." Zage closed his eyes and breathed deeply for a moment. "No, the Fire is flowing to the shops as it should. The disbursal system is carefully controlled."

"What happens if you lose control?" Dara asked.

Zage looked up, his glittering eyes meeting hers.

"Lose control in what way?"

"Like the Surge." Dara swallowed hard, her resolve strengthening. She'd have to ask about it eventually. "Will you tell me about the Surge, Fire Warden?"

Zage sighed heavily, but he didn't look surprised. He stretched an egg-white hand over the Well and drew a stream of Fire up toward it. He poured the Fire back and forth between his palms, letting the raw power pool and spiral in ever more complicated designs. Dara had never seen him do anything beautiful before. His Work was always functional, with a dry precision that belied his true strength. But now he let the flows of Fire morph and curl like Fireblossoms.

"I did not design the containment system," Zage said. "Sovar Amintelle, the First Good King, created it when it became clear his son could not Work. He didn't want the mountain to descend into chaos after his death. He had to stretch out with his considerable will to reach the channels where the Fire flowed naturally and redirect them so the power wouldn't seep through the mountain at random."

Zage continued to twirl the Fire above his hands, sometimes kneading it with his fingertips, sometimes forming it through will alone. The movement of the Fire was mesmerizing. Dara could sense Zage's power, almost like a physical force, as he twirled the Fire into ever more complicated designs.

"You know the Fire is liquid until a Worker completes the solidifying process that holds it in place," Zage said, "whether it be in a Fire Lantern or in the core of a Fire Blade. Sovar's Work solidified the channels of Fire to create the system as we use it today. It is strong, but malleable enough to be modified. When I need to change it, I concentrate on the channels, slowly undoing the Work to allow the flows to split further, and then solidifying the holds on the power anew."

Zage formed the Fire into the shape of the three peaks of Vertigon, sitting on his palm like a statue, then allowed the shape to melt again.

"Sovar's original Work was strong, and it requires a tremendous amount of power to change it. When I first became Warden, I used to put the channels back in place a bit weaker than they started so they'd be easier to unravel for future modifications. The number of people with the Firespark was increasing as the Workers had children, you see. I wanted all Workers to have the opportunity to develop their craft and build a business around a Fireshare."

Zage created a lantern of pure Fire. It glowed between him and Dara like the Orange Star. She looked away from it. Zage's voice was as dry as burning parchment.

"I also knew it would be better to allow the Fire to spread to keep large quantities out of the most powerful hands, as we have discussed. There were enough new Workers that I had to constantly redo the system. I didn't want to make each new channel so strong that I wouldn't be able to open it up and split it without a great deal of trouble. Unfortunately, this continued for long enough that the overall system weakened."

The burning shape of the Fire Lantern melted, and Zage formed the Fire into coils of chain.

"I should have made it as strong as possible, never mind the extra effort to expand it. I shouldn't have allowed even a hint of weakness into the design. Unfortunately, I miscalculated. I thought myself stronger than I was."

Zage's voice took on a bitter note. He didn't meet Dara's eyes.

"I was arrogant, thrilled with my own cleverness and my own strength. I was aware of the weaknesses in the system, but I was too proud. I was convinced I'd catch it in time if anything slipped. I was wrong." He took a shuddering breath, like a gust of summer wind. "The day of the Surge, I was splitting one of the biggest channels, an original artery put in place by Sovar himself. It took extra effort for me to break through. I grew frustrated and forced through the channel too quickly. The Fire surged and burst through every one of those weaker and more malleable bonds I had put in place for my own convenience. Before I could regain control, the Fire had surged through every access point on the mountain."

"Including the one my sister was using," Dara said quietly.

"Yes." Zage finally met her eyes, his gaze unwavering but full of regret. "I bear her death on my conscience every day. She was so young . . ." Zage's face twisted with pain. "You see, it wasn't the concept of disbursal and containment that killed your sister. It was my arrogance. My foolhardiness. My laziness. I thought I could keep track of the system as it got ever more complicated, and I took short-cuts. I failed, and a child paid the price."

"But you didn't pay anything," Dara said. She stretched out a hand and pulled on the Fire Zage had been twirling in front of him. It shot to her hands like an arrow from a bow. "You kept your position. You still control the Well."

"I begged on my knees for King Sevren to remove me from my post," Zage said. "I questioned whether I deserved to live, much less continue in the task at which I had failed. But Sevren was a man of mercy. He believed in second chances. Sevren saw my remorse, and he decided the mountain would be safer in my hands than if he passed the job to someone who hadn't suffered so deeply from their mistakes."

Zage reached out and drew the Fire back from Dara, slowly so as not to hurt her. She let him take it. He twisted the Fire until it formed an ornate leaf. Dara recognized the shape. It was the same as the silver pin Zage wore at his throat to hold his cloak.

"I have never told another soul before today, but I wear this pin in memory of your sister," Zage said. "It is the leaf of a phoenix tree."

"What's that?"

"A tree that grows only in the Burnt Mountains. Legend says that when the true dragons wake and spread their fire over the mountains, the phoenix tree is the first to bloom again. It grows back stronger and more beautiful than ever after each burning. I wear it as a symbol of my penitence and my dedication to making Vertigon a safer place for its children through the Fire, even though a child's death had to teach me that lesson."

Dara swallowed a lump in her throat, thinking of the necklace of misshapen steel beads that her sister had given her, made with her own hands. Renna had been so proud of it.

"Do my parents know that?" she asked.

"Your parents will never forgive me for their daughter's death, Dara, and I do not believe they should. They are correct that I deserved to be removed from my post. But I will work to make the mountain better in their daughter's memory, even though I have no right to invoke her name."

Zage let the phoenix leaf melt away and returned the Fire to the Well. Dara watched it drip down to rejoin the seething lake of Fire beneath their feet. She realized this was the first time Zage had ever used her first name in all the time they had been working together.

She wondered if his remorse over her sister was part of why he had agreed to help Dara learn to Work.

She wanted to hate Zage for what had happened to her sister, but she was all too aware of the sins of her own father. Zage suffered the way she had suffered over her father's responsibility for King Sevren's death, probably more so. She should have been more attentive to her father's schemes instead of staying selfishly wrapped up in her pursuit of dueling glory. She could have warned King Sevren if she'd paid heed sooner. For that, she would be forever culpable in his death. She didn't know if Siv would ever forgive her. But what if she could forgive Zage? He too was trying to atone for something. She only hoped Siv would find it in his heart to be as merciful to her as his father had been to Zage when she finally told him the truth.

Dara looked up at the Fire Warden. He appeared small and thin without his cloak, and telling the story seemed to have drained him further. She could hardly believe that this shriveled, sorrowful man had drawn her parents' ire for the past decade. The Ruminors had grown strong and bitter over the years. She hoped somehow they'd find solace and justice before they burned the mountain down around them.

"Shall we get back to work?" she said.

Zage inclined his head. "Very well, Miss Ruminor."

When Dara left the Fire Warden's home later that night, she felt restless. She thought about visiting Siv to reconcile with him. She had avoided being alone with him since his engagement, but they had to work together against the growing threats from the Fireworkers and the missing duelists. She hated the thought of his coming marriage, but she would not break her oath to protect him just because he had chosen a queen—as she had always known he would.

He'd probably be asleep by now, though. He had been as busy as she had lately.

The night was cold, especially after leaving the heart of the Well. Not many Fireworkers trained so close to that much power. Dara wondered if Zage had her work there instead of at one of the access points in the castle so she would learn control faster. He certainly wasn't coddling her. Strange as it was, she was starting to appreciate Zage.

As Dara left the austere marble house, laughter spilled from the window of the building next to it. She hesitated. This was where Lady Atria lived. She hosted influential people in her parlors every night, facilitating alliances and liaisons amongst important figures. Dara had been here with Siv when he was still a prince. She drew even with the parlor window, listening to the raucous babble. Who was here tonight—and what might they be discussing behind closed doors? Would Atria let her in? She'd become well known in the city of late. Hopefully being a prominent figure on the Castle Guard would be enough to get her into Lady Atria's without a noble escort.

Before she could think better of it, Dara knocked. Quick footsteps sounded inside, and Lady Atria flung the door open, looking as rotund and cheerful as ever.

"Yes?"

"Lady Atria? I'm not sure if you remember me. I'm—"

"Nightfall! Of course, darling, come in. It has been too long." Atria pressed Dara's hand with a fleshy palm and pulled her into the entryway of the greathouse. "We've been taking bets on when First Snow will fall. Care to wager?"

"No, I just came for a quick drink, if that's all right." Dara thought First Snow might happen that very night. It was customary to stop what you were doing for a toast the moment the first snowflakes touched the earth. Many Vertigonians started celebrating early as soon as the clouds hinted at a change.

"Of course," Atria said. "Allow me to—Oh, my dear, one of my guests appears to be trying on the suit of armor. Excuse me. Feel free to go downstairs if you wish. You are always welcome here."

"Thank you."

"Put that helmet down this instant, Lord Farrow!" Atria cried as she disappeared into the front room.

Dara walked down the corridor, peeking her head through open doors to see if she recognized anyone. She was mostly hoping to run into Kel. She needed to find out what Bolden had been up to lately, but it was tricky to get in touch with Kel without arousing suspicion. She still suspected the swordsmen she'd seen training in the cavern might belong to Bolden and his father. She needed Kel to investigate the Rollendar lands in case they'd suddenly acquired dangerous new lodgers.

But as Dara passed one partially open door, she spotted a familiar head of sandy hair. It was Lord Bolden Rollendar himself. She checked to make sure the corridor was deserted and then stopped outside the door to listen.

Bolden paced in front of a large armchair in a wood-paneled sitting room. Someone sat in this chair, too short to be visible except for a slim hand on the velvet armrest. Dara leaned closer, easing the door open a bit more. It was a woman's hand. That much was clear. And there was something familiar about it.

Then Bolden spoke.

"Can't you move up the date? My father grows impatient."

The woman in the chair said something indistinguishable.

"It doesn't need to be a fancy feast," Bolden snapped. "Just enough to keep that silly Guard occupied."

The woman said something else and removed her hand from the arm of the chair so Dara couldn't see her at all. Suddenly Bolden glanced up, and Dara pulled back faster than if she'd been burned. Well, back when she *could* be burned.

She waited a few minutes and then risked another look. Bolden had turned away from the door. He must not have seen her.

The woman stood up from her chair. She had slim arms and a petite, straight-backed figure.

It was Lady Tull.

She approached Bolden and laid a hand on his shoulder, speaking in a soothing voice. He turned around at her touch, and Dara had to leap back again to avoid being seen lurking at the door. Her reactions were slow, though. That was the king's betrothed meeting in secret with a Rollendar!

She hadn't moved fast enough. Bolden said something she didn't catch. Then the sound of footsteps approached the door. Dara darted into the next room and pulled the door mostly shut. Bolden's footsteps reached the corridor. Dara held her breath, gripping her sword hilt. It was silent for a moment, except for the distant laughter of the revelers in the front parlor. Finally, the footsteps picked up again, and Bolden returned to the sitting room where Lady Tull waited.

Dara remained still for a few heartbeats and then peeked into the corridor again. It was empty. When she emerged from her hiding place, the door to Bolden's room was closed. Dara bit back a curse. She needed to hear more of what they were saying. She listened at the door, but the heavy wood muffled the sound too much for her to distinguish any words. Hopefully she'd learned enough.

Dara didn't bother visiting the underground lounge at the back of Atria's greathouse. She didn't want anyone else to know she had been there tonight. With any luck, the armor-wearing Lord Farrow would distract Lady Atria enough that she wouldn't remember Dara had even been there.

She left the greathouse and ran all the way back to the castle. So *that* was why Lady Tull had accepted the engagement. She was distracting the king! And it sounded as if the Rollendars would make their move the night of the engagement feast. *Well, let them come.* Dara and the Guard would be ready for them.

As she ran up the long stairway to the castle, the first light flakes of snow fell from the midnight sky. They coated her eyelashes and clung to her cloak by the time she reached the castle gates. She hurried through the corridors and up to the king's tower, her tiredness forgotten. By the time she threw a quick greeting to Errol Feln and Yuri standing guard and pounded on Siv's door, she had a plan.

25

THE BOTTLE

SIV wished he hadn't made things awkward with Dara. He could sure use her help as the news from Cindral Forest continued to complicate his life. He'd had a meeting with General Pavorran that afternoon. He wanted Dara there to watch for any hints from their conversation, but she had disappeared from the castle yet again after her usual training session. If they'd been on better terms, he might have called her to his room to talk it over afterward or visited her in the dueling hall. But she still treated him extra formally, and she was impossible to catch when she wasn't carrying out her Castle Guard duties.

The meeting with Pavorran had gone as well as could be expected. The man was about as interesting as a rock. Plus, Siv kind of resented him for being involved with the secret force training in the cavern. If he was going to be a villain, he could at least be an entertaining one. Pavorran had delivered a long-winded report on the recruitment of additional soldiers and the subsequent modifications to the army's training regimen. The only mildly interesting part was when he requested the commissioning of a new supply of Fire-infused weapons. Siv told him he would consider it and asked for the details of which Firesmiths he'd use for the job. He didn't plan to approve any new weapons until he determined whether or not they'd be used in his defense. He still wasn't sure whether Pavorran acted alone or whether the whole army would end up fighting on his side. He felt increasingly vulnerable without a strong hold over his military force. He had begun to regret giving Pavorran permission to expand the army in the wake of the news from Cindral Forest. Hopefully Lady Tull had been right to give him that advice.

When Pavorran finally left the castle, Siv retired to his chambers with a plate full of meat and bread and a bottle of wine. Okay, maybe two bottles. It was exhausting to court people's approval, step lightly around those plotting to kill him, and keep everyone from panicking over news of distant wars. Siv was burning tired of it. He had a reprieve from entertaining visitors for once, and he intended to get a bit drunk and enjoy himself. Alone.

Who knew being king would be so hard? He thought he was doing a decent job, but he wished for the simplicity of his prince days. He dropped into a dueling stance and did a bit of footwork across the rug in his antechamber, balancing his wine goblet expertly in his left hand. He wished he could be a Castle Guard instead. It looked like a good life. The Guards got to train, duel, attend carnivals and feasts, and hang out in the castle. They got a warm bed and plenty of food. They could go out for drinks when they liked and kiss whomever they wanted. It was all swords and booze and beautiful, intense eyes admiring you in your uniform.

Siv poured himself another goblet of wine, imagining what it would be like to march around the castle in one of those sharp blue coats. *I wonder if you can drown envy with wine.* He took a huge gulp and walked to the window, his steps wavering a bit. He balanced his goblet on the sill and leaned his forehead against the cold glass.

Of course, the Guards still got to work for the good of Vertigon. They lived on this beautiful mountain and actually had the freedom to explore it whenever they wanted. Plus, their mistakes wouldn't result in someone who didn't have the best interests of the people at heart taking control of the throne. Yes, it didn't sound like a bad life at all.

Siv was thinking about using his secret stairwell to fetch a third bottle of wine from the kitchens, when someone pounded on the door. He tripped on the corner of his Firegold-embroidered rug as he crossed the room. He really shouldn't let his guard down by drinking like this, but his job was burning hard, and he was safe in the castle.

He brushed the breadcrumbs from his table with clumsy hands and dropped onto the couch before calling, "Come in."

"Good, you're still awake." Dara strode into the antechamber and shut the door behind her. She swept off her black cloak, sending droplets of icy water across the room. A bit of frost dusted her golden hair.

"Is it snowing already?" Siv asked.

"Just now. Oh, happy First Snow." Dara reached for a spare goblet from the table without really looking at it and raised it toward him. "I have news, Siv."

"Glad to see you dropping the highnesses and majesties," Siv said, his words slurring a bit. "That was getting older than a Soolen bullshell."

Dara put her hands on her hips. "Are you drunk?"

"Why on the snow-blessed mountain would you say that?" Siv said. He raised his own goblet, which was mostly empty again. That happened so quickly. "Happy First Snow to you too."

Dara narrowed her eyes. *Firelord*, her eyes were pretty.

"Well, pay attention," she said. "The Rollendars are planning something for the night of your engagement feast. And Tull Denmore is in on it."

"Tull? My lady wife? Or future lady wife, or whatever you would call her." His engagee? There was a word for it, but Siv couldn't quite think of what it was. He drained the last of his wine.

"As far as I can tell," Dara said, "she accepted your proposal, but she's working with Bolden. I think they're going to assault the castle on the night of the engagement feast. Bolden said he wanted there to be a lot going on to distract the Guard."

"That sounds like Bolden," Siv said. "But you mean to tell me my future lady wife doesn't love me? I'm shocked."

Dara rolled her eyes, apparently picking up the sarcasm in Siv's tone. "I'm lucky I saw her. She's been around the castle a lot lately. The Guard would have let her come and go as she liked until the feast. She could set up any number of traps for you. Or just open the door for the Rollendars, which sounds like the strategy she picked."

"How did you find this out? It's good detective work." Siv tried to work up the energy to feel betrayed, but there had never been anything personal between him and Tull. In fact, he felt a little relieved that she might be trying to kill him. That probably meant he wouldn't have to marry her after all.

"I got lucky," Dara said. "I went by Lady Atria's parlor and overheard them talking. They looked pretty cozy too."

"Atria's? I miss that place. What do you say we go for a drink there right now? I feel like celebrating." Siv started to stand, his balance off-kilter.

"I think you've had enough to drink, actually," Dara said.

"It's never enough!" Siv shouted.

"Do you want me to have Pool put you to bed, or do you want to hear my idea for foiling Bolden?"

"I don't want anyone but you to put me to bed, Dara." Siv said. "Ever. Ever ever." *Boy, that word's fun.*

Dara grew very still. "You shouldn't say things like that, Your Majesty."

"Why?"

"You know why."

"No, *you* know why." Siv grinned. That would show her.

"Siv."

"Dara."

She blew out an exasperated breath. "Just how much did you have to drink?"

"This is good vintage, Dara," Siv said. "You should try it. Loosen up a little. And maybe stop being so serious around me all the damn time."

"This *is* serious," Dara said. "I think we have a chance to stop the Rollendars for good. We can't keep letting them sneak around and scheme. Let's lie in wait for their men and deal a decisive blow when they least expect it."

"That all sounds grand," Siv said. "But it's First Snow. Celebrate with me. Eat, drink, and be merry, for tomorrow we will be as decisive and kingly as my old granddad was."

Dara folded her arms. "The wine is gone anyway."

"Not true!" Siv said. "I've just remembered I have another bottle. A gift to congratulate me on my engagement."

Siv rummaged underneath a pile of books until he found the bottle in question. It had an unfamiliar label, but he was sure it would be good. People never gave him poor-quality wine. It was one of the definite perks of being king.

Despite Dara's objections, he popped the cork and poured a goblet for himself and one for her. He splashed a bit on the table, but a respectable percentage ended up in the cups.

"To my un-engagement," he said. "And to the brilliant plan that I have no doubt you will tell me about in the morning when my head has stopped spinning."

Dara sighed, apparently resigned to the good sense of his suggestion.

"Happy First Snow."

She lifted the goblet to her lips. Siv drank deeply, watching her intense eyes. This *was* a nice bottle, with a hint of spice and oak. It really ought to be enough to make her smile.

Because he was watching her, Siv had a rather good view when Dara's eyes widened, her goblet dropped from her fingers, and she lunged forward to knock Siv's drink out of his hands.

An instant later, he was flat on his back with Dara straddling him, her hands clutching his shirt and horror in her eyes.

"Siv!" she shouted.

"I can hear you. If you wanted me on my back, you could've—"

"Siv, shut up. There are Firetears in the wine!"

26

FIRETEARS

DARA didn't know what she was doing. She hadn't trained for this. All she knew was that she needed to get the poison out of Siv's body before it killed him.

Firetears could only be used on people who couldn't Work the Fire. It was a simple potion: the Fire pulled together out of its liquid form when it entered the victim's body, forming a single glob or "tear." When the Firetear reached critical mass, it shot upward through the victim's body, wreaking havoc on the way. Depending on the dosage the formation could take hours, but once activated a Firetear would burn through someone's heart, throat, and brain in seconds, stealing their life, their warmth, their light. Firetears were particularly dangerous because they had no taste, and they didn't take effect right away. The speed at which the poison worked varied, but it was always deadly.

Dara knew all of this in an academic sense, but she had never encountered it before. When she put the wine to her lips and felt the Fire contained within it, she knew. By that time, Siv had already drunk half his goblet.

Now he lay flat on his back as she tried to grab hold of the tears of Fire forming in his stomach with sheer will. She had to seize control of the droplets before they joined together, while fighting down her own panic. She'd been getting better at Working the Fire with her thoughts. She relied on the senses she'd been honing during her hours with Zage as she reached into Siv's body. It had to be enough.

"Dara, are you sure—?"

"Quiet. I need to concentrate."

Siv wouldn't feel anything yet. His father probably hadn't felt anything either until his final moments when the fully formed tears burned through him. Dara gritted her teeth so hard she thought they'd crack. She wouldn't let Siv die this way.

She ripped open the buttons on his shirt and pressed her hands against the warm skin of his stomach. The Firetears moved within him, minuscule and fragmented in the wine, but already pooling together in places. There was too much of it! She spread her fingers and tried to capture the droplets, like picking up steel shavings with a magnet.

Siv looked down at Dara's hands on his abs.

"Uh, Dara, I know I'm a bit drunk, but—"

"Shh."

Slowly, Dara allowed a few beads of Fire to pull together in Siv's stomach. She didn't want to leave any of the potion behind. She moved one hand up his chest, guiding the trail of Fire. If she couldn't keep the bits of Fire small they would damage his stomach and throat on the way out. That would be a much more painful way to die than with the quick flash of a fully formed Firetear.

Siv cleared his throat. "As much as I'm enjoying this weird massage, Dara, it's kind of strange, and—Ouch! What are you doing?"

"Stop moving," Dara snapped. "You're making this harder." The droplets of Fire were pooling too fast. He was going to get hurt. She needed to get them out of his body.

Dara kept one hand on Siv's stomach to help her focus on spreading the Firetears out. She moved the other upward, drawing a trail of tiny tears up through Siv's throat. She wasn't sure she could get them out of him without releasing her hold on the rest of the poison in his body. She hadn't practiced controlling this many distinct drops of Fire at once, especially without being able to touch it directly. It was always easier to control the Fire with direct contact. That gave her an idea.

"Open your mouth," she said.

"Why—?"

"Just do it."

She shifted her hand up, resting it firmly on Siv's throat, and then clamped her mouth onto his. Firetears would kill someone who couldn't work the Fire, but Dara didn't have that problem anymore. She breathed in, letting the trail of Fire pass from Siv's mouth into hers, hoping the pieces weren't big enough to burn his tongue. The hot drops sizzled in her mouth as she absorbed them into her own body.

She sat back to begin working the rest of the Fire upward. Siv looked up at her, his eyes slightly out of focus. He had gone absolutely still. The Fire she had drawn from his body ran through her blood now, flowing harmlessly beneath her Firesparked skin.

Still straddling him, she repeated the delicate task of easing the rest of the Fire together in tiny droplets and guiding them up the passageway of his throat. Siv winced, apparently able to feel a bit of what was going on, but he remained still as she put her mouth on his again to draw out the last of the poison.

As soon as it was gone she pulled back a bit, her lips not quite brushing his, and felt for any remaining vestiges of Fire waiting to merge together and slay the man she loved. Their breath mingled between them, warm and sweet. He stared back at her, and for a moment the world was utterly still.

"Is it done?" he said hoarsely.

Dara blinked and scrambled off him.

"Yes, I think I got it all." She sat on the rug next to him and reached for the stone goblet so she'd have somewhere to release the Fire she had pulled into her body. Her fingertips glowed as she let the Fire drain into the stone.

Siv sat up slowly, rubbing his throat. His eyes never left Dara's face. She stared back at him, feeling exposed and vulnerable, but also incredibly relieved.

"You can Work the Fire," he said.

"Yes."

"You're a Fireworker," he said hazily. "Like your father."

"I haven't known for long," Dara said. "I've been practicing, but I wasn't sure if I'd be able to do that." It suddenly occurred to her that she hadn't been touching steel while she worked on the king. She hadn't needed it to focus when his life was on the line. She was making progress. A brief smile started to form on her lips, until Siv spoke again.

"You mean you aren't an expert in Firetears like your father?"

"What?" Ice and dread flooded Dara so rapidly that she wished she'd held on to the Fire.

"This is how my father died. Poisoned by Firetears. A coward's weapon." Siv climbed to his feet, holding on to the nearby table so his balance wouldn't waver. He looked down at her, his face slowly turning to stone.

"Do you know anything about that, Dara?"

"Siv—"

"Tell me. Did Rafe Ruminor kill my father?"

Dara felt as if she were crossing the Fissure on a bridge that had suddenly given way.

"I—"

"And did you know?"

She nodded slowly, keeping her mouth clenched shut. Words wouldn't make this any better.

Siv drew a ragged breath. "You've obviously been keeping more from me than I thought. Tell me: why do you bother saving my life when your father keeps trying to take it?"

"I'm trying to stop him," Dara whispered.

"You didn't stop him from killing my father."

"I didn't know then!" Dara reached out to touch Siv's ankle, but he stepped out of her reach, his movements wooden. "You have to believe me," she said. "I found out afterward, and I've been trying to stop him from hurting you too. I've been trying to make things right."

Siv grabbed his crown, which had been sitting on the table, and clutched it between his hands as if trying to bend it in half.

"So that's why you pledged to give your life in my service?" he said bitterly. "To repay a debt? Well, I have news for you, Dara. His life was worth more than mine. Nothing you do for me can make up for what happened to him. He was a better man and a better king."

"I'm sorry," Dara whispered.

Siv snorted and turned away from her. He walked to the window on shaky feet and pushed open the tall panel of leaded glass. Cold wind swept in, carrying flurries of snow into the room. The temperature dropped fast as the snow and wind and mist swirled in around the king.

They stayed like that for a long time. Siv leaned out into the black night, letting the First Snow fall on his face and hair. Dara sat on the floor, hands pressing into the rug, as she tried to think of something to say that would comfort him. Something that would make up for what her father had done to his. But he was right. Nothing would ever change what had happened.

The Firetears in the wine had to have come from her father. He wasn't giving up, and each time, he got closer and closer to success. Dara had wanted to protect her family despite everything they'd done, but it was becoming harder to justify that course of action. Her parents were sprinting down a path from which they could never return. She'd held out hope that she could convince them of the king's goodness during her visits over the past few weeks. But with this latest incident, it might be time to stop trying to save them.

Finally, Dara stood.

"I will take my leave, Your Majesty. I urge you to continue with the preparations for your engagement feast. I'll prepare the Guard to meet an ambush. Will there be anything else this evening?"

Siv didn't answer. Dara left his chambers and closed the door, leaving him staring out at the snow.

27

PREPARATIONS

SIV went straight to the dueling hall when he awoke the next morning. He laced up his best pair of dueling boots and was already sweating through his first hundred lunges when the Guards arrived. He didn't pause his workout to speak to anyone until all the duelists had assembled. He didn't look at Dara at all.

"I'm training with you today," he announced. "Please treat me as you would any other duelist."

"Yes, Your Majesty," Telvin Jale said with a salute.

"Whatever you say, Your Highness," Shon said at the same time that Dell Dunn shouted, "Your wish is our command!"

"Good." The Guard gathered in a loose ring around him, uncharacteristically shy. The youngest of them looked afraid he might turn into a thunderbird if they moved. "Shall we get started?" he prompted.

They jumped and hurriedly began their stretches, all except for the rangy female duelist, Tora Feln, who folded her arms and faced him head on.

"Sire, do you want us to call you Siv?" she asked. "Like Dara does sometimes?"

"Quiet, Tora," hissed her brother, Errol. "You can't talk to the king like that!"

"He said to treat him—"

"I heard what he said," Errol whispered, as if Siv couldn't hear him plainly. "But he's still the king to the likes of us! Dara is different."

Siv cleared his throat, not looking at Dara.

"Let's just focus on the dueling, shall we?" he said.

The Guards saluted and commenced their warm-ups. Siv just wanted to stab some things for a while. He didn't want to see Dara. Yes, he'd come to the exact room in the castle where he knew she would be, but he *definitely* didn't want to see her.

Dara apparently didn't want to see him either, because she ran the training with the efficiency of a drill sergeant, never once acknowledging his presence. She looked as though she'd gotten as poor a night's sleep as he had. At least she probably wasn't hungover on top of things. Siv was, but that wouldn't stop him from being ready when the Rollendars came calling. He needed to defend himself, his family, and his kingdom. He couldn't trust anyone else to do it.

The duelists divided into pairs for a glove-tossing exercise that Berg used to have Dara and Siv do during their private training sessions. One person would stand behind the other and throw a glove out in front of their partner, who had to lunge and catch it before it hit the ground. The lunging partner wouldn't see the glove until the moment they had to move. It was a good exercise for improving reflexes, plus it was fun. Or at least it was supposed to be, until Dara assigned Telvin Jale to partner with Siv. The former soldier took his job as the king's temporary training buddy very seriously. He was about as enjoyable to work with as a window shutter.

Siv reminded himself he was not here to have fun. Dueling—along with everything else—had to be serious business now that he was a king with enemies on all sides. As of last night, those enemies included his best friend's parents and the woman who was supposed to become his wife. He couldn't afford to have fun anymore.

They did ten lunges and glove catches each then switched places so the other partner could toss. Siv managed to catch most of Telvin's throws, but the man definitely wasn't going easy on him. If anything, he tossed the glove farther for Siv than any of the other duelists were doing for their partners. Siv almost pulled a muscle in his thigh lunging to reach it before it hit the ground. His body ached, but it felt good to be working out again.

The partners switched back and forth until Dara called a halt for a water break. Siv strode over to the window so the others wouldn't feel awkward about relaxing around him. He leaned on the window ledge, pressing his forehead against the cold glass. A fine dusting of snow coated the mountain. The snowfall wasn't thick, and it had already been brushed away from many of the streets and terraces. The few remaining leaves clinging to the trees on the orchard terraces shivered in the sunlight.

"Your Majesty?" Dara came up to stand beside him.

"I don't want to talk."

"I understand," she said. "I just wanted to say that my Fire ability must remain secret. I plan to use it to defend against Fire attacks, hopefully taking your enemies by surprise. It won't be useful for your protection if . . . if my father and his allies know about me."

"Zage can protect me from the Fire," Siv said, resisting the urge to turn and look at her.

"I think the Fire Warden agrees with me on the need for secrecy," Dara said. "He's been helping me learn to Work in case I might be able to defend you with it." She paused for a heartbeat. "Like I did last night."

"Zage knew too?" Siv couldn't help it. He turned to face her. "Is anyone in this castle on my side?" Apparently no one on the whole damn mountain was trustworthy.

"We're both on your side," Dara said. "All of us are." She gestured toward the duelists of the New Guard, who had begun putting on their practice jackets.

"In that case, I expect you to keep me informed about life-or-death situations. And if you know the answers to questions I've spent months investigating."

Dara was silent for a moment. She looked over at the other duelists again. They were giving them plenty of space to talk, but a few kept sneaking not-so-subtle peeks across the hall. Oat and Luci whispered animatedly to each other, punctuated by frequent curious glances at the pair by the window. Siv wondered for the first time how much the Guard knew about his friendship with Dara. *Former* friendship. Errol Feln had even said Dara was different, and he didn't seem like the most perceptive of the bunch. Siv had let himself get in way too deep with her. How could he have been so foolish?

"Okay," Dara said at last, lowering her voice so it wouldn't carry to the overly curious squad. "For your information, I've been visiting my parents to try to get more information about their plans and allies, but I don't agree with anything they've done. I also have a spy reporting on the Rollendars. I'm going to see him this afternoon to find out what he knows about the Rollendars' plans for the feast."

The formality in her tone made something crumple inside Siv. "Do what you have to do," he said, feeling suddenly weary.

"I will. I always have."

"Fine. Great. Let's get back to work."

Siv turned and stomped to the wardrobe to retrieve his gear.

After a few bouts with the Guard, Siv went up to the library to eat his lunch while he awaited Lady Tull's arrival. They had planned to discuss more preparations for their engagement feast this afternoon. It would be downright fascinating to hear what she had to say.

Siv didn't feel much like being alone while he waited for his duplicitous fiancée to arrive, so he invited his sister to join him for lunch. Soraline listened patiently while Siv explained what Dara had told him about Bolden and Tull and her plan to meet the attack head-on.

"Are you sure it's a good idea to let them make their move at the feast?" she asked. "It could be dangerous for the guests."

"It was Dara's idea." Siv grimaced, stabbing at his food. "We don't know where their force is hiding anymore, and it might be our only chance to end this decisively. You're the one who said I didn't stand up to the Rollendars. If we defeat them in front of the court, that could help secure my reign after the dust settles."

Sora twirled a finger through her dark hair thoughtfully. "That's true, but it's a dangerous move."

"I know," Siv said. "I think you should head down to Trure for a while."

Sora looked up, face stricken. "I have too much to do here!"

"I'm sure you can communicate with your Soolen target—I mean future consort—just as easily from Trure. He must have all kinds of romantic things to say now that his army is on the move."

"How kind of you," Sora said wryly. She helped herself to

another serving of goat pie from the platter between them. "No, I think if you're going through with this I should be here. I'll have to put out fires for you later, and it'll help if I'm actually present when the action happens."

"That's very strategic."

"I know." Sora sighed. "It's my specialty."

Siv smiled. At least he could trust his family. He should really appreciate his little sister more.

"I'll assign my best men to join Denn on your personal guard so you'll be protected during the feast," he said.

"Do you . . . do you think you could assign Telvin Jale to my guard?" Sora asked, then she blushed worse than Selivia when she got caught reading romance novels.

"Why?" Siv said. "The man's a bore."

"He's very noble," Sora said, with something suspiciously close to a wistful sigh, "and he was a soldier. I think . . . I think I'd feel very safe with him."

"Sure. Safe. Whatever you want." Siv resolved never to let Telvin Jale near his sister. He wondered if he could fire him for being too burning noble.

"Good." Sora took a large gulp of water to hide her pink cheeks and cleared her throat. "Now that you're not going to marry Lady Tull, have you given any thought to a new alliance?"

"Sheesh, Sora, can't we put one engagement to rest before we start talking about the next one?"

"But—"

"No, Sora, I don't want to think about it."

Sora frowned and picked at her slice of pie. It was their father's favorite kind, Siv remembered, his chest tightening.

"Can I ask you something?" she said.

"Go for it." Siv forked the last piece of pie onto his own plate.

"What's going on between you and Dara?"

Siv coughed. "What makes you think something's going on?"

"You alternate between hanging out with her like she's your very best friend, staring at her like an orphaned velgon cub, and being furiously angry at her."

Siv tossed his fork onto the table and rubbed at his temples. The workout session hadn't fully cured him of his hangover after all.

"I don't know, Sora," he said.

"Do you love her?"

Siv stared at his plate for a long time. When had his little sister become so perceptive? Or, when had he gotten so burning obvious? Well, as the king, he wasn't obligated to answer. He kept his mouth shut.

"So that's a yes, then," Sora said. "I thought so."

"I can neither confirm nor deny—"

"Save it, Siv. I know it's not what you want to hear, but I think the feelings will pass. You can't always feel like your head is wrapped in thunder and your heart's being struck by lightning every time you see hi—her. You just have to wait it out. It's the only way."

Siv raised an eyebrow at Sora, making a mental note to fire Telvin Jale as soon as possible. Sora was definitely not the type to talk about having romantic feelings, much less speak in metaphors. Time to head this crush off at the pass.

A knock sounded at the door.

"Lady Denmore is here to see you, Your Majesty."

"Let her in, Pool. Thanks for the talk, Sora. Do you want to stay for this?"

"No, I have work to do," she said brusquely. "There's a group of prominent Soolen travelers staying on Square Peak, and I am going to craft an invitation for them to dine with me. I'll learn what I can about the invasion of Cindral Forest. Besides, I have to get to know my future people."

"Good. You do that."

Sora left the library, offering Lady Tull a perfectly polite nod on her way out.

Siv greeted Lady Tull as nonchalantly as he could manage, and they set to planning their engagement feast. Tull was full of ideas for how to make the feast spectacular, filling the evening with entertainment and dancing and unique and surprising foods. Siv agreed to most of her suggestions, remaining as amenable as ever to her influence. His lady was in for a surprise of her own, though.

AFTER FIRST SNOW, winter came fast on the mountain. Blankets of white descended from the heavens, weighing down the bridges and softening the sharp peaks. The people turned up their Fire Gates—if they could afford them—and burned paths through the deepening snow with Heatstones. The indoor tasks and leisure pursuits people had neglected while preparing for the winter season resumed in earnest. Fire Lanterns burned bright as people visited back and forth, adding a warm glow to the snowy slopes.

As the day of the engagement feast approached, Siv continued to train with the New Guard as often as he could. He may not actually get a chance to fight, but he'd had enough of relying on other people to keep him safe. It felt good to get back into the rhythm of swordplay. The exercise and the friendly competition with the duelists helped him stay calm and focused while he waited for the Rollendars to make their move.

He still accepted invitations to dinners and teas when he could, tramping through the snow to get to the greathouses that always seemed farther apart at this time of year. Lord Zurren hosted another exhibition dueling match, and the Castle Guard had a rousing argument over who'd get to accompany him, finally fighting a mini tournament for the privilege of guarding him and—more importantly—watching a good duel. Oat and Bilzar Ten ended up winning, and they made full use of the accompanying bragging rights. Dara didn't join the competition for the assignment at all. She didn't seem to want to spend any more time than she had to with Siv. That suited him fine.

They kept the First Snow incident a secret from all but a trusted few. A castle Fireworker accompanied him everywhere now to watch for Firetears in his food, but they didn't want the people to know how close he had come to being assassinated. He still wanted them to believe that Vertigon was safe and stable in the hands of the Amintelles.

Meanwhile, Lady Tull acted as ladylike as ever, Bolden and Von Rollendar were their usual sneering selves, and General Pavorran continued to deliver his dry reports on the state of the army. Siv could almost believe they meant him no harm, if not for the work Dara was doing behind the scenes.

She had reported back to him after visiting her Rollendar spy, who didn't know where the mysterious duelists had gone. Dara wouldn't reveal the identity of her spy, but she reported that the Rollendars had been consuming a lot of food for the amount of staff they had. They must be bankrolling those mysterious duelists somehow, no matter where they were hiding out. Siv suspected it all had something to do with the access road the Rollendars had been so interested in keeping to themselves. Hopefully the New Guard would be a match for the mysterious duelists when they showed up, especially because the attackers expected to catch them unaware.

Siv and Dara maintained a formal distance after First Snow. Despite everything, Siv believed she really was working to keep him safe. He had seen too much to make him doubt that. But he couldn't bring himself to forgive her for keeping the truth from him. At the end of the day, her father was still the one who had murdered his. His gut ached as though he were being stabbed every time he thought about it.

Siv needed a plan to deal with Rafe Ruminor, but he was hoping to tackle that after the engagement feast. If Rafe showed up that night, Zage would be waiting to deal with him, but the Lantern Maker seemed content to work from the shadows. No one knew when the poisoned bottle of wine had turned up, but it was easy enough to guess who was responsible. One of the castle's Fireworkers now checked every bottle and food item that came in for any hint of Firetears. Siv couldn't take any more chances, with his life or with that of anyone else in the castle.

The one area he left vulnerable was the secret tunnel through the kitchens. Instead of sealing it, he and Dara agreed it would be better for Bolden to build his plan around it. Lady Tull had visited the kitchens on several occasions, ostensibly to discuss the menu for the feast. If she was checking up on the tunnel, Siv wanted her to believe it remained unguarded. She couldn't suspect that he knew anything.

When the day of the feast dawned, Siv felt nervous but ready. It was time to show the Rollendars who ruled in Vertigon. And with luck, they would end the threat once and for all and enjoy a winter of true peace.

28

THE ENGAGEMENT FEAST

SNOW fell thick on the castle the day of the engagement celebration. Servants darted back and forth through the courtyard, cloaks flying, bringing in last-minute trappings for the feast. Footprints in the snow marked their paths at first, but soon the flurries thickened, wiping away even the well-worn trails. As nightfall approached, Vertigon was facing its first true blizzard of the season. Heatstones alone weren't enough to keep the paths clear, so the keepers brought out the cur-dragons to fly back and forth over the long stairway up to the castle, breathing fire onto the steps to melt the ice and snow so the guests could make their way up in safety.

Dara led a handful of Guards on a sweep of the castle before the guests arrived to make sure nothing dangerous had found its way inside with the cured meats and baskets full of winter berries. The Guard was prepared, more eager than scared. They had trained hard, and tonight they would get a chance to prove themselves. It was far more exciting than a dueling competition as far as they were concerned.

As she finished her check of the eastern tower, Dara encountered Siv coming down the corridor from the central tower's stairwell. He wore a fine black coat embroidered with Firegold and Bandobar's old Fire Blade.

"Your Highness," she said.

"Miss Ruminor."

Dara bit back a sigh. The king had treated her formally since First Snow, though she'd actually spent a lot of time in his company. He continued to train with the New Guard, and he even sparred against her sometimes. With his renewed dedication to training, he was in better shape than he had been since becoming king. They had talked often as they prepared for what would happen tonight, but their conversations often took place in Pool's presence, and they only ever discussed business. They avoided the topic of their fathers entirely. Dara feared the warmth and camaraderie she once shared with Siv was gone forever. Even though the marriage this feast was celebrating would not take place, she couldn't help feeling that she had lost him for good.

And every time she felt that, she forced herself to remember that she never truly had him. One kiss—okay, several kisses—in a stairwell didn't mean anything. He would never forgive her for what had happened. Besides, he was the King of Vertigon—and she meant to make sure he kept that title.

"Anything to report?" Siv asked, resting his hand on his blade and standing very straight. He looked like a monarch now, grave and sure.

"The Guard is ready, Your Highness," Dara said. "The castle Fireworkers will mingle among the guests, and two of them will be stationed in the kitchens with their own contingent of guards. We'll make sure nothing gets through tonight."

"Good."

"Your Highness, may I have a word?"

"If it's quick," Siv said. "My guests will be arriving in the Great Hall."

Dara waved for the Guards accompanying him, Luci and jittery young Shon, to give them some space. She rested her hand on her own sword hilt, acting the part of a concerned guard. That she was also a concerned friend was no longer relevant.

"I wanted to ask you not to get involved in the fighting tonight," she said. "Those duelists are professionals. I don't think it would be wise for you to join in when the attack begins."

"I can handle myself with a blade," Siv said.

"I know you've been training, but you can't put yourself at risk.

That's the sort of thing a foolish young king would do. We have to show the mountain that you're wiser than that."

"Is that all, Miss Ruminor?" Siv raised an eyebrow, as if it were presumptuous of her to talk to him, as if there had never been anything between them at all. It made anger spike through her, but she forced down the feeling.

"Yes, Your Highness."

Siv turned on his heel, crisp as a soldier, and started to walk away. Dara grabbed his arm just before he stepped out of reach.

"Siv, you can't pretend like nothing ever happened between us," she hissed. Okay, maybe she hadn't forced her anger down enough after all. "We're about to go into battle. We have to be able to trust each other."

"You've proved yourself unworthy of trust."

"I should have told you about my father," she said. "I know that. But if you think I won't do everything in my power to defend you, then remove me from the Guard right now."

"Oh, you'll defend me," Siv said. His face remained impassive. "I don't doubt that."

"We'll put every person in that room at risk if we walk around pretending we barely know each other." Dara's grip tightened on Siv's arm. "We have to be a team."

"The New Guard is your team," Siv said. "You've trained them to do a job. They will do their duty, and so will I."

"But—"

"Miss Ruminor, you do not have permission to touch your king."

Dara scowled at him and released his arm. A shadow crossed Siv's face for a moment, like he might regret what he'd said, but it was gone in an instant.

"Is there anything else?" he said.

"Yes," Dara glanced over at Luci and Shon, but they were turned away from them, gazing politely down the opposite corridor. Before he could stop her, Dara reached up and cupped Siv's face in both hands, making him look down at her. She may not have permission to touch her king, but her friend needed to know she was still with him. Her fingers brushed the edge of his lips.

He stood very still. An image flashed into her mind for a moment, the memory of how he had watched her as she drew the poison from his body, how realization had slowly dawned. She had been so afraid she wouldn't be able to do it. She had been so afraid she would lose him.

"I'm sorry," she said. It may not change things, but if anything happened to him tonight she would never forgive herself for not saying it. "I'm sorry for not telling you the truth, and for—for everything."

"I loved my father, Dara," he said.

"I know," she whispered. "I wish I had been able to do something sooner. You may not be able to forgive me, but I'm so sorry."

Some of the tension released from Siv's shoulders. They stood still for a few minutes as the anger in his eyes slowly changed to sadness. He removed her hands from his face and held them in his, between them so the Guards wouldn't see.

"I know it wasn't your fault, Dara." He turned her right hand over and ran his long fingers from her palm to the blue veins in her wrist, tracing a line like a flow of Fire. "But I wish a lot of things had been different."

"Me too." She breathed, trying to slow her rapid-fire heartbeat. "Please don't do anything foolish tonight."

"I won't," he said. "You be careful too."

"I will." She squeezed his hands once more, tight as a knot, and then strode back toward the other Guards.

"It's time."

More Guardsmen awaited them in the castle entryway. They jumped to attention, uniforms and blades sharp, as the king took his place in their midst. The athletes moved as a unit now, and they looked more alert than they ever had for a competition. Siv straightened his crown, saluted them all, and faced the elaborately wrought doors to the Great Hall. Dara and Telvin pushed the doors open together, and the king made his entrance.

The Great Hall had been transformed into a palace of light. Lady Tull had commissioned special Works to decorate the walls and ceiling. Fire Lanterns usually lit the space, but now curving spirals of Fire-infused metal shaped like vines curled around the hall. They ran up every column and lit every alcove. Dara had been nervous about going near the Great Hall during their construction because the draw of the Fire (even mixed with a liberal portion of metal) was so strong. She gritted her teeth as she entered now, though. The Fire Warden himself would make sure nothing went awry.

To complement the fanciful lighting fixtures, Lady Tull had arranged for ice sculptures and glass candlesticks to decorate the tables. The Firelight flickered off them and cast multicolored refractions around the room. Despite the cold outside, the scene was warm, the lights brilliant. Dara would have been impressed by Lady Tull's efforts if she didn't know the truth behind them. The lights and colors were smoke and mirrors to mask what was about to take place.

Siv sauntered through the crowds of nobles already gathering in the hall, cutting an impressive figure in black. He laughed and joked with everyone he spoke to. He reminded Dara of King Sevren, who had greeted her so warmly when she attended her first feast two days before the Vertigon Cup—and his death.

Dara stayed a few steps away from Siv at all times. She scanned the crowds for suspicious figures, on the alert for unusual jolts of Fire. But the Fire-infused vines decorating the walls made it harder to sense anything. She was glad Zage and his trusted castle Fireworkers were on hand in case anything went wrong.

The nobles mingled while the Great Hall filled up with guests in all their finery. The Rollendars were among the last to arrive. The two sandy-haired men wore scarlet coats—Bolden's open at the throat. They had a bodyguard each, and the pair immediately joined the other noble bodyguards lounging by the back wall. Dara had assigned a few Castle Guards to watch over this group, but none of them had made threatening movements so far.

Lord Von Rollendar marched straight to his place at one of the long tables stretching across the hall and leaned in to speak with Lord Morrven seated beside him. His friend Lord Samanar had been assigned a seat on the opposite side of the hall. Von's relaxed demeanor gave no hints about the scheme he must be preparing to activate any moment now.

Bolden shot a sulky stare at the king then slouched into an alcove with another young lord. When Dara checked on them during her rounds, they were sharing a flask, looking every inch the bored young noblemen forced to attend an official function. They certainly didn't look like men planning a coup.

Tension tightened between Dara's shoulder blades. Something felt off about tonight. She couldn't figure out why. The other Guards looked serious and focused. Everyone was where he or she was supposed to be. Yuri guarded the door to the kitchens on the far side of the Great Hall, and when she caught his eye, he shook his head. All clear still. All they could do was wait.

When the Great Hall brimmed over with guests and noise, Siv strode to the dais. He clapped his hands to call for attention from the assembly.

"Thank you all for coming to celebrate my engagement," he said when the guests had quieted and turned to face him. "It is my great pleasure to introduce you to Lady Tull Denmore, head of the noble House Denmore and the venerable House Ferrington, the next Queen of Vertigon, and my future lady wife."

Applause thundered through the crowd, making the glass on the tables shudder. The doors to the Great Hall swept open, and Lady Tull glided in. Six tall, handsome guards in snow-white uniforms accompanied her. Her gown was a pale shade of rose that perfectly matched the blush in her cheeks. She wore a short cape of white fur around her shoulders and a fabulous red Firejewel at her throat. Tiny Firejewels were fastened in her intricately woven hair, piled high on her head. The ensemble made her look taller than she actually was. She looked like a queen.

The crowd gasped as the beautiful woman stopped a few paces from the center of the Great Hall. Siv strode toward her, confident and grave and handsome. The Firejewels in his crown flashed in the light from the vines adorning the walls, and his black coat shimmered like fine steel.

Dara tensed, hand on the hilt of her Savven blade. She kept waiting for the mysterious swordsmen to rush into the room, or for Bolden and his father to step forward and challenge the king. She had been sure they would pick a showy moment like Lady Tull's entrance to make their move. But Lord Von gazed impassively at the royal couple, and Bolden still hadn't emerged from his alcove.

Dara checked the exits. To their credit, the Guardsmen remained alert, rather than being distracted by the storybook scene playing out in the middle of the hall. But there was still no sign of trouble.

Siv bowed to Lady Tull, and she dropped into an elegant—but

not too deep—curtsy. Siv offered her his arm, and she took it, her delicate white hand a striking contrast against his black coat. The king and his lady strode up the center of the hall as women sighed and men stared after them with envy in their eyes.

Siv's face was solemn and confident. He escorted Lady Tull to the dais, the six guards in white surrounding them on all sides. Dara searched their faces, but she didn't recognize any of them. She moved closer, ready to leap in front of the king if Lady Tull's honor guard tried anything. But still nothing happened.

Siv and Tull rounded the table on the dais. He pulled out her chair, and she sat, settling onto the cushion like a rose-colored cloud. Then Siv raised his goblet, which was full of water Dara had personally tested for poison.

"My people," he said. "Thank you for joining us to celebrate our upcoming union. Let's raise a toast to my exquisite lady."

"Hear! Hear!"

"To King Sivarrion and Lady Tull!"

"Long live King Siv!"

Goblets rose in unison around the room. Dara's grip tightened on her blade. The Guards scanned the crowd, alert and focused. But still nothing happened.

Siv glanced over at Dara, his goblet still in the air. She shook her head slightly. Siv's mouth twitched in response.

"To Lady Tull!" he called to the assembly and downed his glass. "Now, let us eat!"

The feast was the longest meal Dara had ever endured. While the king and his betrothed dined, she strode around the hall, looking for any sign of the threat she was so sure would materialize tonight. She checked and rechecked the kitchens and the castle courtyard and anywhere else it would be possible for enemies to assault the castle. But everything was exactly as it should be: well guarded and calm.

The Rollendars didn't appear to be particularly enjoying the feast, but they were nothing more than surly. Dara almost wished they'd get it over with already.

Lady Tull had arranged for a parade of musicians and dancers to entertain the guests as they dined. Dara had asked Vine to vet all of these groups in advance, and she reported that they were all established acts, no more likely to commit treachery than the average Vertigonian. The Guard had inspected each troupe at the gates just in case, but they showed no signs of hidden weapons—or hidden Firepower. They entertained the diners one group at a time then left the Great Hall without causing any trouble.

And still, the Firelights blazed, the nobles ate, the Guards stood ready, and nothing happened.

Dara completed another circuit of the castle, feeling edgy and tense. She couldn't shake the sense that she was missing something as she returned to her place near the king's table.

If Siv felt as wary as she did, he hid it well. He played the doting fiancé role perfectly. Lady Tull smiled and laughed and looked every inch the blushing bride. That there was no real connection between Siv and Tull was obvious to Dara, but she wondered if any of the nobles even saw it. The feast progressed just as a royal engagement celebration should.

As the meal drew to a close, noblemen and ladies stood to propose toasts and wish the young couple well. The most eloquent speech of all came from Vine Silltine, who talked about the need for married couples to be in harmony with one another and dance to the same rhythm, like the rhythm of the wind. She winked at Dara when she took her seat, as if Dara should understand whatever the heck Vine was talking about.

Then it was time for the dance. As the first notes filled the Great Hall, Siv invited Lady Tull to the center of the floor. Dara edged as close to them as she could get, standing beside the table bordering the dance floor. A pair of ladies sat at the end of the table: Lady Farrow and Lady Roven, if she wasn't mistaken. A bit of their conversation reached Dara as the music swelled and the royal couple began to dance.

"They remind me of King Sevren and Queen Tirra," said Lady Roven.

"Tull is even prettier than Tirra was in her youth," Lady Farrow replied. "And she's from Vertigon, no less!"

"Well, if Sivarrion treats his bride anything like his father treated his mother, she's a lucky woman."

"She's a lucky woman anyway." Lady Farrow chuckled richly. "If I was twenty years younger and there'd been a prince like that on offer, I'd have snapped him up on his eighteenth birthday."

"Cheers to that." Lady Roven sighed, watching the couple twirl around the floor. "My Tellen wasn't nearly as gallant at that age."

"I expect we'll have a beautiful royal baby within the year."

"I'll take that wager." Lady Roven raised her wine glass. "I ought to get my Jully married off soon so her offspring can have a chance at the next Amintelle marriage."

"We must plan ahead." Lady Farrow clinked her own glass against Lady Roven's.

Dara scanned the table beyond the two ladies. Noble after noble gazed at the young couple in admiration. They all seemed happy with this turn of events. Could it really be true that any of them would support the Rollendars if they moved against the king? Von and Bolden were nowhere near as popular as Siv, especially with Tull at his side. What on earth made Tull think this wasn't the best match she could ever make? For a moment Dara doubted what she'd seen at Lady Atria's greathouse. Had she misunderstood them? No. Bolden and Tull had been talking about when to make their move. And they had acted quite familiarly. It seemed unlikely that Tull would hold Bolden's hand and stand as close to him as she had been unless she wasn't intending to go through with her royal engagement. *What* was Dara missing?

Siv and Lady Tull danced alone for the first song, but when the music changed the other nobles stood to select partners for the traditional First Dance. At royal feasts in Vertigon, the nobles always used the First Dance to shore up alliances by dancing with the wives and daughters of men with whom they wanted to curry favor. It was a way to express friendship and admiration for potential business partners.

Dara watched for any strange movements, but the usual shuffle of invitations commenced without incident. More couples swept out onto the floor, gossip following in their wake. The king and his lady still danced, elegance personified.

Wind howled outside the tall, narrow windows of the Great Hall, drawing Dara's attention. Ice had begun to coat the glass. The snowfall thickened. Most of the mountain was invisible, cloaked in frost.

But the Fire-infused vines decorating the room kept the celebration contained within a bubble of warmth and light.

As the blizzard sighed against the windows, Dara turned back to the hall. Bolden Rollendar was striding her way. She tensed, hand on her blade, and checked to make sure Siv was still safe in the center of the dance floor. Then she met Bolden's eyes. She hadn't spoken directly to him in a long time. Though he'd been welcoming when she encountered him as Siv's friend at Lady Atria's, he was the type of man to look right through guards and servants.

But Bolden didn't look through her or walk past her. Instead, he stopped, bowed, and offered her his hand.

"Miss Ruminor. May I have the First Dance?"

"With me?" Dara blurted.

"Indeed." Bolden's eyes never left her face. "It would honor me to dance with our king's favorite Castle Guard, our city's favorite female duelist, and our favorite Lantern Maker's daughter."

Dara didn't want to break eye contact, feeling that it would be the equivalent of losing a duel to Bolden, but she had to check that the Guards were still in position and the king was safe. When she looked back, Bolden waited with his hand outstretched, a slight smirk on his lips.

"Very well," she said. She had to know what this was about. No one offered the First Dance without a good reason. She took Bolden's hand. It was as cold as ice, and just as hard.

They danced at the edge of the floor, drawing only a few curious eyes. Most people not dancing watched the engaged couple spin gracefully across the room. Bolden was a precise dancer. He executed each step perfectly, but Dara felt as if she were dancing with a piece of steel. She was torn between needing to watch over the hall and wanting to stare Bolden down and figure out what he was trying to accomplish here. How did dancing with a member of the Castle Guard win him any political capital, no matter how well known she had become?

He didn't speak at first, but he studied Dara as if she were a mijen game he was determined to win. His hair was messy, and he hadn't bothered to button up his scarlet coat. His breath smelled of brandy, though not as thickly as she would have expected given how long he had supposedly spent chugging from his flask in the alcove. He seemed plenty alert.

Finally, Bolden spoke. "It's been interesting to see what you've done with the Castle Guard."

"Has it."

"They certainly draw the eye." He glanced down at the sigil embroidered on the breast of Dara's trim blue coat. "And they appear to be as loyal to you as they are to the crown."

"They do their jobs well."

"Indeed." The song ended, but Bolden did not release Dara's hand. "Another dance?"

"My lord."

Bolden moved as the music picked up, faster this time. He guided her around the floor with a firm hand on her back.

"So help me understand, Miss Ruminor," Bolden mused as they spun across the dance floor. "You hand-selected a Guard full of your dueling friends. You enlisted your own coach to train them. You made our king their patron and allowed them to continue competing. By all accounts it's a dream position for any duelist, especially since they're unlikely to see much real danger. We are in Vertigon after all." Dara's eyes flickered up to meet Bolden's, but his expression gave nothing away. "So tell me: why didn't you invite Kelad Korran, the one duelist who I know beyond a shadow of a doubt is your friend, to benefit from this dream job?"

Dara fought desperately to keep her expression neutral, even as ice wrapped a fist around her heart. He knew.

"You must have offered him the opportunity," Bolden continued. "It's what any friend would do. The way I see it, the only reason you wouldn't give our friend Kel the chance to join the New Guard is if you had another job in mind for him. Perhaps a job that involved snooping." Bolden's voice lowered to a whisper, and he pulled Dara closer, his skin cold against hers. "Around my father's estate, for example."

"Kel already had a patron." Dara fought to keep her voice steady. "He wasn't interested in joining the Guard."

"Oh, I doubt that very much. You see, Kelad is in my father's custody. It turns out he's not as stealthy a spy as he thought."

Dara tensed. She knew it would give her away, but she couldn't help it. Bolden's smirk deepened. His breath was a hiss in her ear.

"He'll tell us everything. My father can be very persuasive."

Dara fought to keep her heart rate down. What had Von Rollendar done to Kel?

And Bolden wasn't finished. "As you can imagine, I was rather annoyed when I realized Kel had repaid my patronage with treachery. He would still be living in a slum on Square if I hadn't recognized his potential and decided to sponsor him." Bolden's grip tightened painfully on Dara's hand. "I was also annoyed that he compromised some rather carefully laid plans." He looked pointedly around the hall, where the feast continued in peace, the Guard ever vigilant.

"That must be frustrating for you," Dara said. She twisted her hand out of Bolden's grip. She didn't want to be in this man's arms for a second longer. She clutched her sword hilt, waiting for him to say the words that would give her a reason to arrest him.

But Bolden simply inclined his head and said, "It was at first. But instead I've decided on a different plan, one that has been much longer in the works. It will be a bit more dramatic, but then our people love a good show. Thank you for the dance, Miss Ruminor."

Bolden bowed like a gentleman and left her on the dance floor. With a nod to his father, he strode out of the hall. Von Rollendar immediately abandoned his own dance partner and followed his son out. Dara jerked her head at Oat, who hurried after them.

She spun around, scanning the hall, expecting enemies to burst in at any second. But the doors remained secure and guarded. She reached out with her senses, but the amount of Fire in the hall remained stable, still burning steadily from those decorative vines.

Siv must have noticed the worry on her face, for his steps slowed even though the music did not. He met her eyes over the top of Lady Tull's head, and she could only shake her head. She wasn't sure what was going on.

Then the quick pound of footsteps sounded in the entrance hall, and the door burst open. But instead of the flood of mysterious trained swordsmen they had been expecting all night, Telvin Jale charged into the hall alone.

"Square Peak burns!" he called. "The mountain is on fire!"

29

THE MOUNTAIN

CONFUSION spread rapidly through the Great Hall at Jale's announcement. Siv dropped Tull's hand and grabbed his sword, immediately looking to Dara. Her eyes were fixed on the decorative vines tracing the walls. Abruptly, she turned on her heel and darted for the nearest window looking eastward to Square Peak. Siv left Tull in the middle of the dance floor and rushed after her.

"What's going on?" he asked, skidding to a halt by Dara's side.

"I didn't feel it because of all the Fire in here," she said. She pressed her hands to the glass, the ice melting off it faster than should have been possible. "Look at Square."

Snow swirled in the air outside the castle windows, but through the fuzz of ice, Square Peak was starkly outlined against the cloudy sky. Fire blazed in a solid wall around it, with a halo glowing in the mists above. At first Siv thought it was a wildfire, but it didn't have the untamed shape of a random inferno. This was Fire, a solid thing, holding Square Peak hostage within a glowing ring. Snow disappeared into steam as it fell onto the fiery wall, which had to be at least thirty feet tall. It was clear at a glance that no one could pass through the barrier to reach the peak. And no one on the peak would be able to leave.

The nobles gathered at the windows or hurried out into the entryway, no doubt rushing to the eastern portico, where there was a good view of Square Peak. The musicians abandoned their instruments and pressed their faces against the glass with the others.

"Bolden changed the plan," Dara said. "He found out about my spy."

Siv grimaced. So much for ambushing their attackers.

"What's his next move?"

Telvin Jale rushed up to join them before Dara could respond.

"The Rollendars have left the castle," he said. "Oat is following them down the peak. The moment they reached the steps that flaming wall shot out of the mountain all the way around Square."

"Thank you, Jale."

"What are your orders, Sire?" he asked, his composure slipping a hair. "The whole army is behind that wall!"

Siv exchanged glances with Dara. They hadn't shared their suspicions about the army with anyone else on the Guard. But Siv had also decided not to let too many soldiers leave Square tonight because he didn't know how many were under Pavorran's corrupting influence. He'd asked Berg to stay over there too and keep an eye out for any strange movements. Now, if any of the soldiers *had* planned to stay on his side, they were stuck. *Stupid.* He had been so stupid.

"We need to get these people back to their homes," Siv said, looking around at the nobles in all their finery. They didn't need to be in the middle of this. "Jale, have the Guard escort my guests down to Lower King's in groups. Advise those who keep their greathouses on the other peaks to find lodgings on King's. I don't want anyone crossing the bridges tonight."

"Yes, my king." Jale leapt to obey, signaling for more of the Guard to join him.

"Dara."

"Sire?"

"Make sure my sister gets safely to her rooms, then meet me back here."

Dara hesitated, as if she wanted to stay by his side, but then she snapped off a salute and darted toward Sora, who was busily reassuring a cluster of teenage noblewomen that everything would be okay.

Siv returned to the center of the hall and climbed the dais. Four Guardsmen moved in around him, including Pool at his right hand.

He felt oddly calm. They would finally find out the exact nature of the threat against him. For better or worse, this ended tonight.

"I must ask you all to return to your homes," Siv called out to his guests. "My Guard will make sure you get there safely while we assess this new threat. Please remain calm."

The lords and ladies were anything but calm. They gathered up spouses and children and hurried toward the doors. Some muttered about the Fireworkers finally rising up, others said the true dragons had returned, and a few even suggested Soole had come to invade. Some eyed the Fire threading the walls suspiciously, but the decorations didn't jump down to attack them. A far greater power burned on the other peak anyway.

"King Sivarrion," a soft, feminine voice rang out, somehow managing to be heard over the chatter. "I have a message for you."

Lady Tull approached the dais, her pale rose dress swirling behind her. Her six white-clad guards surrounded her, weapons drawn. The Castle Guard moved in around them, not letting them get any closer. A few nobles slowed to listen, if only because the jam at the doors was making it impossible to leave as quickly as they would like. Lady Tull gazed across the hall at Siv, head held high, and ignored the commotion.

"And what is that, my lady?" Siv said softly.

"The reign of the Amintelles is at an end," Lady Tull said. "The Firewielders holding Square are capable of scouring the entire surface of the peak with their wall of Fire. If you abdicate your throne on behalf of House Amintelle, they will withdraw. If you do not, they will burn Square Peak and its inhabitants into nothing." Lady Tull looked at the armed guards around the hall. "If you kill me, it will change nothing."

Siv stared at her for a long time. The final people fleeing through the doors carried Lady Tull's message with them. Within minutes, the whole of King's Peak would know the choice he had been given. Or rather, the lack of choice. His head seemed full of mist and smoke. The entire peak. One third of his realm. Destroyed. Burned beyond recovery. No, this was no choice at all.

Despite her icy threat, Tull looked pale, and she bit her lip until it was as white as her fur cape.

"I am not going to kill you, Tull," Siv said.

Lady Tull blinked. "Throughout our short engagement," she said, "I've observed that you care more for the good of the mountain than for anything else in the world. If you walk away from the throne, not one Vertigonian will be harmed. You have until dawn. I will await your answer at the Fire Guild."

She turned to go. Her guards, blades drawn, glared menacingly at the New Guard, daring them to stop her.

"Who would take the throne?" Siv asked. "If I surrender to your demands?"

Lady Tull looked back, a small smile on her delicate mouth. "You must know the answer to that."

Siv sighed. "Indeed. Tell Rollendar he will have his answer at dawn."

He raised a hand to his guards, and they allowed Lady Tull to leave the hall. The last of the nobles departed on her heels. Some, Siv was sure, had been in on the plot—or at least had promised not to interfere—but he didn't detain them. It wouldn't make any difference at this point. They had one of his peaks, and he had no army. Even his well-trained Guard could do nothing against a wall of Fire.

A few serving men and women lingered at the edges of the room, near the entrance to the kitchens.

"Gather everyone from the kitchens and go to the Guard barracks," he told them. "You'll be safe there for now, and you'll be warm."

The servants hurried to obey, a grim efficiency to their movements. Siv dispatched a few more Guardsmen to accompany them.

Oat edged around the last of the servants at the doors and ran across the hall toward Siv. His uniform was disheveled, and there was snow in his dark hair.

"Von and Bolden Rollendar went straight to the Fire Guild headquarters," he reported, still a bit breathless. "A Fireworker met them outside the castle and escorted them there. The Guild has a wall of Fire around it now too, just like Square."

"Where is Zage Lorrid?"

"The Fire Warden is gathering the castle Fireworkers," Oat said. "They're in the courtyard."

"Good. My sister?"

"Dara has her. She took two Guardsmen with her to post by Princess Soraline's door."

Siv looked around at the remaining Guards. He had sent men to accompany the nobles, the servants, and his sister. There were just four Guards left in the Great Hall: Oat, Pool, Yuri, and young Dell Dunn. The group looked small and unthreatening in the glittering lights of the Fire decorations around the abandoned hall. It mattered little, though. Ten times as many Castle Guards wouldn't be able to stand against the Firewielders. They had only one hope.

"Take me to the Fire Warden," he commanded.

"Yes, Your Majesty."

Oat saluted, and the Guardsmen fell into formation around Siv. They strode through the now empty entrance hall and out into the snowy courtyard. The massive tree in the corner glistened with ice and swayed in the biting wind. The cold assaulted Siv, slicing his cheeks like knives.

Zage Lorrid stood at the courtyard's center. Snow melted in a circle around him, as if he were encased in a burning bubble of Fire. Siv couldn't sense the Fire himself, but Zage quivered as if immense power roared through him.

The castle Fireworkers, those employed to maintain the flows to the Fire Gates and repair the various Works used by the castle's servants and inhabitants, stood around him, each with a smaller ring of melted snow at their feet. There were only five of them. As far as Siv knew, none were especially powerful, which was why they didn't have their own businesses. He could only hope they were loyal.

"It's too much," one was saying as Siv strode up. "I can't Work a tenth of that myself."

"They must have every Fireworker on Square maintaining the Wall."

"How did they even get that much Fire?" said a pudgy fellow not more than a year older than Siv. "Every shop on Square Peak isn't allotted that amount."

"You are correct," Zage said. He acknowledged Siv's arrival with a brief nod. "They have been gathering power for months, siphoning it away from their shares."

King of Mist

"But where could they store it?" the junior Fireworker demanded.

"Underground." A cold voice came from behind Siv. Dara stood on the castle steps behind him, silhouetted against the open door. Snow swirled around her, and ice coated her hair.

"There's a cave system underneath Square, far bigger than anything marked on the maps. They've been amassing Fire there like a second Well."

"We aren't a match for that many Workers," said another Fireworker. He shivered, and a bit of snow drifted down onto his balding head through whatever barrier he had put up. "Begging your pardon, Warden."

"You are correct, but we may be a match for those at the Guild," Zage said. "That is our target. If we bring down the Guild, we will cut this madness off at the head." Zage's eyes glinted dangerously, and Siv could almost see the Fire burning within him.

"Let's go quickly," Dara said. "They could change their minds and sweep the peak any minute." A few of the castle Fireworkers looked askance at her, but they must assume she meant to guard their backs, not that she'd try to help them wrest the power from the Fire Guild's control using her own Fire abilities. Siv wondered how much she *could* actually Work. He'd been too busy being mad at her to ask.

"I agree, Miss Ruminor," Zage said.

"No." Siv's voice was muffled by the snow, but they heard him.

"Your Majesty, if we deal with the Rollendars directly—"

"No. They are not stupid." Unlike him. Stupid. *Stupid.* Why had he let the Rollendars and Fireworkers scheme while he trained up his piddling army of duelists? Swords were no use against magic. He was a useless, *useless* king. Why hadn't he purged the army when he still had a chance and made sure they couldn't be trapped on a single peak? His people would suffer for it. "They could have left orders to burn Square out of spite if anything happens to them. Marching on the Fire Guild won't save the people trapped on that peak."

"My king," Zage said softly. "I cannot bring down that Wall. I didn't think it was possible for them to do such a thing without me sensing it the moment they began. It must have taken time to send the Fire from the cavern to the edges of the peak, but I was monitoring all the Fire in the hall, and I didn't notice until it was too late. I have failed."

"The failure is mine," Siv said. "Go to the Fire Guild. See what you can learn of the men giving the Rollendars refuge. Report back on any weaknesses, but do not kill anyone lest it provoke the Fireworkers on Square. I will remain in the Great Hall while I make my decision. Report back as soon as you can."

"Very well, Your Majesty," Zage said. "Come." He jerked his head toward the sally port in the castle wall. The forlorn group of Fireworkers followed him out into the blustery night.

Dara hesitated on the castle steps.

"Go with them," Siv said. "Maybe you can lend your strength to Zage's."

"I don't want to leave you alone," she said.

Siv looked around at his four remaining guards. Pool's face was grave, and he carried his long knives in his hands. Oat's tall head rose above the others. Yuri's red beard collected a dusting of snowflakes. Young Dell Dunn clutched his blade with both hands. Siv hoped they were all loyal, but there was little he could do if they were not.

"I'll be okay," he said. "I know you still hope your father may change. Talk sense into him if you can."

"And if I can't?"

"I will do what is best for my people," he said.

"You can't think that putting Von Rollendar on the throne—"

"I will do it if I must," Siv said. "A cruel king may be better than a foolish one."

Dara held his gaze, and her eyes seemed to set the world on fire. If the world weren't already burning. To her credit, she didn't try to make him feel better. Nothing would at this stage.

"I'll try, Your Majesty. Stay in the castle. I'll return soon."

Siv inclined his head and kept it bowed as Dara strode past him and followed the Fireworkers into the swirling blizzard.

30

THE FIRE GUILD

THE cold crept into Dara's bones as she walked. She wished she could pull Fire from the stones to warm her body, but she didn't want to give herself away just yet. Besides, there was very little Fire in King's Peak. The castle Workers remarked on it as she caught up to them. The stray traces of magic that normally wove through the stones had been pulled toward a single location.

As soon as she left the blazing Great Hall, she'd been able to sense the Fire Wall around Square. Zage was right. The decorations were a distraction. While she had been worried they would somehow come to life and strangle the king, they had kept her attention elsewhere. Hers, and every other Fireworker in the castle, including Zage Lorrid.

While the nobles danced and the guards worried about defending the castle itself, the Fireworkers—she didn't know how many, but it had to be dozens—had yanked the Fire from that underground lake toward the bridges to form the barrier around Square. The Fire slowly streaming to that central location had welled up enough to engulf an entire peak.

She should have been more worried about what the enemies of the king could do with all that Fire, but she had been distracted by the mysterious duelists, by the treacherous general, by learning to control her own power to neutralize her father. She should have known the sheer strength of the Fire would win out in the end.

And now she marched toward the Fire Guild, on what was sure to be a futile mission. She wouldn't be able to talk her father out of his scheme. He likely wouldn't even be there. He was probably at the center of the Fireworkers sustaining the wall on Square. He would be where the greatest concentration of power was. He was too far gone now anyway, gone down this deep, dark path.

Dara pulled her cloak close with one hand, keeping the other on her Savven blade. She would need it to focus tonight. This wasn't a day for trying to Work without touching steel. This wasn't a day for mistakes.

She kicked herself for not running Bolden through when he dared put his hands on her at the feast. She had never imagined he would do something on this scale. She had underestimated him time and again, and now it was too late. She said a prayer to the Firelord for Kel. Was there any chance he had survived this night? She was glad Princess Selivia and Queen Tirra had left the mountain at least. Maybe Siv and Sora could flee to Trure too when this was all over. She doubted they could win this with Siv's reign intact.

The snow thickened, and the wind howled around the little group of Fireworkers as they descended the steps from the castle and turned along the wooden boardwalk leading to the Fire Guild. The Fire on Square was a beacon at the edge of Dara's senses. She thought of Berg, trapped within that wall, keeping watch on the army. She thought of her old friends inside the dueling school, all the workers and tradesmen and farmers who lived there—and their children. No matter who was in charge of the throne when dawn broke, they had to protect those people.

As they approached the Fire Guild itself, the second, smaller Fire Wall came into view. She could feel it, crackling against her skin and crawling along her bones. The Fire Guild had become a fortress. Could Zage and this small group pull that much Fire away from the Workers within?

They stopped on the boardwalk, before the final stone steps leading to the Guild doors. Zage didn't step onto the stones, which collected neither snow nor ice, anticipating some trap. Their little group waited behind him, clustered on the very boardwalk where Farr had died months ago.

Figures moved in the windows of the Guild, but they were

unidentifiable with that molten wall obscuring them. Tentatively, Zage touched the stone to test it then snatched back his hand.

"He's strong," Zage said quietly. "But not as strong as I thought."

"Who?" Dara asked.

"Not Rafe." Zage met her eyes. "A single Worker holds this Fire Wall. The rest must be over on Square or waiting to unleash other defenses should the wall fail."

"My father isn't in there?"

"Perhaps," Zage said. "Where would you expect him to be?"

"Square," Dara said. "Where the most power is."

Zage's eye glinted as he nodded.

"Are you stronger than this one Worker?" Dara asked. "If you pull down the wall, can the rest of us deal with any others in there?" She wanted a fight. She wanted the one-to-one simplicity of a duel. She hated feeling powerless beneath the threat of annihilation of so many innocent people.

"I believe our king is correct: we would bring down the wrath of the Workers on Square if we harm the Rollendars inside the Guild," Zage said.

"You always think you know best, Zage." A cold, proud voice spoke through the night, a voice Dara knew all too well.

A hole appeared in the wall of Fire in front of a second-floor window. Lima Ruminor, Dara's mother, looked down on the little knot of castle Fireworkers beneath the Guild. The Fire burned around her, setting her proud eyes blazing.

"Evening, Lima," Zage said, so softly that she might not even be able to hear him.

"You haven't even begun to experience the wrath of the Workers," Lima said. Her eyes flickered to her daughter then away again. Dismissing her. "Your foolishness is as clear now as it was the day you were appointed. You took my daughter away, but now I will watch you fall."

From the way Lima said "my daughter" she might as well have said "my only daughter." Dara knew her own presence was inconsequential in the face of Lima's towering fury over Renna's loss.

Zage raised his voice. "Lima, this vengeance you seek will not bring Renna back."

"Do not dare say her name!"

Zage put a hand to his throat, and Dara knew he was clutching the phoenix leaf pin. His tone remained dry and steady as ever, though.

"You cannot allow Vertigon to suffer for your revenge."

"You are wrong again, Zage," Lima said. She reined in her fury, her eyes as cold as the ice gilding the boardwalk railing. "This is bigger than a settling of scores. You and Sevren thought you could keep the power of this mountain in check. You thought true Wielders would allow their power to fritter away. I can't even touch the magic myself, but I know how vain that is. Wielders like my husband, like Corren, like Daz Stoneburner, will not be constrained by your petty limits."

"You are confirming we were right with every breath," Zage said. "Allow me to speak with Lord Rollendar on behalf of the king. This needn't end in bloodshed."

"It is too late for that," Lima said. "Did you honestly believe we would bow to a cold-fingered man like Von Rollendar when we finally made our move?"

Then Lima tossed something from the Guild window. Von Rollendar's head rolled to a stop at the Fire Warden's feet, the sandy hair drenched in blood. Dara bit the inside of her cheek to keep from shouting. A shriek escaped the youngest of the castle Fireworkers.

"He was a fool too," Lima said. "This mountain belongs to the Firewielders." Then the wall of Fire snapped shut in front of her as firmly as a steel door.

Dara didn't wait to see what Zage would do. She didn't look at the severed head or the blood sizzling on the hot stones. Her mother was right: her father wouldn't bow to another nobleman. He would be at the center of power. And though his allies may hold Square hostage, the center of power was still at the top of King's Peak.

Dara turned on her heel and ran back toward the castle. Her father wasn't going to move the crown to a different head. He was going to take it for himself.

And Dara had left Siv behind to wait for him.

31

THE CASTLE

SIV'S footsteps echoed as he paced across the Great Hall. The vines decorating the walls blazed harshly, no longer as ethereal now that the vast room was nearly empty. The Fireworkers had all gone to the Guild, so there was no one to turn down the lights.

Siv paced and paced, from the dais where the remnants of his dinner still sat before the throne to the doors of the Great Hall and back again. The four Guards watched the exits, swords at the ready. Siv hoped Zage and Dara would learn something at the Guild that could end this without provoking the wrath of whoever controlled the wall of Fire around Square Peak. If not, there was precious little he could do.

He didn't need until dawn to give his answer. He didn't want to leave his people in Von Rollendar's hands, but that was clearly the lesser evil. He couldn't let so many of them die tonight on Square. He hated that he would have to give up his father's crown, the legacy of three generations of Amintelle kings, without so much as a fight. But he was supposed to be the Fourth Good King, heir to a peaceful kingdom. He would not sacrifice that long-held peace just to keep his title.

Siv took the crown from his head and twisted it between his hands, wondering what his father would do in these circumstances. Did he have some secret wisdom that would get him out of this situation, something he meant to teach Siv before he was murdered? Siv's insides twisted as he thought of all the lessons he had skipped, all the times he'd assumed he would have plenty of time with his father. He'd thought he would have years to become serious and wise too. Instead, he had failed before his reign had really started.

Siv turned at the dais and paced back toward the ornate double doors. Perhaps if he lived to be an old man, somewhere in exile in the Lands Below, he would figure out what the correct decision was supposed to be in this moment. Perhaps one day answers would come easily, and he could look back with something resembling wisdom. All he knew right now was that he had to protect his people, even if that meant handing over his birthright to the Rollendars.

Pool guarded the doors to the entrance hall. He stepped forward when Siv reached them, before he could turn around and pace back the other way.

"Your Majesty?"

"You don't need to call me that anymore, Pool," Siv said. "I won't be king for much longer."

"I'm afraid, Your Majesty, I find myself quite unwilling to accept that outcome. We may yet discover an adequate solution to this predicament."

"Got any ideas?"

Pool sighed. "Regrettably, no. I find this situation problematic."

"You and me both." Siv rubbed his fingers along the sharp ridges of the Firejewels in his crown. They glittered, as if he held the Orange Star in his hands.

"I wish to state something," Pool said. "Although the current state of affairs is dire, you have acted uncommonly kingly today, Sire."

"What?" Siv looked up.

Pool's expression was as dour as ever, but his voice was gentle. "You remained calm and ensured that your sister, employees, and court were escorted to safety, even though it has left you relatively vulnerable. You displayed wisdom and assurance in the way you conducted yourself, both tonight and over the past few months. Even as you prepare to abdicate your throne, I find myself impressed and—if I may say so—proud of your demeanor." Pool cleared his throat. "Your father would be proud too."

Siv swallowed hard. His grip tightened on the crown, and he studied the toes of his boots. It wouldn't do to give away how much Pool's words meant to him by letting his voice waver.

"Thank you, Pool."

"You're welcome, Siv."

Surprised at the use of his first name, Siv looked up—just in time to see a masked swordsman burst through the double doors and run a blade through Pool's back. Pool's eyes widened in surprise. The tip of the sword glinted, protruding through the front of Pool's coat.

Siv shouted something, he wasn't sure what. Behind him, Oat yelled too, as more swordsmen charged through the doors at the opposite side of the hall. Blades clashed, and the Guards shouted, but all Siv could see was the surprise on Pool's face. The swordsman pulled his blade free as Pool slumped to the floor.

Without pausing to think, Siv threw the crown directly at the man's masked face. The sharp point caught him on the cheek, buying Siv enough time to pull his own sword from its sheath. Then the swordsmen pouring through the doors were upon him.

Blind shock radiated through Siv as he fought. Two, three, four swordsmen joined the man who had stabbed Pool. They were armed with sharpened rapiers, and their actions were unnaturally fast. Fire Blades. Here, at last, were the Fire-Blade-wielding swordsmen Dara had predicted.

Siv met parry after parry, lunging in and out of range, jabbing savagely at the enemy swordsmen. The actions came instinctually, and he was grateful he'd been training over the past few weeks.

And Siv had a Fire Blade too. Dara didn't want him to endanger himself, but he had come prepared. He may not have been a wise or long-living king, but he would go down fighting.

One of his opponents fell with a strike to the upper thigh. He scrambled away, trying to stop the blood flowing from his leg. Siv lunged for the next man, thrusting his blade deep into his stomach. He went down too—and didn't rise.

Siv wielded the Fire Blade, using the swiftness of the magic in the steel, even though he couldn't sense the Fire infusion himself. But even with the help of the enhanced weapon, Siv couldn't fight off that many men unscathed. He took a deep cut to the arm, the pain distant. He missed a parry, and a swipe across the ribs left his coat—and the skin beneath it—in tatters. He narrowly avoided losing an eye as he dove for another opponent's knees.

Pool's murderer launched a compound attack, and Siv barely managed to hold it off. Their blades clashed, pealing like bells. Siv took another stab to his sword arm and retreated halfway across the hall, his blood leaving a scarlet trail on the tiles.

Siv was losing. There were too many of them. He and the three remaining Castle Guards were no match for the masked swordsmen surging into the Great Hall. Within minutes, poor Dell Dunn fell, a slim blade going straight through his throat. Oat shouted for reinforcements, but even if those guarding the other areas of the castle heard him, they wouldn't be here in time. They wouldn't be enough.

Siv retreated to the dais, and Oat and Yuri followed his lead. They stood back to back, three swordsmen against a dozen opponents. It was too little, too late. Giving up his throne wasn't enough. Siv was going to die. He only hoped Sora would be spared and allowed to join Selivia and their mother in Trure. And he hoped Dara would know he had fought well.

An enemy swordsman lunged, and the tip of his rapier sank into Yuri's sword arm. Yuri's hand seized up, and his weapon clattered to the floor.

"Get behind us," Siv yelled. Yuri obeyed, crawling toward the throne at the center of the dais.

Then it was just Siv and Oat facing a room full of assassins. They had the high ground on the dais, but it didn't matter. They were surrounded. There was no way out.

One of the swordsmen lifted a hand, and the others stopped advancing. They kept their weapons raised, though. Siv kept his guard up too, breathing heavily. The blood from his cuts—he had lost count of how many there were—dripped onto the dais and spread across the stones.

Then the swordsman removed the cloth obscuring his face. A red line cut into his cheek, a gash from where Siv's crown had hit him.

It was Bolden Rollendar. Bolden had stabbed Pool in the back. White-hot rage boiled through Siv, unlike anything he'd ever felt before. Bolden had betrayed his kingdom. And now, Bolden stood before him with a sword in his hand.

He sneered. "I always knew I was better than you, Siv."

"With only a dozen trained assassins to help you? Congratulations."

"I have more than a dozen of these men," Bolden said. "The mountain is mine. The Fireworkers too. They've agreed to put me on the throne in exchange for my support. I'll grant them free rein over the Fire and the nobility they've been coveting, and they will make me the strongest king Vertigon has ever known."

"You?" Siv studied the ring of men around them, looking for weaknesses. The longer Bolden talked, the more time he had to live. And maybe to find a way out of this. "What about your father?"

"Oh, I expect he's dead by now," Bolden said. "Courtesy of my allies at the Fire Guild. Did you think I was going to wait another thirty years to become king after going to all this trouble?"

Siv tried to keep the shock from his face. He had never seen much warmth between Bolden and his father, but he hadn't expected his treachery to run this deep.

"Do you really think being a puppet for the Fireworkers is the same thing as being a strong king?" Siv said.

Motion flickered at the edge of his vision. A lone figure slipped into the Great Hall through a side door. He had the familiar swagger of a professional duelist. At first Siv thought it was Dara, except this person was too short and wiry. He was dressed like one of Bolden's swordsmen, but a small group of New Guards followed him, moving slowly to avoid attracting attention.

"I have assurances from the Fireworkers," Bolden said. "You were a fool to keep them subjugated for so long. They were more than willing to help me, especially when they learned I was more accepting of their methods than my father."

"You mean the part about threatening to kill a third of my people?" Siv said.

The wiry swordsman crept closer. The others were focused on Siv and Oat, and they didn't notice when another man joined their number. Siv just had to keep them occupied for a bit longer. The other Castle Guards moved closer too, waiting for the right moment.

"That—and my previous attempts to get you out of the way. You remember a knifeman who took a dive off a bridge rather than be caught? I threatened to kill his family. This is what will make me a better king than you," Bolden said. "I will do what it takes to keep Vertigon strong."

"Including ally with foreign nations?" Siv said, trying not to be distracted by the revelation. That had been Bolden and his Fireworker allies all along? "I know you have Soolen fighters among your men. Do you really think they'll be content to let you sit on a stolen throne? Soole has always coveted Vertigon's wealth and position. And you've let the marrkrats in through the back door."

"I have plans for Soole," Bolden said. A few of his swordsmen stiffened and looked over at him.

Kelad Korran picked that moment to issue his war cry.

The wiry duelist cut down two of the masked swordsmen before they even realized he was there. He was dressed as one of Bolden's men, with the same distinctive wrappings around his face, and they hadn't seen him arrive. Confusion paralyzed the assassins for an instant. Then the Castle Guards who'd snuck in with Kel attacked them from behind.

Siv lunged toward Bolden the moment the assault began, wasting no time.

Bolden parried desperately. Siv's riposte went wide, but Bolden was forced back down the steps. He called for assistance, real fear in his voice. His men were occupied with the new attackers and didn't come to his aid. Bolden cursed and retreated from the dais. Siv chased after him as the clash of blades filled the Great Hall once more.

Kel had rounded up six additional Castle Guards. Battle raged around the hall again. The footsteps and clangs were reminiscent of a dueling competition, but the shouts were more vicious, the actions savage.

Siv focused only on Bolden. This man had ruined the peace Vertigon had enjoyed for a hundred years. This man wanted to destroy everything Siv's father, grandfather, and great-grandfather had worked to protect. This man had killed Pool—and he was going to pay for it.

Siv hadn't dueled against Bolden since they were teenagers messing around with blunted weapons. The man had clearly been training. Perhaps he had even been in the cavern the day Dara and Siv visited it. But Siv had been training too.

He drove Bolden up the center of the Great Hall. Most of the fighting ranged around the dais. Siv forced his opponent closer and closer to the other end of the hall, isolating him from the others. Bolden could only defend as Siv bore down on him. He would make Bolden regret trying to bring down the Amintelles. He would show him what a strong king could do to keep his people out of the hands of a murderer.

Bolden got a quick slice past Siv's guard, opening another cut on his forearm. Siv barely felt the wound as blood seeped into his coat, soaking the black fabric. They neared Pool's body at the back of the hall. The sight filmed Siv's eyes with red, but he could still see enough. He ducked and drove the point of his sword into Bolden's toe.

Bolden cursed and stumbled backward. He was too busy fending off Siv's attacks to taunt him now. Their blades clanged, again and again. Sparks burst from the Fire-infused weapons. Siv's arms grew tired. The blood loss made his head feel sluggish, but he couldn't slow yet.

Bolden's face reddened from the exertion. The cut on his cheek from Siv's crown had clotted, and red-brown streaks spread patterns down his jaw. He roared with frustration as Siv pushed him farther across the Great Hall.

Siv wanted to roar back. He wanted to run the man through, make him pay for all he had done. But he remembered training with Dara, remembered the precision of her style, the way she hit the hand, the arm, the toe, the shoulder. The way she could win a bout without ever delivering a killing blow.

So Siv stayed focused. He didn't allow the rage and grief and frustration burning through him to take control. He focused on making his shots accurate and precise as a surgeon's scalpel.

He gave Bolden a cut on the forearm to match his own. He lunged for his thigh and put a clean slice through Bolden's trousers. That got him another slice along the ribs, but he didn't let it faze him. He retreated a few steps, then as Bolden tried to press what he thought was an advantage, Siv counterattacked with another hit to Bolden's weapon arm.

Bolden cursed and swept his blade toward Siv's neck, the steel moving unnaturally quickly. Siv caught the blade on his guard. For a moment their faces were inches apart. He smelled Bolden's sweat, his blood and fear. Then Siv shoved. Bolden stumbled backward a few steps and tripped over Pool's body. Siv didn't give him a chance to rise. Before Bolden could stand, Siv pressed the tip of his sword to his throat.

"Wait," Bolden rasped.

"Did you really have your father killed?" Siv asked. Sweat and blood dripped into his eyes, but his hand remained steady.

Bolden nodded. It was the lack of remorse in his eyes that made Siv's decision for him, that and Pool's blood cooling on the stones beneath them.

"Then as the King of Vertigon, I sentence you to death."

Siv ran his blade through Bolden's throat. Blood bubbled from his thin lips, and he collapsed on top of Pool's body.

Siv didn't slow to look at the body of his enemy or dwell on the man he had once called a friend. He whirled around, preparing to meet the next swordsman who came his way. But the hall had fallen silent.

The Castle Guards Kel brought with him had managed to subdue or kill the masked assassins. They forced the survivors to gather on the dais and remove their masks. At least half of them had Soolen coloring.

Siv and Bolden were the only ones whose fight had taken them to the other side of the hall. From this distance, Siv had a good view of the bodies littering the floor around the dais. Some were clad in New Guard uniforms. They had beaten the masked swordsmen, but there had been a cost.

Siv slowly lowered his blade, heart heavy, and looked back at Pool's body.

That was when Rafe Ruminor pushed open the double doors and strode into the hall.

Siv scarcely had time to blink at his father's murderer before Rafe raised a hand, and the Fire vines decorating the Great Hall came to life.

The glowing branches of Fire and metal shot down from the walls like vipers. They streaked in between Siv and his remaining

Guardsmen, cutting them off at the other side of the hall. Fast as lightning, metallic shackles wrapped around every man there, Castle Guard or not.

The vines closest to Siv snaked across the floor and wove together, forming a golden cage around him. A bolt of Fire shot forward and melted Siv's Fire Blade into a lump of molten steel. He dropped the hilt just before it scorched his hand. The liquid metal hissed as it fell at his feet.

Siv looked up and met Rafe's gaze. He recognized the intensity and power there immediately. This was definitely Dara's father. He had the same height, the same golden hair, the same deadly focus. He was utterly terrifying.

Siv's heart pounded like a drum, but he kept his voice steady.

"You decided to come out of the shadows," he said. "This is new."

"I would rather not be known for regicide," Rafe said. "The secret way would have kept things much simpler in the days to come. But you've managed to evade my efforts several times now, and I'm not sure how."

"You'd be surprised," Siv said.

"Would I?" Rafe raised an eyebrow.

"So, what now?" Siv said. "You're going to take the crown for yourself?"

"Perhaps. Our young lord's death has disrupted my plans somewhat." Rafe stepped over Bolden's body and strode closer to Siv.

"I can't summon the energy to be sorry about that," Siv said. "I've had a long day."

"Yes," Rafe said.

He moved closer, the cage of Fire still separating them. Siv wished he could dive through it, no matter how much it burned, for a chance to get at the man. His father's murderer, here in the flesh.

"Can I assume you would not be as amenable to working with me as young Rollendar was?" Rafe said, as calmly as if he were discussing the price of soldarberries. "I will spare your life if you agree to the concessions he promised."

Siv took that opportunity to tell Rafe exactly where he could shove his concessions.

Rafe sighed deeply. "I don't know what my daughter sees in you." His eyes flickered to the Castle Guards, standing like statues in the grip of his Fire bonds. "I'm surprised she's not here. I'd have killed the Guards directly if I wasn't worried about her getting hurt." He raised a hand, and the cage of Fire began to shrink. "I'll deal with you first, though."

"You're not killing anyone," said a voice from the door.

Dara had arrived.

32

LANTERN MAKER'S DAUGHTER

DARA felt the Fire moving as she sprinted toward the Great Hall. A gray-bearded man, Yeltin of the old Castle Guard, lay dead in the entrance hall, run through by a sword. But she didn't need that to know the king and his remaining men were under attack. Didn't need that to know she should have stayed in the castle after all.

She slipped through the double doors, Savven blade in hand, and took in the situation in an instant: the Guard held captive, the bodies on the floor, the king trapped in a molten cage.

And her father. The man she had admired for his dedication to his work, the man whose approval she'd sought long after she found out she couldn't Work, the man she'd wanted to protect even after she knew what he'd done. The man she should have brought to justice long ago. Her father was forcing the cage of Fire closer and closer to Siv's skin, about to destroy the man she loved.

"You're not killing anyone," she said.

Her father turned to look at her, not slowing the movement of those bars of Fire. Dara raised her hand toward the molten cage and pulled. She strained with everything she had, calling on her desperation, on her last shreds of focus. She couldn't let him do this, not again, not to Siv.

She pulled.

The cage of Fire stopped shrinking, mere inches from burning

Siv's body. Rafe's eyes widened with shock and confusion. Dara called the Fire toward her, taking advantage of her father's surprise. She didn't hold back. He would know now. He would see that she could Wield his power after all. She yanked harder on the Fire, as she had once seen Zage Lorrid do in the castle courtyard.

And the Fire answered. It roared toward her, streaming heat and power and light. Her father lost his grip on the molten cords as Dara called it all to her in one furious rush.

The metal that had formed the vines, silver and gold, dripped to the ground as pure Fire flowed into her. She couldn't control it. She knew it could incinerate her, but she didn't have time to doubt. She called the power into her body. Heat raged within her. She drove the point of her blade into the stone floor, trying to redirect the massive flow of Fire. The Savven glowed white hot as the Fire blazed through it. Dara forced more and more of the Fire to come to her, to build up in her body. She managed to release some of it through her blade into the paving stones, but not enough.

"Dara! Don't!" Rafe shouted. And through his surprise and confusion, a new emotion burned, one she had never seen on her father's face in her entire life: fear.

It was too much. She couldn't hold it.

Siv stared at her, his mouth open.

"Run!" she gasped.

She had to do something with all this Fire. She couldn't hold it much longer, couldn't release it all through the blade. But the only enemy in the room was her father. And she couldn't hurt him. Even after all he had done, she couldn't bring herself to unleash his own power against him.

So Dara blazed with all the Fire of the mountain, and it threatened to consume her.

Then her father pulled back. He recovered from his surprise enough to try to regain control of the Fire raging through the room. Siv had begun to move toward the door, but he wasn't going fast enough.

Dara fought her father for control. She had to give Siv time to get away.

Now that Rafe was recovering from his surprise, Dara began to see how powerful he truly was. He seized more Fire and broke off molten threads that he sent snaking back toward the king. Dara could barely keep from burning to a cinder, much less carry out any other Work at the same time. She couldn't stop the fiery darts streaking toward Siv. He ducked, and the volley of darts barely missed him.

The Savven blade began to burn in her palm, truly burn, and she smelled the sickly sweet of scorching skin, mixed with the scent of lightning.

"Let go, Dara," Rafe said. "It's too much."

"You can't kill him," Dara said. Her teeth and jaws ached as she clenched them tight. Pain shot upward through the blade in her hand.

She met her father's eyes and once again tried to draw the power from him. Fire welled up in her, like water boiling in a kettle. She was going to explode, she couldn't hold anymore, but she had to keep trying.

Then a streak of silver-gold blurred through the air, and something clunked into the back of Rafe's head. He released some of the Fire as he grunted in surprise. A ring of metal hit the ground and rolled away. Siv had thrown his crown at her father.

"Now, Dara, we have to run!" Siv shouted.

"I can't . . . let . . . go." Dara's bones shuddered and crackled. If she let go now the Fire would destroy her.

"Give it to me," came a dry, papery voice behind her. Then there was a hand on her shoulder, a ring glittering with obsidian. Zage Lorrid gripped her shoulders and pulled some of the raging Fire she held into his own body. Dara couldn't let go, but Zage managed to drain some of the Fire from her, slowly enough that it wouldn't hurt her. The pressure began to ease. She let her teacher take more of the Fire, knowing she had gone far behind the limits of her abilities. She gasped as the power bled out of her.

But then her father raised a hand and pulled the rest of the Fire to himself. It left Dara's body like water bursting through a dam. She dropped to her knees, wrapping both hands around the scorching hot Savven blade. Her vision wavered, nearly going black.

Zage had been concentrating on drawing slowly so he wouldn't hurt Dara. So he was unprepared when Rafe formed a spike of metal from the melted remnants of a sword on the floor and hurled it at him over Dara's head.

She didn't look up, but she heard the thud as the steel rammed through the Fire Warden's body. She crawled forward on hands and knees, dragging her still-hot blade with her. But the Fire Warden didn't fall. He called on the metal, on the Fire, and wielded them against the Lantern Maker.

The air burned as Rafe uttered a guttural sound, full of rage and defiance. Dara looked back. Pure fury twisted her father's face, rendering it unrecognizable. Zage remained utterly silent, face pale and pained. Then both men raised their hands and fought for control of the Fire at last.

The Lantern Maker and the Fire Warden dueled. They wielded the Fire in its raw form. They used its heat to form weapons from the molten steel, silver, and gold coating the floor and hurled them at each other. Thunder boomed around them. They Wielded like the sorcerers of old, and Fire, metal, and stone flew through the air.

The light and power of the Fire were blinding, brilliant. The two master Workers glowed bright with the magic whirling around them. Neither one spoke. Dara couldn't move as the duel raged.

Then Siv's hands were on her arms, and he was pulling her up, dragging her toward the doors.

"We need to go now," he said. "Move."

"I can't leave—"

"He will kill us, Dara." Siv hauled her forward. She could barely stand. Her bones felt like glass.

As they stumbled through the doors, she looked back to see Zage slumping to his knees. Her father sent daggers of molten metal toward him once more, a fierce grimace of victory on his face. As a dozen daggers pierced Zage's thin body, Rafe looked up and met his daughter's eyes for one terrible moment. There was wrath and betrayal and Fire in his gaze.

Dara fled.

33

FLIGHT

SIV held Dara up as they staggered across the entrance hall. He didn't understand everything that had happened back there, but he knew Rafe Ruminor would burn them away to nothing if they didn't get out of the castle. After that furious torrent of rage and power, he wouldn't count on the man's affection for his daughter to save them now.

Dara appeared on the verge of losing consciousness. Fear that she was seriously injured cut through Siv, adding to the piles of dread he'd already felt that day. He knew the Fire could hurt Firesparked people if they lost control of it, but he had no idea how to care for that kind of damage.

"We have to get Sora, then we'll get out of here," he said.

"I can't," Dara gasped.

"Yes, you can." Siv held Dara around the waist so she wouldn't fall. He had to get her and his sister to safety before he could worry about anything else. "Come on, girl, we have to keep moving."

But as they rushed toward the stairwell to the princess's tower, footsteps thundered down it. Siv pulled Dara into an alcove as three masked swordsmen hurried out of the tower. Blood marked the tips of their blades.

The sight of the blood made him recoil. "No."

A fourth man slowed at the entrance to the stairwell and stalked back and forth in front of it, lethal as a panviper. He guarded the only way up to Sora's room. And Siv had no weapon.

"Give me your Savven." He reached for the hilt and hissed as the metal scorched his skin. It was so hot he couldn't even touch it, but Dara held onto it with her bare hands.

"It's too late," Dara said. She leaned against the wall, staving off collapse.

"No, it's not."

"Siv, it's too late for her. I can't fight, and there will be more men upstairs. You're right: we have to get out of the castle."

Siv shook his head and tried to take her blade again, biting back a curse as the metal singed his fingers. He would be useless in a fight if his sword melted the flesh off his bones.

More masked swordsmen darted through the castle toward the main entrance hall. The surviving Castle Guards had wisely hidden when the Lantern Maker and the Warden started slinging Fire, but they'd have their hands full now.

"Is there another way out?" Dara asked. "The kitchen tunnel is too far away."

Siv looked at the swordsman guarding the entrance to his sister's tower once more. He didn't want to leave her. Blood glistened on the swordsman's blade, as it had on those of the other men leaving her tower, too much blood. Grief reared within Siv, ugly and savage as a cullmoran. Sora. Poor wise Sora. He would add her to his list of people to mourn—later. They weren't out of this yet.

"I have an idea." Siv slung Dara's arm over his shoulder, waiting until the corridor cleared. At the first opportunity, he ran toward the entrance to the cur-dragon cave.

"We'll be trapped down there," Dara said when she realized where they were going. But she didn't resist as he hauled her down the tunnel. She must truly be hurt. She normally told him straightaway when he had really stupid ideas.

None of the dragon keepers were in sight. Siv hoped they had taken refuge in the Guard barracks with the servants. The cur-dragons paced across the cavern, snorting restlessly, as if they could sense that something was amiss upstairs. They huffed and sneezed, and smoke drifted above their heads.

Rumy loped straight up to Siv when he opened the gate to the cave.

"Hey, little guy," Siv said. "I need you to prove you're as strong as I think you are."

He helped Dara toward the opening looking out over the mountain, and Rumy trundled along at his side. He was the biggest cur-dragon in the cave now, bigger than he was supposed to be. The creature reared on his hind legs, putting his clawed feet on Siv's shoulder, and stood almost as tall as Siv. Rumy sniffed at the blood on his face. Siv wasn't even sure if it was his own blood or someone else's at this point.

Outside, the night sky sparkled with ice. The blizzard had lessened in intensity, but crystals still swirled through the air. A thick blanket of snow, gray in the darkness, covered every surface. Far off to the right, Square Peak was still trapped behind the glowing wall of Fire. Siv only hoped Rafe Ruminor would take it down and spare the people on Square now that he'd won.

A steep cliff dropped away beneath the cave opening, designed to keep enemies from getting into the castle through the back. A road at the bottom of the cliff wound among quiet greathouses far from the hustle and bustle of the main slope of King's Peak. It would be a steep dive, exposed against the cliff face, but with any luck no one would be looking this way.

"I need you, boy," Siv said to his cur-dragon. "Carry her to the bottom of the cliff, then come back up for me."

Dara stiffened. "Are you sure about this?"

"It's not far," Siv said. "Rumy can handle it." He sincerely hoped that was true. He'd felt how strong Rumy was when he pulled against his lead, felt the power in his wings. He hoped it would be enough to carry Dara to safety.

"I won't leave you," Dara said.

"He'll come right back for me. Won't you, boy?"

Rumy snorted, his breath steaming in the air. A normal cur-dragon wouldn't be able to carry a fully-grown woman, but Siv was pretty sure Rumy wasn't a normal cur-dragon. He had to be part true dragon. It seemed impossible, but then a lot of things he thought were impossible had happened tonight.

"Siv." Dara clutched his hand. "I'm sorry my father—"

"We don't have time for that," Siv said. "Hold on tight."

He lifted Dara onto Rumy's back and wrapped her arms around the creature's neck, careful not to touch the blistering Savven blade she still carried. He kissed her forehead, smelling lightning and metal in her hair, and stepped back.

He would have preferred to test out this escape method himself first, but there was a chance Rumy would be able to carry Dara but not Siv, and he had to make sure she got to safety. He led Rumy forward a few steps along the edge of the cliff. The cur-dragon walked easily enough with Dara on his back. Here's hoping he could fly.

Siv checked once more that Dara's grip was secure and gave Rumy a pat.

"Take it slow," he said. "And don't forget to come back for me!"

Rumy sneezed out a jet of flame and plummeted over the cliff. Siv nearly dove after him, fear sending an icicle through his chest, but Rumy's wings opened, and he soared like a kite caught on the wind. Dara's golden hair flew out behind them as Rumy glided away, carrying her into the darkness.

For a moment, all was still. Siv sat on the edge of the cliff. The other cur-dragons shuffled about in the darkness. He had locked the gate behind him, even though Rafe or one of his Fireworker allies could melt it away easily. And the masked swordsmen could very well have brought bows and arrows to the castle. Steel or Fire could pierce his body any second. But for now, Siv remained utterly still.

As he sat there, savoring these brief minutes of silence, he realized he was bleeding from a dozen different wounds. His black coat hid the worst of it, but he probably looked like a finely scored cut of meat underneath. And he was in all kinds of pain. Siv grimaced and shifted his position, poking gingerly at his wounds. None of the punctures seemed to open directly into any of his vital organs, but he couldn't be entirely sure. He'd need someone to sew him up soon, though, if he had any allies at all left on his mountain.

Siv sighed, trying to ignore the stabs of agony when he moved, his breath clouding the air. He didn't think he could call it his mountain anymore. Vertigon was lost to him.

Siv started to worry something had gone wrong with Dara's

escape. But then a squawk broke the silence, and Rumy soared through the darkness toward him.

"You made it! Is Dara okay?" Siv wrapped his arms around the creature's scaly neck as Rumy landed beside him on the cliff's edge.

Rumy huffed and growled as if he were offended that Siv had doubted him. He strutted back and forth along the edge of the cliff, preening.

"Yeah, yeah, you're very strong. Think you can carry me too?"

Rumy fixed a bright, disapproving eye on him, not unlike the look Dara sometimes gave him.

Footsteps pounded down the tunnel, accompanied by loud voices. Someone was coming.

"Nothing for it, right?" Siv said. He climbed onto the cur-dragon's back, his long legs dragging on the floor, and held on tight. "Please don't drop me."

Rumy coughed out a jet of flame and ambled forward. The brief bunching of his muscles was Siv's only warning, then Rumy hurled himself out over the cliff.

Icy wind ripped through Siv's hair, and his eyes watered from the cold. His position astride the cur-dragon pulled at every one of his many injuries. Rumy didn't show off this time. He kept his wings outstretched, and with something between a glide and a plummet they left the castle behind. They fell faster than Siv would have liked. Rumy wouldn't be able to carry him far.

The cur-dragon swerved, and for a moment Siv had a perfect view of all the peaks of Vertigon. The Village was cloaked in snow, the houses nestled cozily in its drifts. The Fissure was a dark smudge beneath him, occasionally interrupted by the lantern-lit bridges. King's Peak, where he had spent most of his life, looked smaller from the air. And the wall of Fire burning around Square Peak illuminated it all.

They drifted lower, and Rumy beat his wings hard, straining to turn again. Siv held on tight, exhilaration and fear dueling through him. Finally they thumped to the ground and slid to an ungainly stop in a snowdrift. They'd made it.

Siv left smudges of blood behind as he crawled out of the drift.

"Good boy, Rumy," he said, patting his cur-dragon on top of the head. Rumy snorted and flapped his wings like a thunderbird ruffling its feathers. "Now, where did you leave my Dara?"

"Over here," Dara called. She hid in the shadow of a nearby dwelling. The windows were dark, and it didn't look as if anyone had seen their arrival from the air.

Siv hurried over to join her, wincing as each step aggravated his wounds.

"Are you okay?"

"A little shaky," Dara said. "I'm never doing that again."

"Yeah? I think cur-dragon gliding could be the next big thing. Now, let me get my bearings. We're going to need shelter, and soon." Siv shivered. The icy wind wasn't much milder here than it had been in the air.

"You're bleeding," Dara said, resting her hand on his chest above one of the many cuts he now sported.

"That's the understatement of the year," Siv said. The cold really wasn't helping things in that department. His limbs had started to shake, jostling his wounds with each shudder. "Let's see. That's Pen Bridge, which means we're probably at the far end of Eastwind Street."

"Wait," Dara said. "I know someone who lives here."

"Trustworthy?"

For some reason, Dara snorted. "I guess she is at that. Follow me."

Siv and Dara put their arms around each other and trudged through the snowy street. It was unclear at this point who was holding whom up. Siv wasn't sure it mattered. Rumy followed along behind them, occasionally blasting holes in snowdrifts with jets of flame until Siv told him to cut it out.

He was beginning to think about lying down in one of those nice-looking drifts and going to sleep, when Dara slowed.

"This is it." She nodded toward an older-looking greathouse with a wide terrace jutting out from the second floor. Siv was surprised, as he wouldn't have expected her to deem a noble house worthy of trust.

Then Dara sighed heavily and said, "Welcome to House Silltine."

34

DAYBREAK

DARA used her last shred of energy to pound on the door of Vine Silltine's greathouse. An unnatural stillness settled over her. It might be shock. She had faced her father. She had taken his power from him to protect Siv, finally revealing her ability, finally standing against him. She'd managed to stop her father from killing Siv with that fiery cage, but she knew she would have lost if the Fire Warden hadn't shown up.

Poor Zage. She was surprised how much his death saddened her. There had been little warmth between them, despite all the time they'd spent training with the Fire. But he was a good man at his core. His desire for a peaceful Vertigon had been at the heart of everything he did—that and his need to atone for Renna's death. And he had saved Dara's life.

At the same time, Dara understood why her father hated having his power restricted. At the moment when the Fire filled her completely, though she thought her bones would turn to ash, Dara had felt invincible. It was a feeling she never achieved in the duels, no matter how hard she practiced. A new opponent could always come along and defeat her, or she could get injured and never step onto the dueling strip again. But when she held the Fire, the magic in her blood had whispered that no one could stop her. It was a lie, though. It would whisper of indestructibility right up until it killed her.

Still, she could see why her father craved unrestrained power. But he had destroyed the Peace of Vertigon to get it, and in doing so he had compromised his very soul.

Dara pounded on the door again, shattering the quiet of the snowy night.

Slow footsteps approached on the other side of the door. It cracked open, releasing a sliver of light. Vine's butler peered through, holding up a Fire Lantern. A Ruminor Lantern, of course.

"Sorry to bother you in the middle of the night," Dara said.

"Who is it?"

"Is Vine home? I need to see her right away."

"What's happening out there?" The butler kept the door mostly shut. The cold wind whistled at the crack. "We heard such a commotion."

"Please," Dara said. "It's urgent."

"Who is it, Toff?" Vine's voice floated out from the darkness. The butler glanced over his shoulder.

"Vine, it's Dara!" she called, praying she'd made the right choice. She was pretty sure it was their only choice. "Can we come in, please?"

"Dara Ruminor! Quickly, Toff!" Vine bustled forward and pushed her butler out of the way. Her eyes widened when she saw Siv. She had a rapier in her hand as if she had expected a fight at her doorstep, but she tossed it aside to grab Dara and Siv and pull them through the doorway.

"We had nowhere to go, Vine. Could we—?"

"Of course, of course! Toff, run get some bandages and hot water. And don't open that door again."

"My lady! What is *that*?" The butler went rigid as Rumy tried to force his nose through the doorway behind them.

"It's just a cur-dragon," Siv said. He was starting to sound as weak and tired as Dara felt. Blood pooled beneath his boots.

The butler blanched. "A cur—My lady!"

"It's all right, Toff," Vine said impatiently. "We won't leave any living creature out in the snow. Take him through to the kitchen for now."

As soon as Rumy crossed the threshold, Vine closed the door, sealing them off from the dark and the cold. Toff headed down a side corridor, and Rumy followed, stopping to sniff at everything he passed.

Vine wore a pale-green silk nightgown, and her lustrous hair hung loose around her shoulders. She looked absolutely delighted to see them.

"Come!" she said. "You must tell me everything that happened after I left the castle!"

She led them into a parlor on the ground floor and bustled about, pulling heavy curtains over all the windows. Dara couldn't help glancing at them every few seconds, afraid she'd see the tall forms of her mother and father looming outside.

A soft darkness filled the parlor, which was decorated in an old-fashioned style. A few chairs and one low couch spread about the space in a haphazard manner. A table in one corner held an unfinished game of mijen. A large Fire Lantern hanging from the exposed beams of the ceiling, dim with age, was the only illumination.

Dara dropped into a chair and leaned her head back against the ornately carved wood. With Siv's help, she explained to Vine what had happened in broad strokes. Vine's father had apparently come down with a cold, and they'd left the feast early to get home before the blizzard gathered strength. She had missed most of the action.

"I saw the wall of Fire around Square," Vine said, "but only when Toff came to wake me. I swear I shall never leave another party early for as long as I live. Now, take your clothes off, Your Highness."

"Yes, my lady," Siv said. He winked at Dara, an expression that turned to a wince as he eased off his black coat. He wore a white shirt underneath, which showed off the full extent of his injuries. Red lines crossed his ribs in several places, and blood completely soaked the tattered sleeve of his sword arm.

If the king's injuries shocked Vine, she hid it well. Toff arrived with the bandages and a Firekettle full of hot water, and they set about patching Siv up together. Several of the cuts required stitches. Vine spread a blanket over the couch and made Siv lie down on top of it while she worked. Siv gritted his teeth, not making a sound as Vine sewed him up.

For her part, Dara had the worst headache of her life. She felt fragile, as if her bones would crack under too much pressure. She wished she could ask someone if that was a normal feeling—and if it would go away—but there was no one left to ask. Zage was dead, and she would surely never speak to her father or any of the Fireworkers who supported him again after tonight. The enormity of what had happened was starting to dawn on her. She only wished it would dull the pain in her head.

"What are you going to do now?" Vine asked as she tied off another row of stitches. "When my father wakes up in the morning, he'll wonder how long I plan to have house guests."

"We can't stay here," Dara said. Rumy had bought them time. Her father would likely expect them to be hiding in or near the castle. He wouldn't look this far away tonight. And it wouldn't occur to him to look for his daughter at House Silltine, the home of Dara's famous rival, anyway. "Thank you for helping us, Vine, but I think we need to get off the mountain."

"I won't leave Vertigon," Siv said.

"He will hunt you down and kill you," Dara said.

"He tried before," Siv said fiercely. "We'll stop him again."

"Siv, I'm no match for my father." Dara leaned forward in her chair so she could see his face. The light from the Fire Lantern cast a shadow from his high cheekbones. "The Fireworkers are on his side, enough of them to threaten all of Square. Zage is gone. The Guard is decimated. Unless the army will side with you, which I thought was already out of the question, we don't have a chance."

"So you just want to abandon the city to him?" Siv said. "The man who killed my father and my sister?"

"We can't stand against him, at least not now. What if you go to Trure, to your mother's people? Maybe you can gather some support to—"

"To what?" Siv snapped. "Take back the mountain, the unassailable mountain of Vertigon, with a foreign army? And probably kill half my people in the process?"

"You'd rather kill my father directly instead?"

"That seems like the obvious choice to me."

Dara felt her exhaustion like a physical weight on her shoulders. Of course Siv would see that as the only way to defeat her father. He was probably right. But Rafe would have safeguards in place. And she had meant what she said: she was no match for her father. She doubted she ever would be. There was nothing they could do. She wasn't capable of killing her own parents, even if that was what it took to defeat them, even if they deserved it after everything they had done. But she couldn't walk away from Siv either. And he didn't want to abandon his people.

"I'm sensing a great deal of tension in the air," Vine said pleasantly.

Dara gritted her teeth. "Are you."

"Tension and weariness and grief," Vine said. "You have to give yourself time to feel grief, in particular. May I make a suggestion?"

"Go ahead." Siv rolled over so she could get at one of the cuts across his ribs. He bit into a couch cushion as she started the next row of stitches.

"You must sleep and regroup," Vine said. "Neither one of you will be storming the castle in your current state. I suggest you sleep here tonight and begin the journey to Trure tomorrow."

Siv started to object, but Vine poked him in the rib.

"I'm not saying you should return with a Truren army," she said. "But you can regain your health and gather information. I will send word as things develop here. You will be in a much better state to consider your options there. I suspect that whatever move you make will have to wait until spring."

The mere mention of sleep was enough to make Dara want to melt into her chair. Siv's jaw tensed as Vine continued stitching up his side, but he seemed to be considering her suggestion. Then his eyelids began to droop.

"Siv!"

"Huh? Oh, yeah, I think that's as good a plan as any."

"I agree," Dara said. Vine was right: they needed to see where the ashes settled tomorrow, and they needed time to consider their options.

"Oh, lovely," Vine said. "I do think coming to a consensus is best. You're all finished, Your Majesty. Try not to move too much."

Vine sat back to prepare another bandage as Siv reached down with tentative fingers to check the final row of stitches.

"Can you spare some cloaks and food for our journey?" Dara said. "I'm sorry we've already asked so much of you, Vine."

"Nonsense, Dara. You're my friend. And House Silltine has always been loyal to the Amintelles. I'm delighted at the opportunity to actually show what true loyalty means. I shall sleep like a baby after helping the two of you to safety."

"Thank you. I'll find some way to repay you," Dara said.

"Just return safely one day. I would be so disappointed if we never got to compete together again."

"I'll try."

But Dara wasn't sure she could return to Vertigon. No matter what Siv did, she didn't see how she could live here. Her father had betrayed the kingdom. He knew she could Work the Fire now. And she had collaborated with her parents' enemy, the man who'd caused the death of their other daughter. She had learned from the Fire Warden himself. There would be no coming back from that in her parents' eyes. Dara grimaced. She had to stop thinking like that. She knew her parents' true natures now. But she still felt the bone-deep desire for their approval that had once been such a huge part of her life. They weren't worthy of it, but it felt as if the only way to escape their thrall was to flee.

Dara rested a hand on the night-black hilt of her Savven blade, reaching for its familiar comfort. She gasped. The blade was still hot to the touch. No, not hot. It burned with Fire, like a Fire Blade, but far stronger. She had never felt anything like it.

She ran a finger over the weapon, around the intricate curls of the hilt and the Savven mark stamped in the pommel. It hadn't melted from the torrent of power she'd sent through it, and it looked the same as always. But it had changed. Somehow through that furious rush of power and desperation she had transformed the Savven into a Fire Blade unlike any she'd ever encountered.

Dara removed her hands from the hilt and didn't mention the sword to the others. Too much had happened tonight, and she was too tired to even begin unraveling this new mystery. She could barely stand up, much less wield this new blade now anyway.

She was sure the memory of everything she had seen would torment her as she went to sleep, but in the end she didn't have to worry. Vine settled her in a musty guest bedroom in the old greathouse, and Dara dropped into unconsciousness before Vine even closed the door behind her.

SIV EXPECTED the pain prickling all over his body to prevent him from sleeping, but it ended up being remarkably easy. Vine slipped him a tonic she used after particularly trying training sessions. The enormity of everything that had happened that day didn't have time to crash down on him before he dropped to sleep.

When he awoke in the morning, the pain from his wounds returned with such a vengeance that he couldn't think too hard about their situation anyway. Vine cleaned his wounds again and had Toff pack up supplies for him and Dara. While they fussed over the details, Siv hobbled to the window and peeked out through the curtain.

The snow had finally stopped, and nearly three feet of it piled around the greathouse. The mountain was deceptively quiet. A soupy fog hung over everything, giving the impression that the whole world had been painted varying shades of white.

Some time in the night, the Fireworkers had withdrawn the wall of Fire. Square Peak looked safe for now. The only evidence of what had occurred was a stark ring all the way around the peak where the drifts weren't nearly as deep. A thick crust of ice, glimmering in the weak morning light, indicated where the snow had melted and refrozen around the burning barrier.

They had no time to wait for information about who held the castle as day broke. The Lantern Maker would surely send men to search the mountain. Vine wrapped Siv and Dara in thick cloaks and reiterated her promise to send them news in Trure. Siv borrowed rope to make a leash and warned Rumy he'd have to be on his best behavior until they got to safety. Then Siv, Dara, and the cur-dragon began the long, treacherous journey into the Fissure.

Siv looked back at the castle as they snuck from building to building and tree to tree on their way around the edge of King's Peak. It looked the same as it always had. No structural damage. No remnants of the incredible power that had burned within the Great Hall last night. No hint that for the first time in a hundred years, the crown did not sit upon an Amintelle head. His father's legacy was destroyed. Siv didn't know what he could do to recover it. Or if he should even try.

For now, all he knew was that the cuts on his body stung like hell, and he and Dara were going to survive. Whatever it took, they would look out for each other. And even though he was no longer the king, he would not leave his people at the mercy of the Lantern Maker forever.

EPILOGUE

SORALINE Amintelle huddled underneath her bed. She always thought she would be braver than this in the face of disaster. She had imagined what would happen if the castle was ever attacked, as it had been in the days of old before the Peace of Vertigon began. She had read about it in the history books. She had admired the long-ago queens who remained icy and defiant in the face of insurmountable odds. She had hoped she would be as serene as those ancient queens if such events ever came to pass again.

Instead, she curled in a ball underneath her bed, praying that the trouble would just go away. She was only seventeen. She didn't want to die.

Sora shuddered as the door to her chambers opened.

"She's under there," said a voice in a familiar accent. Soolen. She'd had such high hopes for the visitors from Soole. Despite the troubling news from Cindral Forest, she had never guessed the Soolens would be part of the attack on the castle, the attack on her family.

"Did you hurt her?" The second voice was deep and firm.

"No, sir. We killed her guards, but she is unharmed."

"Good."

Sora bit back a sob as a pair of boots approached. She had seen the first guard go down with a sword in her belly. A sweet girl named

Luci Belling. Sora had thought they might be friends in other circumstances. Denn Hurling had been posted outside her door too. He had guarded her since she was small enough to sit on his knee and pull at his red mustache. He had been like an uncle to her as well as a protector. How would she ever tell his twin sister, who was far away in Trure? Sora missed her own sister. And she missed her mother.

The boots stopped beside her bed. Then she saw a pair of knees, and finally, a face.

"Hello, Princess. May I have a word?"

"What do you want from me?"

"I believe that conversation would be much easier if you'd come out, Soraline."

Sora shuddered at the sound of her own name being spoken by that deep, powerful voice. She recognized the face, though it was difficult to see with her cheek pressed against the cold, dusty floor. It was Rafe Ruminor, the Lantern Maker. Why was he working with her Soolen captors?

"Are you going to kill me?" she whispered, her voice sounding unforgivably small. Why, oh why couldn't she be braver than this?

"That depends on you," Rafe said. He waited, but when Sora made no move to emerge from underneath the bed, he continued. "I control this castle. I had intended to place young Rollendar on the throne and see to it that he followed my wishes. That is no longer possible as he got himself killed. Your brother is dead too, by the way, in case you were unaware."

Sora sobbed. Siv. Her loving, infuriating brother. She had been sure he would be such a good king. The world had gone to ruin. Sora felt as if the bed over her head was the only thing keeping her in one piece now. She stared at the Lantern Maker.

"Did you—?"

"Bolden Rollendar killed him," Rafe said. "He attacked the castle with a squadron of trained men."

"But . . . but you said Bolden is dead too?"

"Yes. Most unfortunate." Rafe leaned in closer. Sora wished she could hide the tears slipping onto the dusty stones beneath her. She had never felt so alone. "I believe this transition will be easier if the people do not see it as a coup," Rafe said, his voice soft and firm.

"The army is not fully in hand, and I don't wish to deal with so many complications at once. But if the figurehead bears the Amintelle name, I can see a good many things being different."

"But what do you *want* from me?" Sora repeated.

Rafe Ruminor smiled.

"How would you like to be queen?"

ACKNOWLEDGMENTS

Thank you for reading the second book in the *Steel and Fire* series! It wouldn't be possible for me to tell this story without the help of a few key people along the way.

I especially want to thank Willow Hewitt, Brooke Richter, Sarah Merrill Mowat, Rachel Andrews, Laura Cook, Marcus Trower, Amanda Tong, Rachel Marsh, Kaylee Peelen, Whitney Galletly, Kaitlyn Godfrey, Mike and Angela Chang, Geoff and Alison Ng, all my siblings, and Ayden and Julie Young for their encouragement and advice along the way.

Susie and Lynn at Red Adept Editing and the team at Deranged Doctor Design helped me polish this story and turn it into a book. The Author's Corner continues to inspire me to do better with every release.

Thank you to everyone who read and reviewed *Duel of Fire*. Your positive feedback has made a huge difference. Thanks for skipping some sleep to hang out with Dara and Siv. I can't wait for you to read Book 3!

As always, I'm grateful to my husband for his support and belief in me as I've been on this writing journey. Thanks for cooking me dinner and listening to me think aloud so often.

Jordan Rivet
Hong Kong, 2016

ABOUT THE AUTHOR

Jordan Rivet is an American author of fantasy and science fiction. Originally from Arizona, she lives in Hong Kong with her husband. She is the author of the post-apocalyptic *Seabound Chronicles* and the *Steel and Fire* and *Empire of Talents* fantasy adventure series. She fenced for many years, and she hasn't decided whether the pen is mightier than the sword.

www.jordanrivet.com
Jordan@jordanrivet.com